The ADAMANTINE Palace

Stephen Deas

GOLLANCZ

LONDON

Copyright © Stephen Deas 2009
All rights reserved

The right of Stephen Deas to be identified as the
author of this work has been asserted by him in accordance
with the Copyright, Designs and Patents Act 1988.

First published in Great Britain in 2009 by
Gollancz
An imprint of the Orion Publishing Group
Orion House, 5 Upper St Martin's Lane, London WC2H 9EA
An Hachette Livre UK Company

A CIP catalogue record for this book is
available from the British Library

ISBN 978 0 575 08373 8 (Cased)
ISBN 978 0 575 08374 5 (Trade Paperback)

1 3 5 7 9 10 8 6 4 2

Typeset by Deltatype Ltd, Birkenhead, Merseyside
Printed in Great Britain by CPI Mackays, Chatham, Kent

www.orionbooks.co.uk

The Orion Publishing Group's policy is to use papers that
are natural, renewable and recyclable products and made
from wood grown in sustainable forests. The logging and
manufacturing processes are expected to conform to the
environmental regulations of the country of origin.

With thanks to K. J. Parker for pointing me at John Jarrold, John for putting up with me until Simon Spanton came along, and to Simon for everything since. To Peter and Jean for their support, and lots of others (you know who you are) who helped along the way. To 'Ou sont les dragons?', Kyle and were-ducks. To everyone who picks this up and starts to read.

And especially to my wife, Michaela, for her patience, understanding and much, much more.

Now, on with burning stuff.

The Kings and Queens of Sand and Stone and Salt

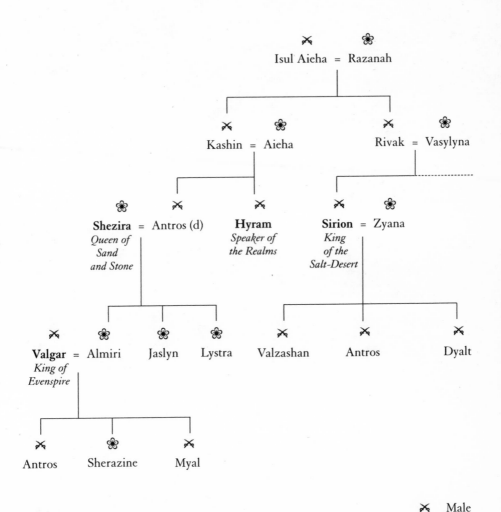

The Kings of the Endless Sea

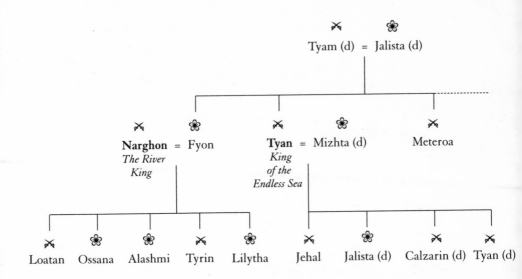

Kings and Queens of the Plains

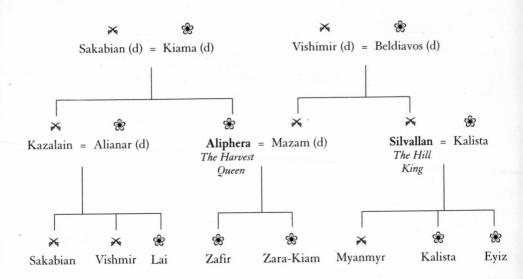

The King of the Worldspine

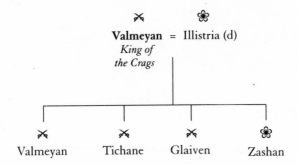

Prologue – Jehal

Prince Jehal felt the dragon take to the air. Curled up inside a saddlebag, he couldn't see a thing. But that didn't matter. He could see it in his mind, exactly and precisely. He felt every stride as the dragon accelerated. He knew exactly when the dragon would make one last bound and unfurl its wings. He felt himself grow heavier as the dragon rose up into the air.

The bag smelled slightly of rotten meat. Jehal wriggled and stretched as best he could, trying to make himself more comfortable in the tiny space. He forced himself to breathe slowly, suppressing the edge of panic that threatened to blossom inside him. Small spaces had never agreed with him, and the smell made him uneasy. It made him wonder what the bag had been used for before. Carrying dragon snacks was the obvious answer.

Is that me? Am I the snack of the day today?

The absurdity of the thought calmed him. Queen Aliphera was as shrewd as anyone, but she was also besotted. Jehal had come to know what that looked like, even in a dragon-queen.

The dragon stopped climbing and began to glide. Officially, Jehal was indisposed. A great deal of effort had gone into his illness, every bit of it spent so that he and Queen Aliphera could be alone and unobserved. All he had to do now was stay hidden until the queen found an excuse to fly away from her riders, her dragon-knights. Months of work and then days of waiting for exactly the right weather, all for half an hour of absolute privacy.

He clenched his fists. One of his feet had cramped. He wriggled his toes. When that didn't work, he tried to rearrange himself so his feet were underneath the rest of him. That didn't work either, but by the time he gave up trying, the cramp had gone away anyway. Eventually, he fell asleep.

*

He woke up to see grey sky pouring in above him. Every muscle in his legs was shouting at him, demanding to be stretched. He yawned, stood up and grinned at what he saw. They were high in the sky, skimming the base of the clouds. Aliphera liked to do that.

Jehal looked around, scanning the horizon, but there were no other dragons in sight. Finally, he looked at Aliphera. She was still half strapped into her saddle, but she was looking back at him, grinning. Her eyes were very wide. They'd flirted with each other for months, in little ways, little stinging touches where no one else would see.

Jehal grinned back. Anticipation, that was the key. And now she had him alone at last.

'You look a little dishevelled, Prince Jehal.'

Carefully, Jehal hauled himself out of his saddlebag. He crawled the few feet towards her, mindful of the thousand or so feet of empty space between him and the ground. It would be stupid to get this far only to plunge to his death.

'I want you, here and now.'

She laughed, but he saw a flash of excitement in her face. 'You're being silly. We'd fall.'

'I don't care.' He didn't let her answer, but covered her mouth with his own. One hand went to the soft skin of her neck. He let it slide down, only an inch or two, and then stopped.

'Loosen that harness,' he said. 'I want to ride with you. Let me hold you while you find a place to land.'

'Yes.' They fumbled together at the clasps and straps that held her fast. Now and then they let their fingers stray.

Finally, the last restraint fell away. Jehal lifted her up, just enough so he could slide into the saddle behind her. He let his hands run slowly down her body and felt her shudder.

'I can't tell you just how long I've been waiting for this,' she breathed.

With a sudden jerk, he rammed his head into the small of her back. She staggered and gasped as he rose and drove forward, punching her as she tried to turn. Once, twice, knocking her forward. Her arms flailed and then she was gone, off into the sky. Jehal sat back down and pressed himself into the saddle, gripping the dragon with his legs while he strapped himself in. A part of him couldn't believe it had been so easy.

The dragon tucked in its wings and dived after her, but that was simply what any hunting dragon was trained to do. It couldn't catch her. All it could do was land somewhere close by and then stay there, howling, pleading for help. Not that anyone could survive a fall like that.

He clung on and peered over the dragon's shoulder, listening to Queen Aliphera's screams, watching until the ground reached out and swallowed her whole.

'That's exactly what your daughter said,' he hissed.

Hatchling Gold

When a dragon-rider wishes a new dragon for his
eyrie, he will write to one of the dragon-kings or
-queens, petitioning them for their favours. If the rider
is wise, the letter will come with a gift. It is understood
that the more generous the gift, the more likely the
rider will receive a favourable response. This gift is
the first of many payments and is made long before
a suitable dragon is even born. This gift is called the
Hatchling Gold.

Naturally, as dragons are few and lords are fickle,
nothing is ever certain.

I

Sollos

There were three riders. Sollos had watched them land away in the fields beyond the edge of the forest. They'd all come down on the back of a single war-dragon, and one of them had stayed behind, keeping the dragon calm. The other two had walked straight towards the trees. Their pace was brisk and full of purpose. Sollos watched as they passed his position and then padded silently after them. They were dressed from head to toe in their dragonscale armour, and Sollos began to think they might as well have let the dragon come with them. It might have made less noise.

He took careful breaths, following behind. As long as the other men who'd been waiting for the riders to arrive didn't get a sudden case of cold feet.

A few hundred yards into the trees, the ground rose into a small mound topped with a standing stone. It had been a place of worship once, back in the days of the old gods, but now the forest had all but swallowed it. The riders went straight up the mound and stopped at the top.

'This is it, isn't it?' said one, in the kind of whisper of someone to whom the whole concept of being secretive was something of a mystery.

The other one was even worse. He leaned against the stone and started fiddling with a tinderbox. Sollos couldn't quite believe what he was seeing, or rather what he was smelling. The idiot was smoking pipeweed.

'It's almost insulting, isn't it,' breathed a voice in his ear. Sollos froze for an instant, and then relaxed. Kemir. 'They're as subtle as a mace in the face.'

'I wish you wouldn't do that, cousin.' Sollos hissed the words between his teeth, hardly daring to make a sound. He could actually feel Kemir's lips brushing his ear, that's how near he was. He found it uncomfortably distracting. How did Kemir get that close without him ever noticing?

'Don't worry. We're downwind, and the men waiting for them are on the other side of the mound. They've been there for a while now. They're getting impatient.'

'They're probably wondering why this lot didn't just crash in through the branches on the back of their dragon.'

'I was beginning to wonder the same.'

'The men on the other side of the mound. Are there still just three or are there more now?'

'Still three.'

Sollos took a deep breath and let it out slowly. He still wasn't sure what to make of all this. He'd had his orders, whispered in his ear, and they'd been quite clear. A pair of Queen Shezira's dragon-knights were going to come to the forest around these parts. They were coming to buy something, something meant to harm the queen. He and Kemir, a pair of sell-swords, were going to stop them. The gold in their pockets came from the queen's knight-marshal, but if anything went wrong they were nothings and nobodies with no ties to anyone who mattered. That was as much as Sollos knew.

'Did you see what they brought with them?'

Kemir didn't answer.

'They must have brought *something*.'

'Maybe they didn't. Maybe they're going to do our work for us and gut this pair of traitors for their gold. If they did, it's small. I didn't see anything.'

The whispering voice hadn't given any clues as to what the something was, either, only that trying to buy it should cost these dragon-knights their lives. Sollos was to wait until the riders met whoever was doing the selling, then discreetly kill the lot of them. The riders would be carrying gold. He could help himself to that, the whisper had said. As for the rest, he would leave the bodies alone and untouched. They'd be found in the morning, by which time Sollos would be back in his barracks. He'd wake up as shocked as anyone else to find that two of the queen's riders had been found murdered.

Which was all very well, but there were three dragon-knights, not two.

'There's another one,' he whispered. 'A third rider came with them. He stayed with the dragon.'

There was a long pause. He could almost hear Kemir thinking. 'We have to let that one go, don't we?'

Sollos nodded. There were supposed to be two riders. From short range with the advantage of surprise, he and Kemir could be reasonably sure of taking down one apiece. A third, though, forewarned, with a dragon at his back, that was a different matter.

'What do you make of them? Not the riders, the others. The sellers.'

'Nervous. They're not swordsmen. They'll run, not fight. We'll have to take them down quickly.'

Sollos shuddered; Kemir's lips were still brushing his ear. He edged away. 'When the purse changes hands, that's when we act. I'll deal with the rider who gives over the money, you shoot the other. Whoever is holding the purse is mine too. Then we go after the rest. Closest first.' From the corner of his eye Sollos saw movement at the top of the hill. He shooed Kemir away and began to creep closer. As he did, he took a careful grip of his dragonbone longbow. It was an old weapon, taller than he was, honed from the wing of some monster of a war-dragon by the looks of it. Too long and clumsy for his liking at such close quarters, but guaranteed to punch through as much steel and dragonscale as a man could wear and still stand upright.

'Have you got what we want?'

'Have you got our money?'

'Show me you've got what we want.'

At the top of the hill three men had joined the dragon-knights. As if all the noise they'd already made hadn't been enough, now they were arguing. Sollos had a fleeting vision of simply walking into the middle of them and seeing how many he could stab before they even noticed he was there.

'Show us the gold, friend. *Then* you see what you get for it.'

'No. You first.'

'Oh, just show them the money. Here ...'

One of them lit a torch. Slowly, Sollos rested an arrow against the string of his bow. One of the riders was holding what looked like a purse. Any moment now ... And they were making it all so easy.

The purse changed hands. As Sollos let fly, he saw the other rider stagger. He didn't even look to see what his own arrow had done, but reached at once for a second.

Both riders were down. The man holding the purse was still exactly where he'd been a moment ago. Sollos could see his eyes, slowly tearing themselves away from the riches in his hands as the dragon-knights toppled over.

The dragon-knights' torch lay on the ground, still burning, lighting the faces of the three strangers still standing on the top of the hillock. Sollos fired again. This time his aim was a little low. The arrow hit the man with the purse in the jaw and ripped off half his face. Good enough. He could see the last two clearly. Still they didn't think to run. Sollos dropped his bow and charged at them, first one hand and then the other drawing a pair of long knives out of his belt.

The furthest pitched suddenly backwards with another of Kemir's arrows in his chest. Finally the last one turned to flee, but by then Sollos was barely yards away and coming at a sprint. A leap and a lunge and Sollos buried both knives into the man's back, one high and one low. That turned out not to be enough, so he slit the man's throat for good measure. Then got up and looked at himself. His shirt was damp and glistening.

'Shit. I'm covered in blood.'

'Better stay away from that dragon, then.' Kemir was standing by the torch, his longbow held loosely at the ready.

'Are you sure there aren't any more of them?' Sollos scurried back to where he'd dropped his own bow. Without it, he felt naked.

Kemir shrugged. 'As sure as I can be. You never know.'

'We should leave. There's still a rider and a dragon waiting for those two to come back. The purse is there. Get it.'

He watched Kemir stoop and pick something up off the ground. Something that jingled with a very pleasant sound. Sollos smiled.

Kemir frowned. 'This is a lot, Sollos. Are you sure we're supposed to take it all?'

'That's the deal.'

That would normally have been enough for Kemir, but he was still standing there, frowning. As Sollos walked towards him, Kemir reached down and picked up something else. 'Have a look at this.'

'Put it back! Whatever it is, it's not ours.'

'Yes, yes, I will, but I want you to look at it first.'

Sollos shook his head. 'Leave it alone.' Do exactly what was asked, no more and no less. Wasn't that a simple enough rule to live by? For Kemir, apparently not, and it was this sort of thing that always got him into trouble. 'Just put it back,' he snapped as he reached him, so of course Kemir thrust it into his hands instead.

'What is it?'

'I don't know and I don't care.' What Sollos was holding was a spherical bottle made of glass, stoppered and sealed with wax at the top. It fitted nicely into the palm of his hand, and from the way its weight shifted was filled with some sort of liquid. In the darkness he couldn't quite see.

Sollos frowned. If it was a liquid, it was a very heavy one. Then he reminded himself that he really didn't want to know. Quickly, he put the bottle back down where Kemir had found it and took Kemir's arm, dragging him away.

Much later, when Sollos and Kemir were both long gone, the shadow of a woman slipped out from among the trees and stepped carefully around the corpses. The woman bent down where Kemir and Sollos had stood. She picked up the bottle and crept silently away.

2

Kailin

The dragon made one circle over the eyrie and then came in to land. Kailin stopped what he was doing to watch. He squinted, trying to make out the dragon's colour, or anything else that might distinguish it. Around the featureless top of the eyrie the other Scales would be doing the same. They'd all be thinking the same question too: *Is it one of mine? Is that one I raised?*

Its shape made it a war-dragon, he decided. Hunting dragons had long tails and long necks and enormous wings and were, to Kailin's eyes, much more graceful. War-dragons were stockier. End to end and wing-tip to wing-tip they were the smaller breed, but they weighed twice as much and ate enough for four. Their colours tended to be drab too. Hunting dragons were brighter. Their bloodlines were more carefully recorded, their breeding more strictly managed, their diet meticulously controlled by the alchemists.

When a mount was old enough, the trainers taught them to take the saddle and the rein, and to understand their riders' commands. The rest of the work of growing a dragon was down to people like Kailin. They were the ones, if they survived, who fed the dragons, watered them, nurtured them, cared for them – the Scales, whose ruined skin, hard and flaking, marked them for life. In the end Hatchling Disease got them all, petrifying them while they were still alive. A Scales did not get to grow old.

If it was a war-dragon, it wasn't one of his. He watched it come down anyway, a steep, hard dive that made the ground quake as it landed. It folded its wings and snorted, blowing a thin stream of fire up into the air. Kailin recognised it now. Mistral. Queen Shezira's second-favourite mount.

Mistral shook himself. He took a few steps forward and then lowered his head almost to the ground. He looked hungry, Kailin thought. Already, several of the nearest Scales were running over, ready to call Mistral away to one of the feeding paddocks. Their other job was to make sure that Mistral was kept well away from the breeding females. One mistake could ruin centuries of careful breeding, and no one in the world was insane enough to get in the way of a pair of mating dragons.

A single rider slid down from Mistral's shoulders, exchanged a few words with the Scales, and then walked straight towards Kailin. As she came closer, Kailin sank to his knees and bowed his head. Queen Shezira was a regular visitor to the eyrie. Lately, circumstances had hurled Kailin into her path.

She stopped in front of him. 'Rise, Scales.'

Shakily, Kailin got to his feet. He didn't dare raise his head.

'How is my Sabre?' Sabre was the queen's hunting dragon. A few weeks ago she'd brought him to the eyrie with a cracked rib. According to the whispers, the queen had taken Sabre hunting somewhere far away, and he'd been charged while on the ground by some beast that sounded like an armoured elephant, except with horns. Sabre, said the whispers, had bitten the creature's head off with a single snap of his jaws.

'Doing well, I understand,' said Kailin, trying to keep the tremor out of his voice. 'Your Holiness knows that I am not the Scales caring for him.'

'Yes, yes. When do *you* think he will be ready to hunt again?'

'If he were in my care, Your Holiness, I would beg for him to be rested another three weeks.'

He could tell from the way the queen tapped her foot that this wasn't the answer she'd wanted. He heard her sigh. 'Then I shall have to ride Mistral. And how is my perfect white?'

Snow, thought Kailin. *She's called Snow.*

'What did you say, Scales?'

'I-I ...' Kailin stammered. 'I'm sorry, Your Holiness, I spoke out of turn.' Had he spoken at all? He wasn't sure.

'What did you *say*, Scales?'

He was shaking. The queen had a temper. Everyone knew what happened to those who made her angry. 'We call her Snow, Your Holiness.' Kailin screwed up his eyes and waited for the blow to come.

'Well then, Scales. Snow. How is she?'

'Still ... still perfect, Your Holiness.' He could feel her eyes on him, but he couldn't bring himself to look at her.

'You see she stays that way. And learn to mind your tongue, Scales. You and your dragon will be the property of Prince Jehal before the next full moon. He will give her whatever name takes his fancy, and he is *not* known for his forgiving nature.' She laughed. 'If you're unlucky, he'll decide you're a spy.'

She left him there, quivering.

3

The Eyrie-Master

The Scales was forgotten almost before Shezira had turned her back on him. Two more days and they were due to fly, almost from one end of the realms to the other. Another two weeks and they'd be in King Tyan's palace. Prince Jehal would be there. She would give Jehal her perfect white and her youngest daughter, and in return he would give her lordship of all the realms. Or rather, he wouldn't object to her taking it.

She smiled. Lordship? Or should it be ladyship? It wouldn't be the first time that the speaker was a queen instead of a king, but it had been long enough. Too long.

The eyrie was built on an escarpment. Most of it was tunnelled underground and so, from the outside, there wasn't much to look at. Scorched rock and blasted earth and the occasional smouldering mound of dragon dung. Further away, fields full of cattle stretched out as far as the eye could see, interspersed with tiny clusters of farmhouses. And there were the dragons, of course, always a few of them out on the rocks, being groomed or trained or saddled or fed, or simply sunning themselves.

The only structure built on top of the eyrie was a massive tower, the Outwatch. As she walked towards its gates, they swung open. Soldiers poured out and formed up in ranks to salute her. In their midst was Isentine, the eyrie-master, dressed to the nines in dragonscale and gold. Shezira stopped in front of him and he fell to his knees to kiss her feet. He was getting old. She saw him wince as he struggled to rise again, which annoyed her. She'd have to replace him soon, which was a nuisance. He was competent and devoted, and it would be hard to find his equal. But if he couldn't bow properly ...

'Come on, come on, get up!' she hissed under her breath. All the soldiers were watching.

'Your Holiness.' Shezira bit her lip when she saw his face. He looked so worn out, almost defeated.

'Eyrie-Master Isentine.' She forced a smile and put a hand on each of his shoulders. 'Your eyes grow ever sharper with the years. You must have seen me coming from quite some way away.'

The eyrie-master bowed again, a little dip from the waist, which didn't seem to trouble him. 'I live to serve Your Holiness.'

'And you do it very well.' She walked on past him. 'We have another hatchling, I hear. One I should see?'

'I'm afraid not, Your Holiness.' Isentine took up his proper position, walking in step with her just behind her right shoulder. 'This is another that refuses its food and wastes away.'

'Again?' A flash of irritation sounded in Shezira's voice, and that made her even more annoyed. A queen should never sound petulant.

'I am sorry, Your Holiness.'

'That's three out of the last four. It's not usually that many.' The eyrie-master could still match her pace easily enough, she noted, so maybe there was some life left in him. For now.

'It is unusual, Holiness, but the alchemists assure me it is to be expected that these things should happen from time to time. I am promised it will not last.'

'And do you believe them?' Shezira shook her head. 'Don't answer. One a month, Isentine. That's what I need from you. One good hatchling every month. But that's not really why I came here.' They were past all the soldiers now. They walked through the gates and into the maw of Outwatch in silence.

'Does Your Holiness desire something?' Isentine asked her. 'We have made all the usual preparations. Baths scented with oils, a feast of delicacies from around the realms, men and women who desire nothing more than to serve your pleasure.' He should have known her better by now, but he was old, and some habits simply wouldn't break.

'If that's what they desire, they can spend their time teaching my daughters some manners and some respect, and making them understand that above all they are required to be obedient.'

It took a long time for him to digest that, which made Shezira smile. She wasn't supposed to say such things in public, and there was no proper formal response. They walked across the grand hall, a gloomy cavern of ochre stone that accounted for most of the lower levels of Outwatch.

'You should do something about this hall. Put some windows in.' The echoes of their footsteps made it seem even emptier, dreary and lonely. 'Maybe I should send my daughters to *you* for a while, eh?'

They reached the far side of the hall, where a maze of intertwined staircases snaked towards the upper levels.

'The study, Your Holiness?' asked Isentine.

'Yes.' The hall wasn't as empty as Shezira had first thought. Here and there she saw soldiers standing guard, still as statues and tucked into little niches where they wouldn't easily be seen.

By the time they reached the top of the stairs to Isentine's study, he was wheezing. What was it? A hundred and twenty steps to this balcony? She shook her head and watched him as he opened the door and then stood patiently waiting for her to enter. This wouldn't do.

She sighed, went in and sat down. 'You're getting positively ancient, Master Isentine.' She watched him as she said it, and saw how much it hurt him. Which was good. He knew what was coming, and that would make it easier for both of them.

'Three score years and then some.' He looked sad.

'And then some more. You've been the master here for as long as I can remember. Twenty-five years almost to the day I came here.' She smiled, thinking back to the first time she'd landed at Outwatch. 'Fifteen years old, betrothed to King Antros, and you were the first person I saw. I thought you looked so handsome.'

The eyrie-master's throat began to bob up and down as though he was trying to say something, but the words were stuck in his throat.

'I haven't forgotten,' Shezira added. 'I haven't forgotten that it was you, more than anyone, who stood at my side when Antros died so suddenly. If you'd turned against me, I would not be queen now. You always had my gratitude in the years after that. You have it still.'

'Then ...' They both knew what he wanted to say. They both knew she couldn't consent.

'You may choose who will be the new master of Outwatch and my other eyries, Isentine. I will respect your judgement. But you cannot remain master of my dragons. Speaker Hyram's reign is almost done. I will succeed him. I can hide you away here, but when I rule the Adamantine Palace I cannot have a weak old man who can barely walk at my side. I am sorry.' She almost reached out and took his hand, because in more ways than one he was the oldest friend she had. But she was a queen, and so her hand stayed still and only the whiteness of her knuckles betrayed her.

Isentine swallowed. He took a deep breath and slowly bowed. 'I understand, Your Holiness. I will find you a man worthy to serve you as I no longer can, and I will take the Dragon's Fall.'

They sat together in silence for as long as Shezira could bear. Then she went and stood by the window. The study looked out directly over the cliffs, and the drop felt almost infinite.

'Or ...'

Isentine didn't move. She could see he was holding his breath.

'My daughters are very fond of their dragons, and very fond of you. Almiri is my heir and has children of her own. Lystra is promised to Prince Jehal and still young enough to be pliable, but Jaslyn ... She spends a great deal of time here, or so I understand.'

Isentine looked at her. He smiled and shook his head. 'You may choose whoever you wish, my queen, but Jaslyn is too young to be mistress of any eyrie. She knows her dragons well enough, better than most I might say, but she has no experience ...'

Now at last he began to see.

'She would need a mentor.' Shezira kept her voice stern. 'You would have to live out your years here, surrounded by these beasts.

I could not permit you to take the Dragon's Fall until you were quite sure she was worthy to succeed you.'

'Yes, Your Holiness. Thank you.'

Shezira looked away. Isentine was almost weeping with gratitude, and that was something she couldn't bear to see. 'You will not come with us to King Tyan's realm. You are too old. Instead you can stay here and think about everything you must do. It will not be an easy task for you with Jaslyn. She's wilful and proud. If I said she was plain, it would be flattery, yet she turns up her nose at every suitor I put before her. Before long you might wish you'd taken the Dragon's Fall after all.'

'I will make her a daughter to be proud of,' whispered the eyrie-master.

I already am, thought Shezira, but that too was something she could never admit. Instead, she began to pace the floor, steadfastly ignoring Isentine's gaze. 'Yes. Now, Prince Jehal. Two more days, Eyrie-Master.'

'All is prepared, Your Holiness.'

'Oh, I have no doubt of that, but still … Summon the alchemist. Haros? Huros? Whatever his name is. Let him bore me with the details of *his* preparations. And in case I fall asleep, please make sure he knows that my knight-marshal has something she wishes to discuss with him. It seems she has acquired a bottle of something that she requires him to understand for her.'

'At once, Your Holiness.'

Shezira watched Isentine leave. He had a spring in his step, one she hadn't seen for a long time. She could almost make herself believe that she'd done something good. A little ray of sunshine amid a much darker storm.

Two more days before I leave to buy Prince Jehal with my own daughter's flesh. Although I, above all, understand that is what we daughters are for.

4

The Speaker of the Realms

'How,' murmured Jehal, 'could anyone *not* covet it? I simply don't understand.'

Beside him he felt Zafir's skin, slick with sweat, move against his own. She turned towards him. 'Covet what, my lover?'

Jehal threw out his arms. They lay together in a carved wooden bed a thousand years old, swathed in silken sheets. In all four walls windows opened out to the sky and the vista of the Adamantine Palace and the City of Dragons below.

'This! All of this!'

Zafir pressed herself against him and began to stroke his chest.

'All of this,' she murmured. She sounded happy, Jehal thought, and well she might. She'd spent most of the night gasping, after all.

Jehal sighed and sat up. 'Yes, all of this. Wouldn't it be perfect? Ah ... I'll never forget the first time my father brought me here. I sat in his saddle with his arms around me as we soared high in the air. The sky was a brilliant blue, the sun burning and bright, the ground far, far beneath us. Dark and green and lush. I could see distant mountains, and then beside them I saw something glitter. I pointed and asked what it was. My father said it was a jewel, the greatest jewel I would ever see, and he was right. The Adamantine Palace, glittering in the sun, the lakes sparkling around it, the mountains of the Purple Spur at its back. That sight is burned into my mind, like dragon's breath.' He smiled and shook his head. 'Awestriker. That's what my father's dragon was called. He was an old one even then, and long gone now. Sometimes I wish my father had gone with him. After my deranged little brother murdered our mother and the rest of our siblings, he was never the same. Lingering like this, drooling and deranged, it's not fitting. A king should live forever or else die in a blaze of glory.'

Zafir draped her arms around his shoulders. 'You have me.'

'Yes. I have you. More than enough for any man. The most beautiful princess in all the realms.'

'Queen,' she whispered, nibbling at his ear. 'My mother is dead. Some wicked man threw her off a dragon, remember?'

Jehal pulled her lips to his. 'That is a dangerous thing to say, my sweet. Your mother had an accident. I'm quite certain of it. And you're still a princess, not a queen. Not until Speaker Hyram says otherwise.'

'Will it be long?'

'I would think an hour, maybe two, before he calls you.'

Zafir snorted. 'Why does it take him so long?'

'Have you seen how he shakes? He's an old man, and twilight is coming fast upon him.'

'He's so dreary. He makes time drag.'

Jehal laid her gently on her back. He gazed into her eyes, so dark and wide, and rested his hand on the curve of her belly. A faint breeze from the windows brushed his skin. 'A clever trick.' He grinned. 'But I can make it fly.'

Zafir giggled. 'When I'm a queen, and you're still only a prince, does that mean you have to do as I say?'

'I will be yours to command.'

'Then I know exactly what my first demand as queen will be.'

'And what is that, my love?'

'As soon as I'm queen, I shall summon you back here at once.' She cupped his face in her hands and pushed him slowly down on her. 'More!' she sighed. 'That'll be what I want from you. More...'

Later, Jehal watched Zafir dress herself and leave. After she was gone, he stood naked at the window, waiting, wondering if anyone was watching him. The Tower of Air was the tallest and grandest of the palace towers, and Speaker Hyram had set it aside for Zafir as soon as he'd known her purpose in coming to the palace. The floors below were full of servants, a few of them

Zafir's but most of them the speaker's. It wouldn't do for Hyram to know whom Zafir had taken to her bed, and yet he stood at the window anyway, daring fate to expose him.

Once he thought Zafir had been gone for long enough, he slipped on a plain tunic and a pair of slightly soiled trousers, and walked out carrying the chamber pot. In the confusion of unfamiliar faces, no one spared him a second glance.

In contrast to the Tower of Air, Jehal's own lodgings were somewhat more modest, almost the meanest that the palace had to offer. Hyram had probably wanted him banished to a leaky hut of mud and straw somewhere outside the city walls, Jehal thought. That would be too overt an insult, but the slight was not lost on him, and he made up for it by being late to Zafir's coronation, loudly bursting into the Glass Cathedral when Hyram was half-way through his tedious speech about dignity and service and the duties of kingship. Kingship, not queenship. Jehal made a mental note to mention that to Zafir once he had her naked again.

Hyram droned on and Jehal picked his nails. The cathedral felt immense and empty. A gaggle of dragon-priests hovered and twittered in the shadows at the back. A few lords and ladies of Hyram's household sat politely, but the only other person who mattered was the potion-maker, dutifully recording the event: Bellepheros, grand master alchemist and First Lord of the Order of the Scales. Jehal watched him and yawned. They could have done all this in ten minutes in Hyram's study with a bottle of fine wine. Oh, but then it wouldn't have been the *same*. Perhaps flirting with death from both boredom and hypothermia at once somehow gave the event gravitas. He should have brought a cloak, he decided. A thick, warm cloak. And a pillow. As it was, the amusement of watching Hyram shake and stutter his way through his speech would just have to do to keep him awake.

Eventually Hyram was done. Jehal slipped out and watched, waiting for Zafir, already thinking about how he would fulfil her first queenly command. But it was Speaker Hyram who came out first, and walked purposefully towards Jehal.

'G-G-Good of you t-to eventually attend,' he stuttered.

Every part of him was trembling. Jehal gave him the slightest of bows.

'I'm quite aware that Queen Zafir could not be crowned without at least someone else of royal blood to bear witness, otherwise I would not be here at all. Are you cold, Your Highness? There's certainly a chill to the air today. I could get a cloak for you, if you like.'

Hyram spat. 'D-D-Don't play the fool with me, Prince J-Jehal.'

Jehal smiled and touched his forehead. 'Of course, Your Highness. I forgot. Your sickness. It seems to be getting worse. It will be a terrible loss to the realms. All that wisdom. Who among the dragon-kings could possibly take your place?'

'And h-how *is* your father, Jehal?' Hyram looked like a broken old man with his constant quivering, but there was still fire in his eyes. Jehal bit his lip. *Careful, careful. He's not a fool. Not yet.*

He tried to look sad. 'His mind, I think, is still as sharp as ever. It *is* hard to know. Most of the time he's rigid with the paralysis. When the shaking comes and he can actually open his mouth, none of us can understand what he's trying to say. It's a wonder we're still able to feed him. The sickness—'

'Sickness?' Hyram snorted. 'I think you will f-find it is almost taken for granted that you're p-poisoning him.'

Jehal clenched his teeth. 'Then I must be poisoning you as well, Your Highness, for your symptoms are the same as his were in the early days. Yes, it's hard to remember a time when he could still talk and feed himself and fuck women and do everything a dragon-prince's father should be able to do, but I would say your symptoms are *exactly* the same.' He spat and turned to walk away. 'It's as well your time will soon be done. How pitiful it would be to have a speaker who can't actually speak. And how's your memory, by the way? Are you starting to forget things yet?'

'Jehal.'

Jehal stopped but didn't turn back. 'Your Highness?'

'Queen Aliphera. They say she f-fell from her dragon.'

'So I heard.' He turned now, so he could watch Hyram's face.

'I knew Aliphera. She l-loved the hunt. She rode her d-dragons as well as any man. This notion – it's p-preposterous.'

Jehal shrugged. 'Yes it is, isn't it. But she'd chosen to fly away from her escorts. No one saw what happened, or no one will admit to it.' He laughed. 'You could always ask the dragon.'

'I'm asking you.'

'*What* are you asking me, Your Highness?'

'D-Did Zafir do it?'

'If that's your question then you should ask her, not me.'

'I d-did. They were my f-first words after I put the crown on her head. D-Did you kill your mother to get this?'

Jehal smirked. 'I imagine that went down very well. If you've suddenly taken to valuing my opinion, the thought did cross my mind. I doubt Zafir murdered Queen Aliphera, though. She may have the ambition to think it, but she lacks the nerve.'

'Y-You, however, do not.'

'Me?' Jehal growled. 'Since it appears I have failed to finish poisoning my own father despite a decade of effort, perhaps I am not as able an assassin as you think. Your Highness.'

'I will send t-truth-seekers to your eyrie. T-To Zafir's as well. B-Bellepheros already has my orders. If you make a-any attempt to interfere with them, I will kn-know you are guilty.'

'Your faith in my character is touching, Your Highness. By all means, send whoever you like, and of course Bellepheros shall have everything he needs put at his disposal. I shall demand that he is as meticulous and thorough as he can be, and when he finds nothing I shall expect you to doubt me no less than you do now. Are you done with me, old man?'

'I-I very much hope so.'

Jehal leaned towards Speaker Hyram and held his gaze. 'What if you're wrong? What if I haven't spent the last few years slowly murdering my own father? What if I've been looking for a cure instead? What if I were to tell you I'd found it?'

For an instant Hyram's eyes faltered. Only for an instant, but Jehal could almost taste the victory. 'Then I look f-forward to seeing him in the s-saddle once more.'

'So do I, Your Highness. So do I.' Jehal walked away, biting his lip, his face stony. When he was sure no one could see, he looked up to the Tower of Air.

'There,' he whispered, as if the wind might somehow carry his words to Zafir. 'Do you think that went well?' He began to giggle and then to laugh until he wept, and after that he didn't know whether it was the laughter or the tears that wouldn't stop.

5

Shezira

The snapper pack was already scattering. Shezira picked one of them and yelled at Mistral. Obediently, the dragon wheeled and dived, tucking in his wings and plummeting towards the ground like a falcon. The snapper was going to be too quick, though. It was going to reach the trees before Mistral was in range. Shezira growled softly to herself. This was what she got for riding a war-dragon on a hunt. They were so vast, their shoulders were so broad, their wings so large, that she couldn't even see what she was doing half the time. Unless she dived like this, in which case the wind almost blinded her instead. She squinted at the scattered trees below.

'Fire!' she shouted.

Mistral spread his wings. Shezira found herself hugging scales as the dragon almost stopped in mid-air. She quickly shut the visor on her helm. She heard the roar and felt Mistral quiver, and a wall of heat washed over her. Then Mistral shuddered and lurched as he landed heavily and stumbled. Shezira felt branches and leaves tear at her armour and heard the crack of a tree trunk. The air was hot and filled with the smell of charred wood. When she opened her visor it was to see a swathe of forest floor a hundred yards long burning. The trees around her were blackened; some were broken where Mistral had smashed into them. Shezira couldn't see whether the blast had reached the snapper. Slowly she backed Mistral out of the wreckage.

'You missed him, mother,' shouted Princess Almiri. Her dragon was already on the ground, some fifty yards away, clutching a headless snapper in its front claws.

Shezira instinctively ducked as something huge flew right over her head, so close that she felt the wind of its passing almost lift her out of the saddle. A sooty grey hunting dragon arched up and flew over the forest, so close that its tail slashed the treetops. Again and again, its head darted down and spat out a narrow lance of fire. Then the dragon climbed, turned and came back to land next to Shezira, squeezing into the space between her and Princess Almiri. Its rider took off her helm and waved an angry fist.

'That was my kill, mother!' Princess Jaslyn bellowed and threw her helm away in disgust. 'What do you think you were doing? You flew right into my path! Silence almost ploughed into you and your clumsy behemoth. You should have borrowed one of Almiri's hunters.'

'Height has precedence!' snapped Shezira. She had to shout to make herself heard. Mistral was scratching at a fallen tree, rolling it over. He could smell something.

'The *chaser* has precedence!' Jaslyn yelled back. Silence folded his wings and took careful steps sideways, until he and Mistral were almost touching. Mistral dropped the tree, shifted and hissed, and Silence hissed back. War-dragons didn't like being crowded. Shezira felt suddenly small. Dragons didn't actually attack riders unless they were commanded. Being accidentally crushed to death, however, was a very different matter.

'I *was* the chaser!' Shezira tried to calm Mistral down. Jaslyn was right. Mistral wasn't made for this sort of flying, and she should have borrowed a proper hunter.

'Only after you practically barged me out of the air!' Silence was baring his teeth at Mistral now. The difference in size didn't seem to bother him at all. *At least being on a war-dragon means I can look down on my daughter while we bicker.*

'Did you get the snapper?' shouted Almiri. She'd shuffled her own dragon sideways too, coming close enough to distract Silence. As the eldest of Shezira's daughters and the only one married with a family of her own, Almiri had taken to the role of family peacemaker. This always made Shezira smile, because she remembered a time when Almiri was every bit as bad as Jaslyn.

'Of *course* I got it!'

All around them, the other dragons were landing on the open ground and the earth trembled as each one came down. At a quick count, Shezira guessed they'd got about a third of the snapper pack, which certainly wouldn't be enough to keep King Valgar happy. Snappers were a menace. Standing up on its back legs, a snapper was half as tall again as a man, twice as fast, and if it got the chance would happily bite your head off. They were cunning, ate anything and everything they could catch, hunted in groups, and weren't averse to slaughtering entire villages. Dragons were by far the best way of keeping them under control, and King Valgar had been holding back from this herd just so they could have this hunt.

Mistral took a few steps towards Silence, barging into him, and growled. Silence hissed again. The dragons were sensing the moods of their riders. Mistral was probably hungry too, and most of the other dragons were eating their first kills now. The scent of blood was in the air, mixed with the sounds of cracking bones and tearing flesh and heavy dragon breathing.

'Would you like to swap, mother?' asked Almiri, still shouting to make herself heard. 'Have a proper mount for the hunt?'

The offer was tempting, but Shezira shook her head. 'It'll be dusk before you're finished here and I need to get back to Valgar's eyrie. I should be keeping an eye on Lystra, in case she does something stupid.'

'You should have let her come.'

'A week before she's supposed to kneel before Jehal? You know what she's like, especially when she's got Jaslyn to goad her on. I want to present her the way she *can* be, perfect and beautiful, not the way she usually *is*, saddle sore and covered in bruises. No. It was nice to fly with you for a while, but I should go.'

Almiri smiled. 'It's a pity, though. I would have liked the four of us to fly together one last time.'

The words cut, although Almiri surely hadn't meant them to be cruel. It seemed only yesterday that she'd given Almiri away to King Valgar. Which had been hard, but at least their clans had been intertwined by blood for centuries and their realms were close. Besides, Almiri was the oldest. She was the heir to the Throne of Sand and Stone, and letting her go had been right and proper. And she'd still had Jaslyn and little Lystra.

Somehow, over the years, she'd lost Jaslyn to her dragons; now she was about to lose the last of her daughters to a prince she barely knew, to live in a palace more than a thousand miles away. A necessary arrangement and certainly not without its benefits, but once the marriage was made, Lystra would be a stranger to her. She was going to have to get used to the idea.

Almiri must have seen something of Shezira's thoughts in her face, for she added, 'Once you sit in the Adamantine Palace, you'll be able to summon all of us as often as you like. You can have as many hunts and tournaments as you want. Prince Jehal will *have* to bring Lystra with him if you tell him to.'

Which was all true, but she couldn't shake the feeling that it would never quite be the same. She sighed. 'There will be a day, Princess. One day. Would you spare Mistral half your carcass? He's restless.'

Half a snapper was little more than a snack for a monster like Mistral, but it seemed to settle his mood. With a pang of regret, Shezira left the hunters to their fun. She turned him on the ground, cumbersome and slow as he was, and then he started to run. *That* made the other dragons sit up and take notice, for the footfalls of a running war-dragon could shake the earth enough to shatter houses, and it took a lot for a beast like Mistral to take to the air. When he did finally spread his wings and soar into the sky, though, all his ungainliness was gone. Shezira had him circle once above them and tipped a wing to wish them luck. Then she put the mountains and forests to her back and headed out over the plains. She allowed Mistral to set his own pace, and let herself enjoy the feeling of the wind in her hair and the utter sense of being alone. It wasn't often that she had the skies to herself, and yet she had long ago come to realise that that was what she enjoyed most. That was when she was truly free, free to pretend she had no titles, no burdens, no family, no daughters to marry off, no plotting nephews to watch, no subjects to rule, no obligations, no responsibilities ...

Catching herself thinking these thoughts made her laugh. *And here I am, set to become the next Speaker of the Realms. Would I really turn my back on that if someone told me I could? Would I really take Mistral and fly away across the Stone Desert to the secret valleys beyond, where no one would know me and no one would find me?*

The answer, she knew, was that she wouldn't contemplate it even for a second. Which probably made her a fool, and that in turn made her laugh even more, and by the time she reached Valgar's eyrie, she felt ten years younger.

She'd hoped the feeling would last after she landed, but it didn't. It died at the exact moment that she saw her knight-marshal, Lady Nastria, walking briskly across the scorched earth towards her. Nastria was already half in her armour, as if in a rush to leave, and was waving something in her hand. She was shouting.

'Your Holiness! Queen Aliphera is dead!'

6

Huros

Huros knew exactly what was going on, because nothing could happen without him. He'd sat with Eyrie-Master Isentine and explained to Queen Shezira everything about the route they would take to escort Princess Lystra to her wedding. Exactly how many dragons would be flying, exactly where they would be stopping and exactly for how long.

They left King Valgar's eyrie at the crack of dawn. Huros was expecting that, because that had been in his plan. Today was the longest stage of their journey, all the way to the Adamantine Palace. They would stay there for one day, no more and no less, to let the dragons rest. He was quietly looking forward to it. He would spend the time with the highest alchemists in the realms, perhaps even with Master Bellepheros himself. It was an opportunity to advance himself, and this had filled his thoughts until late into the night. Thus he wasn't entirely awake when someone knocked on his door. He stumbled outside while the sun was still creeping over the horizon and checked his potions were all carefully packed. Then he wrapped himself in his thick and deliciously warm flying coat, secured himself to the back of a dragon and started to count the others getting ready around him. By the time he reached twenty, his eyes had grown so heavy that he thought he might rest them for a bit. The counting was rather pointless, after all. He knew exactly which dragons were with them and exactly where they were going.

Others climbed up beside him. He felt the dragon start to run and then launch itself into the air. He had a sleepy look around, and then his eyes closed.

When he woke up two hours later, as his belly reminded him

that he hadn't had any breakfast, he was in the wrong place. The mountains of the Worldspine were too close. More to the point, there should have been some thirty dragons in the skies around him. Instead, he could see the white, two other war-dragons, and that was it.

'Er ... Excuse me?'

There were two men on the war-dragon with him. One was a rider, sitting up above its shoulders. The other one looked like a Scales. Huros furrowed his brow, trying to remember the man's name. Kailin. The one who looked after the white.

'Hey! Scales!'

The Scales turned around and gave Huros a blank look. The rider was too far away to hear them over the wind.

'Scales! Can you hear me?'

The Scales nodded.

'Where are we?'

The Scales shrugged.

'Um, don't you know? Where are the others then?'

The Scales shook his head and shrugged again.

'Well. Oh. Then who *does* know?'

The Scales tipped his head towards the dragon-knight. Huros rolled his eyes and gave up. Strictly speaking, Scales were subordinate to Huros and the other alchemists, and all belonged to the order. In reality, most Scales lived in a tiny world of their own that seemed to consist of themselves, their dragons and very little else.

His stomach began to rumble. He decided to have one more try. 'Scales! Um. Have you anything to eat?'

The Scales nodded and passed back a hunk of bread. Huros gnawed on it and quietly fumed. Under *no* circumstances was a squadron of dragons to split without consulting the senior alchemist present. Since Huros was the only alchemist Queen Shezira had deemed fit to bring, that was him. He would have *words*, he thought grimly. Words, yes. Strong and forthright ones.

They flew for hours, and with each hour, Huros clenched his fists ever tighter. Eventually it occurred to him that Queen Shezira might have changed her plans because of the news of Queen Aliphera's tragedy. Huros wasn't sure why that should be, but then he hadn't really been paying much attention. He'd had his own plans to worry about. Besides, that didn't change anything. He should have been *consulted*. Ancestors! He didn't even know where he was any more, except that the peaks of the Worldspine were to the right and there were more mountains to the front. Which meant they were still flying south, away from Outwatch. He furrowed his brow. Or was that the other way round, and the mountains should be on the left?

The pressure on his bladder grew. He pressed his legs together and bit his lip, but eventually he had to give in. Dragon-knights did this all the time, he told himself, and he started to undo the straps that held him onto the dragon. Even the Scales had calmly stood up, relieved himself into a bottle and strapped himself back in again. Except when Huros stood up, the wind buffeted him and almost knocked him over, and he was so terrified that he couldn't go. The pressure turned gradually into pain, and by the time they landed, it was so excruciating that Huros was in no fit state to have words with anyone. He didn't waste any time to see where he was, but stumbled and staggered away towards the nearest tree.

Before he was done, his dragon and its rider were already taking off again, the beast lumbering away and flapping its wings, accelerating up to a speed where it could lift itself off the ground. For one terrifying heartbeat Huros thought he'd been abandoned; then he saw the Scales and a pair of strange-looking soldiers, and when he looked up, the other dragons were there, still in the air overhead. The Scales was sitting by the edge of a wide open stretch of jumbled rocks, next to a pile of boxes and sacks that must have come from the dragon-riders. Here and there sparkling ribbons of bubbling water criss-crossed and threaded their way between the stones and among streaks and strands of silvery sand. Strips of ragged grass, perhaps a stone's throw across, lined the river's course before the forest trees took hold.

The two soldiers walked slowly towards him. They were

carrying some strange contraption between them. From the way they were walking, it was awfully heavy. Huros had a moment to wonder where the queen's precious white dragon had gone, when it shot through the air straight over his head, so close that the tree beside him shook and the alchemist was almost lifted off his feet into the dragon's wake. He clung on to a branch. By the time he'd recovered, the dragon was rolling on its back in the river bed next to the Scales, flapping and splashing its wings. Its rider was standing nearby, soaking wet, waving his arms and shouting furiously at the Scales.

The two soldiers shouted something as well and shook their fists, then carried on with what they were doing. Huros waited until they were close, and then stepped out of the trees. 'You're not dragon-knights.' Both soldiers had longbows slung over their backs. The bows were white and made of dragonbone. Precious things. The alchemist wondered where they'd got them.

The soldiers looked at him. They exchanged a glance and seemed to smirk. 'Clever of you to notice,' said the taller of the two. 'Was it the fact that we're not wearing several tons of dragonscale that gave it away, or that we're not sitting around and picking our noses?'

'We're sell-swords,' said the other one.

The tall one nodded. 'That's right. Currently we've sold them to your knight-marshal.'

'They don't come cheap, either.' The shorter one gave Huros a nasty grin. 'Our swords are long and sharp and very hard.' He definitely smirked.

'Lady Nastria?' Huros frowned. The thought of her sent a jolt through him. She'd given him a bottle of something strange, and he hadn't even looked at it. He was supposed to tell her what it was.

'If that's what her name is.'

The tall one belched loudly. 'That's the one. I'm Sollos. This is my cousin, Kemir. Since you're not the Scales, you must be the alchemist.'

'Huros,' said Huros.

'Well then, Huros the alchemist, make yourself useful. There's half a ton of luggage down there by the river. We'd quite like to move it up into the trees before the heavy brigade come back.' The sell-sword made a rude gesture towards the rider who was still standing over the Scales, waving his arms and shouting. 'I don't imagine he'll be much help.'

'That was pretty good, though.' The short one grinned again. Kemir. 'The white one forgot she had a rider for a moment there. If he'd been any slower jumping clear when she rolled ...' He drew his finger across his throat. 'Pity, really. I would have pissed myself. Still, we don't want all our luggage crushed, do we.'

Huros shook himself. *Words*, he reminded himself. He was going to have words with someone. And these two were very rude. And he was *Master* Huros, thank you very much. They looked a bit big, though. And armed. He bit his tongue. 'Um. Of course. Although ... Excuse me, but where have the rest of the dragons gone, exactly?'

'Their riders have taken them hunting,' said the tall one. Sollos. He gave Huros a pitying look and shook his head.

'For food,' added Kemir. Yes. When the knights came back, Huros would have words about these two as well. *What are they even doing here?*

'Can't have them getting hungry. Never know, they might set their minds to snacking on alchemists.' The two sell-swords were leering and shaking their heads. Every day Huros spent at least some of his time with ravenous monsters who could swallow him in a blink, kept only in check by their training and by the subtle potions that he dripped into their drinking troughs. These two, though, made him far more nervous that any dragon ever had.

'Um. Clearly. I meant the *other* ones. The rest of them. Where's the queen?'

The sell-swords looked at each other and shrugged. 'Keep an eye on the Scales,' said Sollos. 'That's what we were told. We keep an eye on the riders too. In case any of them get any bad ideas about stealing the queen's dragons.' He grinned and stuck out his bottom lip. 'Where the rest of them went ...' He shrugged. 'Don't know, don't care. A clever man might hazard a guess that they flew off to the Adamantine Palace, just like they were supposed to. But you're an alchemist, so I suppose that must mean you're a clever man, and you'd already thought of that.'

'Well ... But why ... why didn't we?'

The tall one sniggered. 'I don't know. Maybe some unsettling news came of late. Maybe your queen doesn't trust your speaker further than she could throw him. I hear he's grown quite large of late. Or maybe we don't know shit.' The sell-swords looked at each other again.

'Did anyone say anything about keeping an eye on alchemists?' asked the short one. The tall one shook his head. Sollos, Huros reminded himself again. His name was Sollos. He seemed to be the one in charge.

'I don't think so.'

'No, I didn't think so either.'

Sollos smiled what was possibly the most menacing smile Huros had ever seen. 'We're just sell-swords. We do as we're told and go where we're sent. No one gives us reasons, and we don't ask for them. Why don't you bother that rider over there, once he's finished laying into your Scales. I'm sure he'll know more than us. As long as you don't expect him to help with the luggage. In the meantime do you think *you* might help us? I believe some of it could be yours.'

The short one nodded sagely. 'It's the stuff at the bottom, I think. It might have been a bit squashed. Crushed even.' He looked at the other sell-sword. 'Come to think of it, did you see something leaking out of one of those boxes?'

His potions!

Huros ran towards the river as fast as his legs would carry him. He didn't need to look back to know that the sell-swords were laughing at him.

A shadow crossed the sun. Huros stopped and looked up. There were dragons in the sky, diving towards the river. Four of them, which was at least one dragon more than there should have been. And they were hunting dragons, not war-dragons, which meant ...

The lead dragon opened its mouth, and the river exploded in fire.

7

The Glass Cathedral

Being alone on Mistral's back was one of the nice things about being queen. All the dragon-knights had to share their mounts with the gaggle of courtiers from her palace, the mob of extra hedge-knights that Lady Nastria insisted on bringing and of course the alchemists and the Scales from the eyrie. Not to mention all the luggage.

Shezira sighed. Everything seemed so small from up in the sky. Over her shoulder, to the west of the realms, the volcanic Worldspine mountains ran from the sea to the desert and, as far as Shezira knew, on to the ends of the world. North of Shezira's eyrie, the dragon lands faded into the trackless Deserts of Sand, Stone and Salt. At the opposite end of the realms, King Tyan's capital was built on the shore of the endless Sea of Storms. When she stood among the mountains or in the emptiness of the desert, everything seemed so unimaginably vast. Yet from up here it was all nothing.

'I hear whispers of lands across the seas,' she whispered to Mistral. 'So do you suppose those are King Tyan's secrets, just like the mystery of what lies beyond the Desert of Stone is ours, eh?'

She sighed again and tried to peer around Mistral's enormous head. Somewhere down there ...

South of King Valgar's eyrie the peaks of the Purple Spur reached out into the heart of the dragon realms. Nestled in their far foothills, surrounded by the waters of the Mirror Lakes, lay the Adamantine Palace. Shezira had landed among its ramparts often enough; still, even now, the first sight of it, gleaming and sparkling like distant treasure in the summer sun, was enough to make her heart skip a beat whenever she saw it.

There! A twinkle, right at the foot of the last mountain. And sure enough a thrill ran through her, as though she was twenty years younger.

Sparkle it might, she thought to herself. For it *was* a treasure. It was a prize, a symbol of power. It was a place where marriages were brokered and alliances sealed, where kings and queens plotted their paths to greatness. It was the centre, the beating heart of the realms.

Above all, it would be *hers*. Soon.

She led her flight to circle around the palace eyrie, waiting for the signal to land. She'd forgotten how immense it all was.

'Do you like it?' She patted Mistral on the neck.

A gout of fire from below told her they were ready. She let Mistral plunge through the air. Like most dragons, he seemed to like that, dropping like a stone from among the clouds. Every time, she was sure he'd misjudge and they'd smash into the stone, but always, just as she screwed up her face and closed her eyes, there would be a clap of thunder as he spread his wings. The force crushed the air out of her lungs and made the ground quiver. She loved it.

As she slid from Mistral's shoulder, Hyram was there to greet her. His shaking, she noticed, had become much worse over the months since she'd last seen him.

'Y-You're going to h-have an accident one d-day.'

It was hard not to grin, but the business of being queen was a serious one, and moments of levity were strictly out of the question. In public at least. She bowed. Hyram held out a trembling hand and Shezira kissed the ring on his middle finger. *Her* ring, soon.

'Speaker Hyram. It is a delight to be in your presence again.'

He nodded brusquely and waved over some of his attendants. He and Shezira walked in silence away from the eyrie, the attendants following. Mouth-watering words gushed from their lips, describing the pleasures of the mind and of the flesh that awaited her, but Shezira barely heard them. *It should be Hyram telling me these things, not his courtiers. Has the sickness become so bad that it's robbing him of his speech? How long before he can't even walk any more?*

Carriages were waiting to take them to the palace. Then they had to wait for Jaslyn and Lystra and Lady Nastria and the other riders Shezira had brought with her, and after that there were endless rituals and formalities to observe, and then the obligatory feast to honour guests, none of which interested Shezira at all. At least Hyram had put some effort into it. Tiny alchemical lamps festooned the vast spaces of the Chamber of Audience. There were hundreds of them, thousands, strung out on lines like little glow-worms, hundreds more studding the vaults of the ceiling like stars so that it seemed they were feasting outside under the sky. Statues surrounded them, larger than life, silent guardians carved in granite. All the speakers who had ever ruled the realms, watching over them. Above them, marble dragon heads reached out from the walls, peering down from the shadows, sullen and brooding. Little lamps were hidden in their mouths to make them glow. As they entered, voices hushed to whispers or stopped altogether, awed by the Speaker's hall. Then the feast began, the noise resumed and the hall filled with servants running to and fro with cups of wine, platters of roasted meat, huge pies and colourful glazed pastries twisted into the shapes of dragons and men.

An adequate effort.

She sat or stood next to Hyram for the entire time, yet she couldn't talk to him. At least not about what she wanted. At the end of the feast, when Hyram stood up and wobbled and declared that he was retiring to his bed, Shezira watched him go, then slipped away to follow him. The Hyram she remembered would almost always slip away to bed early after a feast, it was simply a question of *whose* bed. This time, though, as she watched, he staggered and meandered his way towards the Glass Cathedral. She followed him inside, half expecting to find him locked in an embrace with some dragon-priestess. Instead, she found him prostrate at prayer.

She knelt beside him at the altar and looked up at the face of the dragon glaring down at them. Hyram stank of wine.

'I should thank you for your hospitality,' she said. Hyram didn't seem to hear her. She shivered. Somehow, the Glass Cathedral was always cold.

'This p-place is a lie,' said Hyram suddenly.

'What?'

'The G-Glass Cathedral. It's a lie.' He turned to look at her. His face was flushed and he was either about to burst out laughing or fall about weeping.

'Are you drunk?'

'It makes the t-tremors better. Three bottles of wine and I c-can almost believe I am well again.'

Shezira raised an eyebrow. It was true that Hyram didn't seem to be shaking as badly now, but he couldn't keep his eyes focused on her while he was talking, either. 'Are you sure that's not the wine, lying to you?'

'Does it matter?'

'I suppose not.'

Hyram nodded, as though that was the end of their conversation. He lifted his face towards the stone dragon above them, closed his eyes and sighed. 'Please ...'

Shezira shifted uncomfortably. This wasn't the Hyram she remembered at all, and she wasn't quite sure what to do with him, except maybe help him up and show him to his bed.

He started to climb unsteadily to his feet. Instinct made her offer a hand to help him, but he shied away from her as though she'd offered him a snake by mistake.

'I wouldn't even be here i-if my brother ... if Antros hadn't died. It should have been Antros who got this place. You and him. H-He was supposed to be the new speaker, not me. That was the arrangement. I-I would have inherited my father's throne, not my cousin Sirion. I would have been a king. I was going to m-marry Aliphera. Did you know that?'

Aliphera? Shezira shook herself. She hadn't the first idea what Hyram was talking about. Did he even know what he was saying? She got up. 'You *are* drunk. Let us talk in the morning instead.'

'It had to be one of us, but everyone liked A-Antros better, didn't they. Except you. And Aliphera.' He looked at her suddenly. 'I never quite worked out whether y-you had Antros killed or whether it really was an accident.'

She slapped him. He staggered back and fell over. 'You are *too* drunk, Hyram. You forget yourself.'

Hyram wiped his face and picked himself slowly to his feet. 'You liked Aliphera too.'

'I respected her.'

'Well I *l-liked* her. I was going to marry her once. But then …' His face grew distant. For a moment Shezira thought Hyram was simply going to fall asleep in front of her. 'Things happened. It would have b-been a good match, though. She was always the sensible one from that lot in the south. If I *had* married her, I'd have to have made her s-speaker after me, though, wouldn't I? And that wasn't the arrangement. S-So I did what I was supposed to do. I will honour the p-pact. That's what you c-came here to ask, isn't it?'

Shezira sighed. 'I came here to pay my respects to the Speaker of the Realms. I did not expect to find myself in a midnight tryst with a drunkard.'

Hyram peered at her. 'Promise m-me something.'

'Promise you what?'

'Promise m-me the truth. Tell me one thing, and I will p-promise that you will have this palace after me.'

'I am not, by habit, a liar, Hyram.'

'When Antros died, w-was it you who cut his harness?'

Shezira clenched her fists. 'Everyone who was there saw what happened. We were hunting snappers, as we often do. When we saw the pack, several of the dragons dived. His went with them. He always wore his harness too loose, and on that day, he wore it much too loose. He fell. He shouldn't have, but he did, and it wasn't the first time either. For some reason, his legbreaker rope was too long. It caught him all right, but he ended up hanging underneath his dragon. He was dragged along the ground and through the trees for about a mile before we could make his mount come to ground. I've never seen a dragon so agitated. Antros was dead when we reached him. It all happened in front of a dozen witnesses. No one pushed him and no one cut his harness.'

Hyram gave her a reproachful look. 'You n-never liked him, though.'

'Oh, I was young and he was well into his middle years!' Shezira stamped her foot. 'He was going to be the next speaker one day. He'd already had one wife and she hadn't given him any children. That's what he wanted me for. Heirs. I was a dutiful wife, Hyram, and he was a dutiful husband. I was in awe of him. I didn't have time to *like* him.' She sighed. 'It might have been a little different if I'd given him a son, but all I gave him were daughters, one after another. He never even saw Lystra.'

'Hmmm.' Hyram suddenly sat down. He sounded sad. 'No sons for Antros, no s-sons for me. The end of our line.'

'You can still sire sons.'

The speaker looked up at her, shaking. Shezira couldn't tell whether he was laughing or sobbing. 'L-Look at me, woman. Who would have me? Would *you* have me? You should have done. By rights, you sh-should have. After Antros was gone, you should have married me in his p-place.'

Shezira sighed. 'Yes. But my childbearing ended with Lystra, as you were so keen to point out.' She looked down at Hyram and shook her head. Not the man she remembered. Not the man she wanted to remember. The old Hyram had reminded her of her dead husband. This one ... She didn't know whether to despise him or pity him. She turned away. 'Besides, you blamed me for Antros. You still do. Somewhere in your heart, you think I had a hand in it.'

When Hyram spoke again, his words were so quiet that Shezira almost didn't hear them. 'Aliphera f-fell off her dragon too.'

She laughed. 'That's ridiculous.'

'If Antros could f-fall off, why not her?'

'Antros was arrogant. Aliphera was always meticulously careful.'

'I've sent B-Bellepheros to King T-Tyan's eyrie to find out.' He grimaced. 'Yes, th-that's where it happened, and that's where you're g-going. So I think I should w-warn you to have a care. P-People die around the Viper.'

'The Viper?'

'Prince Jehal. H-He's a snake, you see. A p-poisonous snake. A Viper.'

'Then I will be very careful. *Some* people seem to think he's poisoning his own father. Could that be true, do you think?'

'W-Why don't you find out? Because I'd very much l-like to know. A g-gift for me.' He stood up and spread out his arms. 'In exchange for all this.'

'It's cold in here,' said Shezira. She was tired, and seeing Hyram like this had killed all the joy that the palace had given her. 'I shall retire. I will think on what you've said.'

'I-I remember the first time I came here. I thought the Glass Cathedral would be a palace of light and colour. But it isn't. It's old, cold dead stone, its skin burned glassy by dragon fire so long ago that no one can even remember how it happened.'

Shezira turned slowly away. 'Go to bed, Hyram. Get some sleep.' She walked away.

Hyram stayed where he was, staring up at the stone face of the dragon altar.

'Th-This place is a lie,' he said again.

8

The Attack

A torrent of flames poured from the sky, swallowing the white dragon and her Scales in its fury. The river waters steamed. Stones cracked in the heat. Huros stood stock still. He was fifty, sixty, maybe seventy yards away. A little part of him that wasn't paralysed with fear noted that this was too close. At the last instant he turned his face away, as a wall of hot air and steam seared his skin and slapped him back towards the woods. He caught a glimpse, as he did, of the stranded rider, the one who'd been shouting at the Scales, catapulted into the air, snatched from the ground by the dragon's tail. Of the Scales himself, there was no sign.

'Run! Get under the trees.'

The first of the attacking dragons was wheeling away. As Huros watched, it flipped the rider held in its tail high into the sky. Huros didn't stop to see where the man came down; a second dragon was already diving in. He caught a glimpse of the white, curled up amid the steaming stones, its wings spread over its head like a tent, shielding itself from the fire. When he looked at his hands, the skin on the back of them was bright red. It was already starting to sting. He could smell singed hair. *His* hair.

The second dragon opened its mouth. Huros didn't stay to watch, but turned and ran, hunching his shoulders, trying to shrink into his coat. Another blast of heat punched him in the back. Where his skin was already burned, his nerves shrieked with agony. Up in the sky, when he spared a glance that way, several more dragons were fighting.

'Come on! Come on!' The two sell-swords were waiting for him at the edge of the trees.

'What? What?' gasped Huros. The pain was coming now. He'd

had burns before. Every alchemist had had burns. The backs of his hands, the side of his face and neck. He tried to tell himself they weren't deep, and that was what mattered. The skin would blister and peel, but it would heal …

It didn't work. The pain was excruciating. His hands were the worst. They felt as though they were still on fire.

The sell-swords took hold of him by his arms and ran, almost carrying him away into the trees. A minute ago they'd been so cocksure. Now they were white with fear. Seeing that made Huros's own terror recede, just enough that he could start to think for himself again.

We're being attacked by dragon-riders. Why on earth … ? Who? Who would do this?

This was war. When the queen found out, there would be war. Irredeemable, irrevocable. Unless … Unless there were no witnesses to testify to the attack.

He shook the sell-swords off and started to really run, deeper and deeper into the forest. Another blast of hot air caught him from behind, weaker this time. He caught a whiff of smoke. *We're going to die! They're going to burn us!*

'Stop! Stop!'

One of the sell-swords grabbed him by the arm.

Huros shook him off. 'Why? We have to run. They're going to kill us!' *Oh gods, oh gods, it hurts …*

'Look behind you.'

Huros looked. Back towards the river the forest was full of smoke. He could see flames flickering.

'See. We're far enough into the trees. The dragon fire can't reach us now.'

Huros shook his head. Every instinct he had said run, run and keep running until he dropped.

The sell-swords looked at each other. 'We should scatter,' said Kemir. 'Harder for them to hunt down three of us if we scatter.' Somewhere far overhead, lost behind the canopy of leaves, dragons shrieked and screamed.

Sollos nodded. 'Fire from above. That's how they flush their prey out into the open. Did you see how many of them there were?'

Kemir shrugged. 'Do you think they'll send men into the trees to track us?'

'Doubt it. But they might.'

Huros felt himself start to panic again. Both of the sell-swords were looking at him. What did he know about hunting on dragon-back? Not much. Did snappers always run in a straight line when they reached the trees? Was that how the hunters caught them? 'But, but ... It'll be dark soon.'

'Yes. Be thankful. It makes us harder to find.'

'Dragons see heat,' blurted Huros. He screwed up his face. His hands, they were the worst. He'd have given anything to run back to the river and drench them in blissful cold running water.

The sell-swords looked at each other again. 'Mud,' said Kemir. 'Good for burns.' He pointed higher up the valley. 'I'll go that way. See if I can't lay a false trail or two.'

Sollos nodded. He looked at Huros. 'You make your way deeper into the trees. I'll go downriver. Keep yourself hidden, that's the important thing. Anyone comes after us on foot, we can deal with them. Once it's dark, they won't be able to find you if you keep still and you keep quiet. We'll find you tomorrow, after they're gone. A mile up the river. The way Kemir's going.'

Huros opened his mouth to say something, but the words stuck in his throat. *No, no! Don't! Let me come with you!* But the sell-swords were already turning away. He watched, struck dumb, as they left him standing there. He wanted to cry. His hands, his beautiful hands ...

It's only pain, he told himself. *There's no lasting damage.*

Still ...

He began to run. He had no idea whether he was going in the right direction, only that it wasn't the same way as either of the sell-swords. Kemir was right. Mud. Thick cool slimy mud. That's what he should think about. Mud was good for burns. How did the sell-sword know that? Stupid question – there were dragons in his life, so of course he knew.

He tried not to think about the dragons who might be circling overhead, or the riders who might be racing through the trees in pursuit. When he was out of breath, he stopped running and rested against a tree, careful not to scrape his burns on its bark. The forest was silent. He thought about that for a while, and decided it was a good thing. He had no idea where he was, but with a bit of luck neither did anyone else. It was getting dark too. He tried not to think about wolves and snappers and other monsters that might sniff him out. Shelter, that was what he needed. Shelter and water. Food as well, but that was probably too much to ask for.

Huros made himself think about all these things until his head spun, and then he made himself think about them some more. They were a fragile and uncertain armour, but they just about kept the horror at bay. When they failed, he dug his fingernails into the burned skin of his hands until the pain became so excruciating that it overwhelmed everything.

Stay alive . . .

By the time the light failed and it became too dark for him to see, he'd found himself a place to shelter, nestled into the hollow of a giant tree. He tried to sleep. When that didn't work, he tried telling himself that it was summer, that the nights were short and warm, even here in the foothills of the Worldspine, that the sun would rise before long. He'd make his way back to the river, the sell-swords would be there, the queen and her riders would return, and everything would be fine.

Halfway through the night, it started to rain.

9

The Knight-Marshal

Lady Nastria, knight-marshal and mistress of Queen Shezira's dragon-riders, glanced up and caught a glimpse of herself in the mirror. She saw what she always saw. A short, mouse-haired, nondescript rider who shouldn't have amounted to anything much but who found herself knight-marshal to the most power-ful queen in the realms. An enigma. Sometimes even *she* didn't know who she truly was.

Today, though, if she was an enigma, she was an irritated one. She was having trouble with her boots. However much she stamped her feet, they were never quite comfortable. It was as if, overnight, they didn't fit any more.

'So? Did he or didn't he?' Queen Shezira sat lounging in a corner of the knight-marshal's robing room. She looked distant, Nastria thought. Distracted.

'Short answer: I don't know.' There. Finally one heel slipped into place. One down, one to go. 'If he did, he was keeping it well hidden.'

'We might have been wrong about Speaker Hyram. He's not himself any more. Perhaps we *should* have brought the white with us for him to see before Jehal gets her.'

Lady Nastria snorted. 'Holiness, Hyram hates Prince Jehal. He's also petty-minded and vindictive. You sent the white across the Purple Spur because if you'd brought her to the Adamantine Eyrie, he'd have found a way to ruin her, just out of spite.'

'I don't think Lystra or Jaslyn thought much of our speaker either.' *No. They were both too busy making eyes at Valmeyan's ambassador, Prince Tichane. When they weren't giggling at that vacuous Prince Tyrin and his brothers. Who, ancestors help us, will doubtless be waiting for us in Furymouth in a few days.*

'There's not much to think, Your Holiness, not any more. He was a strong man once. Not exactly a good one, not even a fair one or a just one, but strong enough to exert his will. He's not even that any more. The realms will breathe a sigh of relief when you take his place.'

Shezira got up and started to pace. 'The Hyram I remember, back when we were all a lot younger, he would have mated one of his males to my white while we were sleeping. Oh, he'd have apologised and made some gesture of penitence, but he'd claim the eggs, if there were any, you can be sure of that. But he's not that man any more. If you had seen him last night, you would know that.'

'From the sound of things it's as well I didn't. I might have been compelled to put him out of his misery there and then. Got it!' Nastria took a deep breath and sighed, as the second riding boot finally slipped around her foot. 'No, I think you were wise, my queen, not to bring Jehal's gift here. I didn't uncover anything in Hyram's eyrie to damn him, but still ... I dare say Prince Jehal would have been extremely put out if his wedding present had been spoiled.' She wrinkled her nose and smirked. 'All I found were whispers that Hyram's acquired a fondness for little boys of late. They say that no one's seen him with a woman for months and that his pot-boys keep going missing.'

The queen sighed, and Nastria frowned. Shezira wasn't herself this morning. She was pensive and troubled, and all because Speaker Hyram might actually be dying at last.

'Do you think I should have married again, after Antros?'

'No!' Nastria turned away quickly before the queen could look at her and fumbled with a buckle.

'No. I suppose not. Pointless really.' Then Shezira laughed and pointed to the door, and the two of them walked, and then rode in silence to Speaker Hyram's eyrie.

'It's a good eyrie, this one,' muttered the queen as they dismounted. 'I'll enjoy having it for my time.'

'I prefer Outwatch, Your Holiness,' said Nastria, but Shezira was already walking away, seeking out Mistral and her daughters, leaving Nastria on her own.

Which hardly bothered her at all. Being alone was what she did best.

Later, when they were all high in the sky, riding their dragons with the Adamantine Palace behind them, soaring with the thermals rising over the Purple Spur peaks on their way to rendezvous with Jehal's white and her little escort, Nastria wondered about a certain pair of sell-swords, and how well *they* took to being alone. Probably not so well at all, she thought.

A few hours flight was enough to take them around the south side of the Purple Spur peaks to Drotan's Top, a dome-shaped hill with a flat crest big enough to land a whole eyrie full of dragons. Drotan's Top marked the end of the Adamantine Palace's domain. To the west the land grew ever more rugged, rising up into the Worldspine and the rule of Valmeyan, the King of the Crags. To the south stretched the realm of the Harvest Throne, of Queen Aliphera.

No, Nastria reminded herself. *Queen Zafir now.*

Drotan's Top wasn't exactly an eyrie, but Speaker Hyram had built a small stronghold there with some animal pens. The hunting was supposed to be superb in these parts. As soon as Nastria had seen her mount was well cared for, she went looking for the queen. She knew exactly where to go. Hyram had built a lookout tower on the north side of the Top, where the landscape swept sharply down into the cavernous basin of the Fury River valley, and then up again to the Purple Spur peaks, a dozen or more miles away. Shezira was there, looking out over the valley, eyes fixed firmly to the north.

'I knew I'd find you here.' Nastria stood beside her queen. 'Looking for your white, Your Holiness?'

'Of course.'

'They have to fly up over the mountains. They have a much harder day of it than us today.'

'I know. And yes, I know they probably won't be here for

hours. But still I want to look. I'm afraid I shall be poor company until I see my precious white, safe and sound.'

Nastria allowed herself a secret smile while the queen couldn't see her face. 'I'm a little surprised you're not on Mistral's back and flying out to meet them.'

Shezira snorted. 'We both know where that leads. The sky is immense; we fly along different valleys, around different mountains, never seeing one another. Everyone gets lost. No. I'll bear the waiting. Badly, mind you, but I'll bear it.'

'Your Holiness, may I speak with you about Queen Aliphera?'

'If you must. I had invited her to come here and hunt with us before we flew on to be guests at The Pinnacles.' She frowned. 'It's a shame she's gone. I wondered if her daughter might come instead. The new queen. Which one is the older?'

'Zafir, Your Holiness.'

'Yes.' Shezira smiled. 'Another queen who could only make daughters. All those kings out there must have thought we had a secret conspiracy between us. This Zafir. I've met her, but that was years ago. She and her sister seemed rather bland. What do you know about her?'

'No more than you do, Your Holiness.'

'Really, Knight-Marshal?' Shezira raised an eyebrow. 'That's very unusual for you.'

Nastria felt herself redden. 'We should send a rider, Your Holiness, to the new queen's eyrie. We should ask them for her blessing for our journey. If we send a dragon right away, it will delay us here another day. If we wait until the morning, it will be two days before we hear a reply.'

The queen nodded. 'Make it so. Send Hyrkallan. He's suitable, and he's been chafing at the bit to let his hunting dragon off its reins. Mistral doesn't fly fast enough for his liking.'

The tone of the queen's words told Nastria that she was dismissed. She bit her lip. At the door she hesitated. 'I could stay, if you wish, Your Holiness. We have a few hours yet.'

Shezira shook her head. 'No, Knight-Marshal. Let me alone a while. I like it here. It reminds me of flying, with all this space around me; and I want to be the first to see my white coming in. Besides, don't you have a hundred and one things to do?'

'Only one, Your Holiness.' Nastria smiled sadly as she left. 'Only to serve my queen.'

10

The Ash Dragon

Sollos spent the night snuggled up inside a huge hollow log. He'd covered himself in leaf mould to keep warm, and in the end he'd slept surprisingly well, even after it started to rain. No one had come after him, and when he woke up, it didn't take him long to convince himself that all the dragons were gone. He made his way cautiously back to the river in case any of Queen Shezira's riders had survived, but all he found were the charred remains of the luggage. The white was gone, no one else was there, even the body of the Scales was missing. *Washed away in the river?* he wondered. But while the river was wide, the water was only a few inches deep, and peppered with sandbars and stones.

Maybe the Scales didn't die after all.

He shrugged, washed and drank, and then, more in hope than expectation, rummaged through what was left of their supplies in case something edible had survived.

'Gotcha!'

Sollos almost jumped out of his skin. Kemir was standing right behind him.

'Anything that looks like breakfast left in there?'

'No.' Sollos gave Kemir a glare. 'Burned to the core.'

'They really went for that white dragon, didn't they?'

'Whoever *they* were.'

Kemir shrugged. 'Some other bunch of lords on dragons. Can't tell them apart myself.'

'It matters.' Sollos sighed. 'We're supposed to notice that sort of thing.'

'Well I didn't see any colours, if that helps.'

Sollos gave him a sour look. 'Not really. Did you see what happened to the white dragon?'

'I saw it take to the air after the first couple of flamestrikes. I didn't hang around to see where it went.'

'South. It went south.'

'Took what was left of its Scales with it too.'

'Did it?' Sollos blinked in surprise.

'Hanging from one of its claws. Maybe it was hungry. It hadn't fed, after all. He must have been dead. He was right in the middle of that first blast.'

Sollos sighed. That explained why he hadn't found the remains of the Scales here. 'We shouldn't stay out here. If they come back, this is the first place they'll look.'

'It's the first place Queen Shezira will look too.'

Sollos thought about this, trying to work out how soon the queen would realise that her precious white dragon was missing. 'It'll be tomorrow before anyone comes looking for us. Anyone friendly, that is. Anyway, we ought to try and find that alchemist.'

Kemir looked truly surprised. 'Really? Do you actually think he's still alive?'

Sollos shrugged. 'He might be. You have something better to do?'

They walked in silence up the valley, staying close to the treeline and scanning the skies, until Sollos decided they'd covered a mile. For most of the morning he wandered up and down, calling out as loudly as he dared. The alchemist never appeared. In the end he gave up. For a brief moment he wondered whether it had been right to let the alchemist go off on his own. No one had come in pursuit, despite his fears. They could have stayed together. The man had been wounded too.

No, he decided. Kemir would tell him that when dragons came, it was every man for himself, and the best thing they could have done was to scatter. Kemir would tell him exactly that, and Kemir would be right. He put the alchemist out of his mind.

When he came back, he found Kemir sat against a tree. Next

to him was something large and furry, something shaped vaguely like a rat, except it was the size of a small deer.

Kemir grinned. 'Lunch,' he said. 'Do you think we could start a fire?'

'Absolutely not.' On a clear day like this a plume of smoke would be visible for miles.

'Well you're no fun at all today. They're not coming back. You never know, your alchemist might see it. He's probably only lost.'

Sollos shook his head. 'Tomorrow. By then the queen might be looking for us. Then we'll have a fire.'

Kemir shrugged and started to hack at the carcass. Raw meat was better than no meat at all. They had the river for drinking water. All in all Sollos thought he could come to like being out here, if he didn't have to constantly scan the skies.

Yes. And there's the rub, remember?

He got up and found things to do to fill the time, and eventually he splashed back down the river to the remains of their supplies, in case he'd missed something.

He had. The boxes and bags piled up by the river were all still ruined, and there wasn't a thing he could see to salvage, but when he turned away and let his eyes scan high up the sloping sides of the valley he saw what he'd missed. A great black scar, scratched through the trees. Before, in the light of the early morning, that side of the valley had been in shadow. Now the sun was high overhead, the wound in the forest was obvious.

He blinked and stared, and then looked again, and when he was quite sure, he raced back to Kemir and dragged him to come and look as well.

'There!'

Kemir sucked in air between his teeth. 'Is that what I think it is?'

'That's not a flamestrike.'

Kemir shook his head. 'No. Too big.'

'Much too big.'

'You think there's a dead dragon up there, don't you?'

Very slowly, Sollos nodded. 'Only one way to find out.'

'We've got about four hours of daylight left. Do you think we can get up there in time?'

'No. But we can get a lot closer than we are now.'

They looked at each other and shared a grin. A dead dragon meant dragonscale. Dragonscale meant gold, buckets of it, far more than Queen Shezira's knight-marshal had ever put in their pockets. Suddenly they were simple soldiers again. Simple soldiers out to make their fortune.

Getting there took them the rest of that day and most of the following morning. The smell led them too it in the end, the stink of burned wood laced with something else, something sweet and fleshy. The dragon was there, tangled among the trees it had shattered in its fall. Its wings were twisted and broken, but most of it was intact and still so warm that Sollos could feel the heat of it pushing at him through the air. Here and there its scales were black with soot. Its eyes had already turned to charcoal. Tiny swirls of steam or smoke still curled out of its mouth and nose.

Kemir pulled out a knife, ran up to its flanks, touched the scales and then jumped away yelping.

'Bugger me! Ow! It's hot! *Really* hot.'

There was the slightest sound from underneath one of the dragon's broken wings. Instantly, Sollos had his bow and an arrow at the ready.

'Who's there?'

Slowly, a streaky black figure emerged. For several seconds Sollos stared. Then the man wiped some of the soot off his face, and Sollos breathed out. The alchemist.

'Lady Nastria's sell-swords.' The alchemist slumped to his knees. 'Thank the flames. I got ... Um. I got lost, you see. And then it started to rain, and I was cold and I couldn't sleep, so I started to climb up, looking for somewhere dry. I saw the flicker of the flames up the mountain through the trees. Well, I knew it must have been a dragon come down during the battle to still be burning. Which meant it would be warm and there would be shelter, you see, so when the sun came up I came here instead of going to the river. Um. Sorry if I caused you any trouble. How did you find me?'

'We didn't,' said Kemir, and he pointed to the dead dragon. 'We found this. You just happened to be here, but since you are, maybe you'd like to be helpful. You see, I'd quite like to take some of the scales off this dragon. Think of it as a bonus for rescuing the queen's alchemist.'

Huros shook his head. 'You can't. Not yet. It's not hot enough yet.'

Sollos watched Kemir frown. 'It's blistering. You could cook food on it.'

'Um. Yes. Actually, do you have any? I'm a bit ... Well, I haven't eaten anything since ... Since you know.'

Kemir moved sharply towards the alchemist. He still held his knife. 'Listen, you! I want some of these scales. You can have some too. Plenty for everyone. You know about dragons, so you tell me how to get them. I know about knives, and I'm going to use this one. It can be on you or it can be on the dragon.'

Which was as bald a threat as they came, Sollos thought, but the alchemist didn't seem to get it. 'You can't,' he said. 'You simply can't.'

'Why the fuck not?'

'It's not hot enough. It's only been dead for a day and a half. It's started to burn up from the inside now, but it takes days for the skin to char. Come back in a couple of weeks with a heavy hammer. You'll be able to smash the poor thing up into pieces then. Underneath the scales it'll be nothing but ash. If you've got a cleaver that's sharp enough and heavy enough, you could have a go at getting the bones out of the wings, I suppose. I don't think you'll get very far with a knife, though.'

'A couple of *weeks*?'

'I'm afraid so.'

'But the knight-marshal and all her riders will be back by then.'

The alchemist nodded, and suddenly Sollos found himself

wondering whether the man was quite so stupid after all. 'Yes. I sincerely hope so.'

11

An Act of War

When it became clear that the white and her escort weren't coming to Drotan's Top, Shezira tried to sleep. When dawn broke, she finally gave up trying. The search parties left before the sun had finished clearing the mountains. In the middle of the afternoon the first hunter spotted a column of smoke rising from a river valley close by. Dragon cries echoed through the mountain valleys, and by the early hours of the evening Queen Shezira was sitting by the side of the river yards away from where her riders had been attacked. A dozen hunters circled overhead, keeping watch. She'd already seen one of her war-dragons, Orcus, dead amid the craggy forest. Lady Nastria reported that the hunters had found another. Which left one more still missing, and of course it was the white.

Snow.

Her hands were trembling, she realised. That was how angry she was. Nastria was questioning the survivors. Dragons were shambling about the place, clumsily cracking boulders and trees alike, unattended, swishing their tails and stretching their wings, either one of which could kill man in a blink if they happened to be in the way. It wasn't good enough. No one was talking to *her*. No one was telling her who had done this to her dragons, who was responsible, who had *dared* ...

She stood up. 'Marshal!'

Her call cracked through the air like a whip, and Lady Nastria jerked as though she'd been stung.

That's right. Come running when your queen calls you ...

Nastria bowed, deep and low, careful to observe every protocol and display of respect, and then dropped to one knee. Shezira wanted to hit her for being so cautious. Or maybe she simply wanted to hit *someone*, anyone, whoever happened to be in her way.

'Who survived, Knight-Marshal?'

Nastria kept her eyes to the ground. 'Your alchemist and a pair of sell-swords, Your Holiness. They were on the ground with the Scales and your white dragon when the attack came.'

'Did they see who did it?'

Nastria shook her head. 'No, Your Holiness.'

A savage impulse gripped Shezira. She drew a knife and put its edge against the bare skin at the back of Lady Nastria's neck.

'Have you asked them how they dare still to be alive when my dragons are dead?'

'Your Holiness, there is little—'

'*Have you asked?*' she roared.

'No, Your Holiness.' Nastria shook her head very slightly. Shezira felt the hand that gripped the knife urging her to bite into flesh.

'Who chose the dragon-riders to escort my white, Knight-Marshal?'

'I did, Your Holiness.'

'Who brought in those sell-swords?'

'I did, Your Holiness.'

'Who chose the route? Who chose the numbers of dragons that would fly? Who said that I should not fly my white to the palace for fear of what Hyram might do to her?'

There was a pause. 'I chose the route, Your Holiness.'

'Who said I should not take my white to Speaker Hyram's eyrie?'

Nastria didn't reply.

'Answer me, Knight-Marshal, or I will have your head here and now.'

'Then have it, Your Holiness, for that idea was yours, not mine.'

Shezira froze. For a second she seemed to go numb. Then she withdrew the knife. 'Yes. It was, wasn't it? And you chose the riders, but I would have chosen the same. I wouldn't have sent sell-swords, but I don't suppose they stole my dragon. Very well. Someone has betrayed me, Knight-Marshal, and they will die for this. Get up.'

Nastria rose. She was shaking, Shezira saw. *Good. You should be.*

'I will find them, Your Holiness.'

'Yes. You will. Now where is my daughter?'

'Lystra is at Drotan's Top under guard.' Nastria frowned, confused for a moment. 'As you ordered. With the supplies and as many riders as we could spare.'

'Not her. Jaslyn.'

'Flying guard, Your Holiness.' They both looked up at the dragons circling overhead.

'Get her down. I wish to speak with her.'

Shezira looked blankly around her as her knight-marshal stumbled off. They were in the middle of nowhere, in some piece of wilderness that could have been claimed by any one of three kings, but in reality wasn't claimed by any. The steep sides of the valley were covered in trees with nowhere for dragons to land except the river. No one lived out here.

Two kings and a speaker. Valgar, Valmeyan and Hyram. Any one of them could have flown dragons here and no one would have known. I should add Aliphera's heir as well. All she'd have to do is skirt Drotan's Top, which is hardly a difficult thing to do. But which one of them did this?

She dismissed Valgar at once, since there was no way he'd be able to hide a white dragon without either her or Almiri finding out about it. Hyram then? She'd mistrusted him enough that she hadn't brought the white to the Adamantine Palace. The old Hyram, he might have done something like this...

But ...

She shook her head, trying not to think of the broken and pathetic thing that had masqueraded as Speaker of the Realms. Maybe not Hyram. This new Queen Zafir? Audacious, perhaps, to start a war within days of gaining your crown, but she wouldn't be the first. Or Valmeyan, the King of the Crags?

She paced back and forth. Valmeyan. Yes. Easy to hurl the blame at a reclusive king who hadn't left his mountain strongholds for more than twenty years and showed no interest in the affairs of the other realms. *Not so easy to prove, though, and not so easy to exact retribution against a king who has more dragons than any other two of us put together*. Shezira snorted. She didn't even know where Valmeyan's eyrie was. One rumour said far to the south, close to the sea and King Tyan's realm. Another rumour said it was much closer, near the source of the Fury River, only a day from Drotan's Top. Other rumours said other things. She would have to find out.

'Mother!'

Shezira shook herself back to the present. Jaslyn was standing rigid in front of her, looking as angry as ever.

'Jaslyn.'

'You called Silence down. What do you want, mother?'

Shezira glared. 'Go back to the eyrie,' she snapped. 'Go now, and do not stop until you get there. Tell them that Orcus is dead, and most likely Titan and Thorn as well. Do not tell them *anything* else. Then bring every hunting dragon I have back with you. Jehal can take his pick as a wedding gift, and I do not care which one it is or who it belongs to. The rest I will send back here and they will scour these mountains. We will need another alchemist as well, and supplies to keep a dozen dragons and their riders out here in the wilds for as long as it takes.'

Jaslyn shook her head. 'Send your knight-marshal. I shall stay here until all our dragons are found.'

'You will not! I am your queen, daughter, and you will not forget it! You will do as I say now, and when you return from Outwatch, you will fly with me to watch your sister wed! You will have no part of this search.'

They stared at each other, mother and daughter, anger burning the air between them. Finally Jaslyn cast her eyes to the ground. 'If you find who did this to Orcus, I want them to burn,' she hissed. 'I want to *see* them burn.'

Shezira nodded. 'At last something on which we agree. Obey my command and I'll grant you that wish.'

Jaslyn marched back to her mount, and Shezira watched her go. *You got all that was worthwhile out of Antros but without his stupidity. Such a pity you insist on spending all your time with dragons. You could have made someone a good queen. You could have had my throne when I take Hyram's ring. You'd do better than Almiri will.*

She sighed and clenched her fists. All around, her riders were about the business of setting up a camp. At other times she liked these nights with the stars over her head, with no maids waiting on her hand and foot. Not tonight, though. Tonight her dragon-knights would circle grimly overhead while she slept – if she slept – on watch for a mysterious enemy who would, likely as not, never appear.

The sun set and Shezira retired to her tent. She tossed and turned and snatched a few meagre hours of fitful rest. When she rose, she almost sent them all back to Drotan's Top. Staying out here, so exposed, was dangerous. *It's what Antros would have done, though*. Perhaps that was why she stayed. She didn't know.

They found Thorn two days later, riderless but unharmed. The day after that they found Titan. The white, though, had vanished, and by the time Jaslyn returned with a dozen more dragons Shezira was resigned. The white was gone. By now she could be anywhere. One day she would find who had done this and there would be blood and fire and pain, but for now her perfect white was lost.

One little thing troubled her, as they turned their faces back towards the south, towards King Tyan and Prince Jehal, towards Furymouth and the sea. They never found the body of the Scales.

12

Lystra

'At *last!*'

Jehal yawned and stretched. He'd taken to sleeping through part of the afternoons, simply as a way to make the time pass. Queen Shezira and her flight had been expected five days ago. Dutifully, albeit at the last possible minute, he'd left behind the pleasures of his father's palace in Furymouth and ridden to the eyrie at Clifftop to greet her. Except she hadn't come, and the eyrie was a full day on horseback from the city, and there was absolutely nothing to do except look at his dragons and listen to the noise of the waves crashing against the cliffs.

He'd been on the point of going back, but now the Queen of the North had finally arrived. Either that, or someone else was flying thirty-odd dragons towards his eyrie.

Maybe it was more alchemists. As he dressed himself, he smiled. Hyram had sent twelve of them, including the old sorcerer himself, Bellepheros. They were crawling all over his eyrie, dragging in his men, his riders, his soldiers, his servants, his Scales, even their own kind, the alchemists who served King Tyan's dragons. Every day Jehal made a point of going to watch them at their work. Every day they took a few dozen of his people and filled their lungs with truth-smoke. They asked their questions: *What do you know about Queen Aliphera's death? Do you know how she died? Did you have any part in it?* Every day they got the same answers. They were so sure of themselves, and yet, in the days since they'd arrived, they'd found out nothing. When he was watching them, Jehal would smile a lot and ask how else he might be of help, and try to not to laugh at the frustration on their faces. In a few more days they'd be done with the eyrie and would move on to the palace at Furymouth. It was an intolerable imposition, of course, but one that was almost worth bearing simply to watch them fail.

The speaker's alchemists had almost unlimited power, but there were a few things they weren't permitted to do. Inflict their potions on someone of royal blood, for example. Which was a pity for them, since unless they were going to conjure up Aliphera's ghost and question her, that was the only way they were going to find out what had happened. Jehal had put a great deal of thought and effort into Aliphera's death, and so there was a certain pleasure to be had in watching the alchemists flounder.

But only to a point. Having them here was also a humiliation, an insult that couldn't be ignored and for which Hyram would have to pay.

Jehal pulled on his boots and looked at himself in a mirror, carefully adjusting his clothes to make sure everything was exactly as it should be. He couldn't really complain, he thought. This business with the alchemists would just make him feel that bit more justified in doing what he'd been going to do anyway.

There. He was shrewd enough to see through his own vanity, and he could cut a dashing figure when he wanted to. He nodded to himself in the mirror and walked briskly away, to the stairs that would take him down to the landing fields. It wasn't going to be enough to simply murder Hyram, he decided. Something more was called for. Some sort of vivisection, that would be more like it.

He marched out through the gaping doors of Clifftop and into the open air. Hundreds of soldiers were running to their positions, forming up into wedge-shaped phalanxes. Jehal wasn't sure whether this was supposed to be a show of strength or a display of respect. He ignored them, as he was sure Queen Shezira would do, and looked up. Dozens of dragons were circling overhead. Four were already coming in to land, plummeting towards the landing fields in near-vertical dives. Jehal put Hyram out of his mind; for now he had an entirely more delicious problem to deal with.

The four dragons unfurled their wings, three slender and elegant hunting dragons and one brutish war-beast. They hit the edge of the landing field hard and at exactly the same time; even at that distance the air shook and the earth trembled under Jehal's feet. All four stood exactly where they had landed without taking a single pace forward. Which, he supposed, was meant to show him how skilled the riders were. *Well it doesn't. That's the dragon doing the work, not you. All you're showing me is that your trainers and your Scales are as competent as they ought to be.*

He almost expected to see the four riders slide out of their saddles and march towards him in perfect synchronisation; instead, if anything, they seemed to be arguing.

Then one of them – it had to be Queen Shezira – took the lead and the others fell in behind. Jehal and his eyrie-master, Lord Meteroa, walked out to meet them. In the periphery of Jehal's mind he noted all the other things that were happening: the guards of honour carefully formed up, marching to exactly where they were meant to be, the Scales taking the visiting dragons to the feeding paddocks while the best of his own were lined up for inspection, harnesses and saddles polished and gleaming. None of this mattered at all unless someone made a mistake, and since Meteroa never made mistakes, Jehal largely ignored it. He needed his attention for the queen whose daughter he was about to marry.

Shezira stopped an instant before Jehal. She met his gaze with a stare of her own. Her eyes weren't exactly cold, he thought, but certainly not warm. And relentless. Above all, that was his impression of her.

Good. I could do with a decent challenge. He smiled and took one further step. Queen Shezira held out her hand, and Jehal bowed to kiss the ring on her middle finger. As he did, he was already looking past her, at the three woman behind her, who were presumably her daughters. One with a plain flat face, beady little eyes and an angry look, one rather more delicious, clearly the youngest, shy and nervous but not *too* shy and nervous, peeking back at him through her eyelashes. And the one at the back, who looked the oldest, plain and unassuming, with her eyes cast to the ground and much darker skin than the others. There was something kinetic about that one, as though any at moment she would burst into violent motion. She set Jehal on edge.

Oh gods and dragons, I hope it's the young one she's here to give me.

'Queen Shezira.' Jehal bowed again, deeper this time. 'Welcome to Clifftop.'

He watched her look around. She didn't say anything, but her face told him all he needed to know. *Adequate*, she was thinking. *Adequate.* He felt Lord Meteroa bristle behind him. Apparently her face was telling him the same thing.

He waited. This was where Queen Shezira was supposed to introduce her daughters and he got to find out which one would be sharing his bed before the month was out. And then she was supposed to explain what had taken her so long, and why he'd had to spend days out here when he could have been back in Furymouth, slipping into Queen Zafir's bedchamber every other night and helping himself to an occasional cousin in between.

Finally, Queen Shezira nodded.

'We met,' she said, 'a long time ago. When Hyram was made speaker. Do you remember? Your father was showing you off.'

Jehal smiled and bowed and gritted his teeth. *As if I could possibly forget.* 'Yes, Your Holiness, I remember very well.'

Shezira stepped to one side 'This is my middle daughter, Jaslyn.' She was pointing at the plain one. Jehal breathed a small sigh of relief. 'You won't remember her, because she only wanted to stay with the dragons and spent all her time hiding in the palace eyrie.'

Jaslyn's face tightened a notch. Jehal bowed to her. 'Grown into a most beautiful princess. Dragons are our life, Princess Jaslyn. They are what sets us apart, and without them we are nothing. You are welcome to spend as much time at Clifftop as you wish. We will set aside rooms for your exclusive use while you are here.'

Jaslyn seemed to soften, although only a fraction. Shezira's face didn't change at all. 'The lady at the rear is my knight-marshal, Lady Nastria.'

Ah, the dangerous one. Good. I don't have to be nice to her.

'And this is my youngest daughter, Princess Lystra.'

Princess Lystra bowed to him, but her eyes still never quite left his own. Jehal tried to hide a smirk. *Sweet, with a hint of spice. Now, is that the way you really are, or have you simply taken the trouble to find out what I like?*

'Princess Lystra.' Jehal made a point of not bowing in return for a second or two. 'I ... I ... am overwhelmed. I have heard of the beauty and elegance of the ladies of the north, but you must surely be the most delightful, the most sublime, the most radiant ... Why, I'm not sure I can marry you, for if I do, you will be the fairest of my father's subjects, and every lady in Furymouth will seethe with jealousy.'

Princess Lystra blushed prettily. *So ... she might be clever enough to recognise flattery when she hears it, but she still likes it. Good.*

'Would that not be the case whoever Your Highness marries?'

Jehal blinked. Queen Shezira clearly didn't approve of her daughter being so forward, but Jehal found that he rather did. *Apparently I like a little flattery too. Well who would have guessed?*

'You are too kind, Your Highness.' He smiled and gave a little sigh, and then gestured to the walls of Clifftop. 'Shall we clear the landing field, Your Holiness?' He spoke to Queen Shezira now, who gave a little nod of her head. The best bit, Jehal thought, of being a prince, was that you only had to do the interesting things. The tiresome logistics of dealing with all these dragons, all the riders that Queen Shezira had brought with her, servants, alchemists and so on and so forth, all that was entirely Lord Meteroa's problem.

As they walked, Jehal stole a glance at the skies, looking for Shezira's fabled perfect white. He was wasting his time, though. The other dragons were all still too high to make out any colouring, all circling silhouettes and shadows. He was itching to ask, but that would have been crass.

They paused for a moment at the doors to Clifftop. Queen

Shezira was obliged to survey his men, all dressed up in their gleaming dragonscale. For a moment, all was still and silent except for the distant waves crashing against the base of the cliffs.

'Your riders are a credit to your father, Prince Jehal,' said Queen Shezira, and Jehal couldn't decide whether she meant it, or whether she was simply saying what she was supposed to say.

Either way, there was only one correct response. He bowed. 'You're too kind, Your Holiness. My father will be delighted to hear your compliments. Your own are known throughout the realms for their strength and their splendour.' Which was rubbish, of course. If anything, the riders of the northern realms were known for quite the opposite.

Queen Shezira's face didn't flinch, but Jehal caught a flicker of disdain from Princess Jaslyn. *Full of fire and fury this one. All austerity and determination and not even a flicker of fun. I can thank my ancestors that she's not the one I'm marrying. A real joy she's going to be at the wedding feast.* The thought made him shudder. There were certain duties that fell to elder sisters at these times. *Poor Princess Lystra ...*

'Excuse me, Your Highness, but may I ask what's making that sound?'

Jehal's thoughts fell into disarray. 'Pardon me?'

Lystra was looking straight at him again. 'What is making that sound, Your Highness?'

Jehal cocked his head. 'I'm sorry, Princess Lystra, but I don't hear anything.'

'She means the sea,' muttered Shezira.

For a moment Jehal almost forgot himself. 'Have you not ...?' *Never seen the sea?*

Lystra bowed her head, looking abashed. 'I have seen the Sea of Sand and the Sea of Salt, Your Highness.'

Jehal smiled. 'And I have seen neither, and they are doubtless mighty and magnificent. We have a different sea here, and I will show it to you at once.' He glanced at Queen Shezira. 'If Your Holiness will permit.'

Shezira gave a curt nod. Lord Meteroa and the stewards of

Clifftop would doubtless start pulling their hair out at this diversion from the precise script of the day, but Jehal couldn't help himself. *Never seen the sea?*

He led the way around Clifftop towards the edge, where the land fell away, sheered and shattered by some unimaginable violence.

'Have a care, Your Highnesses. The edge is treacherous. It's a long way down, and many people have fallen over the years. The sea pulls them down, somehow.' He stopped a couple of feet from the edge and offered Princess Lystra his hand. 'The sea, Your Highness. The endless Sea of Storms.'

Lystra took his hand, and so he gave it a gentle squeeze and hoped that Queen Shezira wouldn't notice.

'It's ... breathtaking.' The cliffs dropped a hundred feet to the roaring crashing waves. The sea went on forever, a churning maze of white-capped waves stretched as far as the eye could see, fading into the grey haze of the far horizon, a mighty monster that could sometimes make even a dragon seem small and tame. Jehal smiled at Lystra. Up here on the edge you could feel the spray and even taste the salt in the air. Lystra was staring, mouth agape. 'It goes on and on and doesn't stop! Like the Sea of Sand, except made of water!'

Jehal gave her an indulgent smile. 'The Taiytakei say that if you sail far enough, and can navigate the storms, there are other lands across the waters, so distant that you would have to cross from one end of the realms to the other to even begin to understand how far away they are.' Mentally he congratulated himself. *There. That didn't sound patronising at all.*

'All that water ...' Lystra took a step closer to the edge. Jehal tightened his grip on her hand and she stopped. The cliffs plunged vertically down into the sea.

'There is a path, from the back of Clifftop, that runs down to the sea,' he said. 'The steps are worn and slippery and the way is treacherous, but there is a cave there that can only be reached by those steps. To truly see the waves crash on the rocks and send their plumes of spray up into the air, there is no better place than that cave. I will take you there one day.'

Jaslyn suddenly walked right up to the edge and looked down. For a moment it seemed to Jehal that she swayed in the wind that whipped and swirled up the face of the cliff. If she did, though, she quickly caught herself, and the next thing he knew Lystra had slipped her hand out of his and was standing next to her elder sister, laughing.

13

Furymouth

Shezira had little choice but to bite her tongue and hold her anger. As soon as they entered Clifftop, the rituals began in earnest. First the breaking of bread with Prince Jehal and his lords to assuage the hunger that came after a day on dragonback. Then there were scented baths and massages to ease sore muscles. After that she had to dress, and then came the formal feast, which ran from dusk until the middle of the night and beyond. Parts of it might still have been running when Shezira rose again at dawn.

Then she had to dress for the journey to Furymouth. That was the trouble with being a queen. She always had to be somewhere or do something, which meant there was no time left to keep an eye on her daughters, and it was up to Lady Nastria to make sure they looked the way they were supposed to look, and that they appeared in the right places at the right times. Without Nastria, Shezira was quite sure that Jaslyn, at least, would have sought out Prince Jehal's secret steps and spent the whole time in his cave. Likely as not, Lystra would have followed her.

Finally, the carriages to Furymouth were ready to go. All her riders were mounted up as escort, there was nothing left for her to do and she had her daughters to herself again.

'What do you think you're doing?' she snapped as soon as the carriage wheels were rolling. 'Both of you! Talking back at him? Holding his *hand*?'

Lystra bowed her head and peered back through her eyelashes, but it was Jaslyn who answered.

'He offered it. It is him you should take issue with.'

'And I will.' Shezira glared back. 'But that does not excuse the taking of it. And besides, Lystra should be speaking in her defence, not leaving it to you, as always. *You* will not be here a month from now.'

Jaslyn's eyes flashed. 'No, and I shouldn't be here now. I should be in the mountains, hunting down whoever killed Orcus and stole our Snow.'

Snow. That was the name the Scales had given it, wasn't it? Shezira growled. 'You are a royal princess, whether you like it or not. You go where your duty takes you. And you do *not* dance about like some farmyard peasant.'

'They are more … forward in these parts of the realms,' said Lystra softly.

Jaslyn and Shezira both looked at her. 'What did you say?'

'Since I was forbidden to go to Outwatch for months and months before we left, I spent some of my time in the library. I thought I'd try to find out a bit more about where I was going.' She leaned towards Shezira and her voice dropped. The carriage picked up speed. 'I think they are more, uh … Mother, do you know what a southern wedding is like? Have you been to one?'

Shezira shook her head. 'Knight-Marshal Nastria assures me that their customs are no different to our own.'

'Did Lady Nastria mention what you have to do on the night of the wedding?'

'Me?' Shezira blinked.

'Yes, mother. You. And Jaslyn.'

A smirk died on Jaslyn's lips. 'What are you talking about, little sister?'

Lystra leaned forward even more, until all three of them were huddled into the centre of the carriage. She whispered: 'It's about the consummation.'

'Lystra!' Shezira's feet began to fidget. She reminded herself that she was supposed to be angry with her daughters.

'Mother, I *do* know what happens on a wedding night. I've been watching dragons mate since I was five.'

Inside, Shezira squirmed. This was not the conversation she'd been meaning to have. 'Little Princess, it's not quite the same …'

'Oh don't be silly, of course I know *that*. There are lots of books in our library.'

Antros. Antros and his library ...

'*Picture* books, mother.'

'Lystra!'

'Well that's what you get for not letting me fly dragons with Jaslyn.' She smiled like the sun for a moment and then glanced at her sister. 'And you can stop laughing, big sister, because you and mother are going to have to strip Prince Jehal naked and take him to my bridal chamber, and before you let him in you are obliged to make certain that he's quite definitely ready to fulfil his nuptial duty.' She giggled.

'Lystra! How dare you! That's preposterous.' Shezira clenched her fists and sat back, half filled with fury. The other half of her had gone numb with horror.

'That's what the books in the library say. *With* pictures.'

'Ridiculous.' The queen glared at her daughters, one after the other. *Bloody Antros. It can't be true though. Can it? Are they that different from us here?* 'You should not believe everything you read in books. Whatever they may do in this part of the world, you are my daughters, and you will behave as *I* have taught you. If Jehal wants to parade you like a whore after he marries you, that's his business. But until then, by all the ancestors, you will deport yourselves as princesses should or you will never fly from my eyries again. Do you understand me?'

After that there wasn't much to say, and a sullen silence filled the carriage. At midday they stopped for a while beside a tranquil rocky bay. A small army of servants was already there, clearly having camped the night to be ready for them. Course after course of cold meats and breads and a hundred varieties of strange vegetables marinated in oils were passed in front of them, until Shezira though she would burst. At least this time her daughters behaved themselves impeccably. Prince Jehal remained flawless, flirting effortlessly on the edges of decorum without ever quite crossing the line. If she was honest with herself for a moment,

Shezira could see exactly why Lystra was so taken with him. He was both handsome and charming, after all.

Just a pity he's poisoning his father, eh? Oh, my precious girl, what have I brought you to?

'I spoke to our knight-marshal,' said Shezira when they set off again in the afternoon. 'It seems little Lystra is partially right. Fortunately we are merely invited to take part in this ritual, not obliged. So we can all thank our ancestors for that.'

Lystra giggled, and Shezira couldn't help but smile, and even Jaslyn was grinning and laughing, and the air in the carriage was much better after that.

'What else did your books tell you?' asked Jaslyn.

'Preferably the ones without pictures,' added Shezira.

'I know that King Tyan's realm is the richest.'

'You don't need a library to tell you that.'

'Their eyrie is so far away from Furymouth.'

'Another thing I can see for myself. Did they tell you why?'

She frowned. 'Ships. Dragons don't like them. A pair of ships belonging to the Taiytakei traders was burned by dragons in the time of King Tyan's great-great-great-grandfather. The survivors said that the Taiytakei would never come back unless the dragons were moved away from the city, and so that's what the king did.'

'He moved his eyrie?' Jaslyn looked shocked.

Even Shezira raised an eyebrow.

'Hard to believe,' she said, 'and a story I've never heard before. What of the Taiytakei, then? What did your books say of them?'

Lystra shrugged. 'I think they might be some sort of wizards.'

There wasn't anything Shezira could think of to say to that. Antros had filled his library with all kinds of rubbish. Shezira had never quite understood why, since as far as she knew, he'd never read a book in his life. She'd been the same, far too busy raising daughters and flying dragons and then ruling her realm when Antros was gone.

Maybe I should have gone in there sometimes. Then I'd know about southern wedding-night rituals. The thought made her smile. *Maybe when I'm too old to ride any more ...*

Outside, the countryside rolled past – sandy beaches, little farming villages, fields filled with cattle and corn; wagons and ox-carts, men leaning on staves, gawping as the carriages passed by. *Hot*, Shezira mused, as her eyelids grew heavy. *I'd forgotten how hot it is in the south.*

She dozed. When she woke up again, the sun was darker and the sound of the carriage wheels on the road had changed. *Cobbles.*

She snapped awake, sat up and looked out of the window. They were driving between houses packed together so tightly that they were piled on top of each other. They leaned into the street, reaching out towards each other ever closer, until rooftops almost touched and the sky was pushed out of sight. Now and then crossroads punctured the gloom, bright flashes of sunlight as the carriages trotted past. These other streets fell away, sloping down towards the sea, and with each one Shezira caught glimpses of the harbour, of masts and rippling waves, and the sun glinting on the water. Shielded from the winds by the curves of the bay, the sea here was still and calm. Lystra still couldn't tear her eyes away.

'Now it's just like the Mirror Lakes!'

Shezira nodded. The view from King Tyan's palace, built at the summit of the hill that overlooked the city, was better. She dimly remembered peering over his walls, sitting on someone's shoulders, gawping at the strangeness of it all. The ships with their flags and their masts and their sails had seemed like weird water monsters, and all the cranes around the harbour walls were like a forest of strange trees with no leaves. And the smell, the smell of the sea, reaching out over the ubiquitous stink of the city … She'd been five, maybe six years old.

'You'll see many strange and different sights here, Lystra. Keep your sense of wonder, but keep it to yourself or people will take you for a fool.'

Jaslyn tutted and rolled her eyes, but Shezira could see that Lystra understood.

'Let your eyes sparkle at everything you see, but say nothing.

Do that and Prince Jehal will be yours to command.' She laughed, thinking of Antros. 'And he won't even know it.'

'As long as you spread your legs whenever he asks and give him plenty of sons,' muttered Jaslyn, which made Shezira want to slap her. She didn't, though, because the carriage was slowing to a halt. A moment later the door opened, and Prince Jehal was standing there.

'Your Holiness.' He bowed and offered his hand. 'Welcome to Furymouth.'

They were at the foot of King Tyan's palace now, and the view out over the sea was unbroken. Close into the harbour, dozens of small fishing boats bobbed in the water. Further out, three much larger ships sat in a line.

'There should be dragons, Your Holiness' said Jehal. 'I told the Taiytakei that the next Speaker of the Realms was coming to give her daughter away to be married, and there should be dragons filling the air with their fire. In recompense the Taiytakei offer you this, Queen Shezira, in your honour. A sight never seen before in any realm.'

As Shezira stared out over the sea, tiny streaks of fire shot up into the air from the three ships. High in the sky, they burst into dazzling showers and swirls of colour. Shezira couldn't help but stop and stare. She'd never seen anything like it. She'd never even *heard* of anything like it.

It lasted for a minute, perhaps. When it was done, Jehal bowed to Lystra. 'A pale, ephemeral reflection of your beauty, my Princess. You will light up my father's palace as the Taiytakei light up the sky.'

'I trust we will have the opportunity to thank your guests for their most novel and inspiring welcome?' Shezira slipped carefully between Lystra and Prince Jehal.

Jehal smiled. 'Of course. An ambassador of the Taiytakei will be at the wedding. I'm quite sure he'll wish to speak with you, if you will grant him an audience.' He sidled closer, and his voice dropped until he was almost whispering. 'You should know, Your Holiness, that they have only one desire. They have been coming to our shores for more than a hundred years. We sell them slaves and dragonscale, but that is not why they come. They will flatter you and shower you with gifts, just as they did with Speaker Hyram and my father, but they only want one thing.'

'A dragon's egg, perhaps?'

'Most eggs fail, and they know this. A living dragon, Your Holiness. A hatchling. That's what they want, what they've always wanted, and they will do anything to get it. Anything at all. Why is Clifftop so far from the harbour? To keep our dragons away from the Taiytakei ships?' He laughed. 'No, Your Holiness, it is to keep the *Taiytakei* away from our *dragons*.'

14

The Search Party

Sollos poked at the fire with a stick and glanced up the side of the valley towards the black scar among the trees where the dead dragon lay. Sometimes it would smoke. Sometimes, at night, he saw the flicker of flames. Then it would rain and the smoke and the fire would go away, and when the rain stopped the wound in the forest would steam instead. Today, though, it was quiet. Still and dull.

'You're looking again,' grunted Kemir.

'I know, I know.' The queen had been gone for six days now. Which made it twelve days since the attack. Two weeks, the alchemist had said. Two weeks and a big hammer. Well, he had the big hammer now.

'Hoy! You two! Get that fire going and boil up some water!'

'Aye, milord.' What he also had was the company of a dozen dragon-knights, seven hunting dragons and the alchemist. Sollos poked the fire again and threw on another couple of logs. As the dragon-knight turned away, he muttered an obscenity at the man's back. The dragons probably didn't mind what happened to their dead brother, but the riders and the alchemist certainly would. And while half of them were away searching each day, the other half had nothing better to do than sit around, stuck with guarding the camp.

'Are you sure we couldn't murder them all in their sleep?' muttered Kemir. 'Maybe we could poison them.'

Before Sollos could think of a reply, a piercing rumbling cry echoed along the valley. The first of the dragons was coming back. Every day six went out searching for the queen's white while the seventh circled high overhead, keeping lookout. Since the attack they'd not seen any dragons other than their own, and Sollos was quite sure that they were wasting their time. By now the queen's white was far away.

Still, if it meant waiting here until the dead dragon up the slope cooled down and there was a chance of looting some dragon-scale ...

'He's a bit early.' Kemir was watching the arrival glide down towards the river. Sollos tore his eyes away from the forest and watched the dragon descend. Before it had even come to a stop, the rider on its back was standing up, unstrapping himself from his harness and sliding out of his saddle.

Kemir belched and threw a stone towards the river. 'You don't suppose they actually found something do you?' he said. 'They're not usually back for hours yet.'

Sollos shook his head. 'And there I was looking forward to another peaceful afternoon sucking on grass stalks and scratching my arse.'

'Yeah, and staring up at that dead mound of dragonscale and charcoal up there.'

'We're not going to get our hands on it. You know that, don't you?'

'A *part* of me knows that. We could buy land, you know. Our own little village with our own little subjects. Our own little manor house. With a brewery.'

'And a brothel.'

'Aye, and that.' Kemir sighed. 'Like I said, are you sure we couldn't poison them?'

'Even if we did buy ourselves a title, we'd still answer to the queen.'

'Oh bollocks to her! We could set up somewhere out here, in the mountain valleys.'

'And serve King Valmeyan instead?' Sollos snorted. 'I don't think so. Not him.'

Kemir's voice dropped to a growl. 'No. Not him. Not him at all. Do you think ...'

The rider from the dragon was running towards them. A couple of the sentries were close on his heels.

'Uh oh.' Sollos let his hands drop to his sides and unconsciously fingered the knives at his belt. Kemir stooped down and picked up his bow.

'You two!' The rider from the dragon stopped a little short of them. 'Sell-swords!'

'Sell-swords with names,' muttered Kemir. Sollos took a deep breath, gritted his teeth and bowed.

'Rider Semian. How may we serve?' Semian was the third or fourth son of Duke Semian. Sollos could never remember which, nor did he particularly care. There were some sisters too. They all lived in the vast tract of arid wasteland known as the Stone Desert and the duke served Queen Shezira as Guardian of the North. Sollos wasn't quite sure exactly what the duke was supposed to be keeping at bay up there, other than perhaps the use of first names. This particular Semian was about twenty, skinny and buck-toothed. If he'd been born with a different name, Sollos thought it most likely that he'd have grown up as the village idiot somewhere. As it was he was a Semian, so he'd grown up as an idiot who rode a dragon.

'We have found a town, of sorts. Hidden in the mountain valleys.'

Sollos exchanged a glance with Kemir. 'Then it most likely falls under the dominion of King Valmeyan, Rider Semian.' *It's obvious why Queen Shezira didn't take you south with her.* Rider Semian's helmet was slightly too big for his head, Sollos noticed. It kept slipping forward. *Less obvious why she thought you fit to be part of the search for her precious white. Unless she already knows this is a waste of time.*

Now *there* was a thought. What if the queen herself had been the architect of the attack?

'It is built on the edge of a lake. There is nowhere for a dragon to land. When I passed low over the place, they *shot* at me.'

'And what did *you* do, Rider Semian?' asked Kemir. 'Did you burn them, Rider Semian?'

The dragon-knight took a step back, clearly unsettled by the edge in Kemir's voice. 'Certainly not, sell-sword.'

'Rider, there are, here and there, settlements among the Worldspine that claim freedom from the dragon kings and queens.' Sollos spoke carefully. 'They are home to hunters, trappers and others who live off what the mountain forests provide. They are, to a large degree, harmless.'

'I would have to disagree with you, sell-sword. I am quite aware that such places exist, and that they are dens of vice and corruption. They do not survive off the forest at all. They survive by polluting the realms with Soul Dust, sucking the life out of their hapless victims.'

'Rider, it is true that Soul Dust comes from these mountains, but it is not made in places like the one you have seen. It is made in secret camps that you would not see, flying overhead.'

'Perchance you are right, sell-sword, but how does it permeate out into the realms at large? Through places such as the one I have seen today, that is how.'

Sollos decided he would have to revise his opinion of Rider Semian. Maybe he only *looked* like an idiot. He bowed his head. 'That may be true of a few, Rider, but not of most. And if something *is* to be done about them, it is King Valmeyan's place to do so.'

'The queen tasked us to find her white, and that is what *we* will do. These outlaws may have seen something. They may have heard something. News travels, does it not, among these places?'

Sollos nodded, slowly. 'I see where this is going, Rider. King Valmeyan burns such places now and then, and whether they're filled with honest men or villains seems not to bother him. They see a dragon and they run deep into the trees. They see a knight and they hide. But perhaps a sell-sword ...'

Rider Semian nodded. Sollos heard Kemir give an exasperated sigh.

'Sollos, you know they won't—'

Sollos held up a hand to silence him. 'Rider Semian, we are servants of the queen. We understand our duty.'

'Knight-Marshal Nastria was quite explicit. You know these mountains and these settlements.'

Again, Sollos nodded. 'Yes.' *Now how did she know that?*

'There will be a reward, if you find the white.'

This time Sollos grinned. 'Yes,' he said. 'I'm sure there will.' And it took every ounce of willpower that he had not to glance up the valley to where the dead dragon lay waiting for him.

15

Gifts

Zafir ran her fingers down Jehal's chest. 'So what's she like, this girl you have to marry?'

Jehal smiled. They lay naked together, side by side under the sun, in one of the solars. Over the years Jehal had made a few nests like this around the palace. Private places where he and others who knew of them could come and go unobserved through hidden passages. Small places, but with tall windows to let in the light and the air. Most of this solar was filled by a large sumptuous bed. Others served more delicate purposes.

'A girl, as you say.' He began idly stroking Zafir's thigh. The solar was thick with the smell of incense. 'Naive. Full of wonder at the world, and almost completely lacking in any experience of it, I would say.'

'Stupid, then.'

Not at all. 'Yes. I think she very probably is. Of course, she was barely allowed to open her mouth.'

'Queen Shezira would not want you to know you were marrying an idiot. You might change your mind.'

Jehal laughed. 'Were it possible to avoid this marriage, it wouldn't matter if she was the most clever princess in all the realms. She would still not be the most desirable.' He turned to face Zafir and cupped her cheeks. 'She did speak, though clumsy and out of turn. I dare say she earned herself quite a rebuke as soon as Queen Shezira was able to give her one in private.'

'Is she pretty?'

Yes. 'Not particularly. She was dressed up nicely enough, but she didn't wear it particularly well.' Which was true, he thought. Although unfortunately rather intriguing.

'Tell me she's ugly and deformed.'

'I'm afraid I could only say that about her sister.'

'Then I wish it was the sister that you were marrying. Why can't you marry her instead?'

'It was all arranged, my love, long ago, when my father was still well. My family has given a pledge, and I must honour it.'

'You could still marry her sister.'

'I will ask, if that pleases you, if I might have the choice. I doubt that Queen Shezira would agree.'

'You like her, don't you?'

Jehal's face didn't flicker for a second. 'I hardly know her, my love. She is a doll. All dressed up to look as pleasing as she can, but still a doll.' *Still, I would have to admit to being interested.*

'And you can't wait to unwrap her, can you?' For a moment Jehal was quite sure that Zafir was about to sit up and pout and become unbearably tedious. Instead she pulled him closer. 'I'm afraid I'm going to have to spoil your wedding night. If you have to fuck your doll then so be it, but you'll be thinking of me while you do it.'

Jehal growled contentedly. For a moment, though, he hesitated. 'I should go. Lord Meteroa will already be waiting for me with whatever news there is from the eyrie.'

'Which do you want more? Me or Queen Shezira's white dragon?'

'You, my love. Always you.'

'Then let him wait.'

'He's not stupid. He'll find out about us if we're not very careful.'

'But he's *your* man, is he not?'

'Yes.' Said with only the slightest hesitation.

'Then let him wait.'

Jehal let him wait, and then wait some more. The secret passage out of this particular solar led him right through the palace and back to his own bedchamber. Still he ran, and by the time he reached his own room he was out of breath.

He burst through the doors into his private anteroom. 'Lord

Meteroa! I was resting. I do apologise for keeping you waiting. You should have knocked.' He couldn't help glancing at the floor to see whether Lord Meteroa had worn a groove in it with his pacing back and forth.

Meteroa wrinkled his nose. He didn't bother to bow. 'Resting? You stink of a woman, Your Highness. Should I wonder who you've got in there?'

'See for yourself if you wish.'

Meteroa met his gaze. There was something unnerving about the eyrie-master's eyes. They were somewhere between blue and grey, watery and incredibly pale, and the man never seemed to blink. It was like locking stares with a snake. 'Ah. In one of the solars were you? Which have you got up there? A princess or a queen?'

Jehal pursed his lips. 'Perhaps I had both at once.' He picked up a plum and tossed it through the air. 'Try something sweet to take that sharpness off your tongue.'

Meteroa caught it and tossed it back. 'Thank you, Your Highness, but I had my fill some time ago.'

'Tell me, uncle, since you're so insightful this morning, how is it that, when their lover's thoughts begin to stray, even a blind woman can see through the most finely crafted lies as though they were glass?'

The eyrie-master gave a harsh bark of bitter laughter. '*You* are asking *me?*'

'I learned from a master.'

Meteroa's face became unreadable, the way it always did when he was remembering things from a long time ago. 'That's women,' he said. 'Shower them with pretty words and they'll be insensible to almost anything. Why's that? Because all their capacity to think is occupied with watching every movement of your eyes and listening to every nuance of your voice, searching for the infidelity that they secretly know must be there. Treat them like dogs and they'll fawn at your feet. Throw them a bone now and then and they'll show you far more gratitude.'

Jehal grinned. 'Your advice is as uncompromising as ever. Now tell me about the alchemists. Are they done yet? No!' Jehal clasped his hands together. 'But first tell me about my white dragon. Is she as beautiful as she should be? Is she perfect?'

'So far, Your Highness, she is invisible.'

'She's what?'

'There is no white dragon, Your Highness.'

'*What?*'

Meteroa raised an eyebrow and a faint smile played around his lips. 'Queen Shezira hasn't told you?'

'Told me what?'

'Apparently the wedding gift you were hoping for has not arrived. Queen Shezira has quite a few hunting dragons resting at Clifftop, but none of them is remotely white.' Meteroa cocked his head and raised his other eyebrow. For a moment Jehal felt an almost overwhelming urge to punch him. He carefully unclenched his fists.

'The best dragon in her eyrie. That is what I was promised.'

The eyrie-master bowed. 'I have made some enquiries. As always, it is the alchemists who have been most pliable. It would seem that some sort of incident occurred on the way. As best I can make out, Queen Shezira came here by way of the Adamantine Palace, but the white did not, and someone took advantage of the opportunity to seize it while it was poorly guarded. However, although there were survivors, including the original alchemist who set out with Her Holiness, none of them has come here. A first-hand account is sorely lacking. You are agape, Your Highness.'

Jehal closed his mouth. 'And so I should be, Lord Eyrie-Master, for what you're telling me is preposterous.'

Meteroa snorted. 'If I didn't *know* that none of your dragons has been away, Your Highness, my first thought would have been that this was *our* handiwork.'

'Yes, but since you know that it wasn't, that leaves a rather intriguing mystery, doesn't it? I hope you can solve it swiftly, Eyrie-Master. That white is mine.' He frowned. 'Besides, why would I steal my own present?'

'Why indeed? Shall we move on to the alchemists, Your Highness? I understand they've nearly finished.'

Jehal spat. 'Forget the alchemists! I want to know what happened to my dragon. Unless ...' He grinned. 'Unless Queen Shezira stole it from herself, just so that she didn't have to part with it.'

Meteroa shook her head. 'She isn't you, Your Highness. I think it unlikely.'

'Then who?'

Jehal scratched his head. To look after a dragon you needed an eyrie, and no one could be stupid enough to imagine that a pure white dragon would remain a secret for long, wherever it was hidden. So most likely the dragon would return before long. Meteroa was probably right about Shezira, so what was the point? Attacking Queen Shezira? Wasn't that incredibly dangerous? A huge risk to take, and for what? What could be worth such a gamble? What could anyone possibly gain?

A sudden chill seemed to fill the room. What might he do, confronted with this news? Why, someone who didn't know him too well might wonder if he'd call the wedding off ...

No. No, she couldn't ...

He turned his back on Lord Meteroa, waving him away.

'The alchemists, Your Highness? Grand Master Bellepheros wishes a discreet audience.'

'Yes, yes, yes. Let him come. Now go. I need to think.'

'Yes, Your Highness.' Jehal felt Meteroa bow and begin to back away. 'Once you have finished thinking, Your Highness, I trust you will share whatever wisdom you have found?'

16

The Outsiders

Sollos squelched through the mud with Kemir behind him. To his right, it grew deeper and stickier until it slipped beneath the waters of a mountain lake. To his left, the mud didn't seem to get any better at all, but the forest was thicker and there were even more roots and dead branches in the way. The sun had already dropped behind one of the peaks surrounding the lake, and in another half an hour it was going to be dark. *At which point*, Sollos thought grimly, *we're buggered.*

A couple of hours ago it had seemed a reasonable idea. Rider Semian had flown them deeper into the mountains. Sollos guessed they were about fifty miles south-west of their own camp when Semian had started to descend, and then banked in a half-circle around the shore of a lake. The settlement had been obvious enough, and Semian had found a place to land only a mile or so further around the shore. The day was nearly done, but the distance was short, and Sollos had been confident that they'd easily reach the settlement before nightfall.

Then they'd hit the mud.

'What we need are some boards,' grumbled Kemir. 'A pair of long wide boards. Our own mobile path. With a couple of eyes bolted into them to thread a bit of rope through so you can pull them back up out of the mud again. Do you remember that?'

'Aye. Going back a bit, though.'

'Yes. Being out here does that. I can't wait to get out of these shitty mountains. I really don't know why you were so keen to come back here.'

Sollos shrugged. In a way, it went against his own better judgement as well.

'Not that it matters now, I suppose.'

They trudged on. The sun sank lower, the sky darkened, and the mud didn't get any better. The settlement couldn't have been more than a quarter of a mile away. Sollos's legs were starting to burn with the exertion.

'My boot's stuck. Can I hate you yet?'

Sollos only half heard Kemir's complaint. He stopped. He had the distinct feeling he was being watched.

'Oh . . .' Among the trees, he saw a slight movement. Something *was* watching him. A snapper. Very slowly Sollos slipped the dragonbone bow off his shoulder. He began to string it.

The snapper advanced slowly. One of its feet sank into the mud. It took a step back and returned to watching.

'Do you—'

'I see it,' muttered Kemir. 'I was just thinking that the one good thing about this mud was that nothing big enough to eat us would be as daft as we are and try to walk through it.'

'It's on firm ground over there.'

'Oh good. Let's walk *towards* the half-ton man-eating ravening beast then.'

The snapper stepped into the mud again. This time it didn't withdraw. Instead it took another step, and then another. Sollos looked about, but trying to run away wasn't going to work. Most people faced with a snapper simply ended up eaten. The ones who survived usually did so by climbing a tree and managing not to starve to death before the snappers got bored.

Still, Sollos had a bow powerful enough to take down a dragon-knight. So if he hit the snapper in the right place . . . Except it was going to charge, any second, and his bow still wasn't strung. His hands slipped towards his waist, and to the two long knives he carried there. Waste of time really, facing a snapper with anything short of a lance. He could forget about his armour too. A snapper could bite through anything short of steel plate, and its back claws were worse. Even so, he couldn't bring himself to simply roll over and die. There was always a chance. He could always get lucky . . .

They hunt in packs, remember.

The mud would slow it down, though. From moving like lightning to merely very, very fast ...

Shit. I'm going to die.

The snapper opened its jaws and charged, and time seemed to slow. Even through the mud, Sollos felt the ground shake with its each step. He dropped the bow and pulled out his knives. It was coming for him. For a split second he seemed completely unable to move.

At the last possible moment, his arms and legs finally remembered what they were for. He didn't bother trying to step out of the way, but let himself fall sideways, out of the monster's path. As he moved, he twisted. One knife jabbed straight at the snapper's face, trying to distract it. The other arced in a vicious backhand towards where he hoped the creature's throat would be.

All completely wasted. Maybe if it hadn't been for the mud ...

The first knife missed. The second hit something and was wrenched out of Sollos's hand, and then the snapper smashed into him, the sheer force ripping him out of the mud and tossing him into the air. Teeth tore at his shoulder. There was a sharp pain from one of his ankles, and then he landed on his back, hard enough to knock the breath out of his lungs. The snapper was flying towards him, all teeth and claws. And yet there was something not quite right about it ...

He thrust the knife up towards the monster with both hands and closed his eyes. The snapper fell onto him, jaws gaping. He felt a searing flash of pain, and then everything went mercifully black.

He was in a pool, deep in a cave, far beneath the Worldspine. In one of the secret places that only the Outsiders knew. The water was icy cold. The darkness was absolute and the silence immense. He was alone. He was alone because this was what his clan did when a boy became a man. Except his clan was gone, and he was more alone than anyone had ever been. Only him and Kemir ...

Something snatched his leg. He didn't feel it coming, and it dragged him down so fast that he didn't even have time to breathe. He vanished with barely a ripple and sank like a stone. The water became colder and colder until it began to burn, and then the darkness blossomed into light, and the water wasn't water, but white hot fire, stripping his flesh and searing his bones to ash, and there was a face, the face of a dragon.

Something slammed into him. He opened his eyes and the world and the pain came flooding in. He was lying on a damp dirt floor. Everything hurt. His cheek was pressed into the toe of someone's boot.

'Morning,' said a voice that was both too loud and too far away. His head hurt. He started to retch, but that sent such spasms of pain through his ribs that he stopped. He'd seen someone once, in Queen Shezira's eyrie, caught by the idle swish of a dragon's tail. They'd flown about a hundred feet through the air and they hadn't got up again. If they had, Sollos thought, this is how they'd have felt.

Unless . . .

What happened when you died? He remembered the snapper well enough, so that had to be what had happened. The dragon-priests said that everyone went to the great dragon in the sky to be forged into new souls in the great cosmic fire. But the dragon-priests were mad.

'Are you going to lie there all day?'

'Kemir?' He tried to move. Bad idea. 'The snapper . . .'

'Got an arrow through its head. And so did its friend.'

'This really hurts.' For a moment Sollos had the almost over-whelming urge to get up and look himself over, just to make sure there were no bits missing. One bite was all it took to lose an arm or a leg, after all.

Even the thought of moving triggered fresh spasms of pain. 'My ribs . . .'

'Best I could tell there's nothing broken. Nasty wound on your shoulder. That'll need seeing to. The rest of you looks all right. You took a mighty thump when that thing crashed into you, though. You're probably bruised all over. Lucky it didn't land on top of you.'

'It did. Didn't it?'

'Half and half. It sort of bounced off you and ended up lying to one side. Otherwise only the ancestors know how I'd have pulled you out of that mud. Bloody stuff.'

Very slowly, Sollos rolled onto his back. He started to take a deep breath and then quickly thought better of it. 'My head hurts. Got any water?' He frowned. Instinctively, his hands reached for his knives, if only to make sure they were still there. They weren't. 'Where are we?'

'We're in the Outsider settlement, my friend. Home sweet home.'

'Where are my knives?'

'All right. We're *prisoners* in the Outsider settlement. That would be more accurate.'

Sollos blinked. Carefully, he looked around. Walls made of ill-fitted planks of wood surrounded him. Soft sunlight filtered in through the cracks. 'Prisoners? Why?'

Kemir shuffled his feet. 'There were ... words.'

'What did you say?'

'Oh, nothing to get so upset about. I blundered into the place in the small hours of the morning, which probably didn't help, and since I had you slung over my back, I wasn't in much of a position to argue. And they asked if we had anything to do with the dragon they'd seen earlier, and I said yes, and they asked if the dragon-men were going to come back and burn the place, and so I said yes, probably, since that's what they usually do, either that or the rider was just scouting for a good place to buy dried fish, which, let's face it, was about the only thing this lot have to trade. They didn't take that too well.'

Sollos rolled his eyes. He could do that, he discovered, without anything hurting.

'Don't get all crotchety! Like I said, it was the middle of the night and I woke them all up, so they were pretty grumpy. All right, I might have shouted at them at bit as well, but I'd been carrying you through that fucking mud for hours. I'd lost count of how many times I fell over and I'd had enough. Bloody stuff was bad enough when it was just me.'

'All right, all right.' Sollos forced himself to ignore the pain. He took a deep breath, sat up and then stood. And nearly fell down again.

Kemir caught him.

'Shit! You didn't tell me I'd broken my ankle.'

'Really?' Kemir bent down. 'I didn't spot that. Let me have a look.'

'No! Don't ...' He hopped back and forth, trying to keep his balance. 'Ow!'

'That's not broken. That's just a sprain.'

'How do you know? *Ow!* Stop that!'

'See. No grating bones. Strap that up and you'll be fine. Well, maybe in a couple of days.'

Standing on one leg wasn't working out. Sollos tried sitting down, but then his ribs shrieked at him. He ended up flat out across the floor, back where he'd started. 'So we found the settlement, and now we're stuck here.'

'That's it.' Kemir shrugged. He gave the walls a good shake. The hut seemed ready to fall apart. 'Not exactly stuck. We can leave whenever we want, and I doubt they'd stop us either. Of course, with no bows, no knives, no armour and you being in the state you're in, we wouldn't get very far. Not that we'd know which way to go in the first place.'

'That's fantastic, Kemir. Thank you.'

Kemir snorted. 'Better than being eaten by snappers, I thought.'

'One way to look at it, I suppose.'

'Not as dull as picking our arses back in the valley with those stuck-up knights, either.'

'Since you put it like that.'

Kemir lay on the floor next to Sollos. Together, they stared up at the ceiling. 'I did pick up one thing while we were all busy shouting at each other.'

'What's that?'

'Rider Semian wasn't the first dragon they've seen in these parts lately.'

'Really?'

'Could be they've seen another. Could be it was white.'

'Could be they want to give us our stuff back and then show us where it is?'

'Could be they don't.'

For a long time they lay in silence, looking up at the thatch of reeds.

'Lot of spiders up there,' said Kemir after a while. 'You know, we could ...'

'No.'

'But there's always—'

'Certainly not!'

'Right.'

Sollos could hear men talking outside. Mostly they were the loud confident voices of people going about their normal business, but he could hear whispers too, much closer. Eavesdroppers. He knew exactly what Kemir was thinking, but that was a last resort, something to be kept to themselves until they truly needed it. When they were tying him to a stake and lighting the pyre around his ankles, *then* he might tell them about the dead dragon.

17

Bellepheros

Bellepheros, grand master alchemist, bowed low. Prince Jehal sat on King Tyan's throne. Queen Zafir was to one side of him and Queen Shezira to the other, and then King Narghon and King Silvallan. Both of Queen Shezira's daughters were there, and Bellepheros counted at least a dozen other princes and princesses, not to mention almost every lord or lady of any significance within King Tyan's realm. All here for the wedding.

And this is what passes for a discreet audience?

Strictly, Bellepheros answered only to the Speaker of the Realms. Strictly, no one in this room had any power over him. Strictly …

'Your Holinesses.' He bowed to each king and queen in turn. 'Your Highnesses.' Now to the princes and princesses. 'I have been charged by the Speaker of the Realms to conduct my sacred duty. I have completed this charge, and now it is my duty to report to you, Your Highness,' another bow, this time for Jehal, 'on what I have found.'

Prince Jehal smiled and looked bored. 'We're all gagging to hear it, Master Bellepheros. Tell me first, though, so that we all might hear it – have you had every cooperation from my eyrie-master?'

Bellepheros bowed again. 'Yes, Your Highness. Every cooperation.'

'Have you been able to question every one of the men who serve him?'

'Yes, Your Highness.'

'Has anyone been missed? Has there been anyone you've sought and not found?'

'No, Your Highness.'

'And what of Queen Zafir's men? Her Holiness has remained here as our guest since her mother's death. She has not permitted a single one of her riders, her keepers or any of her men or dragons to return to her own eyrie. Has their cooperation also been complete? Have you been able to question every one of the men who serve her too?'

'Yes, Your Highness.'

Prince Jehal clasped his hands in front of him and leaned forward. 'So in short, Master Bellepheros, you have left no stone unturned, and no obstacle has been placed in your way?'

'The only people I have not questioned under the smoke are yourself and your eyrie-master.'

Jehal nodded. 'Those of royal blood. But you have questioned us yourself, without the smoke, and you have found nothing to contradict what we have told you.'

'That is the case, Your Highness.' Inside, Bellepheros felt the first pangs of unease. Jehal was backing him into a corner.

'So then. To your findings. The speaker sent you here because he believed that Queen Aliphera's death could not have been an accident. Was it?'

Bellepheros smiled. 'Now that I cannot say, Your Highness, for that is *not* what the speaker charged me to learn. My sacred charge here was to determine whether any other man or woman had a hand in her death.'

'There's a difference?'

'A subtle one, Your Highness. And I shall report to the speaker that Queen Aliphera harnessed and loaded her dragon herself on the day that she died. All her fixings and fastenings were checked by one of her own Scales. I have questioned that man myself under the truth-smoke, and he is innocent of any wrongdoing. I am convinced that no one tampered with Queen Aliphera's mount before she left. Indeed, it seems that the late queen was unusually involved in seeing to her dragon herself on that particular day.'

'Did someone kill her or not?' growled Prince Jehal.

'It is a conundrum, Your Highness. I have every reason to think that Queen Aliphera left Clifftop with her harness fully secured. If there was an accident or, for that matter, any malice, it did not originate within your eyrie, Your Highness. I assure you, I will make this very plain to the speaker. Also, there is no possibility that Queen Aliphera was attacked while in the air. The evidence is absolute on this. Her harness was not cut or torn or burned. It was simply undone.'

Jehal cocked his head. 'You haven't actually answered my question, Master Bellepheros. Did someone kill her?'

Bellepheros shrugged. 'I cannot say, one way or the other. No one saw her fall. She had sent her riders away. It is not my place to speculate as to why she would do such a thing, or what she was doing when she fell.' He'd given the truth-smoke to almost every man and woman in Clifftop and found out nothing, except that the queen had insisted on preparing her mount herself. He looked around the room, looking for clues in the faces of the assembled dragon-kings and -queens. Still nothing. Nothing at all. He sighed, and bowed again, this time to Queen Zafir. 'I am sorry, Your Holiness.'

Queen Zafir gave him a curt nod.

Prince Jehal was looking annoyed.

'So you will not say whether this was murder, or that it was an accident. So in fact you say nothing at all, and you have not discharged the duty placed upon you by our speaker despite every possible assistance.'

Bellepheros bowed deeply. 'My apologies, Your Highness.' Understandable, he supposed, that Prince Jehal wanted this to be over, for him to stand up and say it had been an accident. It would be the easy thing too, and yet he couldn't quite bring himself to do it. *Call me a perfectionist, but something is not quite as it should be.* 'If the speaker is not satisfied and demands an opinion that I cannot substantiate, Your Highness, I will say that Queen Aliphera took her own life.'

Queen Zafir almost spat at him. 'And why would she do that?'

Bellepheros bowed again. 'I cannot say. What I can say is that the actions that Queen Aliphera took when leaving Clifftop lead me to suspect she took something with her and that she intended no one to know of it.' He glanced at Prince Jehal. 'Many riders took to the sky that day. Even your eyrie master, Your Highness, and eyrie masters, in my experience, do not leave their eyries when they have visitors. Not without a pressing reason. Eyrie-Master Lord Meteroa flew that day, and when he returned, he also took great pains to conceal something. One might speculate that Queen Aliphera meant to meet with someone in absolute secrecy, and that she took with her something of great value.'

Jehal sneered at him. 'And what might that have been, Grand Master Alchemist?'

'I cannot even speculate, Your Highness.'

'Then have a care with what you imply, alchemist. Trysts? Secret meetings? Suicide? You will find yourself suggesting that my uncle and Queen Aliphera were lovers next.' Which drew a laugh from some of the less civilised, since it was well understood that eyrie-master Lord Meteroa's preferences lay firmly elsewhere. Jehal waved him away, and Bellepheros was glad to go.

Although for now he couldn't go very far. Jehal's wedding was only days away, and the ritual litany of feasts and games and extravagance was already well under way. Bellepheros would have much preferred to disappear to Clifftop among the dragons, or else hire himself a carriage and get back to his laboratories in the Adamantine Palace. But he was grand master, and that meant that Prince Jehal had to invite him or risk being rude. Which meant he had to accept, lest he cause any offence. He had exactly long enough to change from one set of clothes into another, and then he was back among the same kings and queens and princes and princesses as before, only now they were in a completely different part of the palace and dancing. No one paid him any attention now, which suited him well enough. He would wait, he decided, until he could disengage and retire. Tomorrow, he would hire that carriage to take him back to the Adamantine Palace. He wasn't entirely sure whether he was invited to stay for the wedding or not, but he could always cite his overriding duty to the speaker.

'Grand Master. A pleasure to see you.' Bellepheros jumped. He looked around. Queen Shezira was standing next to him, along with a lady knight he vaguely knew. Her knight-marshal, perhaps?

He bowed, deeply. 'Your Holiness.'

'How are you finding the entertainment?'

'Most impressive, Your Holiness.' Of all the people here, Shezira was the one he least wanted to talk to. She would be the next speaker, and thus the one to whom the order answered. Generally, history had taught that grand masters should keep a very low profile when a new speaker was imminent.

'You seemed very sure of yourself when you reported to Prince Jehal. Up to a point. And then very *un*sure of yourself.'

He bowed again. 'I am confident, Your Holiness, that no sabotage occurred in Prince Jehal's eyrie. What happened after Queen Aliphera left Clifftop, I cannot say.'

'Well I'm quite sure that wasn't the answer Prince Jehal wanted to hear. Especially that nonsense at the end. Nor will it be what Speaker Hyram wants to hear, for that matter.'

Bellepheros blinked. 'I do not understand, Your Holiness.'

'Oh come, Grand Master. Prince Jehal wishes you to report that Queen Aliphera's death was an accident. Speaker Hyram wishes to hear that it was murder, preferably with Jehal found crouched over her bloody corpse with the knife still in his hand. You give us neither.'

A chill ran down Bellepheros's spine. Even in his most informal reports he would never have been so direct. For the second time in as many hours he felt himself thoroughly cornered. He bowed once more. 'I give you the truth as well as I can uncover it, Your Holiness.'

Shezira nodded, already losing interest. 'And let us make up our own minds, which we would have done anyway. I'm sure you tried your best, Grand Master.'

Her tone was patronising, and Bellepheros had already taken

a few cups of wine. 'I have a concern, Your Holiness, that I must share with you,' he said. There. The words were out. No going back now.

'And what is that, Grand Master?'

'I understand that one of your dragons is missing.'

It took a moment for Queen Shezira to realise that they weren't talking about Queen Aliphera any more. Bellepheros savoured it. She gave a very slight nod. 'Yes. That is true.'

'Your Holiness, you are a queen of a dragon realm, and so you know the true purpose of our order. We are in every eyrie. We keep meticulous records of the dragon bloodlines and mix the potions needed to make them grow into their different breeds. However, our most vital and most secret task concerning the dragons is somewhat different. Your Holiness, I do not concern myself with the politics of the realms, but from what I hear it is by no means clear that your dragon has found its way into another eyrie. I hear her keeper has not been found.'

'Yes,' said Shezira sourly. 'One of yours.'

'Your Holiness, the dragon-lords may play their games, but we alchemists are charged with the ancient duty of keeping the dragons in check. Even one dragon allowed to reach its full potential is a threat to every king and queen in the realm. I will be obliged to inform the speaker.'

'Grand Master, what is your point? If the dragon has gone rogue, I have eyries filled with many scores more with which to hunt it down. Across the realms there are more than seventeen hundred, as you very well know. How is one wild dragon a threat to the realms?'

Bellepheros bowed yet again. 'My point, Your Holiness, is that my order is at your disposal to help in any way that it can, and that I shall return shortly to the Adamantine Palace, but as I am bound to travel by land, there will be some delay before I arrive.'

Queen Shezira nodded. 'Your offer is noted, Grand Master. I assure you, I am already conducting a quite thorough search. I *will* find my white, and when I do – and I find who took her – there will be blood. Good day.'

The queen moved away. Bellepheros wiped his brow. After that, he decided, he might as well start thinking about who his successor should be. It took him a few seconds to realise that the queen's knight-marshal hadn't followed her mistress away. She leaned into him and spoke quietly in his ear.

'Grand Master. A private word, if you please?'

He left Furymouth the following morning, in a carriage supplied by Prince Jehal and escorted by a company of soldiers. The other alchemists at Clifftop would just have to find their own way back to the Adamantine Palace. Tucked under his seat, carefully packed in straw, was a spherical bottle made of glass, stoppered and sealed with wax. It fitted nicely into the palm of his hand, and from the way its weight shifted, was filled with some sort of liquid. A very heavy liquid. Unlike the knight-marshal, Bellepheros knew exactly what it was. What he didn't know was where it had come from, or how several such bottles would have found their way into the possession of one such as Shezira's knight-marshal. It would be a long journey home, though, with plenty of time to ponder and plenty of inns with wine to help him think.

He didn't get the chance. Two days out of Furymouth his carriage was stopped. Masked men with knives tore open the door. Blood glistened on their blades. He could see bodies on the ground outside. He had time to open his mouth, but before he could shout, a hand clamped over his face.

18

The Price

Twice a day the door to their hut opened and half a dozen Outsiders armed with spears and knives would be clustered outside. One of them would very gingerly place a bucket of water on the floor, together with some dried fish and half-rotten fruit. On the first day, Sollos told them that they had six days before the dragon-riders came. Every morning he reminded them that they had one fewer day to let him go. It took until he was down to two before the Outsiders made up their minds. In the middle of the day the door opened again, and this time there were nearly a score of them. One stepped forward, a heavyset man in his middle years with a thick curly black beard.

'What do you want?'

'Some food that doesn't give me the runs would be nice,' muttered Kemir. Sollos shushed him.

'First of all to thank you for your hospitality.' Sollos smiled. 'Second, I'd like my bow and my knives and my armour back. Then I'd like to know about the white dragon.'

'And what then?'

'We find the dragon, we go away and leave you in peace.'

'We've seen dragons every day since you came.' Curly Beard looked tired. He was frightened.

'We're all looking for the white dragon. You weren't very friendly when they came by, so they sent us instead. When they find what they want, they'll go away. They don't fly for the King of the Crags and neither do we.'

Kemir spat. 'Doesn't mean they won't burn you out if they don't find what they want.'

'What if we help you find the white dragon. What's in it for us?'

'Not being burned?'

Sollos glared at his partner. 'What do you want?'

'Money.' Curly Beard set his face hard. 'A hundred gold dragons.'

'So you've seen one then.'

Curly Beard nodded. 'Could be. Could be we know of someone who's seen one.'

'All right. A hundred gold dragons. That had better buy me a lot of help.' Sollos could feel Kemir behind him, almost unable to contain himself.

'Up front.'

Sollos snorted. 'You must think I'm an idiot.'

'There's been a white dragon seen a few times in these valleys. Not here but somewhere else. I can take you to where they've seen it. And that's all you're getting until I see gold.'

'If you're lying, you know you're going to get burned.'

'Could be that might be coming anyway. So I'll take the gold first if you please.'

Sollos shrugged. 'All right. Not my gold anyway.'

Ten minutes later they were free. Another half an hour and they were in a boat, rowing across the lake with Curly Beard and two of his friends. They were a bedraggled lot, these Outsiders, thought Sollos. Their clothes were ragged and crude, a mixture of animal pelts and cheap cloth that had gone rotten in the permanent damp. Everything they had looked worn and well used, the handles of their knives shiny and smooth and moulded to the shapes of their hands. A few had belts, the leather hard and cracked, the buckles tarnished and bent. Others made do with string. Most of them, Sollos realised, were scarred or damaged; some were missing fingers, others had whole limbs or even faces that had broken and then healed out of shape. Apparently, life was hard as an Outsider. Harder than he remembered.

Sollos had been born and raised somewhere out here. He ought to sympathise, and yet he didn't, because he didn't want to. What was the point, when it was all long gone and burned away?

Curly Beard rowed them to the gravel flats a little way from the settlement, the place where Sollos and Kemir had first landed. They waited for half the morning, patiently standing in the steady rain, until around noon Curly Beard pointed. There was a dragon skimming across the lake towards them. A moment later the three Outsiders were off, fleeing into the safety of the trees. Sollos stood and watched the dragon. He waved.

'I hope that's one of ours,' muttered Kemir with a glance towards where the Outsiders had gone. 'Now would be a fine time to run into whoever started all this.'

The dragon circled over them once, close enough that Sollos could recognise it, and then landed, the wind from its wings spraying a cloud of gravel into the air. Rider Semian beckoned them over. He didn't bother to dismount.

'I almost gave up on you,' he shouted through the rain. The dragon, Sollos saw, was steaming very slightly.

'Well we're very glad you didn't,' shouted Sollos back. Belatedly, he remembered to bow.

'And? What news?'

'They claim to have seen her. They claim they know where she is.'

'Where?'

'Not here, but they claim they can take us to her.' Sollos hesitated. 'They want gold.'

'How much?'

'Two hundred dragons.'

Rider Semian didn't flinch, but his dragon suddenly snorted and snapped at Sollos, who fell over in his haste to get out of the way. The dragon glared at him.

'You ask a lot, sell-sword.'

'I don't ask for anything, Rider,' yelled Sollos, picking himself up and warily watching the dragon. 'That's the price the people who live here are asking.'

'Tell them no.'

'Then you'll never find the queen's dragon, Rider Semian.'

The dragon bared its teeth. Its tail was up in the air, flexing and flicking back and forth like a whip. Among their own kind, dragons usually lashed out with their tails when they were annoyed. It was meant as a warning. But when they did it to humans ... Sollos closed his eyes and tried not to think about it.

'Tomorrow,' shouted Semian. 'Meet me back here tomorrow.' Abruptly, the dragon turned and began to run, launching itself across the flats. The stones hissed and danced with each colossal stride, and Sollos fancied he could see the whole lake ripple. Then the monster unfurled its wings and with a clap of thunder hurled itself into the air and was away. He watched it go. He could actually see it rise through the air with each beat of its wings, he realised, and then dip again between them.

'You should have asked for a thousand,' said Kemir, suddenly standing beside him.

'Apparently so.' Sollos shrugged. 'I suppose it's not his money either.'

19

The Taiytakei

Any other dragon-lord, mused Jehal, wouldn't have these sorts of problems. Any other dragon-lord would simply have gone to their eyrie, looked at the dragons and then gone back to their palace again. Any other dragon-lord would have built their eyrie conveniently *close* to their palace. *He,* though, had to ride out to a field a little way outside the city to look at Queen Shezira's dragons. Not that he minded all that much, but the fact that he had to go meant that everyone else had to go too, and that meant shuffling everyone into carriages. What should have been a twenty-minute jaunt on the back of a horse had taken them an hour and a half, and now the whole wedding was running late. Knowing that the dragon he wanted wasn't going to be here didn't help either.

He tried to keep himself amused by mentally undressing his guests. Zafir's little sister Princess Zara-Kiam was going to be worth undressing for real quite soon, he decided. There were a few cousins and other minor relatives out there who might be worth some attention too: Queen Fyon's youngest, Princess Lilytha, for example, if her brother Prince Tyrin hadn't got to her first. He narrowed his eyes, looking at them standing next to each other, trying to decide.

He sighed. Everyone had been telling him how weddings were supposed to be wonderful days filled with joy and happiness, but looking around him he couldn't see much sign of either. His guests were grumbling and shifting on their feet, already overstuffed with a hundred pointless delicacies. Queen Shezira looked tense. She hadn't actually told him that the white wasn't here, so there was always the chance that no one else had told him either. Jehal had already decided to have some fun with that. Queen Zafir had a permanent angry scowl etched into her face. For himself, he couldn't shake the feeling that the whole exercise was a waste of time. The only person who seemed to be enjoying herself was Princess Lystra.

They sat next to each other on their wedding thrones, shaded by a makeshift awning while everyone else burned up in the summer sun. If he wanted to, he could have reached out and taken his bride's hand, but apparently he wasn't supposed to do that yet. As best he could tell, they were in some sort of interim state between being not married and being married. They'd had a dawn ritual and then a morning feast. After that came the giving of gifts, and then everyone kicked their heels until the evening. There was another feast, a dusk ritual, then the whole humiliating bit about being drugged and stripped naked in front of all the wedding guests. What was that? Revenge for having to stand around and be bored all day?

Finally, after the consummation, once the whole thing was over, they never had to look at each other again, if that was what they wanted. Maybe it was *supposed* to be an ordeal. A warning of things to come? A test of strength?

Someone was parading a pair of horses in front of him. Strictly speaking, they were parading them in front of King Tyan, who sat in his own throne next to Jehal's, drooling and snoring. He was still king after all. Jehal smiled. They were wonderful beasts, pure white, with gold and silver livery. A stallion and a mare. Jehal stifled a yawn.

'Very nice,' he said. 'They will be the most beautiful creatures in my stables. Tell ...' Oh, now this was going to be a problem. He'd let his mind wander so far that he hadn't heard who they were from, and now he was going to look stupid and insult someone all at once. 'I am in awe. Bring them closer.' He glanced around in search of helpful clues. *Horses. Who likes horses? People always give the sort of gift they'd like to receive.*

'King Valgar is too kind,' said Princess Lystra quietly. For the first time since the wedding had begun she wasn't smiling. 'He meant them to go with the dragon. To take us to and from your eyrie.'

So she assumes I know. She doesn't know that her mother hasn't told me. He could have some fun with that too.

'King Valgar is too kind indeed.' He smiled, waving the horses away. Valgar wasn't here so there was no need to waste any time on flattering his presents. 'Let King Valgar know that they are the most beautiful horses in my realm, and that Princess Lystra and I shall ride them to and from Clifftop for a year, as a mark of our respect for his generosity.' He leaned towards Princess Lystra. 'Is the dragon as pure?'

She turned to him, startled, with a wonderful look of horror. 'You don't know?'

'What don't I know?' He smiled again, all innocence, as various shades of panic flew across her face.

Lystra turned towards her mother, sat on the other side of her, and started whispering.

Jehal tapped Lystra on the back of the hand. 'Sorry, did you mean the theft of your white dragon? I know about *that*. Terrible business. I'm sure it doesn't matter.' She was shaking, completely flustered, like a rabbit caught by a farmer's lantern. He kept his smile in place, warm and reassuring, glancing at her from time to time, making sure she caught his eye. *Terrible business?* That was putting it mildly. *I'm sure it doesn't matter?* Of course it bloody mattered. At the very least everyone who had anything to do with the theft was going to die. With a bit of luck, open warfare might break out. There would be trials and tribunals in the Adamantine Palace. It was quite easy to imagine an entire realm falling. Now *that* would be fun.

Somehow, though, tormenting Princess Lystra wasn't as satisfying as it ought to have been. She still looked pale and worried when her mother's dragons were finally brought down to the field and Jehal stood up to inspect them. He picked one quickly, said something nice about it and waved the rest away. He'd had his bride squirming in her seat, and instead of revelling in her discomfort, he found he felt ... well, vaguely guilty.

And that wasn't right. That wasn't how it was supposed to be at all.

Maybe it was the heat. He sighed, stood up and made a pretty speech about how this was the start of a new era, and how proud he was to be joined to such a great clan and yet humbled too. When he was done, he hoped that at least a few of his guests had paid more attention to it than he had.

Riding back towards the palace didn't help either. Having a wife had sounded like a simple enough business, and it had all been arranged so long ago that he'd never thought to question it. However, meeting her in the flesh was somehow ... disconcerting. She would be his queen one day, perhaps sooner rather than later. Which was fine, as long as she was the *right* queen. A simple queen with a demented obsession for needlework or embroidery or something like that, who stayed in her tower all day, had no interest in the world around her and paused only from her handicrafts to pop out a steady stream of heirs, preferably male ones. That was the sort of queen he needed.

'Terrible business,' muttered a voice beside him. Jehal snapped out of his reverie. Lord Meteroa was riding next to him. 'I'm sure it doesn't matter, Your Highness.'

'What do *you* want?'

'I'm afraid you have to attend a little diversion, Your Highness. After all, no one can leave the ceremony of gifts until you and King Tyan lead the way, and yet somehow everyone is required to be in place for the wedding feast before you arrive. In the normal course of things, this would simply oblige you to take a particularly tortuous path from one part of the palace to another, with perhaps a dalliance in the gardens to kill the time. As things are ...'

Jehal raised an eyebrow. 'What, with several hundred relatives all rushing back to the palace as fast as they can, all getting in each other's way? And that's just Aunt Fyon's family.'

Meteroa smiled and nodded. 'Your Highness must be delayed.'

'And do you have something in mind, Eyrie-Master?'

'I do indeed, Your Highness.' Meteroa flashed Jehal a knowing look and kicked his horse into a trot. After a moment Jehal followed him. They turned off the road and galloped down a narrow track lined with trees, then off into the fields. Behind them, a dozen of Jehal's dragon-knights followed, keeping at a discreet distance yet never too far away.

'You weren't thinking about the dragons at all when you picked one, were you?' shouted Meteroa.

'On the contrary,' called Jehal. 'My thoughts were entirely devoted to how none of them was white.'

'Really? I could have sworn your mind was somewhere else. I certainly wouldn't have made the same choice as you did.'

Jehal felt a flash of irritation. Lord Meteroa was clever and loyal and ran Clifftop like a precise machine, and his frankness was usually a refreshing change from the sycophancy that infested the rest of King Tyan's court. Sometimes, though, the eyrie-master seemed to forget that Jehal wasn't King Tyan's little boy any more.

'Well it was mine to choose. Queen Shezira can thank me for not taking the best she had to offer.' Mentally, Jehal kicked himself. He'd *meant* to choose the ash-grey, the dragon that Princess Lystra's elder sister rode. He'd completely forgotten about that, and now he had no idea which one of Shezira's knights would be flying home without a mount of his own. He sighed. He ought to find out. Doubtless he'd made himself another enemy there.

The ground was starting to get rocky. Lord Meteroa dived down another track, where the trees and undergrowth pressed in so close that Jehal kept having to duck while thorns tore at his cloak. *Better change into a new one as soon as we get to the palace. That'll keep everyone waiting another few minutes.* After a little while the wood gave way to great slabs of rock, and the mud below became sand. They were in the Stone Forest, a maze of spikes and spires and walls of rock woven with tracks and trails and clearings, caves and tunnels. Jehal knew it like the back of his hand. It was the perfect place for a secret meeting.

A perfect place for an ambush too.

He slowed and stopped, then glanced over his shoulder. 'What *is* this diversion of yours, eyrie-master? I'm not so sure I shall like it.'

'Wait here if you will, Your Highness. I will fetch them to you.'

'And *who* will you fetch?' Something about Meteroa's manner made Jehal uneasy.

'No one who means you any harm, Your Highness.'

Jehal looked behind him again. His knights were emerging from the woods, funnelling into the cleft between the rocks.

'This is not a good place to stop, eyrie-mas—' He broke off. Emerging from the shadows between the stones, three riders approached, their horses stepping slowly in the sand. They were strange folk, dark-skinned with overly ornate clothes studded with gold and jewels and dazzling rainbows of feathers. They stopped a dozen paces short of where Lord Meteroa waited, dismounted and bowed.

Taiytakei.

The middle one, who wore the brightest clothes, came a few paces closer and then carefully knelt in the sand.

'Your Holiness,' he said. 'We pay homage on this auspicious day.'

With slow deliberate movements, like a cat stalking its prey, Jehal dismounted. He drew nearer, never taking his eyes off the man.

'Sea traders,' he whispered. He glanced at Meteroa. 'What is this?'

'We bring you a gift,' said the dark man. 'A gift for you, O mightiest of princes, to honour your wedding day.'

Jehal forced a smile. 'Forgive me, but it is said that the Taiytakei do not deal in gifts, only trade, and that what may appear at first as a gift will always turn out to have a price.'

The kneeling man beckoned one of his fellows, who brought over something under a cloth and then quickly withdrew. 'We wish nothing more than to bring to you what you desire, and take from you that for which you have no need.' Slowly, the man placed the object on the ground and then backed away, still on his knees. When he reached the others, he rose and turned. All three of them mounted and rode slowly away.

Jehal watched them go, and only when they were long gone did his eyes move slowly to what they had left behind. He took a step towards it.

Meteroa jumped off his horse.

'Let me, Your Highness.'

'Why did you bring me here?'

'Forgive me, my Prince, but I will show you. The Taiytakei wished to give this to you in person and in private. You will see why.' Meteroa tore away the cloth. Underneath was an exquisite box carved from black wood, inlaid with vermilion and gold.

'Open it.'

Meteroa lifted the lid. Inside lay three strips of plain silk, two black and one white, and two tiny golden dragons with ruby eyes.

'Pretty.' Jehal shrugged. He would have said more, but one of the golden dragons turned its head and looked at him.

Meteroa pulled out one of the silks and snapped the box shut. 'Best that others do not see,' he murmured. 'Here.' He handed Jehal a strip of black silk. 'Wear it around your eyes. You will not be disappointed.'

Jehal smiled. Meteroa seemed to be in deadly earnest, and so he wrapped the black silk across his eyes. Immediately the world seemed to shift and shimmer. Voices spoke inside his head: *You are the speaker in waiting, and we are the gift of the Taiytakei.*

For a moment he thought he saw himself, as if looking through another's eyes. He ripped away the silk. Meteroa was still holding the box, but now he had it slightly open again. Four glittering ruby eyes peered up at him.

'In the sunlight they can fly. Or when you will them to,' murmured Meteroa. 'Wear the silk and they will obey your thoughts. They will see and they will listen and you will have their eyes and ears. There will be no secrets you cannot unlock.' He closed the box again and smiled. 'Was I wrong, Your Highness, to bring you to the Taiytakei, so that you might receive their gift?'

'No.' Jehal shook his head in wonder. 'No, Eyrie-Master, you were not wrong.'

He looked at the box and grinned to himself. *You are the speaker in waiting ...*

20

Knights

Rider Semian, when he came back the next day, didn't bring only gold. Three more dragons arrived with him, and on the back of each dragon were three knights. Semian himself brought the alchemist. They landed on the same gravel flats in a flurry of wings and spray. Sollos watched while the alchemist and the riders dismounted and rearranged themselves. Most of the knights stayed on the ground, crouching cautiously behind a protective wall of shields with the alchemist in the middle, while the dragons took to the sky again.

Archers. They're afraid of archers. Which made Sollos think of the last time he'd watched a dragon-knight hand over a purse full of gold to a mysterious stranger.

He stood his ground, out in the open, waiting. Kemir was beside him. Curly Beard and his friends had scuttled off to hide among the trees and watch. Semian emerged from the midst of his men and advanced slowly, looking around, scanning the shore of the lake. Up above, the dragons circled.

Sollos bowed. 'Riders,' he acknowledged. He knew some of the other dragon-knights only by their faces. Despite two weeks of sharing a camp together, they'd never asked his name, never called him anything except sell-sword. Not one had spoken to him other than to order him around.

Semian gave him a disdainful look. 'Where are your outlaw friends, sell-sword?'

'Hiding and waiting to see what you do. Did you bring the gold, Rider?'

'One hundred coins. They may have the other half when we have found the dragon.'

Sollos silently clenched his fists. 'That's not going to work, Rider. They know perfectly well that you'll simply burn their village if they try to steal from you. They expect you to burn it anyway, before you leave.'

'I will honour our bargain if they do the same.'

'I don't doubt it, Rider, but these people are used to King Valmeyan's men, and the King of the Crags is hated here. They expect nothing but treachery and betrayal, and they're not wise enough in the ways of the world to know the different between one knight and another. They probably haven't even heard of Queen Shezira.' Sollos sighed. 'I suppose we'll have to wait until tomorrow for the dragons to come back, and then another day for the rest of the gold.'

'Sell-sword, they will either take us to the dragon today or they *will* burn. That's the only offer I will make. A hundred gold is a fortune for most men.'

Sollos gritted his teeth. *Yes, it would have been.* He shook his head and held out his hand. 'Then give me the gold and I'll see what I can do.'

'No, sell-sword, I will give it to them myself, when they have taken us back to their settlement.'

'With all respect, Rider, that isn't the arrangement.'

'Then change it.'

Sollos shrugged. 'If that's what you wish, but I certainly won't be coming with you. I say again, Rider: these people fully expect your dragons to burn their village whether they honour our bargain or not. Once they've got your gold, I can't see why they shouldn't simply murder us all in our sleep. Either way, your dragons will burn their homes.'

Semian seemed to consider this. 'Then what arrangement do you suggest?'

'These men and women have not seen your white dragon, Rider, but they have heard of others who have and they will take us there. We have to go to another settlement, a smaller one, about ten miles from here. We go directly there. They'll come with us to show us the way. Tomorrow morning, when we're somewhere between here and there, you give them the gold. One or two of them will stay to take us to the man who's seen the white.' It had taken almost an entire day of arguing with Curly Beard to find an arrangement they could agree on.

Rider Semian narrowed his eyes. 'And this other man, will he too demand a hundred gold dragons?'

He will if I have anything to do with it, thought Sollos. 'I'm sure you'll find a way to convince him, Rider.' *Yes. With the point of your swords, no doubt.*

With a curt nod, the dragon-knight turned away. 'Tell them we agree. But *I* will give them the gold, not you, and it will be one hundred dragons, not two. And sell-sword?'

'Rider?'

'We travel in the open, where we can be seen from the skies. Make sure they understand that. Make sure they understand that every step we take will be watched from above.'

'They're not stupid, Rider.'

As Sollos and Kemir walked away towards the woods where Curly Beard was hiding, the knights retreated as far from the woods as they could. Sollos looked up. The dragons were still there, distant specks high in the sky. Which was a pity, because even five minutes of Rider Semian's company was already making him wonder if there was some deal he could cut with Curly Beard that would result in six dead knights and his pockets full of gold.

Probably not, though. Curly Beard would kill him and Kemir as happily as he'd murder a dragon-knight. You were either an Outsider or you weren't, and that was that.

'Well that went well,' muttered Kemir. 'I thought you said he was an idiot. Are you going to tell Curly Beard he can only have fifty?'

'He won't take it. No, he'll get his hundred.'

'Nothing for us then. Hurrah. You should definitely have asked for a thousand.'

Sollos shrugged. 'There's still the dragonscale too. Let's not forget that.'

'Give up. We're never going to get our hands on that.'

'And a reward for finding the white.'

'If we find it,' grumbled Kemir. 'If they pay it.' He snorted. 'Why did they bring the alchemist?'

Sollos shrugged. 'Don't know, don't care. All we have to do is make sure that Curly Beard and Rider Rod-Up-My-Arse stick to the agreement and don't start trying to kill each other. Should keep us busy enough, don't you think?'

'Let them kill each other. I'll help if you like. When they're done, we can have the gold. Suits me.'

Sollos twitched his lips. 'Don't tempt me.'

'You know, we *did* make an oath, a long time ago. We could always—'

'No!' Sollos stopped and took a deep breath. 'No, Kemir. These riders serve Queen Shezira, not the King of the Crags.'

Kemir shrugged. 'A knight's a knight. They all think they're little gods. We could—'

'I said no!' Sollos stamped his foot.

'Look, I'm not saying we should try and overthrow Valmeyan; I'm just saying that sticking a knife into a few dragon-knights would give me a sense of fulfilment, that's all.'

'Those days are gone, Kemir. That oath ...' He shrugged. 'It was a stupid oath. Besides, there are six of them and two of us, and their dragons are watching us.'

He saw Kemir look up at the sky and wince. 'They have to sleep, you know.'

They do. Yes, they do. Sollos shook his head. However much a part of him agreed with Kemir, murdering one dragon-knight or even ten wouldn't change the world at all. As long as there were dragons, there would be men and women who rode them.

As long as there are dragons.

21

The Wedding

Meteroa, of course, timed it perfectly. When Jehal returned to the palace, everyone was waiting for him. He walked briskly into the feasting hall with Princess Lystra at his side and a spring in his step. *You are the speaker in waiting ...*

'Drink!' he cried before he'd even reached the throne at his lolling father's side. 'Drink! A toast! Not to us, but to everyone! To each other! To life!' Then he spun Princess Lystra to face him, kissed her, and then shot a glance along the tables and made sure he caught Zafir's eye. 'Drink!' he shouted again, into the shocked quiet. 'Drink to the pounding of hearts! To the thunder of wings and the wash of fire! To the clash of swords, to the moment of the kill, to the drunken passion of lovers! Drink and shout for joy or shout with rage, I care not which, but do not fill my feasting hall with silence!'

He sat down and thumped his goblet on the table. Everyone was looking at him. This wasn't how a wedding feast was supposed to start, but he simply didn't have the stomach for hours of tedious politeness. Far better that everyone got roaring drunk.

He peered past Princess Lystra at her mother. 'Isn't this more what you're used to, Your Holiness?' He grinned.

Queen Shezira's face remained carefully blank. 'Your exuberance would, perhaps, be more appreciated in my halls than in your own.'

'I mean to make your daughter feel welcome here.'

Shezira said nothing.

'Am I a monster?' he asked her, much later, when the food was almost gone and he'd drunk too much wine. 'Is that what you think of me?'

She met his eyes. 'In another few hours you will be my son,' she said coolly. And that was all.

After everyone had gorged themselves, a troupe of musicians struck up and the dancing started. Princess Lystra came first of course, with her big wide eyes and drooping lashes and that startled look she'd worn since the day had started. Then her mother, which was like dancing with a iron statue, cumbersome and awkward and with nothing to recommend it. And then, out of nowhere, Zafir slid into his arms, sinuous and sensual, pressing herself close and filling his nose with her perfume. Jehal felt himself stir. Her hand slid up his back to the skin of his neck, and he felt a slight pricking sting. He jerked.

'What are you doing?'

Zafir looked at her hand. On one of the rings she wore was a tiny spike, and on that spike the slightest drop of blood. She touched it to her tongue and then wrapped her arm around him again. 'Reminding you that you're not immortal,' she whispered.

'I *feel* immortal.' He pulled her even closer, but this time she resisted.

'I am a dragon-queen, Prince Jehal, not some courtesan, and eyes are watching us.'

'Is that a poison ring you're wearing?'

'Of course.'

'Am I about to die?'

Zafir smiled. This time, when he tried to pull her closer, she didn't resist. 'Not today, my love.' She leaned into him for a second and he felt her breath on his ear. 'I saw the way you looked at her today, your little starling-bride,' she murmured. 'Enjoy the novelty, but remember that it's *me* who can give you what you want. If you plan to toss me aside for her, you may as well take your dagger and run me through and let us both die here and now.'

Jealous? She was *jealous*? For a second he thought about it. 'If you want to see which of you I want, then let us slip away and I will show you,' he said huskily.

She pushed him sharply away with a brittle smile. 'Your starling can have you today. Afterwards … we shall see.' She waved her fingers at him, letting him see the ring again, still wet with a drop of his blood.

You are the speaker in waiting …

He watched her go. Before he could launch himself after her, another pair of arms took hold of him.

'Princess Jaslyn!' Jehal forced a smile.

'Prince Jehal.'

'I cannot say why, but I did not think you to be much for dancing.' Her movements were sharp and aggressive, not like her sister, and as far away from Zafir's as it was possible to be.

'I prefer to dance in the air.'

'With a somewhat more scaly partner, no doubt.' Jehal smiled. 'So do I. So we have something in common.'

Jaslyn looked at him with scorn. 'We have my sister in common now. I am only dancing with you so I can say this quietly, where no one else will hear: whatever hurt you bring her, I will return to you tenfold.'

'And if I bring her joy?'

'Then I will have misjudged you.' She bowed and spun away.

'That hardly seems an equitable arrangement,' he called after her, but she didn't turn back. *Poor Lystra.* He'd expected to see her weep at the prospect of leaving her family and being forced to give herself to a man who she'd doubtless been taught to believe was a monster. Yet she hadn't. If anything, she almost seemed excited.

And now I begin to see why.

Another princess appeared in front of him. Jehal screwed up his face, trying to remember who she was. One of King Silvallan's brood, he thought, as they swept through the crush of bodies. Over in one corner, over the music, he could hear some sort of commotion. Drink had got the better of a pair of his knights. Others were quickly pulling them apart. He thought he heard the scrape of a sword being drawn, but there were no screams and the music didn't stop, so presumably nothing came of it. He tried to dance his way to Zafir's sister, to start laying a few foundations there, but all he got was an endless stream of distant relatives, and they all wanted something.

Suddenly, he was immensely glad that the day was nearly over. Tomorrow the dragon-lords and their courtiers would be on their way back to Clifftop, where they could be Lord Meteroa's problem for a night before they finally left for palaces of their own. He slipped away from the dancing and made his way outside. His head was foggy, and when he tried to shake it clear, it only got worse. Too much wine? Or had Zafir poisoned him after all?

Meteroa appeared at his elbow. 'It's nearly time, Your Highness.'

'I'll be glad when this is done.'

'I would have thought you'd be enjoying this, Your Highness. Prince Tyrin and Princess Jesska have vanished, one suspects to one of your solars; Prince Loatan and Princess Kalista got as far as drawing knives on each other before your guards intervened, and those are merely the highlights. I shall of course have a detailed report waiting for you at your convenience, once you are free of your bride.'

My bride. 'Tell me, eyrie-master, about my bride. How do I look at her?'

Meteroa frowned. 'I would say, with an expression of intrigued interest. Magnificently played.'

Except I wasn't playing. 'Mmm. And how many queens and princesses have been unable to resist the temptation to fondle a drunken prince when he's naked?'

'Queens Shezira and Zafir have both politely declined and will be attending Princess Lystra. Queen Fyon, however, accepted with great enthusiasm. I believe she forbade her daughters from joining her.'

Jehal groaned. Queen Fyon – *Aunt* Fyon – was Narghon's wife. She was grey and sagging, at least ten years older than Aliphera had been. Rumours had once abounded in both palaces that she and King Tyan had been lovers as well as brother and sister. The number of heirs she'd borne for King Narghon certainly spoke of her enthusiasm.

'Princess Jaslyn will also attend you, I believe.'

Jehal almost choked. 'I think you must be mistaken.'

Meteroa looked hurt. 'I am an imperfect servant, Your Highness. On occasion.'

'She made it quite clear in there that she hates me.'

'I'll see to it that she doesn't poison you, Your Highness.'

Jehal snorted. 'See to it that Queen Zafir doesn't poison my bride, if you please. I want Lystra wide awake when I take her. Zafir has an assassin's ring on. Keep an eye on her.' He thought he saw Meteroa smirk, but before he could launch a rebuke a bell began to toll. Meteroa clapped him on the back.

'It's time.'

'A long time ago kings and queens married in the same way as everyone else.' Jehal took a deep breath and rubbed his eyes. His head still felt fuzzy. In the sky above, the stars shone brightly. A silver crescent moon hung on the horizon, out over the sea. A breeze blew up from the harbour, bringing a strange mixture of smells: of the sea and rotting fish and ammonia, and of rose and myrrh and sandalwood from the incense burners strewn across the palace gardens.

'That was before the Seven Princes and the War of Thorns.' Meteroa started to guide Jehal back towards the feasting hall.

'I know, I know, and Speaker Vishmir finally locked Prince Halim and Queen Lira in the Tower of Air and refused to let them out until Lira was pregnant with an heir, and that was the end of the matter. Much as I admire Vishmir's no-nonsense approach, I don't think he meant it to become standard practice.'

'Heirs are important.' For a moment Meteroa's face went as blank as a mask. Then he smiled politely. 'Ask Hyram.'

Jehal laughed. 'Heirs are dangerous. Ask Aliphera. Oh, wait, you can't. She's dead.' He sniffed the air again. 'Whoever arranged the incense burners should be whipped; they're not doing their job at all. Did you put the scent vines around the east window of the bridal bedchamber as I asked?'

Meteroa nodded. He pushed Jehal back towards the feasting hall. The dancing had stopped. Princess Lystra was standing in the middle of the floor. Everyone was looking at him, but he didn't have time to see any more before a gang of knights launched themselves at him. The next thing he knew, he was whisked off his feet and being carried high in the air. People were shouting and cheering. When he strained his neck to look, he could just about see Princess Lystra being escorted away by two queens, her mother on one side, Zafir on the other.

He closed his eyes. They weren't even out of the feasting hall before groping hands started to tear his clothes away. Over the ribald jokes of his riders he could hear Queen Fyon laughing. He shuddered. The women were always the worst.

They carried him high over their heads, parading him in front of everyone they could find, until they reached the Sun Tower in the centre of the palace. They almost dropped him there, trying to carry him up the narrow spiral stairs, but apparently they were quite prepared to risk that rather than let him walk. By the time they got him to the top he was dizzy, but he wasn't given any time to think about that. Someone was already pressing a goblet into his hands. One of Silvallan's nieces. What was her name?

'Maiden's Regret!' shouted a voice to a chorus of laughter. 'The Maiden!'

He drank it down as he was obliged to do, and prayed silently that the riders around him weren't as drunk as they seemed. Mentally, one part of him listed all the dragon-kings and -queens who'd been poisoned on their wedding nights. Another part slowly started counting, ticking off the seconds before the Maiden's Regret took hold of him. It would be longer than most, he'd made sure of that.

They finished stripping him and put him into his wedding shift, a pointless wrapping of cloth designed to fall apart at the lightest touch. By now the room was spinning, but he still had a few minutes before the potion took him completely.

One by one, the riders, the princes, the princesses came to him with ritual offerings of advice for the night to come, and then left.

'Maiden's Regret loosens the tongue!' shouted a voice. *True,* he thought. *That's what the alchemists were using in my eyrie, with their truth-smoke. On my Scales and on my soldiers.* He grinned. *What a waste. All those men and women left half-mad with lust.*

'It loosens everything.' More laughter.

Meteroa must have been beside himself. I must write to Hyram, thanking him on behalf of Clifftop's whores. He started to laugh.

'Are you murdering your father?' Jehal blinked. The question seeped into his consciousness like honey dripping off a spoon. Jaslyn. That's who the voice was. Princess Jaslyn. Because hadn't Lord Meteroa said she was coming? And he didn't remember seeing her before.

Why not? urged a voice inside him. *Why not tell her the truth and be done with it. Everyone wants to know. Make her go away.*

He opened his mouth, but a hand shut it for him. 'Get out of here, you little witch. How dare you! Shoo! Shoo!' The hand let go of him. 'I'm so sorry, nephew. Treat your bride kindly but not too kindly. I'll wager she likes a little roughness that one. Most of us do.'

Jehal looked up and smiled. Queen Fyon, but she was going now, turning away. Hadn't he been about to say something? Whatever it was, it was gone.

It seemed that he blinked, and his knights were gone too. *That's right. Maiden's Regret fools with your sense of time. You haven't got long before it takes you now. Not long at all.*

There was a door. That's what he was supposed to do. Go through the door. And before he'd even finished thinking it, it was done, and up another spiral of stairs, and the stupid wedding shift was already falling off, and then he was naked and standing in a room with eight sides, with windows in all the walls, every one open, with a floor strewn with pillows and blankets and mattresses stuffed with everything from down to straw, and Lystra was standing in front of him. She was far gone with the Maiden, swaying slightly from side to side, and her eyes were black and immense.

A little droplet of fire seemed to fall inside him and gently explode. Princess Lystra opened her mouth and reached for him. He swayed towards her.

Not yet not yet not yet!

He had seconds before he lost any idea of what he was doing. With all that was left of his will he started counting windows. *Second on the left from the door. Faces east. That one ...*

He pushed Princess Lystra towards that window. 'Stars,' he murmured. 'Look up at the stars.' He stood behind her, wrapping his arms around her, and peered through the air to another tower and another window. The window was still dark. Queen Shezira wouldn't have had time to get back to her rooms yet. A pity, because he'd wanted her to see him take her daughter. A sort of prelude to everything else he was going to take, and she wasn't even there.

But then the Maiden came, and Lystra was grinding herself against him, and there could be no more waiting.

22

Scorched Earth

It took the rest of that day and most of the next to reach their destination, picking their tortuous way along the floor of a valley, among hundreds of rivulets that bubbled and splashed among a sea of strewn rocks and streaks of sand and gravel. On either side of them forested slopes rose sharply towards rocky peaks. It rained relentlessly. Every now and then one or other of the riders missed his footing and slipped. By the end of the first day all of them were limping.

Which serves them right for trying to hike in heavy armour, Sollos thought.

In the evening Curly Beard and the other Outsiders sat sullenly silent, huddled under the thickest of the trees, seeking what shelter they could get from the rain. When they looked at the dragon-knights, their eyes glittered with a mixture of greed and hate. The knights glowered back. Sollos and Kemir took it in turns to snooze, but no one else got much sleep. Strangely, the alchemist seemed the most anxious of them all.

As soon as dawn broke, Curly Beard jumped to his feet and declared it was time to move on. With great reluctance, Rider Semian handed over the promised gold. Curly Beard disappeared back down the river with three of his friends and the sack of coins, leaving two of the Outsiders to guide the knights onwards.

'If we went after them, we could still catch them,' muttered Kemir.

It took barely an hour for the other two Outsiders to abandon them. The first slipped away in the woods when one of the knights fell and broke his hand. The other one, when he saw that he was the last, simply ran, trusting the sureness of his feet on the rocks, knowing the knights could never catch him. Rider Semian declared the man a traitor and ordered him shot, but by the time Sollos had his bow strung, the Outsider was too far away. He sent a couple of arrows after the man to keep Semian happy and then pretended to listen while the knight told him how poor a shot he was.

Slowly, Sollos realised that the knights didn't know what to do. He watched them dither and wondered what profit there might be from leaving them to their fate. Six riders and one alchemist, alone in the mountains ...

He looked up. Sure enough, high above, he saw a speck in the sky. The knights had someone to watch over them.

'You! Sell-sword!'

Sollos looked around. He assumed it must be one of the knights, but it was the alchemist, pointing a finger at him.

'Master Huros. Enjoying yourself?'

'I, um ... Certainly not. I require your help. It is clear that the correct course of action is to proceed in the direction we were being led. Please explain this to Rider Semian.'

Sollos cocked his head. 'Why don't you explain it to him your-self, Master Huros?'

'Because Lady Nastria made it quite plain that you two had knowledge of these mountains.' The alchemist made a noise in his throat. 'Um. He will listen to you, and we must press on.'

'Must we? I thought we might go back. Burn those naughty Outsiders for being so ill-mannered.'

'No, Sword-Master Sollos, we *must* press on. If, uh ... if those men were telling us the truth, we cannot be far from the dragon. Turning back will waste days. I repeat, we *must* press on, before—'

'Before what, Master Alchemist?'

'Um. None of your concern. All that matters is that we reach the dragon quickly.'

Sollos thought about that. There didn't seem much to gain from leaving the riders to fend for themselves, but in the end what made up his mind was that the alchemist had actually bothered to call him by his name. With a sigh, he hauled himself to his feet. He didn't bother telling the riders where he was going and didn't bother looking back when they shouted at him, simply gestured at them to follow. Eventually they did.

Kemir was the first to notice the smell. The rain had stopped in the middle of the day, and for the last few hours they'd walked on in glorious sunshine. Apart from his feet, Sollos was feeling almost dry when Kemir abruptly stopped and sniffed the air.

Sollos stopped as well. He wrinkled his nose. There was ... something, something slightly familiar.

'Soul Dust,' muttered Kemir, keeping his voice low so the dragon-knights, a few dozen yards behind them, wouldn't hear.

Sollos shook his head. 'No. There's something right enough, but it's not Dust. Dust doesn't smell like that.'

'It does when you burn it.'

Sollos shrugged. 'It can't be. No one here burns Dust.' He swept his hand across the empty landscape. 'Do you see anyone burning Dust?'

Kemir glared at him. 'No, obviously I don't, because if I did, I'd be pointing at them. Just because you can't see the shit on the bottom of your boot doesn't mean it doesn't stink, and I'm telling you, that's the smell of burning Dust.'

Five minutes later Sollos sniffed again. This time he smelled smoke.

They looked at each other. Then Kemir started to run as best he could over the scattered rocks. The riders shouted. Sollos paused for long enough to yell at them to smell the air, and then set off after Kemir. Around the next bend of the river they skidded to a stop.

Kemir pointed to the scorched scar at the edge of the forest. 'Do you think that's the settlement we were supposed to be finding?' A few charred pieces of wood were still smouldering. The rest of whatever had been here was ash, but that wasn't what caught Sollos's eye.

'Bugger the settlement.' He pointed up the river.

At first glance it might have been a huge white boulder, but there was something too regular about it, too smooth. The boulder, when Sollos looked closely, had eyes that looked back. As he watched, the boulder slowly unfurled its legs, wings and tail and turned into a dragon.

Kemir gave a little whoop of joy. 'Finder's fee!'

Sollos touched Kemir on the arm, a gesture of caution. 'Something isn't right about this. There's no rider.'

'Of course there isn't. We were there, remember. When the other dragons attacked? Fire, shouting, running for our lives? Am I ringing any bells?'

Sollos edged sideways, out of the middle of the river bed, heading for the cover of the forest. The dragon was watching, and there was something altogether too intelligent in the way it was looking at him. 'We never found the Scales.'

'That's because he's dead.'

'Then why this?' Sollos began to step faster. 'Dragons never flamestrike unless someone tells them to.'

'Maybe it was hungry.'

'Maybe it still is.'

The dragon moved. Sollos grabbed Kemir and ran.

Tipping the Scales

For ten years, as the dragon is matured, the gifts must continue, and those whose gifts are found wanting will find their dragon, when they take it, perhaps a little dull in its scales, not as vigorous in its flight or as tight in its turns as they had hoped. When his dragon has finally matured, the rider will visit the eyrie for one last time. A final round of gifts is made, and then rider and dragon are introduced. The dragon is his.

Before the rider leaves, it is customary for one last payment to be made: a small gift to the Scales, the man or woman who has fed and watered and nurtured the dragon since it was an egg. The dragon-princes call this gift Tipping the Scales

23

Snow

A torrent of flames poured from the sky, swallowing her and the Little One beside her in its fury. The river waters steamed. Stones cracked in the heat.

She felt the presence of the other dragons in the sky long before she saw them. Different minds, different thoughts made up of different sounds and colours, but that didn't bother her at first. Other dragons came and went all the time, and the Little Ones never seemed afraid. And then she'd felt their thoughts change, the colours darken and sharpen and fill with fire. She knew what was coming.

An instant before the flames struck, she spread out her wings, tenting them over her head and over the Little One beside her. Instinctively. Protecting her eyes and the Little One. The other Little One, the one who'd been angry and shouting, the one who rode on her back and told her what to do, he was too far away for her to save. She felt his thoughts snuff out, and that made her a little sad. Little Ones burned so easily.

A second flamestrike engulfed her. The fire warmed her, but didn't frighten her. The Little One was afraid, though. Sharply, suddenly filled with fear. She felt it from all of them, but especially from the one beside her. And pain. The Little One was in pain. And panic. And terror. The emotions rolled into her from the Little One. She didn't know what to do with them. She'd never felt these things before. Bad things that made her want to run away.

The newcomer dragons were still close. She could still feel their thoughts, hot and fierce. They were circling around. They meant to come back.

She seized the Little One gently in her left foreclaws and hurled herself down the river, picking up speed with each stride. One of the other dragons swooped over her. She felt its thoughts and held the Little One close as the dragon above raked her with fire.

It passed over her head. As it did, she launched herself into the air and snapped at its tail. She still clasped the Little One tight to her breast. It was out of its mind, screaming and thrashing. Its thoughts were a jumble, disconcerting and incoherent. They made her feel strange. When another dragon swooped past her, she snapped at that one too and lashed it with her tail. She felt its surprise as it veered away.

Up, up, up. Faster and faster. Away. Sometimes she thought the Little One was trying to tell her to let it go, but its thoughts were chaos, broken and messy, and it kept contradicting itself. Three of the new dragons were following her. They were bigger than she was. They felt older. They had Little Ones to tell them what to do too. She could feel their determination, their hostility.

Another dragon dived from the sky above. A dragon she knew, one of the strong ones. One of the dragons that had come from her nest place. It shot down like an arrow and smashed into the closest dragon behind her, sending them both tumbling towards the ground. She heard the shrieks of other dragons echoing around the valleys, and with them came a surge of excitement. The dragons behind her were all gone, spiralling down together, snapping and lashing at her nest-mate.

She felt a shriek of terror from one of the Little Ones, abruptly cut to nothing. Then they were all gone, too far behind for her to hear their thoughts any more.

The excitement faded. The Little One held in her claws was calmer now, and her own thoughts were less confused. A part of her wanted to go back and play with these new dragons, but the Little One's thoughts were clear: it wanted to get away. Far, far away. It didn't know which way she should go and it didn't care, so she flew whichever way caught her eye, along valleys, between mountains, over lakes. She'd never seen this land before, or anything like it, with all its strange shapes and colours and so much sparkling rushing water. She dragged the tip of her tail through shimmering mirrors, soared and dived and snapped at waterfalls, and spiralled around mountains, riding the currents of rising air.

Eventually the light faded, the sun set and the Little One's thoughts went quiet. She could feel herself slowly getting too warm, but the landscape was simply too fresh and exciting to ignore, and so she flew on, playing with it until the heat inside her was positively uncomfortable. Then she landed by a lake. She carefully put the Little One down on the ground, out in the open where she could see him, and bounded into the delicious ice-cold water. She splashed and played under the stars until she was cool again, and then curled up around the Little One and went to sleep.

She dreamed. Far, far away, things were happening. Immense things. Somehow she was a part of them, but they were so far away, she couldn't see them, couldn't hear them, couldn't remember them. She tried to fly towards them, but they kept moving away, eluding her, darting out of the way when she lunged for them.

Abruptly the sun was in the sky again, creeping over the surrounding peaks. She yawned and stretched out her tail and arched her back. The Little One was awake again. She could feel its thoughts. It was hungry.

Yes. Hungry. *She* was hungry too. She looked at the Little One and bared her teeth, as she always did when it was feeding time.

'I'm sorry, Snow. You'll have to find your own breakfast.'

She looked around. She didn't understand most of the noises that the Little Ones made, but sometimes their thoughts were enough. He didn't have any food for her. He was in pain too. And he was afraid. She didn't like those thoughts. They made her feel anxious, and so she stopped listening to them. She thought about being hungry instead, waiting for the Little One to do something about it. When he didn't, she bared her teeth at him again.

'Hunt,' he said. 'You have to hunt.'

Hunt. She knew that noise. It meant flying and chasing and, yes! Catching and killing and eating.

She rose onto all fours and then lowered her neck, inviting the Little One to climb onto her back.

'I can't, Snow. I'm a Scales, not a rider. I'm not allowed.'

The noises made no sense. *Hunt* meant that a Little One sat on her back and told her where to go. She lowered her neck even more, rubbing it against the stones on the ground.

'They'd put me to death if they knew.' The Little One started to walk in circles. Its thoughts were confused, still laced with pain, Still frightened. 'Only riders ride dragons. That's the law. We should go back. What happened? Were we attacked?' It shook its head. 'Oh, I wish you could speak. What if they're still there? The queen won't be back yet, will she? Oh, what to do? I can't ride with you, Snow. There's no saddle; I'd fall. But we can't stay here, and you can't find your way home on your own. I don't even know where we are. Do *you* know where we are?'

She rubbed her neck against the ground again and bared her teeth once more. *Hunt. Hungry.*

'You want to eat. Yes, you must be hungry. Oh, but there aren't any alchemists here. You have to drink the water they make for you. You'll get sick otherwise. We'll have to go back.'

Hunt. Hungry. She made the gestures again. She was starting to get frustrated, and the Little One's thoughts were confusing her. She couldn't make any sense of them.

'I can't climb on your back, Snow. There's no harness. I can't reach.' The Little One walked to her left foreclaws and tried to open them. She didn't understand what he wanted to do, then she caught a picture from his mind, of flying through the air at night, and she was carrying him.

Yes. The way they'd come here. Carefully she raised herself onto her back legs and held out her foreclaws. The Little One nodded and made noises, and in his thoughts she saw that she'd understood him. He climbed into her claws, and she gently closed them around him.

'Hunt!' he said.

Hunt. That was something she understood.

24

A Memory of Flames

They hunted. She ate. The Little One ate too, and then they climbed into the sky together again. The Little One wanted to go somewhere, but it didn't know which way to go, so she flew again as the fancy took her, into a wilderness of crags and broken stone and boulders the size of castles. She tried to hunt there too, but the land was barren and empty. When night fell, she found a place to land and went to sleep. The dreams came again, as distant as ever.

The next day they flew back out among the valleys and rivers. It rained. She liked that, liked the feel of it. The Little One started telling her which way to go. She understood its thoughts: *Left, straight, right, up, down.* She knew the noises too, but when they were racing through the air, the noises were all lost in the wind, and she had to pluck the thoughts out of the Little One's head. She began to wonder whether this Little One was somehow broken. The other Little Ones that sat on her back had thoughts that were much clearer.

'We're lost,' said the Little One. She didn't understand, but she could see in his thoughts that he was anxious. He was always anxious. Mostly she blocked him out.

They looked for dragons but they didn't find any. The next day was the same. And the next. But at night, when she slept, something was beginning to change. The dreams were coming closer. She didn't notice it at first, but after a few days a strange understanding came to her. She wanted the dreams. More than anything else, she wanted them. They were important. More important than food or shelter or even than the Little One. She didn't know why; they simply were. With that one revelation came another. They would come to her as long as she stayed here, away from the others, alone.

The day after that she chose her own way to fly. Instinct drove her towards ever higher places. The Little One was even more upset than usual. It shouted at her. It was angry with her, and that made her feel very bad. She was supposed to do what the Little Ones wanted, and this Little One was the most special Little One of them all, the one who'd been with her since she'd first opened her eyes.

That night the dreams were even closer. She could almost smell them, almost touch them. They were filled with fire and ash and burning flesh. In the morning, when she woke up, she left the Little One behind and went to hunt alone. She felt its anguish and despair as it watched her fly away. It was still there when she came back. It felt joy to see her return and made lots of noises that she didn't understand. When she slept again, the dreams finally let her touch them.

She was a tiny part of something vast. She couldn't see or hear, but she could feel the thoughts of hundreds of dragons, bright and sharp and clear. She could feel other beings too, huge and powerful. Far beneath them she felt a hum of lesser thoughts. Little Ones, she realised with surprise, but that didn't make any sense, because the Little Ones seemed so dull and dim next to the other dragons, and the truth she knew was the other way around.

She tried to grasp the dream, to unravel it, but it fluttered away only for another to come in its place.

She was flying. The air around her was thick with dragons, and on the back of each was a single rider clad in silver. She wheeled and dived and saw that the ground far below was alive. It was crawling, heaving, moving as far as she could see with Little Ones. Thousands upon thousands. Millions upon millions.

Arrows. She closed her eyes and felt them batter against her scales.

She flew over their heads as she would skim over a forest. Little Ones wrapped up in their crude skins of metal. Spears and axes rattled off her scales. She opened her mouth and let the fire burst out of her, filling the world with screams, filling her heart with joy. Everywhere other dragons were doing the same. She could feel the power from the man of silver on her back, driving her on, urging her to kill, kill …

The Little Ones were so many. She burned them by the hundred and they died, and the dead were swallowed up by the horde as though they'd never existed.

And then the dead rising back to life, burned and broken, turning on the living, grasping and clawing. The silver creature on her back was making it so. He laughed, and so did she.

And then something happened, and the silver creature on her back wasn't there any more, and her wings wouldn't fly, and she couldn't move or think, as though a giant claw had seized her mind and was slowly crushing her.

She remembered crashing into the ground, scattering Little Ones around her, as the claws in her mind sank deeper, and then she remembered nothing.

No. Not nothing. She was an egg again. She was a tiny part of something vast. She couldn't see or hear, but she could still feel the thoughts of hundreds of dragons, bright and sharp and clear.

She woke up. Most of the sky was still dark, although the first glimmers of dawn were peeking through between the mountains. The dreams were still there in her head, hundreds of them. They didn't feel like dreams now; they felt like memories. But that couldn't be right. There weren't even a hundred other dragons in her nesting place, never mind a thousand. They didn't feel the same either. The dragons in her dreams had thoughts that shone like cut diamond. The dragons of her nesting place were simple and dull.

She'd never flown far from her nesting place. She knew that. She hadn't been to the places she was remembering. She'd never felt the presence of one of these silver men whose minds burned like the sun. As for flying over a sea of Little Ones, burning them …

Above all the rest, that memory stayed in her mind. She'd enjoyed it. More than that; it was the most exhilarating thing she'd ever done.

But she hadn't done it. She couldn't have done it. They were dreams, not memories, and they couldn't be real. She struggled to make sense of it, but it was far too difficult, and she was already hungry again. She got hungry a lot out here in the mountains. There was plenty to eat, though, if you knew where to look.

She launched herself into the sky as soon as the sun was up, leaving the Little One behind again. She felt his sadness as she went. He didn't like to be left on his own. She didn't understand that. In her nesting place there were always other dragons nearby, and Little Ones too. Even at night in the dark she felt the presence of their thoughts. She'd never been as alone as she was here, and yet she'd never felt so strangely wonderful.

Without the Little One to slow her, she roamed far on her hunts. She looked for river valleys and then followed them, soaring high in the sky, watching and waiting for prey to emerge from the forests to drink. Sometimes it would be a bear, sometimes a few deer, sometimes a herd of snappers. She had to be careful because the animals were never far from the edge of the forest, and once they got among the trees they were as good as lost. So she'd watch them for a while until she was sure they were coming out to drink, and then she'd tuck in her wings and dive. If she could, she'd seize them with her claws and bite off their heads. If they saw her coming and ran, she'd lash at them with her tail, wrapping it around them or sending them flying through the air to pounce on while they were still stunned. If she had to, she'd burn them. They tasted better raw, though.

Today the sky was grey and a steady rain was falling. Rain and cloud were good. She could fly a lot lower before anyone would see her, and that meant they had less time to get out of the way when she fell out of the sky at them. She ate well, and yet something drew her on, further and further down the valleys, as if a part of her knew that something was waiting for her.

There was. She'd flown for half the day, perhaps a hundred miles, when she felt the tickle of stray thoughts. Little Ones. When she looked down, she couldn't see them, only the endless treetops and the little scar of the river flowing between them. She circled down towards the trees and finally landed in the river, peering into the gloom of the forest. Her eyes found nothing, but she knew nonetheless. They were close enough that she could feel their thoughts, each one of them. And they didn't even know she was there.

For a while she wondered what to do. Then she launched herself up into the sky once more.

25

Cinders and Ashes

The dragon trotted a few paces down the river, sending boulders splashing and tumbling, and then stopped and watched them. The air stank of damp charcoal. Here and there, as they dashed for the shelter of the forest, Sollos had to step over charred remains that had once been men and women. Outsiders burned by a dragon. The sight brought back too many memories. It set him on edge.

'Bastard,' grunted Kemir.

Sollos shook his head. 'There has to be a rider. I told you, dragons don't flamestrike unless someone tells them to, and they don't burn their prey. They like their meat fresh.'

They peered through the trees. 'Should we go back and tell Rider Rod?' asked Kemir. 'Or would it be more fun to lurk here and see what happens?'

'No point.' Sollos clucked his tongue. 'It's leaving.' he ran back through the trees to the river. By the time he got there the dragon was already airborne. He watched it go, skimming along the bottom of the valley, barely above the treetops, until it vanished around a bend. *South*, he thought. *It went south.*

He looked behind him, back down the river. He could see the riders and their alchemist now, picking their way through the stones.

'Sollos!'

He couldn't see Kemir through the trees but he heard the urgency. He darted back into the shelter of the trees. 'What?'

'Survivor. Sort of.'

Kemir, when Sollos found him, was kneeling beside a tree. Propped up there with him was an Outsider. Given how badly the man was burned, it was a miracle the man wasn't dead.

'Shit! Give him some water!'

Kemir grunted. 'Done that. He's not going to last. His mind's already gone. He keeps wittering about the dragon talking to him.'

The man groaned and nodded. 'The dragon spoke. It spoke in my head.'

'See.' Kemir shrugged. 'Gone.'

'Go and get the alchemist. He might be able to do something.'

'*You* go and get the alchemist.'

'Get the alchemist!' Sollos pushed Kemir away and crouched beside the dying man. 'We saw the dragon. A white dragon. It left when we arrived. Did it do this?'

'No, it was a careless bloke with a pipe,' muttered Kemir. 'Daft bugger.'

Sollos stood up. This time he shoved Kemir towards the river, screaming at him. 'Go and get the fucking alchemist!'

Kemir jogged off grumbling. Sollos sat down beside the man again.

'We're getting help. Did the white dragon do this?'

The man nodded. He whispered something, too quietly for Sollos to hear, until Sollos bent over and almost pressed his ear to the burned man's lips. 'It spoke. I heard it speak.'

'Who was riding it?'

The man shook his head.

'Was it a dragon-knight?'

The man shook his head again. 'No rider,' he breathed.

'A man then. Not a knight but a man.' *The Scales. We never found the body.*

Another shake of the head. 'No ... rider ... just ... dragon ... on ... its ... own.'

Sollos had never heard of such a thing. Maybe Kemir was right. The man had to be in unbelievable pain judging from his burns. Maybe his mind *had* already gone.

'It spoke.' The man sighed and closed his eyes, and for a moment Sollos thought he was gone. Then his lips moved again. 'It spoke in my head. I heard it. It came for Maryk.'

'Maryk? Who's Maryk?'

The man didn't answer. His chest was still rising and falling, but his breaths were fast and shallow and ragged. Sollos stood up. 'Kemir!' *Where's that cursed alchemist?*

The alchemist was too late, of course. Sollos watched the man's chest heave one last time and then he was still. He'd been gone a few minutes by the time Kemir returned with the alchemist and the dragon-knights.

'He's dead,' said Sollos. He looked at Kemir. 'You told them what we saw?'

'I told them they owe us a bag of gold.'

Semian sneered. 'All we've seen is the aftermath of a fire. For all I know you're lying and the white was never here.'

'If you'd been a bit quicker,' snapped Sollos, 'this man might have told you the same story.'

Kemir pointed up through the trees. 'If your dragon-riders up there didn't see it, they need new eyes.'

'Um ... how long has this man been dead?' asked the alchemist.

'Our dragon-riders are elsewhere, as I'm sure you noticed. And as for this man, perhaps I should look him over for wounds, in case you slid a knife into him to make sure he couldn't contradict you.' Rider Semian cocked his head.

'So there's no one watching to see what happens to you?' Kemir looked ready to hit him. The alchemist was kneeling down beside the burned man now.

'Tread very carefully, sell-sword. Before you raise your hand against me, I would remind you that there are six of us and only two of you.'

Kemir gave him a nasty look. 'I wouldn't dream of sullying my sword with you, *Rider*. Why would I, when all I need to do is nothing at all?'

The alchemist picked up the dead man's hand by the wrist and held it to his cheek.

'You're a long way from your eyrie here, rider. All I need to do is watch and laugh from a distance while you—'

Sollos tugged sharply on Kemir's arm. 'Enough. Leave them.'

Kemir snorted. 'I'd like nothing better.'

'I require an, um, assistant,' said the alchemist. He was squatting by the dead man now, and was pulling things out of his pack.

'You would, would you?' sneered Rider Semian. 'Then let us part ways. You clearly have nothing to contribute after all. We will simply return to our search from the air. It'll be *us* watching *you*.'

'Your, um, *help*, sell-sword.'

The alchemist was offering Sollos a short curved knife, the sort he might have used for paring fruit. Sollos took it. 'What do you want?'

The alchemist tore open a square of waxed paper. Inside was some black powder, which he sprinkled into small clay cup. He held it out to Sollos. 'Knife.'

Sollos took the cup and gave him the knife. With a grimace the alchemist drew the edge along the flesh of his arm.

'Hold the cup so that it catches the blood.' The alchemist clenched his fist. Blood ran down his arm to his elbow. When it dripped into the cup, the powder hissed.

'What is this?' Sollos frowned.

'None of, um, your concern, sell-sword, that's what.'

'Looks like witchcraft to me,' muttered Kemir. He took a step away. Even the dragon-knights had fallen silent.

'He's dead,' said Sollos. 'Potions can't help him. If you'd come sooner ...'

The alchemist glared at him. 'Where did you get your name, sell-sword? Sollos. It's an, er, alchemist's name, not a soldier's. Clearly a, ah, mistake. Or did you choose it yourself?' Inside the cup the powder and the blood had mixed into a paste. The alchemist lifted his arm and wrapped a strip of white linen tightly around his wound. 'Um. You're right that it's too late to help him live. But not too late to help him talk.'

'Master Huros?' Semian sounded edgy. 'I am not easy with this. Blood magic is—'

'Is what?'

'The queen does not favour such practices. They are out-lawed.'

'In, er, her realm perhaps. Not here.' The alchemist gave a little sigh. 'If I smear this on his tongue, he will speak. Um ... if my means don't please you, rider, I am sorry.' He tugged the cup from Sollos's fingers. 'Take this and burn it, if you prefer.'

Semian fidgeted. After a few seconds, when he didn't take the cup, the alchemist shrugged. He dipped his finger into the paste and, before anyone could stop him, smeared it in the dead man's mouth.

25

Awakening

Day by day, Kailin watched Snow change. Dragons, he'd been told, were like little children. If that was so then Snow was growing up fast right in front of him. She was frightening, and yet he felt a strange pride and a sense of wonder watching her. There had never been a dragon like her, not with her purity of colour. She was sleek and perfect, and now she was becoming something else as well. Often she terrified him, but at the same time he was her Scales. He'd been waiting for her since she first started tapping her way out of her egg and into the world, and he'd been with her for nearly ten years now. Slowly he understood. Their roles had changed. He'd cared for her, nurtured her, fed her, and now she was doing the same for him.

They developed a routine. Each morning as the sun rose over the mountains, Snow uncurled and launched herself into the air. Kailin watched her go, peering into the sky long after she'd vanished. Then he sat by his fire, drank some warm water and ate some leftover meat. After that there really wasn't much to do but wait for Snow and wonder if today was the day when she wouldn't come back. Usually he made his way across the mountain, through the snows, to the nearest stand of trees and collected some more wood. When the wind blew, cold enough to flay the skin off his flesh, he huddled up in the lee of some nearby rocks and simply waited. When Snow came back, she always knew where to find him. She would be almost too hot to touch, and her warmth melted the snows, dried his clothes and the firewood, and stopped him from freezing in the night. Each day she brought him food to eat, the headless remains of some animal she'd caught. He'd cook it over his fire, and she'd watch him. When he was done, she'd swallow what was left in a single gulp. He knew perfectly well that without her he'd quickly starve or freeze to death.

He talked to her when she was there. Not expecting any answer, but simply because the mountain was so cold and lonely and he felt better hearing the sound of his own voice. Sometimes, from the way she looked at him, he wondered if she was listening.

He got his answer to that when he trod on a loose stone. The first thing he knew, one of his feet was sliding out from under him. The world tumbled, hit him on the head and wound up lying on its side, dim and blurry.

Hurt? asked a voice inside his head.

He tried to move, but for a moment that didn't work. *Yes*, he decided. *I am hurt.*

The next thing he knew, Snow was standing over him, the tip of her face inches from his own, blotting out the sky, the scorching-hot wind of her breath almost pinning him to the ground. He put up a hand, flinched away, and she retreated.

Is it hurt? asked the voice again.

He groaned and sat up. His head was starting to throb. When he touched it, his fingers came away with blood on them. Slowly, he looked up at Snow.

'Did you speak?' He laughed and then winced. Dragons couldn't speak except in myth.

Its head is broken. Is it going to—

Am I going to what? The thought formed inside his head, but the last part of it didn't make any sense. Something to do with getting hotter and hotter and fading away and then waking up wrapped up tight inside an egg.

Snow peered at him and cocked her head. *Die?*

To Kailin, it seemed as though a giant hand had slapped him in the face. He went numb. The pain in his head washed away. He stood up and staggered away from Snow. 'You … you … I heard you thinking.'

Snow snorted and shook her head, the way she did when she was excited. *It hears! Understands!*

Kailin was trembling. 'You understand me! You understand Kailin!'

Kailin? He got a sense of incomprehension.

'That's my name.'

Name? What is a name?

Kailin didn't know how to answer that, but Snow didn't seem to mind. She seemed to pluck the answer out of his head.

All Little Ones have names. Do I have a name?

'Snow.'

Snow. Why?

Kailin picked up a handful of snow. 'Because you're white.' He held it up to show her and then pressed it against the wound on his head.

Hurt? He could feel the tension in her thought.

'A little bit.'

They tried to talk, on into the night until the sun was long gone and stars filled the sky. Most of the time Kailin couldn't make sense of the images that flashed in his head, nor did Snow seem to understand him, no matter how ferociously he thought. He would feel her frustration build up inside her, and then something would burst and their thoughts would somehow align. It would last for a few seconds, maybe a little more before they drifted apart. Eventually he fell asleep, drained. The last thing he felt from Snow was how awake she was, how filled with wonder and awe.

For days afterwards the thoughts that appeared in his head were strange and alien. They rarely made sense, and he would have to ask again and again what Snow was trying to tell him. As time went by, though, they grew sharper, brighter, clearer. He talked to Snow whenever she was there, and she responded. Every day she was changed, filled with new discoveries. Clearer, more articulate, more intelligent than she'd been the day before. A voracious sense of amazement and adventure infected her every thought, and his as well. No Scales had ever experienced what he was seeing, this blossoming.

It is like a veil is lifted in my mind each night, she told him one day as she left to hunt. He spent the rest of the day wondering what use a dragon would have for a veil, until he understood: she wasn't hearing his words any more, she was seeing into his mind. And when she answered him, she was looking inside him for things that *he* would understand.

'We have to go home,' he told her when she came back from her hunt with fresh blood still on her claws. 'I have to show you to the others.'

I am different. Why?

'I don't know, Snow. It's a miracle.'

Miracle? He felt her confusion. *No. Little One Kailin, I feel as if I have awoken from a sleep that has lasted a hundred lifetimes. I do not understand how I have awoken, nor do I understand how I fell into such a slumber. Nor even how much more is to come.*

'We'll go back home. We can ask Master Huros or one of the other alchemists, or even Eyrie-Master Isentine—'

NO! She snapped her jaws. Kailin scrabbled away from her in sudden terror, before she bowed her head to the ground, a dragon gesture of submission. *I did not mean to frighten you, Little One Kailin. I will not hurt you, but nor will I go back to that place.*

'Why?' Kailin watched warily.

My brothers and sisters there are awake yet asleep. I could not bear to be that way again.

'But all dragons are like that. Except you. You're the miracle.'

No, Little One Kailin. I do not think so. I think we were all this way, a long time ago. I have dreams. Memories of other lives I've lived. Many, many lives, but all of them long ago. I remember when my kind flew in our hundreds. I remember the silver gods and the breaking of the very earth itself, then a hundred lives of bright thoughts and flying free. And then, Little One Kailin, something changed, and everything since has faded into an eternal dull blur, dim and impenetrable. Out of reach. All my kin are still sleepwalking their lives. Somehow, you have awoken me. How, Little One Kailin? How did you awaken me? I will not return to my kind until I have that answer. Until I can bring that knowledge back to them.

'I don't know.'

I know. Your thoughts speak for themselves. There are Little Ones who know far more, who may have the answers. You know of them. You wish to take me before them.

'You would be the wonder of the realms.'

I am not so sure, Little One Kailin. Would you like to see the memories I have of your kind from my lives long ago?

'Of course.'

Visions burst into his head. He saw armies of men, hundreds of thousands, more than anything he could have imagined. He saw himself land among them, lashing with his tail, scattering them like leaves, scores of them, smashing them to pulp in their little metal shells. He felt the fire build in his throat and burst forth. The air grew heavy with the stench of scorched flesh. And he felt the appetite growing inside him. For more, more, more ...

He screamed. The vision abruptly vanished.

Do you understand? In my dream your kind were never anything more than prey, and your thoughts were always filled with hopeless terror. Why would you wish to return to such a world?

'No, no, no!' Kailin shook his head. 'Dragons and men have lived together for hundreds of years. We helped you. You were dying. We looked after you. We've always looked after you. No.' He shook his head again. 'Go back to the eyrie, Snow. Our queen is good and wise. She'll know what to do.'

The dragon cocked her head. *You have seen what we were, and yet you are more afraid of this queen? Curious. I can see that you truly believe everything you say. Perhaps ...* Snow lifted her head off the ground. She rose onto her back legs and flapped her wings a few times. A sign of warning.

No, she said at last. *I will not go back to the place you call the eyrie, Little One Kailin. Not yet.*

26

The Burned Man

The dead man's lips began to move. He gave a soft sigh. The dragon-knights shifted away, shuffling uncomfortably. Sollos heard them muttering under their breath.

'He's all, um, yours,' said the alchemist. 'I don't know, um, how long he'll last. He hasn't been dead for long, so you've probably got at least, um, half an hour.'

Rider Semian was looking at the dead man with a mixture of horror and disgust. 'Ask him what happened here.'

'You can ask him yourself, if you wish, rider.'

Semian's lips curled in distaste. 'No, Master Huros. You made this abomination. It's yours now. The sell-swords will guard you. We will return to the river.'

The alchemist shrugged and turned his attention to the dead man.

'He kept on about the dragon speaking to him,' said Sollos, when the knights had gone. 'It was the white. He said there wasn't a rider. And something about someone called Maryk. I don't know what that was.'

'Leave me with him, Sword-Master Sollos. This isn't for your ears.'

Sollos snorted. 'You heard Rider Semian. We're to watch over you.'

'Thank you, but that's not necessary.'

'Master Huros, there *probably* aren't any snappers or wolves lurking around after a dragon's been here, but you never know. I don't overly mind if you get yourself eaten, but I'm quite sure that Rider Semian would delight in holding us to account for it.'

The alchemist shrugged. 'Stay if you must.' He settled himself and turned to the dead man. 'Um. What's your name, corpse?'

'Biyr,' said the dead man. Sollos shivered. The dead man spoke perfectly normally. He sounded much better than when he'd actually been alive and racked with the agony of his burns.

'Well, Biyr, what happened here?'

'A dragon came out of nowhere. We had no warning. It burned us. I was walking away from our tree shelters when the fire came.'

'Did you see the dragon?'

'Yes.'

'And, er, what colour was it?'

'White.'

The alchemist nodded, pleased. 'Did you see who was riding it?'

'No one was riding it.'

Huros frowned and shook his head. 'Ah. There must have been a, um, rider. Perhaps you missed it? Um … When did you see the dragon? When it was in the air? Did it land?'

'It came down in the river after it burned us. I saw it then, between the trees.'

'Did you see it in the air?'

'No.'

The alchemist nodded. 'There, you see. Um … whoever was riding her had probably already dismounted. Besides, it's not a good view from here through the trees to the river. I'm sure you could see something the size of a, ah, dragon clearly enough, but it would be very easy to miss a man.'

'I didn't see anyone get on its back before it went,' said Sollos quietly.

'That's because it didn't have a harness on,' grumbled Kemir. 'I kept telling—'

'It spoke,' murmured the dead man.

Huros shook his head. 'Dragons don't speak.'

'It spoke in my head. I heard it. It came for Maryk.'

'Um, no. You must be mistaken. That cannot be. Dragons do not speak.'

The alchemist's knuckles had gone very white.

Sollos asked, 'Who's Maryk?'

'One of us,' said the dead man. 'The dragon came after him.'

'How do you know?'

'That's what it said. It had come for Maryk. I heard its voice inside me, full of hate and fury.'

The alchemist shifted uncomfortably and frowned.

'Was this Maryk here?' asked Kemir.

'Yes. He was in the shelters,' said the dead man.

The alchemist raised a hand. 'Enough. Um ... sell-sword, go and bring Rider Semian to me.'

'So he's probably dead then.' Sollos made a face. 'Pity.'

'You should leave now,' said the alchemist.

Kemir grunted. 'I want to know about this Maryk. Where did he come from? Why did the dragon want him?'

'I want you to, um, leave us now, sell-sword. Bring Rider Semian. Um, right now.' The alchemist was chewing his lip in agitation.

'Do dead men lie?'

The alchemist turned and looked at Kemir. For a timid man, there was something very fierce in his eyes. And frightened too. 'About as much as living ones do, sell-sword. I said go!'

Kemir rolled his eyes. 'I'm only asking. Maybe when Rider Rod comes back, you could ask Crispy here whether we stabbed him. Just to make sure, you know.'

'There are no, er, wounds,' said Huros, between gritted teeth. 'It is patently obvious that you did not kill him. Now *go!*'

Sollos turned and left, pulling Kemir away with him.

Kemir chuckled to himself.

'Well he didn't seem very happy.'

'Do you *have* to annoy them so much?'

'Do I annoy them?'

'Does the sun rise in the morning? One day, one of those dragon-knights is going to lose his temper with you.'

'Let him. I'll put an arrow through him before he can remember which side he buckled his sword.'

'Yes. And what will you do about the other five?'

'Run like buggery, I expect.' Kemir laughed again and slapped Sollos on the back.

'I'm not finding this funny.' Sollos wrinkled his nose and loosened his shoulders. 'Something isn't right about this.'

'You keep saying that. As far as I'm concerned, what's not right is that we're helping dragon-knights.'

'We've been helping dragon-knights for months, remember?'

'Then let's just say I liked this work much better when we were helping dragon-knights by killing other dragon-knights. They're so stupid. They deserve to die.'

Sollos shook his head and pulled away, walking briskly towards the river.

'Well they *are*,' Kemir shouted after him. 'No obvious wounds? That's easy. Force open a man's mouth, drive a skewer up into the soft bit in the roof of his mouth and wiggle it about a bit. Or in through his nose, if he's totally out of it. Or up his arse, like Rider Rod. Need a bigger skewer for that, of course.'

'Will you *shut up!*' Sollos shook himself in exasperation. Whatever they both thought of dragon-knights, a fight wasn't going to help anyone, and Kemir was going to have to understand that sooner or later. Preferably sooner.

'Sell-sword!' Sollos emerged from the trees. Rider Semian was there, waiting for him. Sollos sighed. He couldn't bring himself to bow, so he settled for a slight nod.

'Rider. Master Huros has requested your presence. I suppose he has information he thinks you should hear.'

Semian looked at him askance and Sollos braced himself for the inevitable scornful tirade, but it didn't come. 'Very well, sell-sword. You can make yourself useful here instead. I require a fire.'

Sollos looked around at the smouldering embers all around him. 'That shouldn't be too difficult.' *Even for a dragon-knight.*

'I need smoke, sell-sword, and lots of it. No more walking through these cursed river beds. We're finishing this search as we should have started it. On dragonback.'

27

Nadira

The Outsiders came while Snow was hunting. She'd taken Kailin down from the snows of the mountainside into the rain and the constant damp of the mountain valleys. Water was everywhere. Tiny streams boiled down the forested slopes into wide rushing rivers and long still lakes. Whatever wasn't a river or a lake or a sheer piece of rock had a tree growing out of it. Vines grew on the trees and tufts of grass grew on the vines, and all of it was moving and alive.

Kailin was sunning himself on a boulder beside a river when he heard the first scream. He looked up and saw a woman running through the river towards him, leaping from one stone to the next. As he sat and stared at her, he saw that she wasn't alone. Half a dozen men were a little way behind her.

'Help me!' she shouted.

Heading straight for him, she reached his boulder and fell to her knees, clutching his hand. She looked exhausted and terrified. 'I don't know who you are, but help me, please. They're going to kill me.' Then she looked at him, saw him properly, saw his hard flaking skin and screamed.

Kailin screwed up his face and thought of Snow, but he felt nothing. The dragon must be miles away. He stood, paralysed. As the men came closer, they slowed down. There were six of them and they were armed with clubs and knives. Evil anticipation spread across their faces. He stared back, unable to move.

One of the men looked him up and down with obvious revulsion. 'What the fuck are you?' Then he jumped forward and swung a club at Kailin's head. Kailin raised his arms to fend off the blow. The club glanced off his elbow. Everything from his fingers to his shoulder erupted in pain and then went numb. He whimpered, and then the rest were on him, beating him down to the ground until everything faded away into a sea of pain.

'Nice one, Maryk,' he heard someone say.

Kailin returned to the world gradually, reluctantly. His arms felt as thought they were being wrenched out of their sockets. His ribs ached. His head was filled with thunder and lightning.

He opened his eyes. He was hanging from a branch by a rope tied around his wrists, about ten feet off the ground. A thick canopy of leaves and branches blotted out the sky above, filtering the sunlight to gloomy shadows. He was facing the river, overlooking the boulder where the men had beaten him senseless. They were still there, taking it in turns with the woman. Her face was puffy and swollen, and there were fresh scars on her back. They were cursing her, but they swore with such venomous hate that Kailin could barely understand them. *Whore. Thief.* That was all.

When they were finally finished with her, two of them held her down while a third pulled out a knotted length of rope and started to whip her. She spat and kicked at them then, but it was a short one-sided fight, and in the end all that was left were her screams. Eventually even those stopped. Her back was a bloody mess, but the man with the rope only stopped when one of the others put a hand on his arm.

'Leave her. She's almost dead already.'

The one with the rope wiped it clean, then used it to hog-tie the woman. Kailin closed his eyes as they turned away from her, looking up towards him.

'Enjoy watching did you, cripple?' shouted one of them.

'Hey! Thief! Wake up!' A stone hit him in the stomach, and then another one, this time in the shoulder. He managed not to flinch.

'Ah, leave him. He's not going anywhere.'

'Look at him! He's diseased.'

'Well *I'm* not touching him.'

'Was it worth it, thief? Thing? Whatever you are? Look! Look what she got you! Almost nothing. Here, you can have it. Make sure you give your whore her half. She worked for it.' Kailin had no idea what they were talking about.

'When the snappers come by, don't forget to pull your feet up. They can reach you if they're hungry enough to jump. Your whore's not going to be enough for them.'

'They probably wouldn't touch him. Look at him. Diseased, I tell you.'

They went away laughing. When the voices were long gone, Kailin opened his eyes. The woman was still there, tied up, motionless. His arms felt as though they were on fire.

'Hello? Hey?'

She didn't answer, but he saw her move, very slightly.

'Hey! Hey!'

After a while he gave up. He screwed up his face against the pain across his shoulders and tried to pretend he was somewhere else. Maybe that was what the woman was doing, why she was ignoring him. Not that either of them could help the other. All he could do was wait for Snow.

By the time she came, he was so consumed with his own misery he didn't even notice until she landed. Until he heard the woman's screams over his own whimpering.

Little One Kailin! She was crashing down the river, running on her hind legs, flapping her wings for extra speed, straight towards him. With her wings outstretched, Snow was almost as wide as the river, a hundred feet across and more.

The woman's shrieks grew louder and more hysterical, until they turned into a high-pitch keening wail.

You are hurt!

'Get me down from this tree!' shouted Kailin.

How did this happen? Snow skidded to a stop, flapping her wings and scattering boulders the size of Kailin's head. Her head darted forward; her teeth closed around the branch above Kailin's head. She bit through it as though it was putty and lowered Kailin carefully to the ground. Kailin hugged his arms to his chest. The relief was blissful.

I cannot untie you. Snow peered at Kailin, and then sniffed at the woman. *Where did this one come from? Why is it bound? Is it food?*

The woman's wailing subsided to whimpers.

'Snow, leave her alone. Don't hurt her. She's terrified.'

I know. It feels pleasant. It is the way I remember it.

'Talk to her.' Kailin struggled to his feet and started to walk back into the trees. 'Let her know you don't mean her any harm.'

You are in great pain, Little One Kailin. I feel it. I cannot help you. Why did you do this?

He could feel the confusion in Snow's thoughts. The dragon had no idea.

'Other men did this to us. Bad men, Snow. I don't know why.' He tilted his head towards the woman. 'She might.' He winced and walked gingerly among the stones until he found one sharp enough to cut the rope around his wrist. It was painstaking work, but at least when he was done the woman wasn't screaming any more. She was looking at Snow with an expression of bewildered terror. Kailin went over and unpicked the knots that bound her. Once she was free he slumped down against a boulder. The woman hugged her knees. She was shivering badly. He tried to give her his flying furs, but when he came close, she shrank away. He put them close by and then stepped away. Her back was still a bloody mess.

'I'm Kailin,' he said. 'This is Snow. She's my dragon.'

The woman looked at him as though he was mad. She seemed to be almost as afraid of him as she was of the dragon.

Her name is Nadira. She is terrified of you. She thinks you mean to hurt her. She sees you in armour, with a sword and a lance, as most men who ride dragons clothe themselves. And she thinks there is something wrong with you.

He sat down on a stone and watched her carefully. 'I'm not a rider; I'm just a Scales. Do you know what that means? It means I look after a dragon. I do the feeding and the grooming. Like a stable hand. I look the way I do because of her. When they come out of their eggs, dragons carry a disease. It did this to me. Even with the potions from the alchemists, it does this. Don't be afraid, though. This happened to me a long time ago. It's dormant now. Until the next hatchling I'm given to care for. I'm not allowed to ride her, by the way. She says your name is Nadira.'

She is confused. She doesn't understand how we got to be here. She still believes we will hurt her.

'We got lost,' said Kailin. 'We came from Queen Shezira's eyrie. I don't suppose you've heard of her …'

No.

'Queen Shezira's daughter is marrying King Tyan's son. Snow and I were supposed to be wedding gifts. We were attacked by other dragon-knights. I don't know who they were. We escaped and ran away. We've been lost in these mountains for weeks. I don't suppose you know where we are?' Kailin stretched his shoulders and winced.

Very slightly, the woman shook her head.

Little One Kailin, what is Soul Dust?

'I don't know.' Kailin looked at the woman. 'What's Soul Dust?'

She flinched and looked away, and Kailin saw her eyes pause on something lying among the rocks. A tiny leather pouch.

Men who make it bought her for pleasure. She wants it. She needs it like food or drink. She took some and ran away. She was being punished for this. Punishment. Revenge. Retribution. Yes, I understand this. It is wasteful. Foolish.

'They did this to her because she stole from them?'

That is what is in her mind. Another Little One, Maryk, he is the one who did this. I see that name in your thoughts too.

'They raped and beat her and left her to die. They left me to die too. Why?'

We are alike. We both miss our own kind in the same way. We miss what they could be, or should be, but not what they truly are. I have to go now, Little One Kailin. I have not finished hunting for the day. I will not be long.

Snow turned and Kailin watched her launch herself down the

river, the same way the men had gone. That could have been coincidence, but something in the tenor of Snow's last thoughts said otherwise. She'd gone to find them. She didn't look back, and by the time he made himself stand up and call after her, she was too far away to hear his thoughts any more.

When she came back, he meant to ask her what she'd done and to tell her that it was wrong, but he never got a chance. Even as the thoughts were forming up in his head, she came crashing into his mind.

More dragons are coming.

28

The Hunters and the Hunted

When the white dragon came back, she caught them all by surprise. Sollos had barely started on the fire when a great shadow flashed over his head. The knights looked up and stared as the dragon wheeled overhead. She was clutching something in one claw, Sollos saw. She flared her wings and stretched out her massive hind claws, swooping down like an eagle towards them. When she landed in the river bed and took a few steps to steady herself, the mountains seemed to shake. Then she stood there, still, poised on her hind legs, wings not quite fully folded, head raised a little on her long neck, her massive tail stretched out straight behind her for balance.

Sollos retreated slowly from the beginnings of his fire towards the woods. He'd seen dragons stand like that before. So had the riders, who began to fan out across the river bed.

'How long before your own dragons get here, Rider Semian?' Sollos muttered. Semian wasn't there to answer, but Sollos already knew as much as he needed to. *Not for some time.*

Slowly, the dragon reached down with one forelimb. She opened her claws. There was a man curled up in there.

Holy Ancestors, Sollos thought when the man got up. *It's the Scales.* He looked well enough. A bit stiff and battered perhaps, and he walked a little awkwardly, but for a man stuck on his own in the Worldspine for a month he was remarkably alive. *Maybe having skin as hard as stone that flakes like slate helps with that.*

Rider Semian and Master Huros came running out of the trees. They ignored him and went straight towards the dragon. Kemir came after them and stopped at his shoulder.

'Oh well! That's going to make all this a lot easier.' He grinned.

'She's very tense.'

'Who?'

'The dragon, you idiot. Look at her.'

'Mmmm.' Kemir nodded. 'Ready to run. Wouldn't you be? Do you suppose she even remembers her knights after all this time. How do you know she's a she—'

Sollos shushed him. The Scales was walking towards the dragon-knights. He seemed very unsure of himself.

'That's enough!' Rider Semian held up a hand and stopped the Scales when they were still a good twenty feet apart. Semian had the alchemist beside him and one other knight. The rest of the riders were still slowly spreading out, edging towards the trees. Sollos did the same.

'Um, what is your name, Scales?' shouted the alchemist.

The Scales replied, but quietly. Sollos couldn't hear him.

'Scales Kailin. We, er, are here to take you home. You and your dragon.'

'Queen Shezira will congratulate you herself,' called Rider Semian. 'Her dragon is still intact, and has not been lost. She will be greatly pleased. There may be a reward.'

The Scales said something else. Sollos screwed up his eyes and strained forward, as if that might help him make out what the Scales was saying.

Then Kemir had a hand on his shoulder and was tugging him back towards the forest. 'I don't like the way this is going.'

'Did you hear him? What did he say?'

'He said no.'

Kemir was right; Sollos could see that by the way that the alchemist and Rider Semian were standing.

'This is not a request, Scales,' shouted Rider Semian. 'This is an order!'

Kemir was still edging back into the trees. He was stringing his bow.

The alchemist suddenly stepped forward and walked up to the

Scales. Sollos had no idea what they were saying, only that the alchemist looked very determined, and the Scales looked, well, if anything, he looked stunned. Aghast.

Something in the air changed. Sollos felt an irrational anger build up inside him. The Scales was gesturing frantically at the alchemist, trying to make him ... Trying to make him stop? The dragon had lowered itself to all fours. It was utterly still. Sollos could feel the tension radiating from it like waves of heat.

Kemir put a hand on his shoulder again. 'You know what? I think we should back off a little way further.'

'Yes.' He took a step backwards. Then another. 'Yes, I think we should.'

When the dragon moved, it was so quick that Sollos barely saw it. Its head and body stayed exactly where they were; its tail, all hundred feet of it, flicked like a whip. In the blink of an eye it flashed over the dragon's head. The tip coiled around the alchemist, lifted him up into the air and held him inches from the dragon's bared teeth. For long seconds everyone froze except for the Scales, who sank to his knees, wrapping his arms around his head. And then everything happened at once.

29

The Wordmaster

The City of Dragons stood behind the Adamantine Palace, squashed against the mountains of the Purple Spur and the Diamond Cascade Waterfalls. The city was a small one by the standards of the realms, but rich, filled with jewels and knights, lords and ladies. To either side of both the city and the palace lay the shimmering waters of the Mirror Lakes. To the south-west, the only open approach to the speaker's domain, were the Plains of the Hungry Mountain, the fertile grain basket of the central realms. On a good day a man in the palace looking out of the windows at the top of the Tower of Air could see all the way over them to the Fury River gorge, a hundred miles south of the city. Today, though, someone had built a very tall temporary wooden tower not very far from the palace gates, and the air beyond was hazy and tinged with grey. A keen pair of eyes might have made out two figures standing on the top of the tower. They might too have made out that the haze over the plains was the dust kicked up by the ten thousand marching men of the Adamantine Guard, preparing themselves for the ceremonies of the weeks to come.

It would have taken exceptional vision, though, to see that those figures on the tower top were the speaker himself, Speaker Hyram, and a master alchemist of the Order of the Scales. Or that the speaker's shaking was worse than usual, that his face was flushed with what might have been excitement but was more probably rage, and that the master alchemist was looking decidedly pale.

'N-Nothing?'

The alchemist was Grand Master Jeiros, Second Lord of the

Order of the Scales. The possibility that he might now be the first lord accounted for a good part of his discomfort. He bowed as low as he could without falling over.

'Nothing, Your Holiness. Grand Master Bellepheros stated his conviction before the the whole of King Tyan's court. No one tampered with Queen Aliphera's mount before she left and she was not attacked in the air. If there was murder, it did not originate within King Tyan's eyrie.'

'A-And that is all?'

'Prince Jehal pressed him hard in front of many witnesses. Master Bellepheros would not say whether Queen Aliphera's death was malice or misfortune, although he did allude to some sly goings-on between Aliphera and Tyan's brother. Prince Jehal was considerably displeased.'

The speaker spat. 'Tyan's brother? That gelding Meteroa? Nonsense! W-What of Q-Queen Zafir?'

'We have found nothing to implicate her.'

Hyram growled. 'A-And then B-Bellepheros disappears.'

The second lord scraped another bow. 'Taken by force. Prince Jehal reports that all his guards were found dead, most with their throats slit. Of the master himself ...' Jeiros shrugged.

'P-Prince Jehal says!' Hyram spat. 'D-Don't believe a word f-from that viper.'

'Your Holiness, Master Bellepheros chose his words to the court of King Tyan with great care. Implications were presented, not in what he said but in what he did *not* say. He did *not* say that Queen Aliphera's death was an accident, Your Holiness.'

'Of c-course it wasn't!' Hyram stamped impatiently. 'D-Do what you need to f-find out who took him, Jeiros. N-Now, concerning the other matter? H-Have you got to the bottom of h-how Prince Jehal is k-killing King Tyan yet?'

Jeiros squirmed. 'Your Holiness, there is still no evidence that King Tyan is being poisoned at all.' He pursed his lips. 'We have learned, Your Holiness, that there may be some truth to the rumours that Prince Jehal has found something that improves his father's condition. It is a little ...' He frowned. 'It is unclear,

Your Holiness. There are … there are hints of some potion he has acquired.'

Hyram snorted. 'I-If it's a potion, i-it's from one of you. G-Get to the point!'

'Your Holiness, that is the point. It does *not* come from the order. We …' He hesitated, but there was no going back now. 'We think it comes from outside the realms.'

Hyram's face went dark; he started to cough and his tremors seemed to grow more pronounced. It took a while for Jeiros to realise that the speaker was laughing at him.

'Y-you have singularly f-failed, Master Jeiros. Y-You have no answers for me, a-and now this? S-So be it. Go, M-Master Jeiros. I will summon Queen Zafir and P-Prince Jehal and *I* will f-find out who murdered Aliphera, a-and then I will tell *y-you* which alchemist is making p-potions for Jehal.'

The alchemist backed away, bowing as he went. It was a long way to the bottom of the tower, down narrow stairs and rickety ladders. Hyram found himself hoping that the second lord might trip and fall. A broken wrist or some such inconvenience – that would do, nothing more. For all his blathering, Hyram preferred not to lose his second lord as well as his first.

He sighed, alone at last, and let his eyes drift out across the plain. His legions were formed up, twenty phalanxes each of five hundred men. They would be out there every day until the dragon kings and queens gathered at the palace to see him pass his mantle on. Part of the legacy that each speaker handed to the next: ten thousand exquisitely trained soldiers, raised from birth to fight. It struck him as strange, watching them, that so many men should dedicate every moment of their lives to such perfection, and yet be content never to fight. Their loyalty, he was assured, was total and unswerving, hammered into them from the moment they could speak. Their strength and their fearlessness too was total, forged in their relentless and brutal years of training, and then quenched in the alchemical potions that emptied their minds of any doubts that might remain; in their legends, even the dragons couldn't stop them. But didn't they secretly hate him? Didn't they despise him? Didn't they look at their own potency and then look at him and wonder, *Who is this fading king? Who is he to leash us?*

He looked away. A year ago he'd have laughed at such thoughts; then, a year ago he'd been a different man. Still strong, still fooling himself that he was younger than his years. Still with dreams that his days as speaker might go on and on, that he might compel Shezira to wed him as the price of naming her as his successor. Or, old treaties and dusty parchments be damned, marrying Aliphera and naming her instead. Still bedding women as the fancy took him, instead of lying helpless in his sheets, stinking of his own soil after one of the fits caught him unaware, screaming for his pot-boys to clean him.

Now Aliphera was dead, Shezira wouldn't have him, and even the pot-boys kept running away. In another year or two he'd be like King Tyan, dribbling and useless. How fitting that would be, the two of them, old foes that they were, side by side, forgotten, each lying in his own pool of drool. No, he'd rather die a quick death than that. Let them chop him up and feed him to his own dragons, like the speakers of old, before Speaker Narammed clipped the dragon-priests' wings.

He heard the stairs squeak behind him and turned to see a head emerging from the belly of the tower, up into the sunlight. The head didn't have much hair left, and what there was was white. The face beneath it looked pained and out of breath.

'You called for me, Your Holiness?'

Hyram shook his head. 'N-No, Wordmaster Herlian.'

'Then I shall take myself back down into the shade, Your Holiness, and you may tell our dear second lord that I shall corner him when he's sitting down one day and rap his ankles with my stick. I am too old to be climbing these stairs. He seemed to think you wished to issue a summons or two.'

'T-To Prince J-Jehal and to Queen Z-Zafir, but it could have waited. S-Since you're here, though, come and stand with me.'

'If I must, Your Holiness.' The wordmaster struggled out onto the roof. 'But you'd better tell me what there is to see. My eyes are as old as the rest of me.'

'I-I want to know, W-Wordmaster. What will your b-books say of me?'

'Ha!' Herlian's cackle sounded like the snapping of old dry twigs. 'If I write them, they'll say you were a foul-tempered little boy who never attended to his lessons, didn't listen to a word his elders said to him and made his tutor's life an endless sea of misery.' The wordmaster hobbled to the edge of the tower and looked down. 'Long way. Heh. I suppose I might also mention how a headstrong dragon-knight took on the duty that should have fallen to his brother. I know you didn't want it. I don't mean being the speaker, either. I mean being the eldest.'

'H-History, Wordmaster, that's all.'

'History is all I am, young Master Hyram. If it's flattery you want, get yourself a flatterer to walk up all these stairs. I know what you're thinking. You're thinking that there are books and books full of the stories of Vishmir and other speakers of old. Heh. I don't forget, you see. I still remember how your eyes used to light up when I'd finally consent to read to you about them. Your story will be much shorter, Your Holiness. Ten years of peace and prosperity in which nothing of any great significance happened to the realms, and all the little people were left to live their lives and get old and fat. That is what the story of a truly good speaker should be. Let that be enough.'

'I-Is it, though?'

Herlian shrugged. 'It is for the rest of us. If it's not enough for you, then tell me what is. I'll write wars for you if you want. Great victories, epic quests, strings of princesses fawning at your feet. Whatever you like. As much glory as you want.'

'N-No, Wordmaster, that won't b-be necessary.' Hyram shook his head, trying to push away the suffocating weight of hopelessness that seemed to press down on him these days. *That's it, is it? I'll be remembered as a fine speaker, because no one has bothered to write anything else? But then why remember at all?* He sat down, knowing that doing so would allow Herlian to sit as well. 'D-Do you have your q-quill? Let us start with a summons to P-Prince Jehal. M-Maybe you can add an execution as a f-footnote to my reign.'

30

Queen Aliphera's Garden

'I have a gift for you.' Jehal put on his best smile. Zafir glanced at him through her eyelashes. They were walking together, side by side, among many-coloured shrubs and rainbow flowerbeds. The summer sun was bright and warm and a faint breeze ticked Jehal's nose with strange scents, a heady mixture of perfumes and spices.

'Do you like my gardens?' asked Zafir. 'My mother grew them.' They walked just far enough apart to be sure they didn't touch, even by accident. Behind them a little knot of Zafir's ladies followed them around, not too close but never so far away that they were out of sight. In case they were needed to testify that nothing improper could possibly have happened.

'Indeed, Your Holiness.' He *hated* that, having to call her Holiness just because she was a queen now, and he was a mere prince. That would have to change. 'Queen Aliphera's Gardens are justly famous throughout the realms. Even as far north as ...' He let that hang.

'You mean even dear Princess Lystra has heard of them? It defies imagination.' Her words had edges like razors. 'Is she well, your wife?'

Jehal pretended not to notice Zafir's venom. 'When I left, she was a picture of health and very bored.'

'You should have brought her with you. It would have been a delight to welcome her as a guest within my walls.'

Yes. Especially now that she's carrying my heir. Of course, he didn't know for sure that Zafir knew this; in fact he didn't even know for sure himself, but the signs were there, and as far as he could tell Zafir's spies were making sure that she was at least as well informed as he was. *I should probably ask her whether it's going to be a boy or a girl.*

He smiled again. 'She would have been overjoyed, I'm sure. Given her condition, however, I have had to order that she be confined to the palace. It is concern for her health, you see. The risk of miscarriage.' Zafir didn't blink. *So that's that, then. She knows.*

Zafir sniffed. 'I'm told that my mother was still flying three days before I was born. Queen Shezira probably gave birth to one of her daughters while still in the saddle.'

The risk of miscarriage that would come from letting you anywhere near her. 'Dear Queen Zafir, it should be plain to you that I've been seeking an excuse to lock my darling wife away since before I married her. Would you deny me my freedom?'

For a moment Zafir didn't answer. Then she stopped and turned to face him, and her face lit up. 'Is marriage so unhappy for you?'

'Deeply.'

'I'll help you get rid of her then,' she said quietly. 'I have a debt of that sort, after all.'

'In time, my love.' Jehal glanced back at the ladies-in-waiting. They were twenty, maybe thirty yards away, chatting among themselves, casting the occasional glance towards their queen. Well out of earshot.

'But not before she gives you an heir?'

'It *does* keep her out of the way, my sweet.'

'I suppose you, of all princes, can find a way to make sure she never gives birth. What a string of tragedies she has to look forward to.'

'Actually, I was thinking of birthing them in secret and then sending them away with the Taiytakei to be raised in secret in some far-off foreign land.'

She smiled. 'To come back in twenty years and challenge you for your throne? How romantic. And stupid. Get rid of them, Jehal. Them and her.'

'As soon as I can, my love. When I find the right potion.'

She drew a little closer, almost close enough to touch. 'Where do you get them from? Do you have a pet alchemist? He must be very good.'

Jehal bowed. 'Why, I make them myself, Your Holiness.'

'No you don't!' She laughed.

'I have a new one now. Something that makes my father's illness subside, at least for a while. I have a few flasks of it with me to dangle under Speaker Hyram's nose. Doubtless he intends to accuse me of killing your mother yet again, though without a shred of evidence. He's going to start sounding quite foolish soon. When he's done, I shall let him taste a little of my bottled salvation so that he can see how much better he might be, and then he'll never, *ever* taste any more.' He shook his head and laughed as well. 'Well, unless he makes me speaker, but I can't see that, can you?'

'I think he'd rather hand himself over to the dragon-priests.'

'Yes.' Jehal scratched his chin. 'Would he rather go slowly mad, though? I suppose he would, but it will be fun to find out.'

'Make him suffer. After he crowned me, he took me aside and asked if *I'd* killed her. I couldn't believe what I was hearing. And then he asked whether it was you.'

Jehal put on a face. 'Well I hope you told him no.'

'Of course I did. Still, I think he had rather more of a secret desire for my mother than I realised.'

'I don't think it was *that* secret.' *Not that secret at all. Just not reciprocated.* 'Don't worry, my sweet, it's me that he wants to hang, not you. Smile him a pretty smile and he'll melt like butter.'

'Like this?'

'Exactly like that. I feel my blood quickening already.' He glanced back at the watching courtiers and sighed. 'Is there some way we could ...' he whispered.

Zafir's smile faded. She shook her head sadly. 'No. Not until this is done. That's what you said.'

'I know, but ...' He grinned and bared his teeth. 'Now I'm here, it is a physical pain that I can't touch you.'

She blushed and looked at her feet. 'Do you like this dress?' she asked.

'On you, it's perfection.'

'It was my mother's. I think she wore it on the day she first met Speaker Hyram. I had to make some adjustments, of course. I spoke to some of my mother's old servants and learned how she carried herself, how she dressed herself, how she wore her hair. When Hyram sees me, it won't be me he sees – it will be my mother, as she was when he fell in love with her. I shall drive that dagger in deep and then twist until the blade breaks.'

'Oh, that's cruel.' Jehal grinned. 'Between the two of us, we should have him weeping on his knees.'

Zafir shrugged. 'He accused me, moments after he *crowned* me.'

Jehal grinned some more. 'Well, he *was* right.'

She peered at him and pouted. 'You said something about a gift and then wandered off into all sorts of unpleasantness. Is it a *nice* gift? Shall I want it?'

'Oh yes, I think you shall want it very much.'

She wagged a finger at him. 'We agreed, remember.'

'My love, it's not *me* I'm offering. Well I am, but not here and now. Although ...' He glanced back at the courtiers again. 'I have a steel sword as well as the one *you're* after. I could butcher them all and then we could—'

'Jehal!'

'I'm sure they're all very tedious.'

Zafir laughed, and Jehal felt a tension inside him ease and fade away. He still had her. That was what mattered. However much she hated him for marrying Princess Lystra, he still had her. He handed her a strip of black silk.

'You have to put this on,' he said, 'like a blindfold. No! Not here!' He lowered his voice until he was absolutely sure that no one else would hear. 'But it's not a blindfold, my love. When you put it on, you will see things. You won't want anyone else to know, so do it when no one is watching you.' He offered her a box. It wasn't as pretty as the one the Taiytakei had given him, but it was close. This one, though, only had room for one little golden dragon with ruby eyes.

Zafir ran her fingers over the carved wood. He could see the hunger in her eyes. 'What is it?'

'Open it when you're alone. Take a good look at it, and then put on the blindfold. When you do, you'll understand. I could tell you a lot more, but where would be the fun in that?' He winked and his voice dropped even lower. 'Anticipation is often the greatest pleasure.'

'Oh really?' She was almost purring. 'Will you be staying in the City of Dragons after you've finished taunting poor old Hyram?' He could see the desire flashing through her. *A real shame that we can't—* He bit his lip. *Not yet, not yet. Not while Hyram's watching us so closely.*

'Of course. Though no one will know of it.'

'How can you be sure?'

'Leave that to me. Do you trust me, my love?'

He wasn't sure what to make of the look she gave him, but decided to take it as a cautious yes. He smiled as he felt the hairs prickle on the back of his neck. They'd dallied for too long, and the queen's chaperones were drawing closer. Slowly and cautiously and giving plenty of notice of their advance, but nevertheless with the same relentless purpose as a hostile army.

Later, when everyone was supposed to be asleep and he was alone in his carefully guarded and watched bedchamber, Jehal opened the shutters on his windows, slipped out the second strip of black silk and wrapped it across his eyes.

So, my love, let's see how far you've got.

31

The Adamantine Guard

Watching Zafir play with her new toy was far too much fun, and of course the first thing she did, as soon as she discovered she could make the little dragon fly, was to send it to spy through his window. He took off the black silk and then let her watch him for a while, tossing and turning in his sleep, then pretended to awaken. The tiny dragon flew up to his face as if to announce its presence. He tried to look sheepish.

'You are very wicked,' he whispered in the dragon's ear, 'and if you were here, I would show you *how* wicked you are.'

The tiny dragon danced around him, taunting him, and then darted back towards the window.

'Zafir,' he hissed, and the dragon paused and hovered. 'Nothing I've given Lystra comes near to this. Send it to watch us, if you want, and you will see.'

The dragon paused and then left. Jehal shuttered the windows behind it and then put the black silk back across his eyes.

Both of them rose late the next morning, and as Zafir rode with him to her eyrie, she seemed to glow.

'I'm sure you have another one,' she whispered in his ear as he prepared to mount his dragon, Wraithwing. 'We could watch each other when we're apart.'

Or I could tell her about the second silk, he thought. *Tell her that I can share the eyes of her little spy with her, that I can watch her through its eyes whenever I want, if she keeps it near.*

Tempting, very tempting, but that wasn't why he'd given it to her. 'Wait for me, my love,' he said thickly. 'I'll find you, after we're both done with Hyram.'

'Hmmm.' Her eyes flashed. 'You'd better.'

He climbed into the saddle and wiped his brow. *Maybe the Taiytakei can get me some more.* That made him laugh as he watched Zafir and her courtiers back away from his dragon. *For all I know, these are the only two such creatures ever made, and I ask for more simply so I can watch my lover when she's not in my bed? Not that they'd know, of course, but still.*

'Fly!' he shouted, and immediately felt the huge muscles of the dragon stir beneath him. Wraithwing lifted his head, rose onto his hind legs and began to run across the flat ground. Jehal closed his eyes. He could feel every stride as the dragon accelerated. He knew exactly when it would make one last bound and unfurl its wings. He felt himself grow heavier as it rose up into the air, and he sighed. Nothing, but nothing, compared to that moment, the second that the ground let go. Such a pity that it only lasted for an instant; then it was gone, and everything that followed was tame and flat. He thought about getting out the black silk again and letting his eyes ride with one dragon while his body rode on another, but that was just a quick way to lose the silk to the wind. He tried to think about Hyram instead, but Zafir kept getting in the way. He wondered sometimes if he should have spurned Princess Lystra and taken Zafir to be his bride instead, but that would have ruined everything. It was a shame, though, because one day, because of what he'd done, Lystra was going to be in the way. Maybe he should have turned them both away. He could have done that. Rejected Lystra because Queen Shezira hadn't brought the perfect white dragon that she'd promised him.

He smiled. Instead, in a few days he'd be joining the search for it, even though he was absolutely sure that the dragon was safely locked away in some distant eyrie. Shezira was putting on a very good show. She'd kept it up for two months, and all sorts of little rumours leaked from her camp.

Another thought crossed his mind. Maybe it *was* all a ruse, just not the ruse he thought it was. She had some two dozen dragons and a hundred riders in the search, and all of them so very, very close to the Adamantine Palace. A lot closer than anyone else.

Yes, he thought. *Definitely worth a look,* and he let his mind wander over the possibilities as Wraithwing powered through the air. They flew over miles of rolling hills covered in trees, and then the ground fell away, faster and steeper, diving down into the Fury River gorge, which effectively cut the realms in two. To the south Queen Zafir ruled. To the north, the speaker. Jehal thought about that too, as he guided Wraithwing down into the gorge and shot along the roaring river. He skimmed the line between the two as closely as he could, while Wraithwing dipped his tail into the waters and threw up a cloud of spray behind them.

He flew along the gorge for an hour and then climbed out again, veering north across the dullness of the Hungry Mountain Plain. He made Wraithwing fly high. *No point in scaring all the peasants.* For a while he closed his eyes and dozed, but as the Purple Spur mountains slowly grew out of the haze and he could see the first glitter of the Adamantine Palace, he saw that there were other dragons in the air. Hunting dragons, by the look of them, half a dozen or so. At first Jehal wondered what they were doing there. Then he saw that Hyram had his legions out.

Perfecting them so he can show them off before he stands down as speaker. Jehal nudged Wraithwing into a tight spiral, diving straight through the other dragons towards the men on the ground. As he fell towards them, each legion bunched together, presenting a seamless wall of gleaming shields towards him. The shields were made of dragonscale, large enough to hide a man, and if he'd ordered Wraithwing to flamestrike, the fire would have stopped at the shield wall. As he passed over the heads of the soldiers, the shields came down and a hedgehog of scorpions popped up in their place. Each could fire a bolt the size of a javelin with enough force to punch through a dragon's scales, but it wasn't the dragon they'd be aimed at; it was the rider.

When he was past them, Jehal climbed again and had Wraithwing tip his wings to salute them. *Best to be nice. One day they're going to be mine.*

He landed at the Adamantine Eyrie, almost expecting to see Speaker Hyram waiting for him with a posse of guards, ready to drag him straight off to the dungeons. Not that the old goat would dare such a thing without any proof. Not when Jehal was married to the next speaker's daughter. *Ah, Lystra, all these little uses I have for you. A pity I'll have to be rid of you in the end.*

He frowned. Thoughts like that left him feeling strangely uncomfortable, so he set them aside and concentrated on what was around him. Instead of the almost-expected armed escort, the eyrie was almost deserted. A couple of hunting dragons were ripping into a pile of freshly slaughtered cattle. A few Scales were going about their duties; one of them ran to help him dismount and care for Wraithwing. There were soldiers too, but not very many, and he supposed that he'd already passed most of the Adamantine Guard out on the plains. He'd brought a dozen riders and half as many dragons of his own in case he needed them; now he felt almost foolishly overdressed. All in all, he had the distinct impression that the eyrie-master, when he came running out of his little tower, hadn't even known he was coming.

'Prince Jehal!'

'Copas.' Jehal smiled. The man looked horrified, taken completely by surprise. 'Did the speaker not warn you of my arrival?'

'Ah, of course, Your Highness. We were expecting you tomorrow.' Lies. Jehal could see straight through them. *Strange. Why would Hyram assume I would ignore his summons? Does he think I'm scared of him?*

Well if he did, he was in for a shocker of a day tomorrow. Jehal widened his smile and let out a few more teeth. 'I can't help but wonder why, since it always has been and always will be a three-day flight from Furymouth, and when the speaker summoned me, his words were quite terse and direct. "Immediately" I believe was his demand.' *I shouldn't blame him. Most of the men here belong to the order, not to Hyram. One day he's going to be mine too.*

'Your Highness, I am at a loss. Do you intend to proceed directly to the palace? I can arrange accommodation here, if you would prefer.'

'In case no one at the palace is expecting me either?' Jehal cocked his head. 'No, thank you, Copas. It's hardly your fault if the speaker's staff failed to warn you. I'm sure they can't have made the same mistake twice. However, my riders will stay here, if you would so oblige me.' *If Hyram does plan me any ill, they'll do me no good in the palace.*

He watched as various Scales unloaded his baggage into a pair of carts. For a few minutes he wondered whether he was going to have to ride perched on the back of one of them. Eventually Copas brought up one of his own horses. He hung his head.

'I'm sorry, Your Highness. We have disgraced ourselves.'

'Someone has. I'm sure it's not your fault.'

Copas had at least managed to send a rider ahead so that the palace gates were open and the servants and the guards could pretend they hadn't been taken entirely by surprise. But everything took far longer than it should, and by the time he was finally alone, he had to admit that whatever mad game Hyram was playing, it was starting to work. What was it that Hyram thought would keep him away? *What is it that I don't know?*

It turned out to be two things. The first he discovered when he unpacked his precious potions and found all but one of them were missing. The second became clear when Adamantine Guard smashed their way into his room in the middle of the night.

32

The Alchemist and the Dragon

Kailin was terrified. He had no idea what he should do or say. In front of him were dragon-knights from Queen Shezira's eyrie. He didn't know them by name, but some of the faces were familiar. And the alchemist, of course. He knew Master Huros. They'd all want him to bring Snow back home, and a Scales always obeyed. That was his life. Look after the dragons and do as he was told. Except that behind him was a dragon who didn't want to go home. He walked through the shallow rushing water of the river as though lead weights were shackled to his feet.

'That's far enough!' The dragon-knight standing next to Master Huros held up a hand. Kailin stopped. They were still a good twenty feet apart. The other riders were spreading out, edging towards the trees.

Snow spoke in his head. *Make them understand that I will not come back. Not yet. They should cease their pursuit of us.*

Kailin winced. *I don't know how. They won't listen.*

'Um, what is your name, Scales?' shouted Master Huros.

Kailin looked at his feet, too used to averting his eyes from his masters. 'Kailin,' he said.

'Scales Kailin. We are here to take you home. You and your dragon.'

'Queen Shezira will congratulate you herself,' called the knight. 'Her dragon is still intact and has not been lost. She will be greatly pleased. There may be a reward.'

He didn't know what to say. He shook his head. He couldn't force the words out of his mouth. As soon as he did, they'd kill him. They'd take him back to Outwatch and string him up for all the other Scales to see, and then they'd very slowly execute him.

This is what happens to a Scales who does not obey.

Tell them no!

He was shaking. He glanced up at the dragon-knight and at Master Huros, pleading with his eyes. 'I can't. I don't know how to. What if ... Snow doesn't want to—'

'This is not a request, Scales,' shouted the knight. 'This is an order!'

Master Huros stepped forward. He walked over to Kailin and put a hand on his shoulder. 'Um, listen to me, Scales. Whatever has happened out here, it, er, it doesn't matter. If you've ridden the dragon, that doesn't matter. Whatever petty crimes you may have committed, they can be forgiven. The rules that we live by do not extend to circumstances such as these. You've done your duty and done it well. The dragon is intact but, um, she *must* come back to an eyrie at once.'

Kailin still couldn't meet the alchemist's eyes. 'I can't. She won't.'

Tell them no! Or I will.

'Scales, you do not understand. There are, er, things you don't know. She must come back to an eyrie. If she doesn't, she will change. You might even have noticed little differences in her behaviour already. We have to take her back.'

Change? He could feel Snow's curiosity grow.

'I should not even have told you this much, Scales. These are the secrets of our order, but you must believe me, and so I tell you that without the elixirs I and the other alchemists at the eyrie will prepare for her, she ... she *will* change. She will become a wild thing. She'll be dangerous, not just to you but to everyone.'

What does he mean? Ask him what he means!

He felt the edge in Snow's thoughts, the suspicion, the horror, the incipient fury. He felt it in himself. 'No! Stop!' He wasn't sure whether he meant it for Master Huros or for Snow.

The alchemist suddenly looked very surprised. 'Yes,' he said. 'Yes, that's right. More intelligent. More independent. How did you know?'

Kailin went rigid. 'Master, Master Huros, please—'

Leave him be!

'How did you know this, Scales?' The alchemist's voice had dropped to a whisper and he was glancing back at the knights. 'Yes. They remember things. That's exactly what happens, and that cannot be, cannot be *allowed* to be! But, but you shouldn't know this. *How* do you know this?'

Something in the air began to change. The anger inside his head was growing, blooming, pouring into him. 'Master Huros! She's in your head! She's reading your mind! She knows!'

He caught a glimpse of abject horror in the alchemist's eyes, and then Snow moved so fast that Kailin didn't even see it happen. One moment the alchemist was there in front of him, the next he had shot up into the air, the tip of Snow's tail wrapped around him. He dangled helpless in front of Snow's face – shrieking, screaming, pleading – while everyone else froze and watched. Stray thoughts flickered through Kailin's mind, thoughts that weren't his and were filled with such a frenzied rage that he fell to his knees in the water, clutching his head. *Preparations? Memories? How? How long? How long have you done this? HOW LONG?*

He didn't see the moment when Snow squeezed the knot in her tail and crushed the life out of the alchemist, almost splitting him in two. He saw the body, though, flung through the air like a stone from a catapult, straight into one of the knights, so hard that the force of it lifted him off the ground and both sprawled like broken rag dolls. He felt the sky go dark as Snow leapt straight over his head. She landed, shaking the ground where the knight had been, and snapped up another in her claws. The man screamed as she crushed him, and Kailin heard the metal plates of his armour bend and break. The other knights were bolting for the cover of the trees. Snow's tail whipped around again, casually flinging a rock the size of half a man. It caught another rider, smashing him into a tree. He didn't get up.

Then came the fire. She swept her head from side to side, sweeping the edge of the forest with torrents of flame. The knights, if they were quick enough, would cower behind their dragonscale shields and the heat would pass them by.

But if they were crouched behind their shields, they weren't running. Snow sprang out of the river and up the bank to the forest. The fire came again, and this time her tail cracked into the trees. She plucked out one knight, cartwheeling him a hundred feet into the air, and then another, this one smashed head first into the stones of the river bed. Kailin whimpered and covered his face. He couldn't bring himself to watch. He heard men scream, branches crack, tree trunks bend and break.

Sprinting footsteps splashed through the water towards him. He heard a voice: 'What are you doing? Are you mad?'

Arms roughly pulled him up and gripped him tight. Raw steel touched his throat.

'You tell that dragon to fucking stop, right?'

Another voice: 'Kemir! Get away from him, you idiot.'

Kailin screwed up his face. 'I can't.' *I can't stop her. She's not listening to me.*

'Kemir! It's gone berserk! You can't stop it!'

'He's right.' *Snow. Stop! Help me!*

The man with the knife at his throat tensed as if preparing to make his killing cut. 'Well then, you're coming with us.' He started to drag Kailin out of the river. 'If it's going to burn us, it's going to burn you too, you bastard.'

The man was doomed. They were all doomed. Kailin knew it as soon as they started to move. He could feel Snow had sensed his plea. She wasn't done with the other knights yet, but as soon as she was ...

'Shit!'

They had almost made it when Snow exploded out of the inferno on the other side of the river, showering ash and embers and burning branches all around them. The fire flashed again, and the other man shrieked.

'Sollos!' Kailin's captor stumbled and the two of them went down together on the soggy grass. The man didn't let go, but rolled so that he was lying on his back with Kailin on top of him, both of them staring up at Snow, who glared back down at them. Her teeth were bloody, her eyes blazed, and she had someone in her tail again. Through the haze of smoke and gibbering terror, Kailin thought he recognised one of Knight-Marshal Nastria's sell-swords.

'Let him go!' roared the man with the knife. 'Let him go or I'll kill your rider.'

Where are the alchemists? The thought hit Kailin like a hammer. *Where are they? Burn them! I will burn them all!*

Don't know! Don't know! Inside, Kailin curled up into a little ball and just waited to die.

Where are the others? Where are they?

'I know where they are!' shouted the man with the knife. 'I know how to find them.'

The fire in Snow's eyes died. She snarled and dangled the man held in her tail close. Kailin could see him clearly now, and he *was* one of the knight-marshal's sell-swords. Sollos. He couldn't remember the name of the other one.

Tell me!

Kailin blinked. High up in the sky he thought he could see a dark speck or two moving against the clouds.

33

Jehal's Cure

There were seven or eight of them, all wearing veils to hide their faces. They dragged him out of bed and away through the palace. He shouted and screamed but they ignored him. When he struggled, one of them hit him hard enough to split his lip and knock loose a tooth. They took him out into the courtyard, across to the Glass Cathedral and to a hidden staircase behind the altar. Far underground, they hauled him through dim passageways murky with smoke and into a gloomy cavern of a room. A scattering of torches shed enough light for him to see the torture machines lining the walls. Hyram was sitting in the middle of the chamber, a small brazier glowing beside him.

'Are you mad, old man?' shouted Jehal. 'Have you completely lost your mind?'

Hyram didn't say anything, only watching as the veiled guardsmen chained Jehal to a wheel.

'No one will stand for this – Narghon, Silvallan, Zafir, even Queen Shezira and King Valgar. Even the Syuss will rise out of the sand to shake their fists at you.'

Hyram simply watched, trembling slightly. The veiled guardsmen finished their work and slipped away into the shadows. Jehal and Hyram were alone.

'Y-You missed someone.'

'Yes, even the King of the Crags might swoop from his lofty throne if he ever finds out that you've imprisoned a dragon-prince.'

'Y-You know, I simply d-didn't think you'd come.' Hyram rose painfully to his feet and snapped his fingers. 'I-I am not imprisoning you, Jehal. I'm t-torturing you. When I'm done, you can g-go.' Another pair of veiled men emerged from the shadows in the corners of the room. 'I have h-had letters from Queen Zafir. She says that you and Queen Aliphera were lovers.' Jehal's heart skipped a beat. *Letters from Zafir? Ancestors! What's she done?*

Hyram was pacing up and down. The two men with veils were standing patiently, waiting. 'Z-Zafir blames you. She thinks that her m-mother killed herself because you were about to marry s-someone else. Were you lovers?'

Jehal spat at him. 'Does your interest in my bed stem from the emptiness of your own, old man?'

'Were you l-lovers, Jehal?'

'None of your concern, Speaker, but yes, I fucked her every way you can think of. She couldn't get enough of it.' Even in the gloom he could see Hyram's face tighten. The speaker gave a little nod, and the two torturers set to work. One pulled his head back so he couldn't see what the other was doing. He could feel it, though, the waves of agony they sent through him.

'No!' he shrieked. 'No, we weren't lovers!'

Hyram gave another nod, and the torturers let go and stepped away. Jehal hung his head, slowly catching his breath as the pain faded away. Sweat dripped down his face. He didn't even know what the second torturer had done. *Have they marked me? Scarred me? If they have, I will return the favour a thousand times.*

'No. Q-Queen Aliphera was t-too wise not to see through you, Prince V-Viper. I want to k-know why you had her k-killed. And how.'

'I didn't.'

The torturers reached for him again. This time they didn't stop for a long time. Jehal gritted his teeth, but in the end he screamed and sobbed like everyone else. There was only one thing he could cling on to: *I didn't have her killed.*

Eventually it stopped. Jehal slumped, exhausted. Hyram looked him up and down.

'C-Can you still hear me, Viper?'

Jehal made no response. Best to pretend he'd passed out. Then Hyram slapped him.

'Don't p-play coy with me, boy. My man knows h-his work. I know you can h-hear me. Would you like a r-rest, Jehal?' Hyram dragged the brazier closer. His hands were shaking.

'You should get some help with that, old man,' breathed Jehal. 'Before you hurt yourself.'

'M-Master Bellepheros gave everyone in y-your eyrie the truth-smoke.'

'Master Bellepheros stood up in front of my father's court, in front of King Silvallan, Queen Shezira, King—'

'Yes, yes. He found n-nothing. Q-Queen Shezira found nothing. She even s-sent her daughter to ask you while y-you were reeling with M-Maiden's Regret and f-found nothing.'

Ah. So that's what that was about. 'Because there is nothing to find, old man.'

Hyram finished moving the brazier closer to Jehal and sprinkled dust over the coals. Wisps of white smoke coiled up into the air. 'I will show them h-how it is done. Master Bellepheros could not bring his s-smoke to you. N-Not allowed. But I can. Breathe deep, Prince V-Viper. The torture was only a b-bit of fun for me. Now you'll c-confess it all and be hanged. I w-win.' Hyram began to totter away.

'This is a war you're starting, Speaker. Everyone will turn on you. *Everyone!*'

'N-No they won't.' Hyram almost seemed to smile, but the twitching muscles in his face twisted it into a sneer. 'Even if I'm wrong. N-No one cares, Jehal. Why b-bother? In a few months I'll b-be gone anyway, one way o-or another.'

'If that's truth-smoke, old man, then ask me about the potion I brought with me. The one that eases my father's pain. The one that might cure your symptoms. Ask me about that, you old cripple, and then ask me what it would take from you to ever, *ever* get your hands on any of it. Ask what you'd have to give me. You're sick. You're dying, and it's the slowest, most degrading death you can imagine. I will relish every day of watching you ebb away. Ask me, Hyram!'

Hyram seemed to chuckle. 'W-What makes you think I would

have to g-give *you* anything at all?' He walked away and Jehal was left alone. The smoke risking from the brazier grew thicker and thicker. He could smell a sweet aroma with a strange sickly perfume. Truth-smoke.

Now what? Truth-smoke wasn't perfect. The alchemists liked to pretend that it was, but a clever and determined man could still fool an inept interrogator. *Or do the alchemists spread that rumour too, so that we always pay them to do our truth-seeking instead of doing it ourselves? Never mind. I'm clever. I'm determined. Is Hyram inept? No. He's clever too. But what if... I have to make him stupid. How? Can I do that? We'll have to see.*

The smoke was getting to him. His head was light and he was starting to lose track of where he was. *I didn't have Aliphera killed. She fell off her dragon. It was an accident. I wasn't there. I was sick in bed.* He stopped. He couldn't remember what he was thinking about. There was someone else in the room. He couldn't move and he wasn't sure why. And he was hurt. He couldn't remember how that had happened either.

'You were m-mumbling to yourself,' said the voice. Jehal forced his eyes to focus properly. Ah yes. Hyram.

'You're old.' He giggled.

'They say that the w-words a man mumbles to himself as the s-smoke takes him are the lies he wants to tell. What do you think about that?'

Jehal grinned. 'I think that sounds very clever.' A very distant part of him, he realised, *did* know where he was and what was happening to him. It was as though that part had been locked away in a faraway place. It was jumping up and down and shouting at him, trying to tell him things, but he couldn't hear it.

'So. L-Let's start with what you said. You didn't have Aliphera killed. I-Is that true?'

'I didn't *have* her killed.' Jehal yawned. 'I was there. Why can't I move my hands?' The faraway part of him was shouting and screaming something. If he tried, he could *almost* make it out.

'Because they're t-tied to a wheel. You were there? What do you mean you were th-there?'

'I was with her.' He stared at Hyram. 'On the back of her dragon with her when she fell off. I wasn't ill that day. Your alchemist was so close to the truth of it. She *did* hide something when she flew out of Clifftop, and Prince Meteroa too, when he came back. Me. We went to such trouble, she and I, so that no one would ever know I was with her. Weeks of careful thought. And now here you are with your silly smoke and now you know.'

'You were w-with her?'

'Why, Speaker Hyram, you don't look well at all. I was in her saddle pack. I'd been seducing her for months. Little glances, little touches. She wanted me, old man. Oh, she *ached* for me. I just had to look at her and she got wet. So she smuggled me onto her dragon so that no one would know, so we could fly away and just fuck all day.' He leered at Hyram.

'No!'

'Yes, old king.'

'I a-asked you if you were l-lovers. You said n-no!'

'You were torturing me. I lied so you'd stop. You didn't want to hear it, but you should have believed Queen Zafir. Devious little bitch that she is.'

Hyram's shaking was getting worse. He was clenching and unclenching his fists, pacing up and down in front of the brazier. The faraway voice in Jehal's head was still shouting things. Something about Hyram. Jehal frowned.

'Does it bother you, old man?' he asked. 'Does it trouble you?' He twisted his head from side to side, trying to hear what the voice was saying. *Goad him? Make him angry?* He looked at Hyram again. 'Does this make you angry?'

Hyram hit him. 'Yes. D-Did you kill her?'

Good. There was blood in Jehal's mouth. 'The ground did that. When she fell. Do you want to know why she fell? You do, don't you. Do you want to know why she wasn't strapped into her riding harness? Can't you see it for yourself? Do you want to know whether her body was naked when they finally found her?'

Hyram hit him again.

'Did she fall or did I push her? Is that what you want to know? Or do you want to know whether it was before or after I'd had her?'

This time Hyram hit him in the stomach. 'Shut up!'

'Maybe you'd like to know how many times I took her?'

'*Shut up!*'

Jehal coughed. 'No. You wanted to know the truth, old king, and so that's what you're going to get. I was her lover. I was with her when she died. I wanted to have her on the back of her dragon. Have you ever fucked on the back of a dragon in flight, old man? It's a thrill, but it's stupid. People fall.' He cocked his head. *Keep talking.* 'Do you want to know what she was like, Aliphera? Do you want to know how she moaned when she came? Do you want to know what she liked best of all? Do you want to know that she liked it from behind? Do you want to know what she would whisper when I slipped my fingers inside her? Is that what all this is for? Because you can never have her for yourself and you want to know what it was like? Ask away, old man. I can tell you *everything*.'

That was as far as he got. Hyram, rigid with rage, let out a roar. He swore and screamed at Jehal, hitting him again and again. When it stopped, Jehal had a vague idea that it was because some men in veils had finally dragged the speaker away. Throughout it all Jehal grinned.

I win.

34

Kemir

He was lying on his back. He was soaking wet and freezing. Ice-cold water rushed around him. The tumble of stones that littered the river bed pressed into his back. He had a death grip on a man he vaguely knew, a knife held at the man's throat, and an enraged dragon glaring down at him. It already had Sollos, crushing him in its tail. Kemir's mind froze. He couldn't think. He was going to die.

Where are the alchemists? The words came from somewhere. He was staring at the dragon's mouth, waiting for the moment when the fire would come. Its mouth didn't move, but the words came anyway. *Where are they?* They filled him up on the inside, as big as the dragon itself. *Where are the others? Where?* He thought his head would explode. *Alchemists! Where?*

He could feel the Scales' skin, soft underneath, hard and brittle as glass where it was flaking away. *Will a knife even cut him?* 'I know where they are!' he shouted, if only to make the noise in his head go away. 'I know how to find them.'

The rage in the dragon's eyes faded to a simmering anger. It peered at him and snarled, and then it threw Sollos up into the air and caught him with its tail again, holding him head down just inches above Kemir's face.

Tell me!

'Don't tell it!' croaked Sollos, and then he screamed as the tail tightened around him.

Kemir squeezed his arm into the Scales' throat. 'If I tell you and let this one go, you'll burn me.'

Mountains. I see mountains in your mind. They are close. Tell me or I will burn you both.

'There are mountains all around you, dragon. Burn me and you'll never know which one.' Above him, Sollos screwed up his face in agony as the dragon flexed its tail again. Then the monster looked up. Abruptly, it let go of Sollos, turned and ran down the river. A few seconds later, it was rising into the air. Kemir could see two dark dots moving against the clouds high above. Reluctantly, he let go of the Scales and ran to Sollos.

'Are you all right?'

Sollos sat up. Blood covered his face from a shallow gash in his scalp and he held his left hand gingerly. 'Nothing that won't get better.'

'Do your legs work?' Kemir glanced over his shoulder. The Scales was standing up, looking into the sky, dazed and lost. Sollos got up.

'Well enough.'

'That's good. I'll grab him. Let's get running.'

'Wait! The riders.'

Kemir grimaced. 'What about them? They're all dead.'

'No, they're not.' Sollos pointed. In the middle of the river an armoured figure was staggering to his feet. Kemir grinned. *Rider Semian. What luck!*

'Well that can soon be corrected.' He raised his voice. 'Hey! Rider Rod! Over here.'

'Wait.'

'I'll make it quick. We'll get out of here before his friends come back.'

'Wait!'

Kemir growled. 'What?' Rider Semian was stumbling through the water and the stones towards them.

'Who was telling the white dragon what to do?'

'I don't think *anyone* was telling it what to do.'

'But that's not right.'

Kemir shrugged. 'Maybe, maybe not. I know shit about dragons, except what they do when they have riders on their backs.' He fingered a knife. Semian was getting closer. He looked bewildered, as though he hadn't the first idea what had happened. *Easy prey.*

'Let me talk to him.' Sollos picked his way over the stones towards the dazed dragon-knight. From above, a series of soul-rending shrieks echoed through the valley. Kemir winced.

'Rider! Rider Semian! Are you all right?'

Semian didn't say anything. His face was strangely blank. Kemir felt the hairs on his neck prickle. *Danger!* He took a step towards them. 'Sollos!'

Semian's mouth was half-open, his eyes vacant and distant, but when he moved, he moved with a sudden speed and purpose. In the blink of an eye he had drawn his sword and run Sollos through. Sollos gave a little grunt and doubled up. As Semian pulled free his sword, Sollos crumpled and fell into the water. Kemir found he couldn't move.

'Sollos!'

Semian lifted his sword and thrust down, burying the point in the exposed skin at the back of Sollos's neck.

'*Sollos!*'

Semian turned to look at Kemir. The vacant stare had gone.

'You *bastard!*' Kemir hesitated. Fury and revenge surged through him, demanding retribution, immediate and bloody. Yet Semian was armoured. He was a knight. And he'd been so unexpectedly quick.

I'm afraid of him. The realisation was horrifying, almost as bad as seeing Sollos die. *If I fight him, he might actually win. I'm afraid of him. And he's not afraid of me.*

Semian came slowly towards him. There could be no doubting his purpose now. He knew exactly where he was and exactly what he was doing.

'You and me, sell-sword. That's what you wanted.'

'He never drew his sword. He was trying to help you. You're filth. You and your kind.'

'It's clear.' Semian's eyes were wild. 'You were a part of this all along. Both of you. You made a fool of me, but I will redeem myself with this.' He waved his sword in the air. 'Now I have the vile stain of a traitor on my blade, I can barely bring myself to hold it in my hand. Quick now, man, before I can stand the stink no more. Let us be done. Kill me if you can, or add your blood to his.'

Kemir took a step away, keeping his distance. 'Killing you here and now, that would be too quick. I want to watch you die slowly.'

'Are you too great a coward to fight me, sell-sword?'

The rage surged again, but the fear kept it in check. 'One day there'll be a shadow in an alley, and I'll be in that shadow with my bow, waiting for you. You'll never know. You'll never see it coming.' Kemir scuttled away through the rushing water and the rocks, putting more distance between them. Semian would never catch him dressed in so much dragonscale, and he didn't try. The knight simply stood and watched him retreat.

'Coward.'

'You'll never know!' Kemir turned and ran. When he'd crossed the river and reached the trees, he looked back again. Semian was still standing there, stock still, out in the open. A perfect target. Kemir took his bow from his shoulder and started to string it. *Seventy, eighty yards. A man in armour. If he's stupid enough to stay still, I'll probably hit him. I won't kill him. Then I can finish him slowly. Yes, that would be perfect.*

He'd almost forgotten the dragons when there came another shriek, so loud and close that he flinched. A moment later the entire river exploded. Water and stones flew everywhere as two dragons crashed into the river bed, locked together, teeth and claws sunk into each other. One of them was the white. The other was dark brown with flashes of iridescent green on the insides of its legs. It had a rider on its back, but he quickly disappeared as the dragons thrashed and rolled in the water. Then the thrashing stopped and the dragons parted. The white dragon was limping. The darker beast got up, nosed at something in the water and roared. One of its wings was clearly broken, and it seemed to barely notice the white now.

It was still in the way, though. Kemir ran a few dozen yards through the trees, following the river, but Rider Semian had gone.

The Scales was still alive. Somehow. Stumbling blindly though the stones. The white dragon picked him up in one claw, turned and ran.

Kemir watched them go. Inside him something broke.

35

The Dragon-Queen

Hyram went out to watch Zafir's dragons fly in to the Adamantine Eyrie, but his mind was still on Jehal. After the debacle of the truth-smoke, he'd been left with three choices. The most appealing was simply to have Jehal killed while he had the chance, but that would have been war, and above all the point of the speaker was to make sure there was never another dragon-war. Keeping him in the dungeon had some appeal as well but wouldn't achieve anything. When Shezira succeeded him as speaker, she'd let him go however much she thought he was guilty. Better to set him free sooner rather than later and see what he did.

Except that hadn't worked either. Instead of flying south, where Hyram could have kept an eye on him, Jehal had flown west, to Drotan's Top. From there he'd gone north, supposedly to join Queen Shezira's interminable and futile hunt for her missing dragon. Shezira knew all of her riders far too well for Hyram to have a spy among them, and so now the Viper was at large. He'd show up sooner or later, but Hyram would have felt a lot more comfortable knowing what Jehal was up to. *He wants to be speaker. He knows I'd die rather than betray Shezira for someone like him, so perhaps he's thinking of who comes next. Who will she name in her turn? Does he think that marrying Princess Lystra will make it him? She'll name Valgar surely? If he's still alive.*

Queen Zafir's dragons landed one after the other. A twitch started in Hyram's cheek and wouldn't go away. *Valgar's getting old. In ten years he'll be as old as I am now, and Jehal the perfect age. Maybe that's what he has in mind.*

After everything he'd learned in the last few days, he wasn't sure how he should approach Queen Zafir. She'd told him that

Aliphera and Jehal had been lovers and she'd been right. She'd told him that she didn't think Jehal had murdered her mother, and she might have been right about that too. He wasn't even sure he cared any more. Aliphera had soiled herself with the Viper, she of all people. She deserved to die. If her death was an accident, Hyram's only regret was that she hadn't pulled Jehal down with her. *I should put her out of my mind. Even if Jehal didn't kill her, he's still murdering his own father. He could hang for that. Best that I forget her forever.*

Except there she was, standing in front of him, exactly as he remembered her from twenty years ago, glorious, radiant, beautiful beyond compare. He felt a fool and ashamed of himself. Old and crippled. How could he stand before her?

'Your H-Holiness.' He bowed. *It's not her. She's gone, remember. It's her daughter. But she looks so much like her. I'd never really seen it before, but she does.*

Queen Zafir bowed and kissed his ring. 'Speaker. You flatter me.'

He looked at her. He couldn't stop looking at her. She was Aliphera at her best, her hair piled up on the top of her head to show off the curves of her neck, the same deep red riding clothes, the same carved amber dragon hanging at her throat, the same russet folds of furs to keep her warm against the wind. Everything about her glowed.

'Y-You're wearing your m-mother's furs.'

Zafir bowed her head. 'Since she died I've taken to always wearing something that was hers. To honour her memory. I hope you're not offended.'

'C-Come.' Hyram offered her his arm, which she took with a smile. 'I-I have to apologise to you, Queen Z-Zafir. I once l-loved your mother very much. I should n-not have said what I did after you were crowned.'

She met his eyes with sadness. 'No, Speaker, you should not. Prince Jehal killed my mother. We both know that now.'

He looked away and bit his lip. 'I d-don't know. I-It may have been an a-accident.'

'I think he was on her dragon with her when she died.'

'I kn-know he was.'

For a moment Zafir tensed. 'You know?'

'Y-Yes. H-He told me. I was n-not very kingly while he w-was here, but I did learn a g-great deal.'

'Then I am keen to know more.' She was still tense. Idly, Hyram wondered why.

'I know that e-everything you told me was true. I kn-know I should have paid more heed to your l-letters. I know I d-did you an injustice. P-Please forgive me. Tell me, how are the rest of your family?'

She seemed to relax. 'My sister still grieves. Uncle Kazalain has sworn an oath of vengeance. He stomps and shouts and drinks and bellows for war and has no idea who he should fight.' She gave him a thoughtful look. 'Mostly he vents his anger at Queen Shezira. He has this foolish notion that you might have defied the old pacts and chosen Aliphera to succeed you. He has his sons beside him, but that is all. As for the rest, the whole realm is shocked with sadness.' Then she smiled at him, and he couldn't help himself.

'Y-You are every bit as beautiful as your m-mother, Queen Zafir. I hope you know that.'

'You're too kind, Speaker. But tell me more about Jehal. I came here thinking you would ask me lots of questions, and how clever I would seem to know even some of the answers. But you already know far more than I do.'

He led her to the edge of the eyrie, where a line of carriages waited to carry Zafir and her entourage to the palace. There he left her while a hundred servants buzzed about, carrying cases and sacks and boxes to the four corners of the palace. He'd given her the Tower of Air again, hoping she'd understand that he meant to honour her. When he'd summoned her, a part of him had meant to accuse her. He might even have treated her as he'd treated Jehal, with a bit of mild torture and the truth-smoke. Now the thought appalled him. What was he thinking? The Viper deserved it for a hundred and one other things, but Queen Zafir?

She was exactly as he remembered her mother. Her clothes, her hair, her jewellery, the way she spoke, the way she held herself. A part of him knew that she must have done it deliberately; another part didn't care.

In the evening they dined in the great hall of the palace, with the golden carved heads of the previous forty-four speakers looking down on them. Zafir walked in with a dozen gleaming dragon-knights behind her, all dressed in the deep reds and autumn browns that Aliphera had favoured. She wore Aliphera's own favourite dress, and the sight of her brought tears to Hyram's eyes. *So much regret.*

As they ate he quietly told her everything he'd done to Jehal, and everything Jehal had said in return. She listened quietly. Her eyes seemed to tell him that he'd done the right thing.

'It doesn't matter whether he pushed her or whether she fell,' she said softly, when he was done. 'He is responsible, and I hate him for it. I used to like him. There was a time when ...' She looked down. 'There was a time when I hoped he would marry me and not Princess Lystra. But now ...' She shuddered. 'She's welcome to him. I should have listened to you a long time ago, and so should my mother. There will not be a war, Speaker, I promise you that. But I will have vengeance. I can promise you that too.'

He got drunk. It lessened the symptoms of his illness, but that was only ever an excuse. Mostly, it lessened the bitterness and the regrets and the pain, the other illness that ate away at him from deep inside. Except tonight it didn't; it made him worse and filled him with maudlin sighs, until he found himself telling Zafir everything. It was all he could do not to break down into tears. In front of all his knights and hers that would surely have been the end of him. Through it all, she watched him. She didn't say anything, but her eyes seemed filled with sympathy. He'd expected her to tell him that he was stupid, that he was a fool, that what he'd done to Jehal threatened the peace of the realms, that he was an idiot for mourning a woman he'd barely known, and that death was death and he should be glad of the years he'd had.

Instead, when he was done she leaned towards him and spoke into his ear.

'I can't bring my mother back, Hyram,' she whispered. 'But your sickness, if it truly is the same as King Tyan's, now there I may be able to help you.'

'The V-Viper claims he has a p-potion,' Hyram slurred. 'The a-alchemists know nothing about it. You s-said you had some i-information. In your letter.'

She leaned further towards him. 'He gets his potions from the Taiytakei, but I can do better than that.' From somewhere she produced a small vial. 'He was bringing a sample with him when he came to the palace to answer your summons. I dare say he meant to taunt you with it.' She giggled. 'I stole it when he spent the night at my eyrie on his way here.' She opened the vial and poured a few drops into his wine and then a few into her own. 'I thought about asking my alchemists what it was, but you know what they're like. A year from now they might come back with an answer or they might not. I've had it tested.' She lifted up her goblet and swallowed. 'It's not poison, I know that much. It's a bit …' She giggled again. 'It's a bit like a mild dose of Maiden's Regret. Of course, I don't know if it will help you with your sickness, but I'm sure it can't do you any harm. If you can believe anything Jehal says, it doesn't make the sickness go away, only keeps it at bay for as long as you take the potion. If you stop taking it, the sickness comes back again.'

Hyram stared at his wine. He sniffed it.

'It tastes terrible. It doesn't go well with wine either. Brandy is better.'

'Y-You tried it before?'

Zafir shrugged. 'I wanted to know what it would do before I offered it to you. Obviously I didn't try it until I knew it wasn't poison.'

'B-But it came from the Viper.' Hyram shook his head. The room was blurring before his eyes. 'It c-could be anything.'

She sat back in her chair, moving away from him. 'You don't have to drink it, Speaker. If you do, and it works, I have more.'

'How m-much more?'

Now she laughed. 'Enough for a few months. Enough to see you to the end of your time here. I know where he gets it too. I can tell you, if you want me to.' She leaned into him again. 'Drink it, Hyram. Don't let Jehal win. Be young and strong again, the way my mother wanted to remember you.'

Her closeness, the warmth of her through his clothes, made him shiver.

'What have you got to lose?'

He stared at his wine. He was still staring at it as the feast came slowly to an end. When he meandered away to his bed, he took the goblet with him, still half full. *In the morning*, he decided. *In the morning I'll ask her for another dose. Jeiros can take it. He can tell me what's in it. He can tell me if it's safe. In the morning.* He put the goblet on the table beside his bed and tried to sleep, but sleep wouldn't come, and the goblet seemed to stare at him.

If you were Antros, you'd drink me, it seemed to say. *If you were you, you'd drink me. If you don't, then who are you? Queen Zafir is right. What have you got to lose?*

'Everything,' he whispered, and hoped the goblet would hear him and leave him be, but instead it seemed to laugh.

Everything? You've already lost everything. And here I am, offering it all back again, and you turn me away? Who are you? What are you? Are you already a ghost?

Trembling, he reached out and took the goblet in his hand. She'd put some into her own cup, hadn't she? And drunk it down. He'd seen her do it. She was right, wasn't she?

That's right, murmured the goblet, as he put it to his lips. *Drink me down. Be a man again. Be a man.*

Be a man.

36

An Accommodation

Kemir crept out from the trees. In the middle of the river the wounded dragon paused from its howls and turned to look at him; quickly Kemir retreated, but the dragon didn't seem very interested in him. He couldn't see Rider Semian anywhere.

Maybe he got crushed in the fight.

That would be too much to hope for. Kemir ran through the forest beside the river until he rounded a bend and the dragon couldn't see him. Then he crossed over and crept back again. Still no Semian. The dragon hadn't moved either. He watched it for a while, searching for the courage to go out into the water where Sollos lay.

When he finally found him, he wondered why he'd bothered. Sollos was dead, and he'd known that from the moment he'd seen Rider Semian drive down his sword. He helped himself to Sollos's bow, his arrows and his pack.

'Goodbye, cousin.' He turned Sollos over and very gently removed an amulet from his neck, then turned his back on the body and picked his way into the trees. He carefully buried the amulet. Next he set about looking for any tracks that might have been Rider Semian's; he didn't find any, but as the sun slipped behind the mountain peaks two more dragons swooped silently into the valley and landed in the river. Kemir watched them come in through the trees. He strung his bow and crept closer until he could see them properly. The dragons were splashing in the water, cooling themselves down, while their riders clustered by the shore. Four dragon-knights. No, five.

He clenched his fists. He could see Semian again. Still alive. He strained his ears to hear them. The breeze, such as it was, carried their words towards him.

'We saw Storm's Shadow on the way in as well,' said one of the others. Kemir couldn't see his face. 'Mias was riding her, wasn't he? No sign of him though. What happened?'

'We found the white. The Scales was with her. He wouldn't give her back. He set her on us.' Semian shook his head. 'All the others are dead. The alchemist too. Everyone except one of the sell-swords. They were in with the Scales somehow.'

Kemir nocked an arrow to his bow. The breeze carried the scent of the dragons too, a light whiff of ash and charcoal. He savoured it. If he could smell them, then they couldn't smell him. *You lying, murdering bastard. I could kill you where you stand. Right now.*

'Mias and Arakir got back before they were done. The white attacked them in the air. I didn't see what happened to Mias. The white must have got him.' Semian glanced towards the dragon with the broken wing. 'Arakir was on Tempest. I saw him and the white come down into the river, fighting each other. Arakir was crushed, Tempest has a broken wing and I think a broken foot as well. The white was hurt too. She headed upriver. She was limping and I didn't see her fly. The Scales was still with her and the surviving sell-sword escaped as well. I suppose he's long gone now.'

No, I'm right here. Kemir squinted down the length of his arrow. *Where should I shoot you, Rider Rod? In the face? In the throat, as you did for Sollos. Not in your heart, because there's nothing there.* Slowly he lowered the bow. This was too easy. Semian could die here and now. Vengeance would be served, but Sollos would still be dead.

There was the little matter of the four other dragon-knights too, but they were armoured and Kemir was sure he could vanish into the forest before they could turn their dragons on him. But merely putting an arrow into Semian wasn't going to be enough. There had to be pain and suffering. He had to die slowly, piece by piece.

'We saw the white. It's a couple of miles further up the river,' said one of the other riders. 'We'd seen Storm's Shadow, and then we saw Tempest. Ancestors! What do we do? Should we go on to the white? It's getting dark.'

Piece by piece. Kemir raised his bow again.

'No.' Semian screwed up his face. 'Yes. No. Was Storm's Shadow hurt?'

'It's hard to say.'

'Go and find out. If Storm's Shadow can fly, take her back to the camp. Tell them what happened and that we need another alchemist. Tell them we've found the white and bring them back here. Someone will have to stay here with Tempest. The rest of us—'

The first arrow struck Semian in the leg, just above the knee. Semian howled, staggered and fell back into the water. The second arrow struck one of the other riders in the back. The third arrow hit the wounded dragon in the neck, which only made it hiss and snap. Kemir didn't stop to fire a fourth; instead he jogged a little deeper into the forest and then turned and followed the path of the river. The knights wouldn't follow him into the trees, he was quite sure of that, and the dragons would never find him in the dark. Not killing Rider Semian, he discovered, was immensely satisfying. Killing him was something he could only do once. He smiled to himself. *I can put arrows into his arms and legs again and again and again.*

It took him well into the night to find the white dragon and the Scales. The dragon was curled up next to the water, sleeping. The Scales was huddled next to it. As he crept closer, he saw another body too, gently snoring. He slipped up to the sleeping Scales, crouched beside him, slid out a knife and slowly pulled back the man's cloak.

'Scales!' he hissed, glancing up at the dragon. He gave the man a gentle shake. 'Scales!'

The man stirred. The dragon's breathing didn't change.

'Scales!'

The Scales opened his eyes. Kemir touched his lips with the point of his knife. 'Quiet, Scales. If I was going to hurt you, I'd have already done it. But if you wake up your dragon ...'

'Who are you?' The Scales was looking up at him, still dazed with sleep, not quite understanding.

'My name is Kemir. I was a sell-sword working for your queen until one of her knights murdered my cousin. I want to help you.'

The Scales blinked and rubbed his face. A part of him looked terrified; another part looked vaguely surprised and seemed to be looking past Kemir rather than at him. Kemir felt a coldness. He started to turn and caught a glimpse of the tip of the dragon's tail snaking through the air towards him. He swore and dived away, but the tail was too quick. The next thing he knew, he was being lifted up into the air.

'Scales! Damn you! Call it off! I'm here to help.'

Help? What do you mean?

The thought seemed to come from outside him, but that was a ridiculous idea and he dismissed it. 'You left one of the dragon-knights alive. Now there are more of them. They're coming. I tried to slow them down, but they're coming after you. Call it off!'

How many are coming?

'Four knights. No, five. But two of them are too hurt to worry about.' This time he couldn't shake it. The question had come into his mind, but the Scales hadn't uttered a word. 'How … ?'

The ground fell away. The dragon was rising, lifting its head, lifting him up into the air at the same time. He hung helpless as it snorted and growled. A rush of warm rancid air engulfed him.

How many dragons are coming?

Very carefully, Kemir looked down at the Scales standing on the river bank twenty feet below him. The one who'd been sleeping, a woman he now saw, was looking up at him as well. She looked pasty and pale in the moonlight, and was shaking.

'Scales. I think your dragon is talking to me.' *Have I gone mad?*

No. How many dragons?

'Snow!' The Scales was wringing his hands. 'Don't hurt him. No more! Please!'

Thoughts tumbled through Kemir's mind so quickly that they tripped over one another. *The dragon can think.* That was terrifying enough. *The dragon can hear what I think.* That was worse. *The dragon killed half a dozen knights.* That was better. *It did it because it wanted to, not because someone told it to.* That was either the best or the worst; he wasn't sure which.

He regarded the dragon. A calmness settled inside him, a mixture of hope and resignation. Shitting himself wasn't going to do much good just now. 'Two new dragons. They were going to send one after you. To watch. The other was going to go for help. By the middle of tomorrow morning there might be a dozen dragons looking for you. You want to escape, don't you?'

I want to free the others of my kind.

'My name is Kemir. I want to help you.'

No, Little One Kemir, you do not. All I see in you is death and vengeance. You want to kill dragon-riders. I am simply a means to that end.

'No dragons, no dragon-knights.'

The tail squeezed a little tighter. *Your fear has a sharp and pleasant tang to it. How will you help me, Little One?*

Kemir tried to pull himself free. The dragon hadn't pinned his arms, but all his struggles were futile. He still had the knife that he'd used to threaten the Scales. If he stabbed the dragon's tail, would it drop him? Would it even notice?

I will crush you before you blink, Little One. Again: how will you help me?

'I'll help you kill dragon-knights. Any way I can.'

I do not wish to kill dragon-knights. I wish to free my kind.

'Then I'll help you kill alchemists. You asked where they were. I can tell you.'

The dragon looked at him for a long time and then slowly lowered him to the ground. *Then we have an accommodation, Little One Kemir. Alchemists. So be it.* The dragon turned to look at the Scales, but Kemir still heard its voice inside his head. *More dragons come, Little One. We must fly. Now.*

37

The Mirror Lakes

The Mirror Lakes, clustering around the City of Dragons, were generally thought to be perfectly round and perfectly bottomless. The ground didn't slip gently and gracefully away under the water; it simply stopped. In the myths of the dragon-priests the Divine Dragon moulded the world from clay and then baked it hard in the flames of his breath. The people of the city weren't the most religious of folk, but they generally agreed that if the priests were right, the Mirror Lakes must have been where the dragon-god stuck his claws into the clay to hold it tight while he did his work. Strange and monstrous creatures were rumoured to inhabit the lakes, rising to the surface sometimes in the middle of the night, swallowing boats whole and then sinking again, disappearing without trace.

From where Jehal sat, perched at the top of the Diamond Cascade falls, one could see that the lakes weren't perfectly round at all. He was fairly sure they weren't bottomless or inhabited by monsters either, but no one had ever proved that, one way or the other. Vanishing boats, he thought, were more likely to be the work of thieves, and any monsters that inhabited the lake were probably of the human variety.

He could see the city too, and the Adamantine Palace, all laid out some half a mile beneath him through the haze of spray from the falls.

Mine. It's all going to be mine.

Behind him Wraithwing splashed in the waters of the Diamond River. A shadow passed overhead and moments later another dragon came in to land. The two dragons looked at each other curiously. The newcomer dived into the water and started to drink. Its rider sauntered towards Jehal. She took off her helmet.

'I was wondering whether you'd come. You have some explaining to do,' said Jehal. He had to speak loudly to be heard over the roar of the waterfall.

Zafir smiled. She didn't say anything but sat beside him and looked over the edge.

'You should be careful,' said Jehal. 'You could fall.'

'We could both fall.'

'I watched you come up from the eyrie. You didn't bring any riders with you. No one knows where you are. No one knows who you're with.'

She put a hand on his arm. 'Did *you* bring any riders, Prince?'

'Of course not. You never know who might have lined their pockets.'

'How far did my mother fall?'

Jehal shrugged. 'We're higher now. You stole my potions. And you've been writing letters to Hyram.'

She didn't look at him. 'You've been to see your new family. How *is* Queen Shezira?'

'Do you feel threatened, my love?'

'Not at all. Do you?'

'Not in the least.'

'I didn't steal your potions. I took them because you told me to.'

'I told you to take *one*.'

'Hyram's got them now.'

'I know.'

She looked at him, and the flicker of a smile played at the corner of her lips. 'And I know you know. I saw your little golden dragon sitting on the windowsill, watching us with its beady ruby eyes. How many more of those have you got?'

'Only that one and the one I gave to you. They were a wedding present from the Taiytakei.'

Zafir raised an eyebrow. 'It was almost worth marrying your little starling then. And what do they want, the Taiytakei?'

Jehal shrugged. 'To see me prosper, I suppose.'

'That doesn't sound like the Taiytakei.'

'They want what they always want and what they can never have. A hatchling.' For a few seconds Jehal stared out into the void over the city below. Sitting up here with his feet dangling over the empty air, he almost felt he could fly. No dragons, just him. It would be easy, wouldn't it? To let go and soar and be free of it all. No more Hyram, no more Shezira. No more watching his father's glacial crawl towards death. No more constant battling of wits with the Taiytakei and all the others that surrounded him, fawning at his feet for favours while all the while hiding poisoned daggers behind their backs. No more—

No more Zafir. He turned and looked her squarely in the eye. 'Well?'

'Well what?'

'Did Hyram tell you that he tortured me?'

'No. He said he hadn't been very kingly.' She spat. 'As if that was somehow a change.'

'Well he's not a king, is he, so I suppose we shouldn't be surprised. He wasn't very good as a torturer either. Maybe I should send him one of mine for next time. In fact he was so inept I had to show him how to make a proper job of it. We're beyond words now, he and I. I think I have to muster my dragons when I go south.' He shook his head. 'I'm at a loss. I didn't think he'd dare anything so bold.' Now he laughed. 'I almost had some respect for him, for a moment, until he let me go. Now if he'd killed me outright and taken the consequences, why I think I might even have given him a round of applause. And then I think of him rutting with you after I left, and I just want to paint the palace with his blood.'

'Don't!' Zafir shuddered. 'He doesn't deserve even to exist in your thoughts.'

'Ahh.' He took her hand and kissed it. 'You're very sweet, my lover.'

Zafir pulled her hand away. 'Don't touch me. I don't want anyone to touch me. I tried to think of you when I let him have me, and now when I think of you, I think of him.' She shivered. 'It's horrible.'

'Antros was always supposed to have been quite the lover. Hyram didn't share his talents?'

'He was drunk, selfish, boorish and pathetic. I had to do everything for him. Didn't you see with your little Taiytakei toy?'

'I saw you writhe and wriggle under him. I heard your squealing too. Quite a show, I thought.'

'Mercifully quick.' She made a face. 'If you saw it all anyway, don't ask me any more. What's Shezira up to in the Purple Spur? She's making Hyram nervous, and you going there didn't help that at all.'

Jehal laughed. 'Really? Why now, I would *never* have thought of that. Yes, a little more distrust between them can never hurt, but I'm afraid Queen Shezira has returned to her eyrie. I had her delight of a daughter to waste my charms on instead.'

'Almiri?'

'No, not the nice one; the one that's made of the same flinty stuff as her mother. The one that thinks she's a dragon born human by mistake. Jaslyn. The one who asked me whether I was poisoning my father while the Maiden's Regret had me.' He laughed. 'I shall have to thank Queen Fyon for that. She's a bit sharper than I've given her credit for. No, I had a frosty welcome to say the least. I might have said one or two things out of place. Perhaps she was kind enough to put that down to my exertions of the previous days.' He laughed again. 'They were still trying to find their missing dragon, and now they've lost another one.'

Zafir raised an eyebrow.

'Seems they tracked their white down, and it turned on them. Princess Stone did her best to make sure I didn't find anything out, but there's a dragon out there with a broken wing. They've lost an alchemist and I saw a rider in a pretty poor state. Apparently someone put an arrow in his leg, so the white's not flying around aimlessly on its own, that's for sure.' Not *the* white. *His* white. 'When I left, they were trying to work out how to put their injured dragon down.' Jehal scratched his chin. 'They had quite a lot of alchemists there, now I think about it. More than I would have expected. And of course I now know exactly how many dragons she's got out there and have a shrewd idea how many riders too. She didn't like me paying attention to that sort of thing.' He shrugged. 'Still, I'm quite impressed. They're up to something, and I still haven't got the first idea what it is.'

Queen Zafir shook her head and looked away. 'Prince Jehal, that won't do at all. They may make Hyram nervous, but they bother me too – so many dragons so close by.' She stopped and peered down at the city. From the Adamantine Eyrie the tiny distant shape of a dragon was rising into the air. 'You're going to have to go.' She stood up.

'Pity. I'd been hoping to have you for rather longer.'

'I'm sure you had.' Zafir whistled. Her dragon looked up from where it was splashing in the river with Wraithwing. 'But we can't risk anyone seeing us together now. You need to be gone before that dragon gets high enough to see Wraithwing and Emerald Mirror together.'

Reluctantly, Jehal got to his feet. He was going to have to explain to Wraithwing that he couldn't simply throw himself over the precipice and spread his wings, that he'd have to take to the air the hard way. He sighed, and then to his surprise Queen Zafir launched herself into his arms, pressing herself against him.

'I wish we had longer too,' she murmured.

Jehal stroked her hair away from her face and purred, 'I thought looking at me made you think of Hyram.'

Zafir made a face. 'It did until I got up here. Now it just makes me think of you without your clothes on.'

He kissed her and let his hands begin to wander. 'It won't be for much longer, my lover.'

'Give me the strength not to murder him in his bed, Jehal.'

'Give me the patience to wait for you.'

'*I* have to lie with that crippled oaf. All I think of is you with your starling-bride, and then all I want to do is slit his throat and then hers and be done with all this.'

With a great effort Jehal let her go. 'You keep that thought close to your heart, my Queen, and keep your mind on Hyram.'

She snorted. 'No fear there. For as long as I can bear it, he'll think of nothing but your potions, my mother's face and the hole between my legs.'

Jehal reached out to stroke her face one last time, then turned towards Wraithwing. He waved over his shoulder. 'Once he marries you and makes you speaker, you can cut as many throats as you like.'

'I'll hold you to that, Jehal,' she called after him. 'He'll be first. You can choose who comes second, you or your starling.'

38

The Ravine

The dragon was hurt. Kemir hadn't noticed that when they'd taken to the air in the middle of the night. In fact, he hadn't noticed much, clutched in the dragon's claws and hurtling through the night air at speed. The ground flashed past in the moonlight, not far beneath him but quite far enough to smash him to pieces if the dragon let go. The monster's wingbeats rippled through the air like thunder. For the second time in his life, he prayed.

In the dragon's other foreclaws the Scales held on tight to the woman, whoever she was, while she in turn screamed and shrieked herself hoarse.

The air got colder. Finally the dragon landed in a field of snow, tumbling in a spray of powder, while Kemir thought for the umpteenth time that night that he was going to die. The beast took them to the edge of a narrow ravine and jumped in, gliding down into total darkness. When it landed at the bottom it let them go and fell asleep almost at once. Kemir huddled up against the dragon's warmth and fell asleep as well, drained beyond exhaustion.

When he woke up, he knew something was wrong. The dragon's breathing was laboured, and the Scales was sitting by its muzzle, stroking its nose. This close, in the daylight, the dragon seemed even larger than it had the night before. Its head dwarfed the Scales; its amber eyes were larger then an open hand; its teeth ...

Kemir didn't want to think about its teeth. Instead he looked up. The ravine was steep and narrow, so narrow he was surprised that a dragon could fly into it at all. He wasn't sure how any of them were going to get out again, and he was hungry. And if it wasn't for the dragon, they were all going to get very cold very quickly. The Scales didn't have any flying furs, while the woman, it seemed, didn't have anything else.

'I've seen you before,' he said to the Scales. 'What's your name?'

'Kailin.' The Scales didn't look up.

'What about her?'

'Her name's Nadira.'

'What's the matter with her?' When she wasn't screaming, she looked dull and vacant. She was sweating and shivering.

The Scales didn't answer.

'Who is she?' The Scales didn't answer that either. Kemir shrugged. 'What's up with your dragon then?'

'Her name is Snow. She's hurt.'

'Is it bad?'

'I don't know. She must have damaged herself when she fell into the river with Tempest. It looked like she broke Tempest's wing.' Kailin shook his head sadly and looked nervously at Snow. 'If she did, they'll have to put Tempest down, poor thing.'

'Poor thing?' Kemir scratched his head. 'How *do* you put a dragon down?'

The Scales flashed him a warning glance. 'Be careful. She's sleeping, but you saw what happened in the river. I don't know for sure, but I've heard stories that the alchemists give them something in their food. They go to sleep and then they burn from the inside.'

'I've seen that.' Kemir nodded. 'That's what happens when they die.'

'I wouldn't know. I've never seen a dragon die.'

'Well if it happens with this one, we won't have to worry about staying warm for a while.' He looked up at the walls of the ravine. *No. Just staying fed.* 'I don't suppose you have any idea where we are?'

The Scales shook his head. It didn't take long to discover that the Scales didn't have any food, water, shelter, spare clothing or any of the basic necessities for surviving out in the wilderness. He'd had a dragon, though. Apparently that was enough.

He left them to it and set off down the ravine, following the trickle of water that bubbled along the bottom. As he pressed on, the ravine grew gradually steeper and narrower. He passed countless caves. *That's the Worldspine for you. Riddled with holes like a honeycomb. Yawning caverns big enough for an army and tiny holes barely enough for a man to crawl into.* He began to see overhanging trees above, casting everything into shadow. The sides pressed in closer and closer; the trickle of water grew into a rushing stream that ran faster and deeper around every bend. Abruptly the cliffs on either side fell away and he emerged into the middle of a steeply sloping forest. He circled around to the top of the ravine and sat on the edge, looking out through the gap in the trees. He was high up in the side of a mountain valley. One that looked exactly the same as every other mountain valley.

Great. Nice one. That really helped. Shall we walk all the way back now?

He sat there for a long time, staring, until finally he muttered something and Sollos didn't reply, and it hit him, hard, that his cousin was gone forever. They'd spent a good part of their lives with only each other for company, although it hadn't always been that way. They'd roamed the realms, selling their sword arms, but this was where they'd been born, here in the Worldspine. They'd killed perhaps a dozen dragon-knights between them, but only because other dragon-knights had paid them to do it.

And now Sollos was gone. Their contract with Knight-Marshal Lady Nastria was finished and he was back where it had all started. He had his bow, his knives and his wits, which ought to be enough to survive out in these valleys. He didn't owe anything to the poor fools he'd left in the ravine. He was entirely free to do whatever he wanted.

And entirely trapped. He couldn't walk away from what he and Sollos had been. Not on his own. Not while Rider Rod was still alive. And then there was the dragon, and the glimmer of a possibility that he couldn't ignore no matter how unlikely it was to bear fruit. Trapped. Utterly trapped. Revenge was what he wanted. Revenge, not just for Sollos but for all the others, for every Outsider who'd ever burned. Which meant staying with the dragon and the Scales and the woman, whoever she was.

Which meant keeping them alive.

'Bollocks!'

The shout echoed around the valley and faded, lonely and unanswered. He sighed, clambered down from his rocky perch and strung his bow. It took him a couple of hours to track down a decent meal and another hour to skin and fillet it. Hiking back up the ravine took twice as long as walking down it. By the time he got back, he was exhausted and hungry. As far he could tell, he'd been gone for about ten hours and none of the others had even moved. Maybe the woman had rearranged her legs. He threw himself down and closed his eyes.

'Is your dragon up to starting a fire for us?' he asked.

The Scales shook his head. 'She's in torpor. They do this when they're hurt. She'll sleep until she's better.'

'Well how long is that going to be?'

'If she's broken a rib, two or three weeks.'

Kemir opened his eyes again and looked up at the sky framed by the sides of the ravine. He laughed. 'Two or three weeks?'

'Yes.'

'So all we have to do for all that time is hide her from Queen Shezira's riders and not starve to death. Oh, and we can't actually move from this spot, because if we do, the two of you will die of exposure.' He closed his eyes again and shook his head. 'Curse you, dragon. Curse you for everything.' And he set about keeping them alive.

The Scales was useless; all he did was sit beside his dragon and stroke her scales. The woman spent her time staring into space with her mouth hanging open. Or else she shivered and shook and screamed about things that made no sense. Some sort of fever, Kemir thought, and it went on for so long that he was sure she'd die. She didn't though, and eventually the fever broke. At least when she was well again she had some idea of how to survive. After the first few days she took to coming with him. She didn't even have have any boots, but it didn't seem to bother her to clamber over the stones and the moss in bare feet. Each day she came with him to the end of the ravine and then waited while he hunted. When he was done he'd start a fire, and they would sit and watch the flames. They didn't speak, but there was a sense of something shared between them. Of surviving whatever the cost. Every day he'd give her the choicest piece of whatever he'd killed, and then they'd lie down next to each other and doze. She didn't say much, and she often seemed to drift away. Lost somewhere far away. Or else she had fits and screamed. She seemed to understand when he wanted to be alone. Sometimes, when he touched her, she flinched and froze. And sometimes, when he remembered again that Sollos was gone, he saw in her eyes the same fierce hunger for revenge as he felt inside.

She suited him, he decided. He didn't mind keeping her alive.

As each day began to fade they slowly made their way back, chewing on raw pieces of meat. The Scales was always there when they returned, waiting for them. Every day they came back later than the last, but he never said anything. He didn't eat much either. He was slowly wasting away, waiting for his dragon to come back from wherever she'd gone.

Twice Kemir saw other dragons in the distance. He watched them, little specks in the sky, until they were gone. They never found Snow's ravine.

Snow slept for four weeks, not two. By then the Scales was little more than skin and bone. Kemir and Nadira had left him there with his dragon as they did every morning. When they came back, after dark, he was gone. The dragon was awake. The air smelled of gore.

Meat!

Kemir froze for a moment, then pushed Nadira back the way they'd come. 'Run! Now!' He lowered the remnants of the wild pig he'd killed to the ground. He could feel the dragon inside his head, almost insane with hunger, eyeing him up.

'Alchemists,' he said loudly. 'I'm going to take you to the alchemists, remember. Eat me and you'll never find them.' He stepped back away from the pig. The dragon lunged forward and snapped it all up in a single gulp.

Hunger! Feed! There was a tinge of anger in there as well.

'Where's Kailin?'

The dragon withdrew slightly. He could feel something in its thoughts that might have been shame.

Little One Kemir, it spoke in his head more quietly this time, *I have been gone for a long time. I am very, very hungry. I need to feed, and I cannot hunt until I have sunlight. It is best that you leave.*

Kemir retreated back down the ravine and spent the night huddled with Nadira, shivering, trying to keep warm. Without the heat of the dragon, a night on the mountain, even out of the wind, was unpleasantly cold.

By morning the dragon was gone. They made a quick search for Kailin, but there was no sign of him, and Kemir's heart wasn't really in it. When the dragon came back, late in the afternoon, its snout and claws were stained with blood, and its breath was foul. It looked fat, Kemir thought.

They flew north because that's where the alchemists laired. The dragon never said what had happened to the Scales, and Kemir never asked.

The Dragon-King's Tithe

The rider, if his Hatchling Gold has bought him favour, may visit many times before a suitable dragon is hatched. On each visit he will bring a gift to the eyrie-master, and these gifts are of the utmost importance, for their quality and generosity will determine the care with which the chosen dragon is raised. When a suitable dragon is finally hatched, a price will be set by the dragon-king himself. This price is the Dragon-King's Tithe.

Usually the tithe is agreed far in advance, yet until the price is paid the rider can never quite be sure that it will not change. Sometimes the tithe is everything that the rider possesses; sometimes it is nothing at all.

39

Parting

Jehal awoke from a restless sleep. His dreams had been troubled – always running, always being watched, always chased, always having to look over his shoulder – and everywhere he ran the walls, the trees, even the rivers would burn and melt and the heat would force him to run again.

He slipped out of bed and padded to the window. Kazah, his pot-boy, was slumped on his stool, snoring loudly. Jehal opened the shutters to let in the light. Kazah didn't stir. That was what Jehal liked best about the boy. Aside from being a deaf mute and blessed with a loyalty that put Jehal's hunting dogs to shame, Kazah slept like the dead. Jehal could have an all-night orgy, and the boy would be none the wiser.

Outside, the sun was creeping over the horizon. Ships bobbed on the water out in the estuary of the Fury River. In places the water seemed to be on fire, burning in the dawn sun. Jehal shuddered and turned away. The sight of it reminded him too much of his dreams. There wasn't a little golden dragon with ruby eyes perched on the sill outside. That was the important thing.

He padded back to his bed, sat down, pulled a strip of white silk out from under his pillow and wrapped it around his eyes. His sight blurred, shimmered and shifted, and then he was somewhere else. He was in the Tower of Air in the Adamantine Palace. In Zafir's bedchamber, out of sight under the bed.

He listened. He could hear breathing. *Her* breathing. Relaxed and restful, as though she was asleep. He didn't hear any snoring. If Hyram had been there with her, there would have been snoring. Then again Hyram rarely came to her, and when he did, he rarely stayed. Usually Zafir went to him and then slipped back to her own bed once he was asleep. Sometimes when she came back in the middle of the night, barefoot, hugging her clothes to her, she looked desperately sad. Other times she looked angry. Yet other times she would look around the room, searching for his little golden dragon, and then she would stand in front of it naked, and blow him a kiss, or mime being violently sick or slitting someone's throat. Whether she meant him or Hyram, he was never quite sure.

Sometimes, in the morning, she would look for him too, and if they were both alone, they'd whisper to each other through little golden ears and watch through little ruby eyes.

That would be later, though. This was much too early for Zafir. Under her bed the little golden dragon twitched its head and skittered across the floor. It flapped its wings, so fast that they vanished into a blur, and lifted off the ground; then settled itself at the head of the bed, a couple of feet away from Zafir's head, and stopped, staring at her. Jehal took a deep breath. She was fast asleep. Sometimes when she was sleeping, she was breathtaking. He could have stared at her for hours.

He shook himself, took the white silk off his eyes and slipped it back under his pillow. Then he put on the other silk, the black one.

Well, my lover, let us see who you've been spying on today.

The answer wasn't much of a surprise. Zafir's Taiytakei dragon had secreted itself in Lystra's room, where it usually was. Zafir clearly had nothing better to think about than how often he was sharing Lystra's bed. Which was pleasantly predictable of her. Jehal grinned to himself and kicked Kazah's stool. The trouble with Zafir's jealousy was that it was a challenge. It made him want to see how many times he could bed his wife without his lover and her spy-dragon catching them at it.

It was depressingly easy too. But then if it had been harder, he'd probably have done it even more.

He kicked Kazah's stool again. The pot-boy jerked upright and then fell over sideways. He jumped to his feet, ramrod straight, and saluted.

Message for my wife. Jehal and Kazah had their own sign language, a bastard hybrid of the signals that the dragon-knights used when they were flying together, the signs that some thieves used, and other bits that they'd simply made up themselves. Jehal was having the boy taught to read and write too, but he was so slow that one of them would probably be dead before he got anywhere.

Kazah nodded. Having a private language meant no one else understood what Jehal was telling Kazah to do. Several times he'd sent Kazah to Lystra to arrange a rendezvous knowing full well that Zafir was watching him.

Wake her up. She is to come to my bed. Tell her I want her. Kazah smirked and Jehal grinned back. *That* gesture wasn't particularly hard to translate. *Tell her to shut all windows and doors first. Tell her that eyes are watching her.* He gave Kazah a kick and watched the boy scurry away. Then he closed the shutters, blocking out the dawn light, lay back in his bed and sighed.

He didn't have to wait long. He heard footsteps outside and then giggling, and then Kazah slipped back in with Lystra behind him, still in her nightclothes.

Jehal grinned. 'Did anyone see you?'

Kazah shook his head. So did Lystra. 'Only the guard you put on my door.' She flung her arms around him and snuggled her head against his chest. He always flinched for a moment when she did that. It reminded him too much that he was going to have to let Zafir have her way one day.

But not yet. He pushed her gently away and put a hand on her belly. She had his heir inside her, and that made her the safest person in the world just now. He'd have to wait another couple of months before he could feel it move, they told him, but he put his hand on her anyway. After this morning they might not see each other for a while.

She held his hand there for a second, then moved it up to her breast. 'I still don't see why I can't come with you.'

Of course you don't. He smiled at her. 'You need to conserve your strength.'

'Oh Jehal, I hardly know it's there.'

'You're sick every day. Don't pretend you're not.'

She made a face. 'That's nothing.'

'Besides, you're safer here.'

'But why? At the palace I'll have you and my mother and my sisters and all their riders as well.'

He laughed. 'You know the answer. There might be people who would prefer your mother not to take Hyram's place.' *Me, for example.*

That was the trouble. She simply didn't understand that anything might happen, that someone might break their word, that the dragon-kings and -queens weren't all fast friends working together for the good of them all. Which made it very difficult to look her in the eye sometimes. And if she'd really thought there *was* any real danger, she'd either insist on going to be at her mother's side, or else insist that he didn't go so he'd be safe too. She didn't insist on things very often, but when she did it was a timely reminder of who her birth-mother was.

He kissed her lightly. 'I don't want to trouble you.'

'I think you're just bored with me.'

Inside his head Jehal rolled his eyes. *That* old chestnut again. *How* many times had he heard that? And from *how* many different women? 'If I was bored with you, my love, would I have risen at dawn and called you to my bed for one last time before I leave?'

She stuck out her bottom lip and then took hold of his other hand and put it on her other breast. She smiled. 'I suppose not.'

She stepped a little closer, until he could felt the heat of her right from her knees to her neck. Jehal swallowed. He looked at Kazah and nodded at the door. The boy was smart enough to know when to make himself scarce.

'I'm leaving in the middle of the morning for Clifftop,' he said thickly. 'Everything is packed. It'll take me—'

Lystra put a finger to his lips. 'I know, husband, I know.' She called him that a lot, and for some reason his head went fuzzy every time she said it. 'Four days to reach the palace, a week as

Speaker Hyram's guest, and then a week more after my mother succeeds him. And then another four days back to Clifftop and yet another day to return here. Almost a month. I know it all by heart, my Prince. Every day, where you'll be and what you'll be doing.' She smiled at him. 'One very long and lonely month. I might come out to Clifftop to meet you when you come back.'

'You shouldn't.'

'Yes, but you won't be here to tell me not to.' She pressed herself against him and kissed him, and he lowered her down onto his bed.

'I shall miss you greatly,' he said, and was surprised to find that he meant it.

'But not as much as I shall miss you.'

He rolled her over and silenced her with his lips. Best not to let her say anything else. Sometimes when they were together like this he found himself questioning his whole purpose, and that wouldn't do. Instead, he set about making sure she really would think of him for every single day that he was away. Together, for an hour or so, they stopped time.

When they were spent she fell asleep in his arms, which was something she always did if he let her. To his surprise he fell asleep as well; the next thing he knew, Lord Meteroa was banging on the door, shouting at him that it was time to go. Lystra yawned and stretched. She got up and looked at him, a muzzy smile on her face.

'Do I have to go?'

'I'm afraid you do.' Jehal shouted at Meteroa to leave them alone for a few minutes and started to look for his clothes. 'Don't go back to your rooms for a while. Go out for a ride. Or go to the baths. Send someone to air them while you're away.'

'Why?'

'Because I ask you to.'

'But I wanted to wear—'

He looked at her sharply. 'Humour me. A favour to me for giving you this time.'

For a moment she looked hurt and he felt as though she'd knifed him. Then she smiled. 'If that's what you want.'

'It would make me happy. Listen!' He cupped her face. 'While I am gone, trust Meteroa. Don't trust Princess Jesska, Prince Iskan, Prince Mazmamir or any of their clan. We might have the same blood, but we also have the same ambition. Trust Queen Fyon but don't trust her sons, particularly Tyrin.'

When she was gone, he called Meteroa in to help him dress. 'Keep her safe while I'm gone. Whatever happens to her happens to you, my friend. You understand?.'

Meteroa gave him a sceptical look. 'Then I shall eat a lot and get fat for you, but please be back before she gives birth, Your Highness.'

'There's always the chance I won't come back at all.'

Meteroa cocked his head. 'Then I shan't have to worry about her. Tell me, Your Highness, which one pleasures you the most? Your wife or Queen Zafir?'

Jehal felt his chest tighten. He snarled, 'Get out!'

'Your Highness—'

'I said get *out!* Before I find something sharp.'

Alone, he slowly finished dressing himself. Meteroa was getting above himself, he decided. The man would need taking down a peg or two after this was all done.

He's right, though. It's a question that demands an answer, and I don't have one.

The last thing he did, before he left, was take the black and white silks from under his pillow and tie them around his wrists. Southern knights often tied strips of cloth to their arms; worn on the left they were signs of conquests, on the right they signalled obligation, which made it an easy way to keep the Taiytakei silks innocently to hand. Generally, Jehal wore the black one on the left and the white one on the right. It seemed right, somehow.

Almost as an afterthought he took the black silk off again and put it across his eyes. The little golden dragon was still in Lystra's room, buzzing madly about the place, looking for a way out.

Jehal smiled. As he left, he started to whistle.

40

Arts of War

Jaslyn called Silence into a tight turn and dived. Five of Queen Shezira's riders, flying in a tight line alongside her, suddenly scattered, seemingly at random. The ground was straight ahead now, rushing to meet her. In the centre of her vision a cluster of soldiers raised their dragonscale shields. Silence belched fire at them and then spread out his wings, pulling out of the dive. An immense hand pressed Jaslyn into the dragon's neck, knocking the breath out of her. She didn't have a chance to see whether the fire had done anything useful, but she doubted it. The soldiers were a half-legion of the Adamantine Guard and they'd had plenty of time to lock their shields together. Then again, the point of the dive hadn't been to burn them; the point had been to distract them, to give her knights a chance, to lead them into battle in such a way that she didn't get herself killed.

Behind her, the five knights strafed the soldiers from five different angles at once, wheeled and flew away. They'd spent years perfecting that manoeuvre, all for this one day.

When she was safely away from the soldiers on the ground and their vicious scorpions, Jaslyn let Silence pick up a little height and turned to look for her riders. Three of them were following her; the other two were already on the ground. Which meant that, after they'd sprayed their fire and turned away, the soldiers had managed to hit them. Which meant that, had this been a real fight, they'd be dead.

'Two?' Jaslyn patted Silence on the neck. 'They got two. Did you see that? Do you think mother's going to be angry?' She smiled to herself as she flew Silence over the soldiers, tipping them a salute. 'So much for our clever plan, eh? Do you suppose we got any of them?' From up in the air it was hard to tell whether any of the soldiers had been burned. Even if their shield wall failed them, their dragonscale armour would deflect the worst of the flames.

Scattered around the Hungry Mountain Plains, other legions of the Guard were under attack, as each of the dragon-kings and -queens put them to the test. Jaslyn circled for a while, watching in case any of the attackers had come up with something original, but as far as she could see, none of them had. In the distance she saw one group of knights try exactly the same ploy she'd used herself. They didn't get the timing right. When the first knight unleashed his fire and pulled up his dragon, the other five should have been right there and they weren't. They weren't out by very much, only a few seconds, but it was enough for the legion to adjust its wall of shields and scatter the flamestrikes. A hundred and sixty years ago, when Master of War Prince Lai first demonstrated the technique, he'd left a hundred men dead or injured behind him.

Jaslyn sighed. For every pattern of offence, the legions had a counter. Nothing ever changed. It was almost like a ritual dance where everyone knew all the moves by heart. Supposedly, Prince Lai had invented four of the fifteen recognised tactics. The other eleven were even older.

She turned Silence away from the battlefield and spiralled down. In the middle of the legions Speaker Hyram had his tower, where he and the dragon-kings and -queens who weren't participating in the mocks fights could stand and watch. Her mother was there, and Almiri too. Lystra had stayed in the south, slowly getting fat with Prince Jehal's heir. As she flew past, she searched the tower for Prince Tichane but she couldn't see if he was there. The thought of the Crag King's ambassador left a strange sensation inside her, one that she usually reserved for her dragons.

She pushed all that away, landed Silence at the foot of the tower and handed him over to the alchemists and Scales who'd set up a makeshift eyrie around the tower. Then she bounded up the steps. Out over the plains, most of the other dragons were circling now, waiting to come back, watching the few who were still sparring with the legions.

'You lost two of my riders,' said Shezira as soon as Jaslyn reached the top of the tower.

'Prince Lai's pattern of Autumn Leaves.' Speaker Hyram smiled at her. 'Ambitious. Difficult to execute properly.'

'Which you didn't,' added Shezira.

Jaslyn clenched her teeth. 'What do you mean?'

'Your timing was wrong. The knights behind you were too slow. The legion had time to adjust.' She shook her head. 'Don't feel too bad. Someone else tried the same pattern and made the same mess of it.'

'Prince Jehal.' Hyram spat out the name. 'Your execution of the pattern was better.'

Shezira shook her head. 'I disagree. They were both equally poor.'

Jaslyn looked around, taking in all the faces. There were two men she'd never met who were Speaker Hyram's cousins, and a cluster of advisers around him. Next to her mother, Knight-Marshal Nastria was staring out across the plains, seemingly oblivious. Behind her, King Tyan sat in a chair with his tongue hanging out, his head lolling and his eyes staring up at the sky, constantly quivering. She recognised a few others from Lystra's wedding too. Queen Fyon, who smiled at her while her eyes filled with daggers. And Valgar and Almiri, of course.

Almiri caught her arm. 'The signallers on the field flagged seven injured from your attack. Their shield wall wasn't quite perfect.'

'And Prince Jehal?'

'Four.'

For some reason that made everything better. 'It feels strange, burning men I don't know for no better reason than entertainment. I hope they weren't killed.'

'The signaller indicated injuries only.'

'Who's winning?' Jaslyn tried to sound like she didn't care.

Almiri laughed. 'Not you. Queen Zafir. Six dead, thirty injured.'

'*What?*'

'She lost all her five riders doing it. She charged them. On the ground.'

'She did what?'

'She put her five knights on their dragons on the ground, and they charged the legion as though they were cavalry. Ran straight into it. Scattered men everywhere. Broke their shield wall completely. Then she flew in behind and burned them. They got all the men on the ground but they didn't get her.'

'But that's *cheating*.'

'Not according to Speaker Hyram. He let it stand.'

Jaslyn clenched her fists and ground her teeth. 'There are traditions! No contact. No one would land their dragons to attack a real enemy. They'd be killed at once! They're not supposed to do that.'

'The riders who charged across the ground would all have been dead. Speaker Hyram has ruled that, since it was Queen Zafir's dragon who did all the damage, and since she escaped unscathed, the score stands.' Almiri put an arm around Jaslyn's shoulder and led her towards the far corner of the tower roof, away from twitching ears. 'If you want my advice, you don't say anything.'

'It's *cheating*,' Jaslyn hissed again.

Almiri forced her to sit down. 'It's only cheating if the speaker says so, and the speaker doesn't. When was the last time you saw Speaker Hyram? Before this, I mean.'

Jaslyn spat over the edge of the tower. 'On the way to Lystra's wedding. When mother practically invited someone to steal our white dragon.' She frowned. 'If Prince Jehal can get King Tyan onto the back of a dragon to come here, why can't he bring Lystra with him too? That's not fair.'

Almiri ignored her. 'Have you noticed anything about Speaker Hyram?'

'Not really.' Jaslyn shrugged.

'Have you noticed that he's not shaking or stuttering any more?'

Jaslyn glanced back at the speaker. 'Oh. Did he use to?'

'Little sister, do you notice *anything?*' Almiri laughed. 'Speaker Hyram has been slowly dying for this last year. Alchemists' disease. Do you know what that is?'

Jaslyn shook her head.

'It's what King Tyan's got. Take a look at him.'

'I know he's sick.'

'It starts with trembling and shaking. Over the years you slowly lose all your capabilities. Eventually you probably die, but generally people either starve because they can't feed themselves any more, or else their family sends them quietly on their way. King Tyan has had this disease for nearly a decade.' Almiri shook herself. 'Anyway, what I'm trying to tell you is that Speaker Hyram has been sick, but now he's better, and it's Queen Zafir who found him the cure. There are quite a lot of other whispers about Speaker Hyram and Queen Zafir too, so if I were you, I wouldn't say anything to his face.'

Jaslyn sniffed. 'Cheating is still cheating.'

Almiri grabbed Jaslyn's arm and squeezed it hard. 'Listen to me, little sister. You do nothing to annoy the speaker. You say nothing about Queen Zafir. Do you understand?'

'Why?'

'Because mother will tear off your head if you do. She's nervous. I haven't seen her like this for a very long time. She thinks Hyram might change his mind about who's going to be the next speaker.'

'But he can't.'

Almiri's grip tightened until it started to hurt. 'Yes he can. He's the *speaker.*'

'We have a pact!'

'Which can easily be broken.'

'But ...'

Almiri let go. Her mouth twitched with amusement. 'Little Jaslyn, these are kings and queens, not your dragons. They don't simply do what you tell them.'

41

Kings and Queens

Hyram put down his cup and stood up. He looked around the immense ten-sided table at the kings and queens, the knights, the lords, the master alchemists, the priests. He couldn't remember the last time he'd felt to young, so strong, so powerful. His head buzzed with Zafir's potions. They left him on edge, hyperactive, almost priapic, but they made the shaking go away, and the stutter – that was what mattered. He wore the Speaker's Robe and held the Speaker's Spear, and the weapon's power coursed through him. He couldn't remember the last time he'd felt so strong.

Around the table the masters and mistresses of the nine realms interrupted their feast and gave him their attention, one dragon-king or -queen on each side of the table. Beside him on his side of the table sat Sirion, the loyal cousin who had inherited his crown and throne when he, Hyram, had become the speaker. On the tenth side, opposite him, sat the grand master alchemists and the dragon-priests who would anoint his successor. As expected, one side of the table was almost empty: the King of the Crags hadn't deigned to join them. *No surprises there.*

He banged his cup and cleared his throat. 'These words are said once every ten years. You will hear them today. Some of you have heard them before. Some of you have heard them twice or even three times. They are old words and wise words. They are not my words, but the words of all speakers, crafted and honed over the decades. You will hear them now, and then you will not hear them again for another ten years, so I beg you to listen and remember.' He looked around the table from face to face. Some were listening, some were simply pretending to listen. It didn't matter. His voice sounded strong, and he wondered if any of them could understand the simple joy of being able to speak again, to have the words come out of his mouth pure and fully formed, not wrecked and ruined by the twitching that used to plague him. In particular, he looked at King Tyan, his old friend and enemy. Now there was one king who wasn't listening. Tyan was asleep. Trembling a little, but mostly still.

Prince Jehal, sitting next to Tyan, caught Hyram's eye and cocked his head. Hyram bared his teeth and moved on.

'We keep histories of our dragons now.' He nodded towards the alchemists at the end of the table. 'We know when they were born, who was their sire and who was their dam. We breed them to our liking, but it was not always so. They were once wild creatures. We have no histories of them from that time. Not because there was no ink, nor because there were no books, but because they were all burned. There were no towns, no cities, not because there were no bricks and no mortar, but because they were all burned. There were kings and armies, perhaps, but they are forgotten, because they were all burned. We hid in the forests where the dragons couldn't reach us. We lived as the Outsiders live, filthy and starving.'

He let his eyes wander over their faces again, and then banged his cup on the table a second time. This time the kings and queens banged the table with him. 'That was before the alchemists came.' He raised his cup to the far end of the table, where Jeiros gave an embarrassed nod. 'Now the dragons are tamed and we are their fragile masters. You, Kings and Queens of the Nine Realms. *You* are their masters. You want for nothing and you answer to no one. Except ...'

Now was the time. He took the Speaker's Ring, carved into the likeness of a sleeping dragon, from his finger and put it gently down. His finger felt strangely naked. Then he laid the adamantine spear beside it.

'Except to these,' he said. Strange. He'd dreamed of doing this so many times, and it had always felt like the end of his life, as though it was the only thing keeping him together. He'd take off the ring and put down the spear and feel himself immediately begin to fade. Yet now, when the moment was real, he felt light-headed, as though this was the beginning of something and not the end.

He picked up the ring again and held it out for all to see. 'This. This ring binds you. Binds you to ancient pacts made long ago between the ancestors of all our clans. Every ten years you shall choose from among yourselves one who will take this palace. To be the judge of your actions and the arbiter of your disputes. Ten years ago you and your forefathers chose me. My time is done. In one week you will choose another. I will guide you, but the choice, in the end, lies with you.'

There. Done. The speech they'd all heard before, the speech made by every speaker since time began. His last duty. Speaker Hyram was no more. He wasn't even 'Your Holiness.' Just another dragon-lord sitting at the speaker's table. He put the ring down and banged the table with his cup one last time.

Someone started to clap. Very slowly. Jehal. It had to be Jehal.

'What a fine speech.' The Viper was smirking at him. 'Pity I've heard it all before. Yet unexpectedly clear. I confess I've been dreading it. Th-Th-The l-l-long a-a-ag-g-gonising w-wait for each word. Truly, the potions that your darling lover stole from me have worked wonders.'

Around the table everyone froze. Some paused only for a moment and then continued to eat. Others stopped, waiting. No one said anything. They were all looking to Hyram. His feast, his hall, his palace, his job to admonish such crass behaviour. Even if the insult was directed at him, Jehal was making fools of them all by being so direct.

Hyram sat slowly down. He smiled and folded his arms. 'What *did* make you think I would have to give you anything for your elixirs?' He felt strong. Strong enough to challenge Jehal to a duel of the sword and the axe. He could do that now. One of the perks of being a simple dragon-knight again. Yes, and another perk was that he didn't have to be the diplomat now. It wasn't up to him to keep everyone in line any more. 'Never mind, eh? Go back home.

Go back to poisoning your father.' *I can say that now. In public. In front of everyone.*

That got them all. Even Zafir, even Shezira, who'd tried to pretend that Jehal hadn't said anything, even they couldn't ignore that. They stared at him in mute horror. All except the Viper, of course, whose mouth would probably still spew its villainous bile long after the rest of him was dead.

'Oh no, I couldn't do that. Since it seems you're going to live a while longer, I suddenly have something to keep me from growing bored again. I'll not forget your hospitality, Hyram. Perhaps now I'll be able to repay it one day.' Jehal turned and stroked his father's head. 'Or perhaps not. The potions haven't done much for King Tyan. He's too far gone. How long, do you suppose, before you follow him?'

'Perhaps he'd get better if you *stopped* poisoning him?'

This time Jehal got slowly to his feet. Several others rose as well: Narghon, Shezira, a couple of Hyram's own cousins. The rest were too stunned to move. Jehal leaned across the table. 'Slander me one more time, old man, and I'll take you out to the challenge fields. I won't kill you, but you'll wish I had.'

'Slander?' Hyram stood up as well. 'Or the truth?'

'If it's the truth, why don't you show all these worthy lords and ladies some evidence? Oh!' Jehal slapped his forehead. 'What a fool I am. Of course. That's because you *haven't got any*. Not one little shred.'

'Then challenge me. I accept. Axe and sword. Ahh, please, *please*, little Viper, let us play.'

Someone slammed a fist into the table. It took a moment for Hyram to realise that it was Shezira. 'Enough, both of you. Hyram, don't be a fool. Prince Jehal, you began this childishness. Perhaps you should leave.'

Jehal shot Shezira a look of pure hate. 'Of course, Your Holiness. How rude of me to be accused.' He took a step back and bowed. 'King Narghon, King Silvallan, King Valgar, I bid you and yours a pleasant evening. The rest of you can choke.'

In silence the table watched him go, his riders and King Tyan with him. When the door slammed, Queen Shezira resumed her seat. King Narghon was still on his feet. He shook his head. It made his jowls wobble.

'Lord Hyram, Prince Jehal is right. You should show us your evidence or still your tongue. And Queen Shezira, why should Prince Jehal be forced aside when he is the one who has been wronged.'

'Because, save for those of you who choose to be blind, we all know that I'm right,' Hyram spat.

Shezira drummed her fingers on the table. 'King Narghon, this is Hyram's hall until another one of us takes that ring. He cannot be sent from his own hall, and one of them had to go. Hyram, you might be right that there are several around this table who have their suspicions. Nevertheless, you have no proof. I am quite certain I know who was responsible for the theft of my white dragon.'

'Aye, the King of the Crags. Pity he didn't bother to come. Where's Tichane to answer for him, eh? Not here either.' Hyram smirked. The potions and the wine were making him light-headed, but for once it didn't matter. He didn't have to care.

'Does he ever come?' asked King Valgar.

'I'm not sure he even exists any more. How would we know?'

Shezira cleared her throat. 'When I have *proof*, I will pursue them, *whoever* they are' – she glared at Hyram – 'to the end of the world. Until then I will keep my silence, and I suggest you do the same.'

'I've had enough of silence.'

He stopped. Zafir was leaning forward to catch his eye, shaking her head. 'The wine is making you reckless,' she said, quietly enough that most of the others wouldn't hear. 'And the potions.'

Hyram blinked. 'Queen Zafir is quite right: I have made a fool of myself. Perhaps it is the prerogative of any man relieved of such a burden, but King Narghon is also correct. If the Viper has insulted my table and all who sit at it then so have I. Queen Shezira, it is me you should have sent away, not Prince Jehal.'

Shezira pursed her lips. She didn't reply.

'Oh, I think you should both have stayed,' said Queen Zafir pleasantly. 'I was looking forward to watching you spill that murderer's blood!'

Narghon shot to his feet again. 'I will not have these accusations!'

Zafir raised an eyebrow. 'Didn't you know? Prince Jehal was with my mother when she died. They'd slipped away for a little tryst, and only one came back. I have drawn my own conclusions. You may do the same.' Her brow furrowed. 'Maybe she fell, or maybe she was pushed. Who knows? He did it, though. Either way, Prince Jehal has her blood on his hands. If he pushed her, I have to wonder why. Why would he do such a thing? If Aliphera had been here instead of me, what might have happened? Would Lord Hyram still have honoured his brother's pact? Of course he would. So I can't help but wonder what madness is going through the minds of those who suggest that Prince Jehal would have killed her to remove a possible alternative successor.' She was looking straight at Queen Shezira now. 'Or to guarantee his bride. Or to ensure that he would be speaker one day.'

The air chilled. It took Hyram a second or two to unravel what Zafir had said. By the time he'd worked it out, Shezira was already bright red.

'*Who* suggests?' she hissed.

Zafir shook her head. 'Utter madness. So perhaps Aliphera wasn't pushed; perhaps she simply fell, but I'll call him—' She coughed and gagged. 'I'll call him—'

She started to rise, slipped and fell to the floor, clutching at her throat. Whatever she was going to call Jehal, the dragon-kings and -queens never found out.

42

Poison and Lies

The Adamantine Eyrie was full. It was more than full. Makeshift pens had been set up out on the Hungry Mountain Plains, more for the herds of cattle to feed the dragons than for the dragons themselves. The speaker had laid out a tented village to shelter all the extra workers that had been drafted in. Some dragon-lords had also brought a few men of their own. And with the eyrie workers and the drivers and carters came the hangers-on, the traders, the fortune-tellers, the fortune-seekers, the thieves, the pickpockets and the desperate, all of them sucked out of the countryside, drawn in by the knowledge that wherever there were dragons, there was wealth. The tented village had grown into a a tented town long before the last dragon arrived. It was a crowded chaos where every other face was a stranger.

For two riders set upon a very private piece of business, it was perfect. They didn't look like riders; they looked like simple soldiers, sell-swords perhaps, or a pair of off-duty swordsmen of the Adamantine Guard. They moved with purpose through the stalls and traders, right to the heart of the makeshift town, certain that no one would recognise or remember them.

They were wrong. A boy, not quite a man, in a dull brown cloak and with a dirty face had been following them for quite some time, ducking and weaving through the throng. But the riders didn't know anything about that, not yet.

Near the centre of the market they stopped at a little table set up in front of a tiny tent barely large enough for a man to stand inside. There *was* a man there too, a strange fellow with uncommonly dark skin. The clothes he wore were tattered and faded, but they'd been rich and ornate once. Any gold and jewels were long gone; only a dazzling rainbow of feathers remained. The riders seemed unimpressed by his strangeness. The boy hung back and watched them all with an expression of puzzled interest.

A purse changed hands. A heavy one by the looks of it. The dark-skinned man vanished into his tent and appeared again a moment later. He held out a leather satchel. The taller of the two knights took it and they moved quickly away. Too quickly. Too quickly to be innocent at any rate. The boy followed them to the edge of the market and into a large beer tent. In the middle of the day there weren't many people inside. The boy glanced at the riders and then padded across the sticky straw floor and sat down at a table.

'Oi! You! Clear off!'

It took a while before the boy understood that the shout was meant for him. He didn't look up but fished in his pocket and put a silver quarter down on the table in front of him. Out of the corner of his eye he watched the two men he'd been following. The taller one reached into the satchel, took something out and stuffed it inside his coat.

'Where'd you get your grubby hands on a bit of silver then?'

The boy still didn't look up. Off to one side, the satchel had passed to the shorter of the two.

'Thieving, is it? Picked some rich pillock's pocket, did you?'

The tall one was getting up now. Leaving. The boy didn't move.

'Ah, what do I care.' A mug of something bitter-smelling landed in front of the boy, splashing across the table. The boy reached out and sipped at it. Eventually, the other rider got up and left. The boy followed. He eased closer this time, inching into the man's shadow until they were side by side. The boy waited for exactly the right moment.

He snatched the satchel from the rider's shoulder and dived down a narrow gap between the tents, skipping over the ropes that held them up. The man roared and gave chase, hurling himself after the boy, shouting and screaming for someone to stop him. The boy was the more agile of the two, but the rider was fast and strong and made a good show of keeping up. The boy led him away from the centre of the tented town and in among the cattle pens that surrounded it.

Away from the crowds, the boy turned a corner. Instead of running, he hunched down into a corner among the shadows. When the rider barrelled round a moment later, the boy let him pass and then stood up behind him.

It was done in an instant. The man's steps faltered as he wondered which way to go. A blade, blackened so it wouldn't catch the sun, flicked out of the boy's sleeve and into the rider's side in one fluid stroke. The boy was already running again before the man even knew he'd been stabbed.

The rider launched himself after the boy again. He took a few steps. His hand went to his side, and then he stopped. He looked at his hand and at the blood streaming out of him. Inside he was suddenly burning. He couldn't speak. The pain grew and grew, filling him up from his core to the tips of his fingers and toes, and yet he couldn't speak, couldn't move, couldn't even scream. Mercifully, when the pain reached his head, everything went white and then dark.

The boy dropped the knife and kicked it aside. He zigged through the maze of wooden pens out of caution, but no cry went up behind him. He sprinted. He'd chosen the place to murder the knight quite carefully, but now time was against him. He ran to the edge of the pens, to where another rider, this one in full dragonscale, was waiting with two horses. When Rider Semian saw the boy, he nodded and climbed into his saddle.

'Is it done?'

The boy gave a curt nod and mounted the second horse.

'What about the other one?'

'I recognised him. He's another one of Jehal's.' The boy threw off his cloak. When he took off his hat, long dark hair streamed out. He wiped the dirt off his face and suddenly wasn't a boy any more, but Lady Nastria, Knight-Marshal to the Queen of the North. 'Go! We need to be quick.'

Nastria wheeled her horse and pushed along the muddy

paths between the pens, retracing her steps. As they got close to the dead dragon-knight, a couple of old women got up and ran away. They hadn't had time to steal much more than the dead man's purse, and Nastria didn't begrudge them that. The two dismounted and tied the body across the back of Nastria's horse. Together, they galloped towards the Adamantine Palace and the City of Dragons. As they drew close, Nastria dismounted again, put her peasant cloak and hat back on and led both horses up to the palace gates.

'Rider Semian, pledged to Queen Shezira,' declared the knight. The gate guards looked him up and down, took a good look at the body on the other horse, then nodded and let him pass. Nastria carefully stared at her boots. The guards barely noticed she was there at all.

They made their way to the Tower of Dusk in the western wall of the palace. There were many towers scattered through the palace, and each one had been given over to a different dragon-king or dragon-queen while the next speaker was being chosen. Queen Zafir resided in the Tower of Air. King Valgar had been given the Tower of Dawn on the eastern wall. King Tyan had the smallest of them, the Humble Tower. Kings Narghon and Silvallan had the Tower of Water and the City Tower over in the northern section of the palace. The Tower of Dusk had been given over to Queen Shezira. Nastria led the horses right up to the tower doors. Rider Semian opened them and they went in, dragging the body of the dead knight with them.

Inside, several other of Queen Shezira's riders were waiting. As soon as the doors closed behind him, Nastria threw off her disguise again. She pointed at the body. 'Get that down to the cellars. Where's the queen?'

'The queen is with the speaker.'

The riders parted as Lady Nastria pushed between them. Two reluctantly picked up the body by its arms and legs. 'Your Ladyship, this man isn't dead.'

Lady Nastria paused and frowned. 'Just get him down there. Let Master Kithyr know that he's needed.'

The knights exchanged nervous glances. Nastria shooed them down the stairs. In the wine and food cellars they cleared a heavy wooden table and laid out the body. Nastria looked him over. They were right. The man wasn't quite dead after all.

She slapped his face. 'Can you hear me, traitor?'

The man didn't move, so Nastria moved around him and jabbed a finger into the wound in his side. This time he moaned and opened his eyes.

'Hurts, does it?' She pushed her finger further in. The man wailed and screwed up his face. 'Rider Tiachas. A few months ago, you flew your dragon out of Outwatch with your two other brothers in treachery to the edge of the Barnan Woods. You took them to meet some outlaws. They went to buy something. You took them to the edge of the woods and they never came back. Do you know what happened to them? They were killed. I paid a pair of sell-swords to do it. I often wondered what went through your mind when they didn't come back. Were you afraid? And then, slowly, as the weeks turned into months and no one came for you, there must have been hope. Pointless, useless hope, Tiachas, because there's always been someone watching you. Can you hear me?' She wiggled her finger and Tiachas squealed. 'All I want to know, Tiachas, is who poisoned your soul. I was there, just now, when you bought the poison from that Taiytakei clown. I saw you with Prince Jehal's man. Was it Jehal, then?' She forced open his eyes and held out the satchel. 'What is this, Tiachas? Some sort of poison? Did Jehal pay you to murder our queen?'

Tiachas rolled his head from side to side. His tongue lolled out of his mouth. Blood was pouring freely from the wound in his side again, pooling on the floor under the table. Noises bubbled in his throat, but if he was trying to speak, the sounds made no sense.

'No? Are you trying to tell me that I'm wrong?' Nastria pulled a knife out of her belt and started to toy with it. 'I don't think I believe you, Tiachas, but I don't mind. You're trying to pretend you still have some courage and honour, and that's a good thing.

So I'll humour you. All I want to know is who, Tiachas. Who bought you?'

The head-shaking intensified.

'I *will* torture you, Tiachas, and you *will* tell me. And when you have, I will parade what's left of you in front of every court in the realms before I hang you. I will destroy your family, root and branch. They will lose everything, and they will hate you because *you* were the traitor who brought this down on them. Do you understand?'

Tiachas lunged at her, but he was feeble and slow, and Lady Nastria moved easily out of the way. The pair of riders caught him and held him down before he could roll off the table.

Nastria turned away. 'Let him go, and leave us. Please encourage Master Kithyr to hasten himself.'

The riders released Tiachas. They seemed uneasy and left slowly. Nastria watched them go.

'You know what disturbs them so, don't you? No, perhaps you don't. Master Kithyr is not a torturer but a blood-mage. So you *will* tell me what I want to know. And if you were hoping to die before I found out what I wanted, I'm afraid you're going to be disappointed there too.'

Nastria walked slowly around the cellar. Everything here had been laid in by Speaker Hyram's stewards for Queen Shezira and her knights. Hyram must have done the same for all the dragon-kings and -queens. How easy it would it be to poison an entire clan.

She put that thought aside. No speaker in two hundred years had murdered a guesting king or queen, and she doubted Hyram was about to start. She selected a bottle of wine, opened it and poured some for herself. Eventually she heard Kithyr padding across the stones towards her, but she didn't look round.

'Tiachas is a tool,' she said softly. 'I want to know who the craftsman was.'

It took the sorcerer an hour. There weren't even any screams, but then that was always the way with Master Kithyr. Always quiet. Throughout it all Nastria didn't look round. She stood statue-still, sipping at her wine, and by the end the bottle was empty. She didn't feel even slightly drunk. Instead she felt cold. Blood-magic. Another necessary evil. Like sell-swords.

When the blood-mage was done, she heard him padding softly back towards her.

'Well? Am I right? Was it Jehal?'

'No,' whispered the sorcerer. 'The Taiytakei.'

She thought about that for a while. The mage didn't move.

'He met one of them, who gave him something,' said Lady Nastria after a while. 'A flask. Filled with liquid silver. Like the last one. I still want to know what it is and what it's for.'

'Ask your alchemists. There are plenty of them. You know there's only one liquid that is of interest to me, and it is not silver in colour.' She could hear the sorcerer's disdain.

Nastria spat. 'Every time I do that I lose another alchemist. Huros, Bellepheros ...' A second of silence passed between them.

'What should I do with the body?' asked the sorcerer. 'Shall I leave it here?'

'No, Master Kithyr. Make it go away. Where no one will ever find it.'

She sighed as the sorcerer went about his work. So much for parading her traitor in public. It simply wasn't the same when all you had was a collection of bits.

43

A Crack in the Stone

High above the city, perched on a tiny plateau of rock overlooking the top of the Diamond Cascade valley, Hyram and Queen Shezira stood side by side, watching the water rush by hundreds of yards beneath their feet.

'Queen Zafir. How is she?' Shezira stood inches from the edge. Hyram was even closer. The tips of his boots were actually sticking out into the void. One good push and both of them would be dead.

'Recovering well.'

'That's good to hear. So was she poisoned or wasn't she?'

'She's been a little unwell of late.'

Shezira cocked her head. 'A little? Hyram, when she collapsed everyone thought she was dead.'

'She choked. That's all.'

'Well then I'm sorry for you that she ruined what was left of your feast.'

Hyram laughed. 'We both know it was ruined already. When Queen Zafir collapsed, most of you couldn't get out of my hall fast enough. She was doing you all a favour. Giving you a polite excuse to leave.'

'Very kind of her, I'm sure.' Shezira swayed slightly as a gust of wind whistled along the valley. 'I would prefer to return to the pavilion now.'

Hyram didn't move. 'This always used to be one of my favourite places when I was younger. You can see right across the realms from up here.'

'I prefer to be on dragonback.'

'I know. But standing here is a reminder of how far the likes of

247

you and I can fall. One missed step and we plunge to our dooms. It's been more than two years since I came here, you know. I couldn't stand like this when I was sick; I would have fallen.'

'Hyram, when we ride we wear harnesses to secure us to the backs of our dragons so we cannot fall, no matter what we do. That is what the dragons do for us. We can be as foolish as we like and our dragons will save us.'

'They didn't save Aliphera. Or Antros.'

'They won't save anyone who refuses to wear a harness.' Shezira turned away. 'If you stand there on the edge for long enough, Hyram, you *will* fall. Learn from your brother's mistake.'

Set back from the edge was the small pavilion built by Speaker Mehmit some two hundred years ago. The Purple Spur mountains were littered with little follies like this. Most had fallen into ruin, but this one had been popular with the speakers who'd followed him. From the bottom of the cliff it was invisible, and even from above it was almost impossible to spot unless you already knew it was there. It had become a little secret that the speakers had shared, passed down from one to the next. It was also an excellent place to spy on the Diamond Cascade, which had always been a popular place for dragon-lords and dragon-ladies who hungered to be away from the eyes of the palace court.

She went inside. There wasn't much to the pavilion, only a single airy room with open arches instead of windows. At the back were two wide alcoves, both generously piled with luxurious furs and soft cushions. It wasn't hard to guess what the speakers had used *those* for.

Has he brought Queen Zafir up here? Shezira pursed her lips. Of course he had.

She heard Hyram come in behind her and turned. 'It's good to see you in such good health, Hyram.'

'I can promise you, no one is more pleased than I am.'

'Are you going to marry her?'

That stopped him. For a moment Hyram froze. 'I think Queen Zafir stole the secret of the potions from the Viper to spite him. She knows how I feel about him.'

'*Everyone* knows how you feel about him.' Shezira cocked her head. 'But I'm not quite sure I understand it.'

'He's poisoning his own father.'

'Is he? Is he really?'

'I am certain of it.' Hyram's brow furrowed. 'Can't you feel it from him? The coldness? He's not human like the rest of it. He's vicious, callous, arrogant, self-obsessed—'

'You could be describing any of us.' She smiled slightly.

'You don't understand, do you?' Hyram shrugged. 'Ask Queen Zafir. She knows exactly what I mean. Maybe she'd be able to explain it better.'

Shezira's smile faded. 'Yes. So are you going to marry her?'

Hyram didn't smile. 'Yes, Shezira, I am.'

'And are you going to name her speaker, so you can carry on in the shadows behind her?'

This time he didn't say anything.

'Does she understand that she has to give up her throne, her crown? Does she have an heir ready to take on those burdens?'

That made him laugh. 'Do you?'

'We have a pact, Hyram. If you name Zafir instead of me, I will challenge her. And you will make a bitter enemy of me. Isn't Jehal enough?'

He looked at her. After a few seconds he turned away.

'I think I shall leave now.' Shezira strode past him back out into the open air. She signalled to the dragon-knights circling high overhead to take her back down to the palace. Almost at once a dragon tipped its wings and almost fell out of the air towards her, landing perfectly on the flat area of rock outside the pavilion. The rider threw down a rope ladder but didn't change position. Shezira frowned. Her riders knew better that that. Whoever it was should have moved aside so that she could take the reins.

When the queen didn't move, the rider lifted her helmet. 'Are you coming up or not, mother?'

Jaslyn. Shezira climbed up to sit behind her daughter.

'I would like to fly Silence back to the palace, please.'

Jaslyn looked at her as though she was mad and didn't move.

Shezira bit back her irritation and buckled herself into the second harness. Jaslyn clucked at Silence, who ambled towards the edge of the cliff and flopped lazily into the air, gliding down over the Diamond Cascade valley, out over the falls and into the immensity of space over the City of Dragons.

'You're upset, mother,' shouted Jaslyn.

Shezira kept her lips tightly pressed together. *Upset? Upset?! I'm furious, you stupid girl. More than furious, and you would be too if you knew. If you had any ambition, you'd be seething!* There wasn't any point in saying anything to Jaslyn, though. *I suppose I should be grateful that she's noticed anything at all.*

'Mother, you're making Silence anxious.'

For an instant everything went red. She twitched in the saddle, half of her set on lunging forward to wring Jaslyn's neck, the other half determined to stay in control. Underneath her she felt the dragon twitch too, and lurch suddenly forward.

'Mother!'

Shezira clenched her fists. Jaslyn could tell something was wrong because her *dragon* could tell something was wrong. *That* was much more like her daughter.

'Take me straight to the palace,' she snapped.

Jaslyn tipped Silence into a dive. The dragon tucked his wings into his body and simply fell, head first, tail stretched out behind him, towards the palace. They dropped like that, half a mile vertically through the air. The wind was immense. It was impossible to say anything; by the end, as the palace spread out before them, it was almost impossible even to *feel* anything except the rush of it, and the sharp terror, tightly held in check, that they were going too fast, that they couldn't possibly stop ...

Silence spread out his wings. Shezira pitched forward, helpless as the dragon slowed. She couldn't breathe. She must have blacked out, because one moment there was a crushing weight on her back and everything was grey, and the next the weight was gone, and they were floating down in looping circles, already below the tops of the palace towers. When they landed, Jaslyn threw down the ladder. Shezira climbed down very slowly and carefully. She was shaking. When she got to the bottom, Jaslyn was looking down at her with a big grin on her face.

Shezira didn't smile. 'Hyram is going to name Queen Zafir the next speaker,' she said. 'Why don't you take her for a ride and see if you can crush *her* to death.'

She turned away and strode towards the Tower of Dusk.

44

Semian

Rider Semian's leg still hurt. On the outside the wound had scarred over and healed weeks ago. Inside, though, it ached. If he tried to run, the ache got worse. Climbing the stairs of the Tower of Dusk left him sweating at the pain. Even if he simply stood still, it slowly grew worse until he had to sit down. The sell-sword's arrow had hit the bone in his thigh. He must have chipped or fractured it, and it was never going to be quite right ever again. He tried not to let it show, but the other dragon-knights were slowly realising that he was a cripple.

He stood stiffly straight as Lady Nastria climbed wearily up from the cellars. She looked very tired, more drained that Semian had ever seen her. A strange smell wafted up from behind her. Something bitter and acrid. Then the sounds started. Soft tearing sounds at first, then bones cracking. He shuddered and tried not to think about it.

At the very moment that Lady Nastria emerged from the cellars, a dragon landed in the yard outside. Semian recognised it at once. Silence. Others opened the door as the queen strode in. She looked angry and shaken.

'Your Holiness.' Lady Nastria stepped out in front of her. 'I have found—'

Queen Shezira waved her away. 'Hyram is going to name Queen Zafir the next speaker.'

Everything in the room stopped. People froze. Whispers died. Everyone stared at the queen.

Shezira cocked her head and looked at Lady Nastria. 'You were saying?'

Nastria bowed deeply. 'One of your knights has betrayed you.

He has been bought.'

'Ah.' The queen pressed her lips together. 'Another poison plot, knight-marshal?'

Lady Nastria nodded. 'I believe so, Your Holiness. I have the poison. I need to take it to the alchemists' redoubt to identify it.'

'Out of the question.' Shezira shook her head emphatically. 'Now that Hyram has betrayed our pact, I need you here. I will challenge his decision, and I need to be sure I have enough dragon-lords behind me. I would not wish this to become a war.' She paused and looked suddenly thoughtful. 'Send Princess Jaslyn. Let her do it.' A slight smile crossed the queen's face. 'Yes. It would be good to get her away from here for the next few days.'

By the door Rider Jostan was already running into the yard, waving and shouting, trying to call back Silence before he and the princess launched into the air. He was too late. Semian watched the knight-marshal's face. She looked far from happy. But whatever her doubts, she bit them back and bowed again.

'Of course, Your Holiness. I would like to send an escort.'

Shezira frowned. 'We still have an encampment in the Spur. It's only a few hours away.'

This time Nastria stood her ground. 'Nonetheless.'

'Very well.' The queen sighed. 'Two riders, no more. Make sure they are replaced from among the encampment.'

Which wouldn't upset any of them, Semian thought ruefully. Since the day he'd been shot by the sell-sword, they hadn't found a trace of the white dragon, nor of the Scales who was with her. Almost certainly they were both long gone, and the search had become a complete waste of time. But no one had dared tell that to the queen, and so they carried on.

The queen wrinkled her nose. 'What *is* that terrible smell?'

Lady Nastria blanched. 'It's the cellars, Your Holiness. Something has rotted. It will be removed shortly.'

'And the smell with it, I hope.' Shezira strode on, starting up the sweep of spiral stairs that rose through the middle of the Tower of Dusk. 'Someone tell my steward to prepare for guests this evening. And send an invitation. I think I should spend some time with my son-in-law and see what sort of impression Lystra has made on him. As soon as he is willing. Marshal, with me. You look like a peasant, and I'll be wanting you at your best. And since we're having guests, that smell had *better* be gone.'

The queen vanished around the curve of the stairs. Lady Nastria followed, but before she did, she pressed something into Semian's hands. 'Take this to Princess Jaslyn at the eyrie, and be quick about it.'

Semian's mouth fell open. *She's a princess. How can I tell her what to do?*

'Take Rider Jostan with you. The princess has an eye for both of you.' And then Knight-Marshal Nastria winked at him, which left him even more speechless.

On horseback he raced with Jostan to the Adamantine Eyrie, his leg getting steadily worse all the way. As they arrived, Princess Jaslyn swept out of the eyrie, heading towards one of the queen's carriages.

'Your Highness!' Semian jumped off his horse. In his haste, his leg almost buckled under him. Jaslyn gave him a cold look, certainly not the sort the knight-marshal had been talking about.

'Semian?' She didn't break stride.

'Your Highness, Her Holiness commands you to the stronghold of the alchemists.'

Jaslyn threw back her head and barked a laugh. She opened the carriage door.

'Your Highness! Lady Nastria has executed Rider Tiachas for treason. He is implicated in a plot to poison the queen.'

Jaslyn climbed into the carriage and made to close the door.

'Prince Jehal is also implicated.'

That made her stop. Breathlessly, Semian explained what the queen had ordered them to do. Jaslyn's eyes narrowed.

'So mother is sending me away, is she?' She spat, and storm clouds flashed in her eyes. 'Will this be enough to bury Jehal, do you think, Rider Semian?'

Semian lowered his eyes. 'I cannot say, Your Highness.'

The princess snorted and slowly climbed back out of the

carriage. 'Why does she send me, Rider Semian? Why not you? Are you not competent to run errands?'

Semian stayed carefully silent.

'Or you, Jostan?' She barked out another harsh laugh.

'Rider Nastria would have gone herself, Your Highness,' said Jostan quietly. 'It was the queen who ordered otherwise.'

'Of course.' Jaslyn bared her teeth. Without another word, she strode back into the eyrie.

By the time they were flying again, the sun was already sinking towards the horizon. Dragons were nervous in the dark, but Jaslyn drove them on at a merciless speed. They'd all spent months among the valleys of the Purple Spur looking for the white dragon. Even blindfold, Semian could have flown among them and been almost sure to reach his destination.

A dozen dragons and three times as many riders, together with several alchemists and scores of camp followers, were still camped out in the Worldspine. Over the months the tents had gone, replaced by a neat row of log cabins alongside the river. Sections of the forest were still being cleared, making way for cattle, driven up from the nearby valleys in King Valgar's realm.

A bonfire, lit at the highest end of the camp, guided them in. The dragons circled overhead, spitting blasts of fire to announce themselves, and then glided nervously down along the river, dipping the tips of their tails, feeling for the ground. As soon as they touched water, they tipped back, spread their wings and stopped dead in the air, dropping the last twenty feet onto the rocks of the river bed. Rider Semian's dragon lurched sideways and almost toppled over. Semian screwed up his face and closed his eyes, but Matanizkan found her balance and righted herself. By the time Semian dismounted, Princess Jaslyn had gone, vanished into the same cabin that she'd lived in for most of the last two months. Semian and Jostan looked at each other, shrugged and went to bed.

By first light they were in the air again, flying north through King Valgar's realm, skirting the edge of the Worldspine. In the afternoon they reached an apparently makeshift eyrie that was little more than a field with a small fortified manor house. Semian took it to be the provincial home of some bumpkin baron at first, a convenient place to stop and then move on. It didn't take him long to realise that he was wrong. The house was run by the Order of the Scales and contained alchemists, several of them. There were soldiers here too, and not any soldiers, but Adamantine men. The speaker's soldiers.

He listened as Princess Jaslyn and the alchemists talked, and he slowly understood. Somewhere a few miles to the east was the start of an old hidden road that ran deep into the Worldspine. At its far end was the alchemists' hidden stronghold, the source of their power – a day on dragonback, but a week or even more on foot or on the ox carts that carried the barrels filled with the alchemists' potions. Every week, no matter the weather, a convoy left the stronghold, feeding the eyries of the realms. The secret of the alchemists' potions was a precious one, closely guarded by the order and shared only with the kings and queens of the realms. Semian knew better than to ask exactly what they did, but it was something to do with taming the dragons. Everyone knew *that*.

Princess Jaslyn still carried storm clouds on her shoulders, the alchemists were taciturn and suspicious, and when he left, Semian was glad to go. He was bored too. Flying beside the princess was something of an honour, and certainly better than sharing a tower with a blood-mage, but after a while all the mountains looked the same. Back at the palace the tournaments and games would soon be starting. There was glory to be had, and gold too. Out here there was nothing. Nothing to do and nothing to see.

Nothing at all.

45

The Valeford Track

Snow dived out of the sun. Stretched out along the mountain track were five wagons, a couple of men on horses at the front and perhaps a dozen soldiers at the back.

'Burn the soldiers first,' screamed Kemir, trying to make himself heard over the wind. He had a saddle now, and he and Nadira rode on Snow's back instead of being carried in her claws.

'You don't need to shout,' yelled Nadira in his ear. Kemir closed his eyes. He still hadn't grown used to Snow plucking the thoughts out of his head.

No.

Snow ignored the soldiers. Instead, the first burst of fire hit the riders at the front. They had felt the rush of wind, perhaps, because Kemir thought he saw one of them look up and behind him just as Snow let loose. A blast of hot air hit Kemir in the face and he hugged Snow's neck.

They heard you shout.

Kemir felt Snow land. The air smelled of burning. He sat back up and saw that they were straddling the mountain track, blocking the way. The first wagon was on fire. Either side of the track smoke rose from a swathe of smouldering heather and gorse. Snow dropped to all fours, exposing Kemir and Nadira. She sent a second blast of fire along the road across the remaining wagons and towards the soldiers. Then she snatched up one of the dead horses and bit it in two, swallowing the back end whole.

Somehow, one of the horsemen was still alive. Staggering to his feet among the ashes, he started to scream. His clothes were burned to his skin; every part of him was either blackened or raw and red. And he was obviously blind. Kemir put him down with an arrow.

The smoke and flames from Snow's flamestrike cleared. All the wagons were blazing now. The soldiers at the back were still there, though. They'd formed up behind a wall of interlocking shields, and as Kemir watched, the shields dropped for a moment. Behind the shields, the soldiers had a crossbow. A big one.

They were pointing it at *him*.

'Shit!' Kemir threw himself flat against Snow's neck, but what saved him was Snow herself. She lifted up her head as the crossbow fired. Instead of hitting Kemir, the bolt hit the dragon in the shoulder. Kemir felt the shock, the surprise, the unexpected pain. The bolt must have been as long as his arm, and the crossbow had enough power to puncture Snow's scales and drive the missile deep into her flesh.

Then came the rage. It rose up from somewhere deep inside, in a tight seething ball, and bloomed, filling Snow's thoughts; and as it filled the dragon, it filled Kemir too. He started to unbuckle his harness so that he could get at the soldiers with his knives, then stopped himself. Snow leapt forward. She smashed the five carts to pieces, hurling their burning wreckage far away across the valley as she went. The soldiers scattered, some of them struggling through the gorse on either side of the track, most running away down the trail. A few of them actually ran past Snow, dodging between her legs. The dragon flicked her tail back and forth over the track, and at the same time sent another spear of fire down the trail ahead. Kemir glanced over his shoulder. One soldier had been knocked flying. Another seemed to have dived into the gorse and was still alive. A third had somehow ducked under Snow's tail, but she caught him just as he was getting away, cracking the tip against the side of his head so hard that Kemir could actually see the man's neck snap.

Behind him Nadira unleashed a scream of banshee violence. Kemir's fingers were fumbling at the harness again, tearing at the straps that kept him on Snow's back. The anger was overwhelming. He *needed* to fight.

Snow reared onto her back legs and pounded along the track, picking up soldiers as she caught them. She crushed one, hurled the next high into the air and tossed the third into her mouth, biting down so hard that his armour shattered. Finally Kemir freed himself. He slithered down the back of Snow's wing and then down her leg. He landed hard, almost got himself trampled, had to dive out of the way of Snow's flailing tail, but none of that mattered. The dragon-rage had him and he couldn't feel anything else. He leapt up to his feet again and jumped into the gorse, chasing one of the fleeing soldiers. His bow was still tied to Snow's saddle, and that was fine. He didn't want to shoot these men in the back. He wanted the joy of driving his knives into their bones.

The gorse was dense and the soldiers were in heavy armour. The man he'd set his sights on stumbled; Kemir bellowed and threw himself on top of him, wrestling him, hacking at him with his knife. The soldier was wearing dragonscale plates, which would turn his knives no matter how hard he stabbed, but armour always had gaps. In the crotch, behind the knees and elbows, around the throat. The soldier half rose to his feet, raised an arm to ward Kemir off and reached for his sword with the other. Kemir's first knife found the soldier's armpit, driving up into his shoulder. The soldier opened his mouth in shock, and Kemir drove his other knife down the man's throat. He pulled both blades out as the soldier fell, howled in exultation and looked for someone else to kill. Snow was a few hundred yards down the track now. She'd stopped and was sweeping the bushes with flames.

He remembered the soldier who'd dived into the gorse to escape Snow's tail.

Alive. We need one alive. Although it was hard to remember that through the haze of murder in his head.

Nadira was off Snow's back as well. He saw her in the gorse, lifting up a heavy stone and smashing it down again. He couldn't see what she was crushing. *Someone's head, most likely.*

He couldn't see any soldiers now. They were all gone, lost among the thorn bushes, most of them shattered or burned by

Snow's wrath. If any of them were still alive, they were hiding. You couldn't outrun a dragon.

'She can hear your thoughts,' he shouted. 'You can't hide from her.'

The dragon had finished burning soldiers. She came pounding back along the track, shaking the earth, past where Kemir was standing, back to the ruins of the burning wagons.

Alchemists. Where are they? She didn't make a sound, but the thought was so loud in Kemir's head that it made him wince. He started back towards the wagons as well. Snow was rummaging in the bushes, clawing out the half-burned bodies of the wagon drivers, the ordinary men who'd happened to be in the way. She gave each one a cursory glance and then tossed it into the air.

Dead.

When the bodies came down again, she caught them in her mouth and swallowed them whole.

Dead.

Nadira staggered out of the gorse onto the track. Her hands were bloody, her face a strange expression of exultant shock. She came towards Kemir. Her eyes were very wide.

Dead.

'I killed one!' She sounded amazed. 'I never killed anyone before, but I did it. I smashed his head with a rock.'

Dead.

The bloodlust was still there, still strong, but no longer overwhelming. Kemir took her hands in his. 'Do you know who these soldiers were?' She shook her head. 'These were Adamantine Guardsmen. The speaker's men. The best soldiers in the realms, or so they say. They train to fight dragons.'

Dead.

He looked around at the carnage and laughed. So much for the Guard, but then what were they thinking? What was anyone thinking? How could a man fight a dragon? How could even an army of men fight a dragon?

Dead.

He left Nadira to search the corpses for anything worth stealing and went to look at the weapon they'd used to shoot at him. It was smashed, crushed under Snow's claws as she'd run past, but the remains told him enough. He'd been right – it *was* a crossbow, the biggest one he'd ever seen. It probably took two men to even carry it. The mechanism for cocking it was splintered beyond recognition, but Kemir guessed it was some sort of crank. It probably took three or four soldiers to use the weapon. Grudgingly he found himself impressed that the soldiers had been quick enough to use it at all.

Alive! Kemir, there is one alive. Ask it! Make it tell you where the alchemists are to be found!

A shriek echoed between the mountains. A dark shape swooped out of the sky towards them. Kemir's heart sank.

Shit. Ash.

46

Ash

When he'd set out with Snow to find the alchemists, Kemir had soon realised that he didn't know where they lived after all. What he knew was that the blood-mages who had first conquered the dragons had lived somewhere in the north of the Worldspine, and that the alchemists had raised their stronghold in the same place. It had never occurred to him how vast the Worldspine was. They'd searched for days, and the mountains had stretched on forever in every direction they looked. The days had become weeks. All they ever found were bleak snow-covered peaks, lush forested valleys and, when they strayed close to the realms, occasional Outsider camps.

You lied to me. You do not know where the alchemists live.

All he could do was let Snow peer into his thoughts, let her see for herself that he'd never meant to fool her, that he'd always thought that his knowledge was enough. Sometimes, when she was angry with him, she was terrifying. It was hard to live with a creature that could extinguish him so easily, over which he had no power.

Because of your alchemists, it is my kind who have no power, she'd replied.

He'd gone into a couple of Outsider settlements with some of the weapons and money they'd stolen from Queen Shezira's dragon-knights. The first village had given him a cautious welcome and taken his gifts, but they hadn't known any more about the alchemists. The second had taken him captive. They probably would have killed him if Snow hadn't crashed in first. She'd destroyed the village and anyone who wasn't quick enough to run away into the trees. She was pitiless. Man, woman or child, if it moved, if it thought, it burned. Some of them got away, and Kemir almost had to beg her not to hunt them down. Snow had given him a curious look, an expression he'd come to recognise as a mixture of incomprehension and indifference. She'd let the survivors go in the end, but the memories made him shiver. They'd been Outsiders, which sort of made them his people. Snow didn't care. She'd squashed them with all the compassion of a child crushing ants.

They'd flown south again, deep into the Worldspine, still searching. There, Snow had spotted a lone dragon in the far distance. Kemir couldn't even see it at first but then made out a tiny black speck in the sky, miles away.

There is another dragon, Kemir. Alone.

'Where there's a dragon, there's a rider. Maybe *he* knows where the alchemists hide away.'

Snow climbed higher and surged through the air. The dragon-knight saw them coming but didn't seem particularly bothered until Snow swooped down and almost landed on his dragon's back. She ripped the knight out of his saddle. The other dragon shrieked and did what they always did – it dived for the ground. Snow banked into a steep spiral, following it down. This new one was shorter than Snow, but heavier, squat and compact. A war-dragon, Kemir decided. A poor one too, since its scales were a dull dark grey, almost black in places, and barely gleamed at all.

Alchemists! Where are the alchemists?

It took Kemir a moment to realise that Snow wasn't thinking to him, but to the rider she'd seized. The two dragons whirled towards the ground. Kemir's fingers gripped into Snow's scales. Riding behind him, Nadira's arms around his waist were like a vice, crushing the air out of him. The wind took his breath away. Nadira might have been screaming, but he didn't hear it so much as feel it reverberating through him.

Where?

His heart almost stopped as the ground hurtled towards him – he could almost believe that Snow was so set on having an answer to her question that she hadn't noticed – but, as always, at the last moment she spread her wings and he nearly fell off her back, and then they were suddenly down on the ground.

The near-black dragon was eyeing them mournfully. Snow hurled the rider at it. The beast sniffed the body and then curled up around it, head held erect and alert. It never blinked, Kemir noticed.

Your kind are too fragile, grumbled Snow.

'Did you get an answer?' Kemir was shaking and Nadira was sobbing. He badly wanted to get off Snow's back and feel the solid ground beneath his feet, but the sight of the other dragon made him stay where he was. For all he knew, Snow might simply fly off and leave him there.

I might, conceded Snow. *You have been little use to me.*

Kemir tried not to think about that. 'Well, did he tell you anything or not?'

No. He was in pain and fear and then he died. I saw a place in his mind, very briefly. It is somewhere in the realm of one of your kind called Valgar.

'King Valgar.'

You know this man?

Kemir couldn't help but laugh. 'He's a king, dragon. He wouldn't spit on my corpse, much less know me. I know where to find him. It's north again. Where we've already looked.'

Then we will look again.

He sighed, ready for Snow to take to the air straight away expecting to find the alchemists before the sun set. And then when she didn't, she'd fly into a rage, and he and Nadira would cower and pray to whatever gods might hold sway over a vengeful dragon, and he'd wish that Sollos was here because somehow Sollos had always known what to do.

'I should run off and leave you,' he muttered.

I would not let you, Kemir. Not now.

But Snow didn't take off; she cautiously stepped closer to the other dragon.

Get down and hide among the trees for a while. This one has a deeper rage than mine inside it.

They didn't fly away to continue the search that day, nor the next, nor the one after that. Instead, Snow stopped looking for the alchemists and stayed with the dark dragon for a month. Sometimes she ignored him for days at a time. She hunted alone and brought back food for the other dragon. Kemir, in his turn, hunted with his bow. He kept himself and Nadira alive. The mountain valleys were cold and wet and treacherous. Ordinary men died in places like this, but there was always food and water, and shelter as well, if you knew where to look for it.

Finally Kemir decided he'd had enough. He'd barely even seen Snow for four days, and the two dragons were flying together now.

'They don't need us any more,' he said to Nadira. 'They've forgotten us. When they remember, they'll eat us.'

They packed what little they had and left, striking west. He didn't know where they were, but the Worldspine ran from north to south, so heading west was bound to take them back into the realms sooner or later.

Snow caught them three days later. She landed as close as she could, while the other dragon circled over their heads.

There are two of us now. Her thoughts didn't seem angry, but Kemir felt the conviction behind them.

'Is that one of you for each of us?' he asked. He couldn't help himself.

There is one harness for your kind. It is of no consequence to me to wear it.

'And what if I don't want to ride you.'

Ash will burn you where you stand.

'Ash?' Kemir glanced up. From below, the war-dragon simply looked black.

Ash. That is the name your kind gave him, and now that he has awoken, he hungers for the same vengeance. So, Kemir, will you ride with us?

'Do I have a choice?'

You always have the choice to die.

Wearily, Kemir climbed up the ropes onto Snow's back. It took him a good part of the day to adjust Ash's harness so that it fitted her properly and didn't threaten to tip them out every time Snow launched herself into the air. They turned north once more, Ash flying alongside them. The black dragon made Kemir's skin crawl. Snow's indifference was bad enough – but to Ash, Kemir and Nadira simply didn't exist. His thoughts, when he spoke to Snow, were clear enough. Men and women were food, nothing more.

They resumed their search. One fruitless day passed and then another, and then, in the middle of the wilderness, Snow spied a cluster of wagons driving along a hidden track.

Amid the burning wreckage Snow rose onto her hind legs. In her foreclaws she was holding a body. *Alive! Kemir, this one is alive. Ask it! Make it tell us where the alchemists are to be found!*

Kemir shouted, 'Then put it down before you break it!' As he walked towards her, Ash swooped low over the track.

Hungry!

Snow looped her tail around one of the bodies and hurled it into the air. Ash caught it on the fly.

You should have waited, Ash thought reproachfully. *The smell of them burning has given me an appetite, yet you've left me nothing to sate it. At least, nothing still breathing that I can chase.*

Kemir shivered.

Soon. Snow cocked her head as Kemir came closer, and gently lowered the twitching soldier onto the ground in front of him.

'I said don't break him,' Kemir growled. 'When you want to know something, all you have to do is pick someone up and shout inside their head. When they've stopped screaming in terror, the next thing they'll do is tell you anything you want to know. Even if they lie to you, you'll know it. What you don't do is crush his ribcage while he's still shitting his trousers.' He looked at the man and cursed. 'You're as impatient as a two-year-old.'

Snow snarled at him. *I am seven years hatched, Kemir.*

'You're as impatient as a *human* two-year-old. You have to wait until whoever you've got can properly understand what's about to happen to them. *Then* ask your questions.' He turned quickly away and knelt beside the soldier. If Snow decided that now was finally the time to eat him, he didn't want to see it coming. 'Have you got any more? This one's probably past caring.'

No. Make this one tell me what I want to know!

The soldier was coughing up frothing blood. Snow had caved in one side of his chest. It was a miracle the man was still alive.

'Soldier?' Kemir got down onto his hands and knees so he could talk into the man's ear. 'Soldier? Can you hear me? What's your name?'

The soldier mumbled something that Kemir couldn't make out.

Iyan. He knows himself as Iyan of the house of Liahn. Next to Snow, Ash came to watch. The war-dragon looked bemused. Then he seemed to sneer and turned his attention to the bolt still embedded in Snow's shoulder.

'Iyan? The dragons are their own masters here. They mean to burn the alchemists. Every one of them. They will stop the alchemists from making their potions. All the dragons will be free. They'll burn us all. Every man, woman and child, every last one of us. No matter what it costs us, we must not let these dragons know where the alchemists are. Do you understand? If you know where they are, you must not even think about which way they are to be—'

That was as far as he got before a claw came down, and Ash drove the crossbow bolt into the soldier's chest, pinning him to the ground. The soldier gasped and was still.

Clever, Little One. Very clever.

'Well I hope he had a good think about all the things I told him not to tell you before you skewered him.' Kemir backed away from the dead soldier. Ash had never even acknowledged him before.

When we have all we need from you, I will 'skewer' you too. The dragon gestured with a wing along the track. *That way. I have seen a place in his mind.*

Ash didn't bother to wait, but that didn't matter since he was slower than Snow in the air.

As Kemir and Nadira strapped themselves into the harness on her back, Snow spoke in his head again. *When you spoke to the broken man and told him of the things that would come to pass, and that he should not tell us or help us, I could not tell whether you were speaking only to trick him, or whether you meant every word. Which is the truth, Kemir?*

Kemir grunted. 'I don't know. I couldn't tell either.'

47

Alliance and Betrayal

'The trouble is,' drawled Prince Jehal, 'that I'm simply not important enough.' He was lounging against the battlements on the top
of the Tower of Dusk, quietly enjoying himself.

The night air was cool and fresh and clear. If he looked over
the wall, he could pick out the night-watch patrols in the City of
Dragons by the light of their lamps. Beyond the city the moon
shimmered in the sky and in the Mirror Lakes below, and then
the Purple Spur rose like a black wall, creeping up from the
horizon into the sky, eating the stars as it went. Queen Shezira's
feast had been sublime, far better than Speaker Hyram's. He felt
sated, serene and relaxed. It helped his mood immensely to see
that Queen Shezira was anything but. She paced back and forth
across the top of the tower, face set in a deep frown.

He smiled. 'Hyram is a bastard,' he added. 'Did you know
he summoned me here about Queen Aliphera, and then when I
dutifully came, he tortured me? I wasn't going to make anything
of it when it looked like he was going die very slowly and miser-
ably. Didn't seem much more I could do than nature had already
done. Now, though ...' He shook his head and sighed. 'What
difference can *I* make? Hyram will oppose your challenge and so
will his family. So will Zafir, and so will Narghon and Silvallan.
So should I. A speaker from the south is overdue, and I've no
reason to dislike Queen Zafir. As I said, the trouble is that I'm not
important enough.'

Queen Shezira stopped her pacing and looked at him directly.
They were alone on the battlements by her insistence. No one,
she said, was to hear what they had to say to each other. Even
the rooms below the roof had been cleared, and the stairs were

guarded by her most trusted rider. And one of his as well, so they could keep an eye on each other.

'You're important enough. I already have King Valgar and one other that I can count on. Valmeyan won't be here and so won't have a say. Neither do the Syuss. I only have one question for you. What do you want?'

Jehal's smile widened. 'I told you, sweet Queen. The trouble is, I'm not *important* enough.' He met her gaze. If she was too stupid to understand what he meant, she didn't deserve his help.

She wasn't stupid. Slowly, she nodded. 'The Speaker's Ring. You want to succeed me when my years are up.'

'That would be a most enticing prospect.'

'And the most obvious demand. Yes.'

'And will you make Lystra your heir? To take your crown when you take Hyram's ring. So she need not worry so much about my rabble of half-cousins sniffing after my father's throne?'

She pursed her lips. 'Perhaps. If you'll give me your word to pass the Speaker's Ring on to Lystra when your time is done, and let Almiri become Queen of Sand and Stone in her place.'

Jehal nodded, then made a show of looking concerned. 'Wait. Begging your pardon, Your Holiness, but isn't all this the same assurance that Hyram gave to you. His word?'

'Are you calling me a liar, Jehal?'

He folded his arms. 'Let's just say I'm still a little irked that you dismissed me from Hyram's table two nights ago. One might have the impression that you think Hyram is right, and that I *am* poisoning King Tyan. Perhaps I've been poisoning Hyram as well, who knows? But if you did think such a thing, I would have to wonder as to the worth of your promises. Your word given to a prince may bind you, but your word given to a poisoner? I don't think that means very much to you.'

'If I had thought there was any truth to Hyram's suspicions, I would never have given you my daughter, Jehal.'

A warm feeling spread out from somewhere deep inside him. Jehal smiled again. 'Thank you, Your Holiness. I cannot describe how grateful I am to know that. You will declare me your successor when you make your challenge? In front of everyone?'

'Yes.'

Jehal bowed. 'Then King Tyan's vote will be yours, Your Holiness.'

'Good. Our business is done. Return with me to the feast, if you will.'

'Leave me here a while, Your Holiness. My mind is filled with ways to turn Silvallan and Narghon against Hyram and Zafir. Your victory would surely be even more pleasant if the two of them stood alone. I will rejoin you shortly, Your Holiness.'

Shezira hesitated, then nodded. Jehal watched her go, sinking slowly down the stairs into the guts of the tower. As soon as he was alone, his eyes shifted. He looked across the Tower of Dusk into the palace beyond, to the tall and slender Tower of Air, which looked down on everything. He was smiling.

'Speaker. At last. So sorry, Zafir. Nothing personal.'

Then he turned to look out to the mountains, leaning out over the stones, wondering what it would feel like to know that everything he could see was his.

He didn't look down. If he had, he might have seen a tiny pair of glittering ruby eyes.

48

The Eyrie of the Alchemists

Princess Jaslyn was the first to see the smoke. It hung, a slight haze staining the air, a mile or two ahead of them. When she waved at him and pointed, Semian saw it too. As they got closer, he made out the remains of the wagons on the ground, and the gleam, here and there, of shattered swords and armour.

The three dragons split smoothly. Semian and Jostan dived low, one to the left and one to the right. Silence and Princess Jaslyn powered up. While she circled overhead, the two knights swooped over the battle site from opposite angles. They made a second pass and then climbed back to Princess Jaslyn.

'Wagons and soldiers. All dead,' shouted Rider Semian at the top of his voice. 'Dragon attack.' He had no way of knowing whether Princess Jaslyn had heard him. There was a crude sign language that all dragon-riders learned, but it didn't cover things like this. The best he could do was: *Friends. Dead. Dragon spoor.*

He heard Jaslyn shout something back, but all her words were stolen by the wind. She signed: *How long?*

One hour. Two hours. 'Recent. Not long ago.'

Danger?

No. 'Whoever did this, they've gone.' Or at least he hoped so. There wasn't any sign of anything alive and moving on the ground, and whoever had burned these men could be miles away by now.

She told him to land and followed him down while Jostan circled overhead. They dismounted and picked their way through the wreckage. Parts of the wagons were recognisable – scorched axles and wheels. Most of the rest was charcoal and ashes, some of it still too hot to touch. There were a lot of bodies. *No. Bits of bodies. Soldiers.*

'These were the speaker's soldiers,' said Princess Jaslyn. With a start Semian realised she was right. Adamantine Guardsmen. Most had been eaten, and all that was left were hands and arms and legs and pieces of crushed armour chewed and spat out. The few bodies still in one piece had been burned and crushed. There was one impaled to the ground by one of the Guards' own scorpion bolts.

'They're all dead, Princess,' he said, and she nodded. 'Do we search for who did this? They cannot have long gone. They may be resting their dragons or letting them hunt.'

'Or they may be gone.' Jaslyn shook her head. 'We go on as we were. We'll tell the alchemists when we reach them. Once my mother is speaker, she'll put an end to these outrages.' She walked back to Silence and climbed onto his back. 'We fly at three levels now.'

Semian nodded. Three levels meant that one of them would fly close to the ground and the other two much higher, separated by thousands of feet and impossible to surprise all at once. Which was Jaslyn's way of saying she thought they were in some danger. They took to the air once more. Jostan stayed high, so Semian flew low, with Princess Jaslyn somewhere between them. Flying in the middle put her in the safest part of the formation, but also meant that they were relying on her eyes to spot any danger. Semian tried not to think about that and concentrated on following the rutted track leading to the alchemists' stronghold. In a lot of places it was almost invisible. It vanished into wooded vales, twisted over flat slabs of rock and skulked under overhangs, almost as if it had been designed to be difficult to find and almost impossible to follow.

Late in the afternoon the track led Semian over a high pass and down into a lush green valley. A village lay spread out beneath him nestled against a rushing river and surrounded by fields and cattle. The track followed the river, past the village and through a stretch of woodland. The sides of the valley grew steeper and closer together until he was flying between two sheer walls of rock hundreds of yards apart. The cliffs were pitted with fissures stained with streaks of black and dark green. Tiny trickles of frothing water bubbled over the cliff edge and dissolved into clouds of spray. In every possible crack stunted trees and bushes struggled to grow.

The cliffs came steadily closer together. Semian could feel Matanizkan's unease. She didn't like flying in such a confined place.

Abruptly, the cliffs closed completely. At the base where they joined, a loose collection of stone buildings hugged the rocks. Among them Semian could see the mouths of several caves, shafts of darkness disappearing into the earth. The river vanished into one of them; beside it was an eyrie, small but unmistakeable. There were no dragons.

Matanizkan pulled up. There was nowhere left for her to fly. The walls of rock spun wildly as she pitched over. For a moment, Semian was hanging upside down; and then she'd turned and was diving towards the valley floor. Semian gritted his teeth and gripped his harness. Somehow she found the space to spread her wings and levelled out, her claws skimming the ground.

'Down,' he told her, and she seemed almost grateful to land and catch her breath. He stayed in the saddle and walked her slowly back to the head of the valley, to the eyrie. By the time he got there, several alchemists were waiting for him. There were soldiers too, and several scorpions pointed in his direction. Cautiously he dismounted. He glanced up for Jostan and Princess Jaslyn but couldn't see either of them. Sandwiched between the walls of rock, he couldn't see much of the sky at all.

'Rider Semian in the service of Queen Shezira,' he called. The soldiers relaxed as he walked away from the dragon, and one of the alchemists approached.

'Keitos, senior alchemist.' He bowed. 'Apologies, Rider. We had no warning you were coming, and these are troubled times.'

Semian wasn't sure what Keitos meant by that but kept his silence. They walked away from Matanizkan. 'I'm riding escort to Princess Jaslyn. There is one other dragon-knight as well. Rider Jostan. They'll be arriving shortly.' He forced a grin. 'Interesting landing.'

Keitos nodded gravely. 'It was certainly an unusual approach. You haven't been here before, then. This is place is difficult for dragons. That's one of the reasons it became a stronghold for us in the old times, before our order mastered them.'

Back when you were blood-mages. But reminding the alchemist of his order's sordid origins would have been poor behaviour for a guest, so Semian held his tongue. They waited at the edge of the eyrie as Matanizkan was lured out of the way. Eventually, he saw Jaslyn and Jostan flying down the valley towards them. They'd clearly seen him almost crash into the cliff and even Jaslyn was coming in low and slow. They landed gracefully, one behind the other, and dismounted. Keitos left Semian and went to greet them. When the alchemist returned with Jostan and Princess Jaslyn, he looked grim. Jaslyn was telling him what they'd passed on their way.

'Everyone was dead,' she was saying, 'and it was clearly a dragon attack.' She looked at Semian. 'Would you not agree?'

Semian nodded. Keitos bowed his head. 'And the wagons, Your Highness?'

'Everything was destroyed. You know, I imagine, that several of my mother's knights were attacked some months ago.'

'We are aware, Your Highness. One of your dragons was never found.'

'A perfect white. We're still searching for her.'

Keitos nodded vigorously. He led them into a crumbling stone longhouse. Semian noticed that the roof leaked. Everything here was damp.

'We don't have much by way of lodgings, Your Highness. There are a few rooms but ...'

Jaslyn waved him away. 'We won't be staying long, Master Keitos. I have something of a mystery to show you. When you can tell me what it is, we'll be on our way. I hope to leave at first light tomorrow.'

'A mystery?' Keitos paused and his eyes lit up. 'How unusual. I'm sure Your Highness will be most well received. Forgive me, Your Highness, but since many of our elder masters are now guests of the speaker for Queen Shezira's accession, might I ask why you came here? I'm sure their knowledge of potions would have sufficed.'

'It's not a potion, Master Keitos. It is something more like liquid metal.'

Keitos bowed. 'We shall do our best, Your Highness.'

'Good. And you will do it today, and then I will leave in the morning with all the proof I need to destroy Prince Jehal forever.'

For the first time since they'd left the palace Semian saw something like a smile flicker across Princess Jaslyn's face.

49

The Dragon-Priests

Hyram stood at the window of the Tower of Air. Over on the Tower of Dusk he could see two figures on the battlements and nothing more. Then Zafir wrapped the black strip of silk around his eyes and he was *there*, clinging to the stonework only a few feet from Jehal. He couldn't see much, until the end when Jehal leaned out and stared over at the City of Dragons. But that didn't matter. He heard it all. Every word. Even after Jehal had gone inside and there was nothing to see except the stars in the sky and nothing to hear but the wind, he stood there, silent and motionless. He felt as if his heart had been turned to stone. Very slowly he took off the silk.

'She's going to make the Viper speaker after her,' he said. He still didn't quite believe his own ears. Shezira was almost a part of his family. It was unthinkable that she'd do such a thing, and yet he'd seen it. He'd *heard* it.

'I told you she would plot against you.' Zafir's soft hands took his.

'But the *Viper*. How can she?' He shook his head in disbelief.

Zafir stood close beside him, close enough that he could feel her heat. She was wearing a thin silken shift that clung to her in the breeze from the window. 'Your family gave her their word that she would follow them. She's a proud and stubborn queen.' Zafir shook her head. 'And look at how much she's prepared to give him. She almost makes him king of her own realm while he waits.'

'I would have had one of her daughters succeed you as speaker. She herself, if she was still sound of body and mind.' Hyram wrung his hands. 'Why? Why did she have to betray me like this? With the *Viper* …'

'It doesn't matter, my lover. Whatever you decide, I will be there for you, and surely you can rely on your own clan. What does Shezira have? King Valgar and King Tyan?' She snorted. 'Not enough.'

'Jehal will bring Silvallan and Narghon with him.' He shook his head. If Zafir hadn't been holding him, he would have been pacing back and forth. He should have thought of this. Stupid to let Shezira see what was coming, and now he was going to pay for it.

'No.' Zafir squeezed his shoulders and whispered in his ear. 'I can promise you at least one, if not both.'

'How?' Still, no decision was made. He could always name Shezira, as he'd first intended. He could still marry Zafir and live out his years as a king. Would that be so bad?

'Trust me, Speaker Hyram.' Zafir slipped the black silk out of his hands. 'I need to bring back my little spy.' She wrapped the silk around her eyes and moved to stand right in front of him, facing the window, leaning very slightly into him. 'Hold me,' she breathed. 'I lose myself sometimes when I do this. Don't let me fall.'

'Yes, of course.' One hard push and she'd fall out of the open window. The ground was a hundred feet below. She'd be smashed to pieces. *Just like Aliphera.*

No. He couldn't let Jehal win. He couldn't change his mind. Not now.

'Hold me tighter.' Zafir was pushing herself into him, swaying slightly, gently grinding against his groin. She might have been doing it deliberately or she might not; either way, he felt himself respond. His arms reached around her, pulling her closer still. His fingers caressed her skin through the gauze of her shift. She was shivering.

'Are you cold?'

'No.' She took one of his hands and moved it slowly over her until it reached her throat. She held it there. 'If you thwart Prince Jehal in this, you'll be the centre of his life. Everything he does will orbit around the hate he'll have for you.'

Hyram nuzzled her ear and whispered, 'Not for long. You'll hang him for the murderer that he is.'

'Will I? I steal the potions that keep you a man from Jehal, but he's the one who knows what they are, and only he knows where they come from. Tell me, Speaker, what means more to you? Is it me? Is it Jehal? Or is it the potions? Would you give them up for all this? Would it be worth it?'

Hyram didn't answer. A decade ago he might have said it was Jehal and vengeance that mattered the most. Two decades and he would have said Zafir and the smell of her skin. Now, though ... He closed his eyes. The potions. It was the potions.

Zafir gripped him tightly. 'I know. I understand. Just remember that we might need Jehal for a little while longer, until we can find out where he gets them.' As she spoke, a little golden dragon fluttered through the window on metal wings and settled on the bedpost. Zafir moved his hand down to her breasts. 'Close the shutters. What's done is done. Queen Fyon is Jehal's aunt. She'll try to sway King Narghon behind Jehal. I can do something about that. You make sure of Silvallan and your cousin. That will be enough for us.'

Hyram reached to untie the knot in the black silk around her face, but she turned deftly to face him and took his hands in hers.

'Let it stay there. I'd like to watch with the dragon's eyes.'

She pulled him onto the bed, and as he pulled back her gown and pushed his way inside her, he forgot about Jehal and about the potions and there was only her. With the silk covering her eyes, it was easier to see Aliphera's face gasping beneath him.

He tried to slip out of her bed in the middle of the night, but she pulled him back and made him forget himself until the sun was creeping over the horizon once more. Then she slept, and Hyram lay wide-eyed and awake, staring at the ceiling, and at the two pairs of ruby eyes that stared down from the bedposts. Hadn't there been only one mechanical dragon the night before? He tried to remember and found that he couldn't. When he looked at his hands they were shaking. Not a lot, but enough that he could see it. Fear gripped him. Potions! He needed another draught already.

He dressed quickly and hurried away to his own rooms. The potions were still where he'd left them, waiting for him. He gulped down a mouthful and looked at what was left. Slowly but surely they were running out. He was getting through them faster than he had at the start.

Best not to think about that. Once all this was done, once Zafir was the next speaker, he could concentrate his energies on the alchemists. Find out what these potions were and where they came from. Make as much as he'd ever need. Yes. That was the way it would be. And he'd have to make Zafir speaker, because if he didn't, what then? To lose her was to lose everything now.

The potion took hold of him. The shaking went away and he felt strong again. He dressed himself properly and hurried to the Glass Cathedral, then stood at the altar and waited. He tried not to remember being here months ago, at his weakest, with Queen Shezira standing over him, cold as ice and hard as stone.

'Lord Hyram.' Out of the dark recesses of the church, the dragon-priests filed towards the altar. They formed a circle around him and bowed as one. They never once spoke of it, but he could feel their hunger for him, urging him to go the way of the speakers of old, on a pyre lit by dragon fire, his charred remains to be carted to the eyrie as fodder for the beasts.

'High Priest Aruch.' Hyram didn't bow. As speaker he was bound to respect the traditions of the Glass Cathedral, but as plain Lord Hyram he would treat them with the disdain they deserved. 'I have not come to be reforged, if that's what you're hoping.'

Aruch didn't move. 'Your Lordship was so close to the ultimate mysteries,' he whispered. 'So close. Closer than any speaker since the time of the Narammed. You are fallen, Lord Hyram. Fallen by the hand of woman. So tragic. You could have been one with us.'

'Oh please, anything but that. Cut out my organs while I'm still alive and take them to the eyrie. Even that would be preferable.'

'Your words are meant to wound, but you cannot pierce our scales, Lord Hyram. We pity you, now and forever.'

'You can do something else for me, Aruch, *if* you can spare the time. I intend to marry the woman you so despise.'

'We know. We are prepared. And we do not despise Queen Zafir. We despise no one, and all are welcome within our walls. Always.'

'Well, there will be a lot of us within your walls and sooner than you might have thought. The wedding is to come forward. Tomorrow, at dawn. Everyone is already here, so why not.' Yes. It was an impulse, but it felt right. Bring it forward, if only by a day. Let everyone know. Let the battle lines be drawn. Let all his enemies array themselves out in the open where he could see them. Antros would have done the same, and Shezira too. So be it. Hyram turned and strode out of the circle of kneeling priests.

'Some even find comfort here, if you remember,' murmured Aruch as he passed.

Hyram snorted.

'Some will, some won't. It will be interesting to see, don't you think?'

'Thy will be done, Lord Hyram. Thy will be done.'

As he left, he felt the priests silently rising and returning to their shadows.

50

Rebirth

They left the wagons still burning, the soldiers all dead and broken. Nadira watched as they shrank away into nothing, until even the pall of smoke was gone. She was a survivor; she prided herself on that. She'd had a husband, four children, the pox; she'd lost herself in Soul Dust and been attacked by dragons, raped by their riders and she'd survived it all. She thought about surviving for a long time as the dragons flew, and she thought about the soldier she'd killed, hammering his head with a stone until there was nothing left of his face. It had left her with a strange feeling, an empty floating sensation that she didn't understand.

She had no idea where they were any more except somewhere in the Worldspine. The mountains she was used to were huge towering things that glowered at one another and kept their distance across deep wide valleys. Here, everything seemed all squashed together. The mountains were piled up right next to each other, sometimes on top of each other. The valleys were more like ravines. No one could live here. Or that's what she thought until she saw the village.

The dragons passed over it and then turned and soared away. She could feel their excitement. No thoughts came to her but she knew they'd found what they were looking for. They spent the rest of the day hunting, gorged themselves, and when they were done they curled up on a tiny plateau to sleep. Nadira sat resting her back lightly against Snow's scales. The air up here was bitterly cold, but in places the dragon was almost too hot to touch. Kemir stood up, strung his bow and went off. She understood men like Kemir. He was strong. He brought food. He kept her alive and made her feel safe, and in return she would stay close to him. If he asked, she would close her eyes and imagine herself somewhere far away and give herself to him. As far as Nadira knew, that was the way of the world for someone like her, as good as it could be. She should count herself lucky.

He came back an hour later empty-handed, looked at her and shrugged an apology, then walked off again. After a while she got up and followed him. He was standing at the edge of a precipice looking out at the mountains. Away from the dragons, the cold air quickly worked it way through her clothes to her skin. She shivered and huddled next to Kemir.

'There's no food up here,' he said. 'We go hungry tonight.'

He didn't speak much, and usually she was glad of that. The dragons spoke even less. The white one said things to her sometimes. The black one only spoke as though she wasn't there. Hearing them inside her head had been a terror at first. Now, when they flew into a rage she flew into one too; apart from that, she barely noticed. They were all quiet company. She liked that, but not tonight.

'I've been hungry before. This is it, isn't it? They've found what they're looking for.'

Kemir nodded.

'Good.' It ought to frighten her, but it didn't. Instead, she felt a sharp stab of anticipation.

'Might be. Might not be.' Kemir shrugged. 'When they've done what they've come to do, I don't know what happens to us. They might leave us here. They might eat us.'

'I don't think so. We'll find some way to be useful to them.'

'We should run away again. They might not look for us this time.'

Nadira put her arms around his shoulders. 'Come back to the dragons. I'm cold.' When he talked at all, Kemir mostly talked about running away. She wasn't sure how much he meant it. They'd tried it the once, and that was all.

He shook her off, so she went back to the dragons on her own and curled up beside them to sleep. Kemir came back a few minutes later. He lay next to her, wide awake, staring at the stars.

'I was born in a settlement,' he said. 'I lived there until I was fifteen. Then the King of the Crags came. He was only a prince then. I wasn't there. I should have been, but I was off larking about with one of my cousins. When we came back, it was all gone. Nothing but ash. All we had was each other. On the day that you first saw me, they'd just killed him too. I can't run away. Not now. I want to see it all burn. They know that too, Snow and Ash. They know I'll stay.'

Ash had started to snore. The sound was so deep that she didn't hear it so much as feel it gently shaking the mountainside.

'Riders came to my settlement too,' she said quietly. 'It was deep in the forest. Everyone thought we were safe. It was all trees. There was nowhere nearby for a dragon to land. Didn't help though. The trees weren't big enough. They found us and burned us through the leaves and branches, and then the dragons crashed into what was left and knocked it flat. The riders came after us, those they hadn't burned. Everyone was either killed or they took us as slaves. I wasn't good enough to be a slave. Too old, too ugly, too something. They took my boys though, the ones they didn't kill. I saw them.' Her eyes glistened. That was the one memory she hung on to, watching her two boys, one eight years grown, one ten and almost a man, being dragged away. They'd been weeping and cowering, but it was a happy memory in a way, because at least they might still be alive, even if they were chained to the oars of a Taiytakei galley somewhere.

'They did what they always do,' she said quietly. Kemir was still staring blankly at the sky, so she lay down next to him, forced herself to rest her head on his chest and run her fingers though his hair. 'When they were done with us, they killed all the other women too old to be sold. But not me. They took me back to their castle and helped themselves whenever they wanted. After a few days I must have bored them. They took me back to where they'd found me and left me there in the cold ashes to die. The others were still there, their corpses already chewed to the bone. I suppose they thought that some snapper would find me before I could reach another settlement.'

Kemir muttered something and draped an arm over her shoulder.

'The snappers must have eaten their fill. But it was all wrong after that.' All wrong because she was useless. She was too old and no one wanted her. Among the settlements a woman on her own could mean only one thing. She'd moved from one place to the next, never staying long, selling herself to stay alive, stealing when she could, until she got caught and sold to a Dust gang. She didn't remember too much for a while after that, just doing everything they asked. Anything.

'Whatever it took to get more Dust,' she breathed, and felt a pang of craving inside her. Even thinking about it, even after all this time ... 'And then they had enough too, and left me for the snappers again. Them or the cold.' She laughed bitterly. 'Snappers don't like me, I suppose. Too skinny. Not good eating. I thought I was seeing things. There was a huge white dragon. And then there was Kailin Scales. And then there was you, and then Kailin Scales went away, and I was still alive, and even the Soul Dust was gone, as much as it ever can be gone.'

And she'd survived.

She felt the rise and fall of Kemir's chest. He was sleeping. She rolled away and lay next to him, watching the stars, feeling the heat from the slumbering dragon on the other side of her. She ran a hand over Snow's scales. They should have run away. They both knew it. They should have left when Snow found Ash. Right then, when the dragons were so distracted they might have got away. Instead they'd waited too long. Now the dragons would never let them go, but it didn't bother her; if anything it made her feel special. There were worse places to be.

Snow was deliciously warm. She could feel the sense of purpose that filled the dragons now, even while they were sleeping. It hadn't been there the day before. It was infectious. She wanted to *do* something. She had no idea what. She'd never had a purpose before, never had time for it. Not starving, not being eaten, not dying of cold and exhaustion – all that had been purpose enough. Suddenly she didn't have to worry about those any more.

Kemir had a purpose. The dragons had a purpose.

She'd thought about that all through the day, as the mountains grew shorter and steeper and sharper and more pressed together.

'I want to help kill the dragon-knights,' she whispered. She wasn't sure if she'd meant it for Kemir or for Snow, or whether she was simply speaking to the wind. 'Every one of them,' she added. 'I want to kill them all.' This surprised her. It wasn't the purpose she'd expected. Maybe it wasn't her purpose at all. Maybe the dragons had made her want it, in the same way that when they grew angry she grew angry too. Or maybe she'd caught it from Kemir. In the end it didn't really matter, did it?.

Nadira hunched her shoulders and closed her eyes. She made herself small and snuggled next to Snow. The dragons were dreaming, and from their dreams she knew exactly what was coming.

Yes. There were far worse places to be.

Returning the Cinders

There is one last price a dragon-rider must pay. When a dragon finally dies, it burns from the inside so that all that remains beneath the scales is charcoal and ashes. The scales survive. They are light and strong, and above all fire and heat will not penetrate them. Thus they are much sought after as armour. When a dragon dies and only the scales remain, the rider must gather them and return them to the eyrie and the dragon-king from whence they came. Thus the dragon returns to the place of its birth. Only from the cinders, say the alchemists, can a new dragon be born.

51

The Alchemists

Jaslyn had come to see the alchemists once before. She'd been thirteen years old. Lystra was eleven, Almiri sixteen and very soon to be wed to King Valgar. They'd come with their mother and Lady Nastria on the backs of two dragons, both dead now. Jaslyn's memories were of huge dark caves and wizened old men and damp stone, and of Almiri being unbearable. Their mother had taken them down through endless tunnels to a place that had never seen the sun, lit only by a few lamps. The rush of some underground river had echoed everywhere they went. They'd come out into a huge cavern, and her mother had pointed at the purple stains on the walls.

'This is where our power comes from,' she'd said. 'These tiny little plants. The alchemists make them into potions. The Scales feed the potions to our dragons. The dragons do as we command them. Without these little plants we are nothing. Remember that, always.'

Jaslyn had hated every minute of it, but what she had hated most was the thought that her dragons did as she asked of them because of some little plant. They were supposed to do it for *her*. For their love of *her*.

She was older and wiser now, but the feeling was still there, and it hit her in the pit of the stomach as soon as she landed. *I hate this place.* She looked at the cave mouths and trembled, and so it was a relief when Keitos led them through the jumble of stone houses instead. He bowed and nodded his head and mumbled platitudes, none of which she really heard, and took them into a squalid little hut where an old man sat at a bench squinting through a piece of coloured glass at a leaf. They stood in the doorway and waited, but the old man didn't seem to notice them. He just looked at his leaf. He was deathly pale, and all that was left of his hair were a few white wisps.

Eventually Keitos coughed.

'I know you're there, Master Keitos.' The old man didn't look up. 'I know you have visitors too. Three dragon-riders. I felt them land. Whoever you are, you'll just have to wait.'

'This is Princess Jaslyn, Master Feronos, daughter of Queen Shezira, our next speaker. Soon to be our mistress. With her, Rider Semian, also in Queen Shezira's service.' Jostan had stayed at the eyrie to see their dragons were well cared for.

The old man sighed. He stared at his leaf for another few seconds and then put it down and looked at them. 'Princess Jaslyn. Yes. You came once before with your mother. Five years ago, in the winter, when we were all covered in snow. Yes, yes. I remember.' He didn't get up or bow, or do any of the things Jaslyn was used to. 'Shouldn't you be at the palace?'

Jaslyn stared at him.

'Master Feronos is the wisest of us in the lore of stones and metals,' said Keitos nervously. He shuffled his feet and took a step into the room. 'Her Highness has brought something that she says is a mystery, Master. A liquid that is like metal.'

'A liquid that is *like* metal or a liquid that *is* metal?'

'Prince Jehal may be poisoning Speaker Hyram or King Tyan with it. Maybe both. And someone has used it to try and poison my mother,' snapped Jaslyn. She pushed Keitos out of the way and thrust the clay pot, still sealed with wax, in front of the ancient alchemist.

A gnarled, trembling hand reached out and took it from her. Feronos wasn't ready for how heavy it was. It tumbled from his fingers, and Jaslyn barely caught it before it smashed on the floor.

'Ahhh.' The old man nodded. 'I know this. It's been a long, long time since I've seen it. It doesn't surprise me that you don't know what this is. There aren't many that would. You have to be old like me to remember.'

'You haven't opened it, old man.' Jaslyn clenched her fists. 'How can you know what it is when you haven't even opened it.'

Silently, Feronos put the pot on his table and broke the seal. Very carefully he opened it. 'A metal that gleams like silver and runs like water. Very heavy. Nothing quite like it. Very hard to find.'

'I know *that*.' Jaslyn stamped her foot. 'Where does it come from? Who made it?'

'No one *made* it, girl. You cannot *make* this. As for where it comes from …' He shrugged. 'Not from within the realms we know, I can tell you that. We had some once. It came across the sea, I think.' His brow furrowed. 'Oh, now … who was keeping it? Not here. Somewhere in the west. Old Irios had some in Shazal Dahn, but he's gone now. Long gone.'

The old man seemed to drift away.

Keitos bit his lip. 'Our stronghold in the western deserts,' he said reluctantly. 'We like to keep it a secret.'

'But that's …' Jaslyn's gaze shifted to Semian. 'That's Speaker Hyram's realm!'

'It was a long time ago,' whispered the old man.

Jaslyn rounded on him.

'But it's poison, yes? It *is* poison?'

He shrugged. 'Drink enough of it and you'll sicken. Like a lot of things. Irios liked to work with it, but he went mad. They say the liquid metal did it to him. Sailors used to bring it to him. The alchemist's disease, they call it. Old age I say. Couldn't stop shaking. In the end he just walked out into the desert and never came back. Or that's what someone told me once, I think. Fumes in the air. But not a poison. Not unless you want to spend a decade waiting. No. Quicker to let age take its course, I would think.'

Jaslyn gripped the table. The world seemed to spin and rush around her. 'No. It *is* poison. Alchemist's disease. That's what Almiri called it too. And King Tyan, yes, he's been dying of it for nearly a decade, and Hyram, he's been ill for more than a year. Slowly getting worse. It *is* a poison. It *is* Jehal.' She clenched her fists. 'He's killing them so slowly that they don't know they're being murdered. Hyram has the right of it, and no one else believes him!'

Master Feronos carefully sealed up the pot and put it on the floor. He seemed slightly disappointed. Jaslyn strode back out of the hut and filled her lungs with fresh air.

'Highness!'

'Rider Jostan!' She looked at him in surprise. 'You're supposed to be at the eyrie, seeing to it that Silence is cared for exactly as I requested.'

'Highness, there are other dragons nearby. The white has been seen.'

Jaslyn blinked. 'What? Here? With the alchemists?'

'No. But two dragons were seen near the village a few hours before we came. A black war-dragon and a white hunter. It can only be ours. There *are* no other whites.'

She snorted. 'And who told you this, Rider Jostan? A peasant already in his cups? A farmer? Or was it the village idiot?'

'Your Highness, a captain of the Adamantine Guard. A legion of them protects the alchemists' redoubt.'

'I've never heard of such a thing. Nor did I see any Guard as we flew in.'

'They camp within the forest, under the cover of the trees.'

Jaslyn shook her head. 'No matter. We must return to the palace at once. Go back to the eyrie and have our dragons readied. Queen Shezira is on the point of making a pact with Prince Jehal. We must be back before the speaker is named. So we must leave *now*.'

Jostan looked unhappy. 'Your Highness, by the time the dragons are fed and readied the sun will be almost set. I beg you, please do not camp in the wilds of the mountains in the middle of the night while there are other dragons nearby. We do not know if they are friends or enemies or what their purpose is, but if one is the white ... Remain here, Your Highness, in safety. We can leave at first light and still be back in time.'

'Rider Jostan is right,' said Semian from behind her. 'We will fly with you if we must and die to defend your life, but it is unwise to leave in such haste.'

Jaslyn growled and clenched her fists, but they were right and she knew it. She stamped back into the hut and snatched up the pot of poison. *The Viper's venom.*

'Very well. First light. Not a moment later.' She swept up her cloak and marched away, striding impatiently across the ground without knowing where she was going. *Nastria should have come. Too many mysteries. Wait, wait, wait; we should leave now; I should be with mother. And what does Jehal get from poisoning her ten years from now? Why would he do that?*

And why is the white here?

52

First Light

A low droning hum filled the Glass Cathedral. Hyram and Queen Zafir stood on either side of the altar. They wore jewelled dragon masks and and long robes of gold and silver leaf that flowed and spilled across the floor. They were supposed to stand absolutely still, like statues, while the sun rose, until the first light of the day spilled in through the windows.

Shezira watched them carefully. She'd been through the same ordeal when she'd married Antros. She'd had to be still for nearly half an hour, and apart from giving birth to their daughters it remained the hardest thing she'd ever done. Antros, of course, had fidgeted constantly. Now Zafir was so still that she might have been made of stone. Hyram, she thought, was trembling very slightly.

The droning of the priests grew very slightly louder. The sun was nearly at the window. Shezira glanced over her shoulder. Jehal was sitting somewhere at the back with King Tyan. Tyan had gone into one of his moaning phases, and she could hear him even over the hum of the priests. If he was trying to say something, he'd long ago passed the point where anyone could understand him.

She'd made a point of going to see King Tyan and spending some time with him. He seemed to recognise her. He couldn't talk and hardly moved, and when he did, he trembled so violently that everything around him went flying. Yet she couldn't shake the feeling, when she looked into his eyes, that he was still in there somewhere, hopelessly alone and mad with despair. Afterwards she'd found it hard to be angry with Hyram any more. She'd even suggested to Jehal that he should give Hyram some of his secret potions himself, that they should make peace, but Jehal had only shaken his head.

'Never,' he'd whispered. He was doing everything he could to discover how Queen Zafir had stolen them. It was all her doing. She had an iron wickedness inside her. A true dragon-queen.

Shezira looked at her, across the altar, trying to see it, but she could never get past how young Zafir was. *Too young to be a speaker.*

Finally, the first light spilled in and struck the altar. The priests stopped their moaning and closed in around Hyram and Zafir, waving their arms up and down, reaching for the sky and then the earth and then back to the sky. Whatever the symbolism of all these rituals, Shezira doubted that anyone but the priests understood it. No one cared about the dragon-priests any more.

They backed away and fell to the floor, leaving Hyram and Queen Zafir standing alone in the orange dawn light. The masks were gone. They each reached out one hand towards the other, their fingers touched, and it was done. They were bound together, joined as one in the Cathedral of Glass, never to be split apart. Hyram was a king again.

Afterwards, as the kings and queens walked amid a surfeit of petty princes towards the enormous breakfast feast that awaited them, Almiri fell in step beside Shezira.

'Is King Valgar well?' asked Shezira. They both knew she wasn't enquiring about his health.

'Resolute. King Tyan?'

'Bought.'

'King Narghon?'

'Will do whatever Fyon tells him to, and Fyon has always doted on her nephew. Silvallan's going to be the hard one. He has reasons to be friendly to both Hyram and Zafir, but if Hyram's cousins turn against him, Silvallan will go with the tide. What have Sirion and his court got to say for themselves?'

Almiri pursed her lips. 'They've said very little.'

'Yes.' Shezira glowered at Hyram's back, some yards ahead of them. 'He's put them in a difficult position. He was their king before he became speaker, and acts as though he still is. But he's not the one who will suffer. If he gets his way and names Zafir, he'll stay at the palace. Sirion will remain on the throne and wear the crown, but Hyram's shadow will still be there. What does he do? He's an honourable man, I know that. Hyram's breaking a pact that their grandfather made. He needs to understand that I'll win without him and without Silvallan if need be. But it would be much better if the dragon-lords were united.'

Almiri smiled. 'Hyram's not quite himself. Ten years of peace and harmony shouldn't be ruined by one mistake of judgement. Let Zafir be the villainous witch that she is. Who can say what else she might put in the potions she feeds him? And she says she steals them from Prince Jehal, but does she?'

'King Tyan has hardly made a miraculous recovery, has he?' King Valgar was watching them. Shezira nudged Almiri away. 'Go back to your husband.'

'There is one thing, mother.'

'Yes?'

'Prince Dyalt needs a bride. I know Hyram asked after Lystra a year or more ago.'

'Yes, and I told him that Lystra was already taken. I thought Dyalt was supposed to marry some Syuss princess.'

'He was, but she died. Drowned in a lake. You know what the Syuss are like when they see water. Besides, Dyalt is the king's youngest son and so not far removed from the throne. His father thinks he ought to do better than one of the Syuss, and I think you should offer Jaslyn's hand for Dyalt.'

Shezira snorted. 'Would they have her? Just as well I sent her away.'

'You bought Valgar with me and Jehal with Lystra. Jaslyn is your daughter and your most likely heir. Dyalt could be marrying himself to your throne, and if you do become speaker, they will wonder which one of us will succeed you.'

'Will they?' Shezira tried not to laugh.

'They can always hope. Mother, they'll have her.'

'Dyalt is fourteen; Jaslyn is too old for him.'

Almiri laughed and shook her head. 'Mother, how old is Hyram? How old is Zafir? Make the offer.'

'No.' Shezira shook her head. 'No, I can't do that.'

'Why, mother? Why?'

'Because that would be far too direct and Hyram would be certain to learn of it.' She grimaced. '*You* make the offer. I have made no decision as to who will succeed me, but by all means let them think it will be Jaslyn. For the peace of the realms. If they stand by the pact, and only if they stand by the pact.'

Almiri's eyes sparkled. She smiled and turned away to walk at her husband's side. Shezira went on alone. She wondered about her daughters sometimes. Were they all they seemed to be, or did they manage to hide some part of themselves, even from her? Offering Jaslyn to Dyalt was a clever ploy. Jaslyn would probably never speak to either of them again, but Dyalt could hardly say no.

My most likely heir? She chuckled to herself. *You all have to get rid of* me *first.*

53

The Fire Within

The dragons took off as soon as the sky was light enough to fly. The very tips of the mountains shone like they were on fire, while the slopes below were still dark with shadow. Snow and Ash knew exactly where they were going, which was more than Kemir did. He tried to spot the alchemists' valley, but the first he knew of it was when Snow flew between two mountains, over the top of a narrow cliff, and plunged vertically down.

Walls of rock raced past on either side. He tried to breathe, but the wind was icy; it ripped the breath out of his lungs and brought tears to his eyes. He could see the ground hurtling towards him, blurred shapes rushing at him, and then Snow shuddered and he closed his eyes as the wind suddenly stopped and the air became blistering. She shot over the ground, pouring fire over everything. Ramshackle buildings made of stone, trees, little yards, men running screaming to get away, the flames engulfed them all.

There were dragons on the ground. Snow banked sharply, heading towards them. Three figures hurled themselves flat as she flew over them, scorching the ground where they lay. As one, Snow and Ash spat fire at the three dragons below. The dragons shielded themselves with their wings.

'Do dragons burn?'

Only our eyes. Soon there will be three more of us that are free. Ash landed in the makeshift eyrie, smashing buildings with his tail and burning anything that came out of them. The three harnessed dragons all watched, alert and wary but otherwise still. Snow stayed in the air, circling back round.

I knew those dragons before I awoke. I remember them.

Kemir glanced down as Snow flew back over them. They were

hunting dragons, he could tell that much. Otherwise, they looked the same as any others: dark grey or black scales with occasional flashes of of deep metallic blues and greens, all three of them. Just like the dragons from the camp in the mountains.

He started in surprise as his eyes shot to the three figures Snow had burned. Instead of lying still and smouldering in the dirt, they had got up and were running. One of them seemed to have a slight limp.

'It can't be ...'

Snow strafed them once more, and again they threw themselves to the ground. This time Kemir got a better look at them. They were riders, all three of them. Dressed in their dragonscale armour, which explained why Snow's fire wasn't putting an end to them. Two of them had large shields which they held up to deflect the worst of the blast. Kemir kept his eyes on them as Snow passed. As soon as the dragon was overhead, the three riders got up and started to run again.

'Rider Rod!' Kemir felt breathless. 'Luck *is* with me today. Let me down, Snow. Let me down! *Now!*'

No. She flew back over the buildings. Most of what would burn was already ablaze. Kemir tried to keep his eyes on the three riders. Among the wreckage, men were still running about, most of them dashing for the shelter of a few large caves. Snow landed amid the ruins and Kemir lost sight of the riders behind a cloud of smoke. It was hard to do more than simply hold on as Snow bucked and lunged and lashed her tail and burned whatever lay before her until finally everything was still.

'*Now* let me down.'

The dragon ignored him. She trotted to the largest of the caves, where a river poured out of the cliff. She stepped slowly inside, splashing through the water. The entrance was large enough, but it quickly shrank. She squeezed in as far as she could and gushed fire into the depths.

Minds. I sense minds in here. Many of them. Many have escaped. Many are still alive.

They must all burn. The ground shook as Ash ran in from the eyrie. The two dragons surveyed the caves, then, one by one, burned them out.

They are still there. I feel them. Ash pawed at the ground. *Let them taste our fire!*

I cannot reach them.

Then we will wait, and sooner or later they will starve.

'Let me down! I'll go in there and get them out for you.' The last he'd seen of the three riders, they'd been heading for the cave closest to the eyrie. He couldn't see their bodies, which meant that they must have reached it. That or Ash had simply eaten them.

Snow stamped with frustration. She lowered herself onto all fours and let Kemir slide down to the ground. Nadira stayed where she was. She frowned at Kemir as if she disapproved. He ignored her and ran to the cave where he thought the riders must be, but then hesitated. Three of them and one of him. Poor odds.

He crept slowly in. The sun only reached the ground outside at its zenith; inside, the cave grew very dark very quickly. He touched the walls, feeling his way forward. They were warm and dry from Snow's breath. That would tell him how far her fire had reached. It would tell everyone inside as well. They'd know how deep they had to go.

About a hundred yards into the cave it became too narrow for a dragon. Another hundred yards and the walls weren't warm any more. Everything was pitch black except the circle of daylight behind him, yet when he squinted he thought he could see lights ahead of him, faint pinpricks of white light that looked more like stars than like lamps or torches. He moved slowly, feeling for each step with his feet, creeping silently forward. The pinpricks became brighter. They were lights, definitely lights. Which made him wonder how many other people might be hiding in this cave.

In the nearest of the lights he caught a faint glimpse of a face. He raised his bow, but the figure wasn't wearing the armour of a dragon-knight. The face vanished; the light bobbed and moved away.

Kemir moved faster, fumbling silently through the darkness

towards the light. Whoever he was following stopped by the next light and took that too. And the next and the next. Kemir was close enough to see that the lights were like little lamps, but their flame was a cold white and he didn't smell any smoke or oil. The man carrying them wasn't a soldier and didn't seem to be armed. Kemir drew a knife then sprinted the dozen yards between them. The man heard him at the last moment and turned around as Kemir bundled into him, knocking him down and sending the lamps flying. In an instant he had his knife at the man's throat.

'Please please please ...' The man was weeping with fear. There was a bad smell.

'Three dragon-knights came this way, didn't they?'

'Yes. Yes. I don't know who they are. Please, please don't kill me.'

'Where did they go?'

'I don't know.' Kemir pressed the knife harder against the man's skin. The man squealed. 'Deeper! I don't know. Into the gatehouse.'

'Gatehouse?' Kemir felt a sudden coldness inside him. 'How many other people are down here?'

'I don't know!'

'Then guess.'

'I don't know, I don't know. I'm just a servant. Please ...'

'One? Two? Ten? A hundred?'

'A hundred? More, I think. I don't know. Please.'

A hundred? Kemir's eyes grew wide. He slowly withdrew his knife. 'Soldiers?'

'Yes.'

'How many?'

'I don't know. A century? A legion? I don't know!'

A legion? In these caves? That can't be right. Still, a dozen, even half a dozen, was quite enough. Kemir gripped the man by the throat and hauled him to his feet. 'One of the dragon-knights is called Rider Semian. Tell him that Kemir, the sell-sword who ruined his leg, is outside waiting for him.'

He let the man go, picked up one of the lamps so he could see where he was going, and started back towards the entrance to the cave. He didn't run. In fact a part of him wasn't sure he wanted to go back at all. The dragons weren't going to like this. If they meant to starve this lot out, they were likely to be in for a long wait. And so far they hadn't exactly impressed him with their patience.

54

The Two Speakers

In the middle of the ten-sided table lay the Speaker's Spear and Ring. Hyram was on his feet; everyone else was watching him, waiting for him to sit down. Some of the dragon-lords looked bored, some looked impatient, some were simply annoyed that he was taking so long. He was shaking again this morning. Only a little bit, but Shezira could see it. Either the potions that held his sickness in check were losing their effect, or he was running out.

Opposite Hyram sat Acting Grand Master Jeiros and High Priest Aruch. On each other side of the table sat a dragon-king or -queen and one other knight. That was all. Two sides were empty. The Syuss had few dragons and were invited to the palace only as a courtesy, and the King of the Crags had held himself aloof from the rest of them for over a generation.

Shezira couldn't help but stare at the ring. *Seven of us, then.* Her hands gripped the table. She'd been waiting for this day for a decade. She'd done everything right; even this foolishness with Queen Zafir seemed nothing more than a last test to see if she was worthy of that ring. Sitting at the table, staring at it, she could almost believe that Hyram was testing her, nothing more, that Zafir wasn't even real.

Hyram finally sat down. Jeiros stood up and made a speech. Aruch followed him. They were the same speeches that were made every ten years. Jeiros spoke of responsibilities and burdens. Shezira knew all the words, yet now they were meant for her she found herself soaking up every one of them. When it had been Hyram, a decade ago, they'd simply been dull; this time they made her skin tingle. When Aruch spoke of humility and the grace of the dragon-god, she didn't roll her eyes as Jeiros did beside him but found herself wondering: *Is it true? Could it be the priests who keep the dragons at bay? Do the potions only work because they will them to?* Stupid thoughts that she would have laughed at on any other day seemed suddenly profound.

She pinched herself. *You're the Queen of Sand and Stone, the Queen of the North, not an idiot princess seeing her first dragon.*

When it was Hyram's turn again, he spoke of everything he'd done in his time at the palace. He spoke of peace and prosperity, of the unsurpassed strength of the Adamantine Guard, of the value of continuity. Then, in the same voice he'd used to inventory the armoury of the Guard, he named Queen Zafir as his declared successor and sat down. It took Shezira a second to realise what he'd just said, that he'd actually done it and broken their pact, that it wasn't a test after all.

Sirion will back me. Valgar too. And Jehal and King Narghon. Silvallan if he knows Zafir's cause is lost. The silence lasted for a second, then another. Everyone was looking at her. Hyram's mouth was slightly open. Anticipation shone in his eyes. With a start she realised that she still hadn't said anything. At the end of the table Jeiros was staring at his feet. He had two rolled-up scrolls in front of him. He reached for one.

'No,' she whispered. It took her another second to fully find her voice. When she did, she rose smoothly to her feet. There would be nothing hurried or angry about her. Her voice would be calm when she spoke. Almost gentle. As though she was chiding an errant child. Jeiros looked at her. He had the scroll in his hand now, the words to anoint the next speaker. She met his eye and shook her head.

With a sigh Jeiros put down the scroll in his hand and picked up the other one. Aruch rose beside him. They looked tired, Shezira thought. Almost bored. She suddenly realised that everyone had known this was going to happen. They might as well have rehearsed it. In a way, wasn't that what they'd all been doing for the last few days?

'Are there any other challenges?' asked Jeiros. When no one spoke, he went on. 'Seven times the anointing of a speaker has been challenged. Three times the challenge failed. Of the four that succeeded, three threw the realms into turmoil. Queen Shezira, for the good of the realms, will you withdraw your challenge?'

'No, Grand Master, I will not.'

'Then, Your Holiness, what is your challenge?'

'Hyram, there is a pact between our clans that was made generations ago. If you violate that, you sully us all. Wiser men and women than I decreed long ago that only a reigning king or queen may take the office of speaker. They decided this because they understood that to govern the nine realms a speaker must first prove themselves worthy. Queen Zafir does indeed sit on a throne and may make an excellent speaker – twenty years from now, when she has proved herself. I call on you to honour the pact between our clans and name me as your successor.'

'And who would be *yours*, Shezira?' hissed Hyram, glaring at Prince Jehal.

Jehal smiled back at him. 'Someone who is wise and able, Hyram, and who does more to earn the honour than spread their legs.'

Hyram shot to his feet. 'Viper!'

Shezira glared at them both. 'Prince Jehal, this is a sacred time. Show some respect.'

Jehal lolled his head. 'For what?'

Hastily, in the moment of silence that followed, Jeiros unfurled the scroll and read the text aloud: 'As was written in the time of Narammed, the word of the speaker has been challenged before the assembled Kings and Queens of the Nine Realms. This council will disperse and reform one day from now, at dawn, when a new speaker shall be chosen, by the word of the speaker, or by the vote of the Kings and Queens of the Nine Realms should the challenge remain.'

Jehal groaned and slumped across the table. Shezira wondered for one startled moment whether he'd somehow been poisoned, but then he raised his head. 'Do we have to? *Another* day of acting like startled rabbits? Not daring to eat anything, keeping away from high places, constantly being surrounded by our armoured dragon-knights.' He bowed at Shezira. 'As you say, Your Holiness, this is a sacred time, and I apologise for my previous words. But let us end this now, while we are all here and unquestionably alive. No more childishness. We all know where we stand.'

Shezira frowned. 'I sympathise, but there is a proper way, Prince Jehal.'

Lady Nastria leaned into her and whispered. 'You should agree with him, Holiness.'

Shezira looked at her. She cocked her head. *Why?*

Nastria drew closer. Her words were so quiet that Shezira could barely hear them. 'Because Princess Jaslyn will return from the alchemists at any moment, and when she does, Prince Jehal is finished. Use him now, Your Holiness, and then throw him away.'

'Are you sure of this?' she mouthed back.

'As sure as I am of anything, Holiness.' Nastria straightened and turned back to the table.

Shezira did the same. *Perfect.* It was hard not to smile. She looked at Hyram and then at Jeiros. 'I am agreeable.'

Hyram smiled back at her. 'No. I say we wait.'

Jeiros was looking at Queen Zafir. And Zafir was nodding. Jeiros appeared uncomfortable. 'Apologies, Lord Hyram, but this is a matter for the Kings and Queens of the Nine Realms. You no longer have a voice in this.' He avoided Hyram's gaze. 'Do any object?' When everyone was silent, he sighed. 'Very well. Queen Shezira, Queen Zafir, one by one you shall each call a monarch to your cause. Whoever the kings and queens decree shall be speaker.' As he finished, Shezira glanced at Zafir. *This is your last chance to end this, to avoid making a fool of yourself.* But Zafir's face was a mask. She met Shezira's eye for a moment and her expression didn't flicker at all. She walked slowly to stand in front of Hyram. Shezira took her place by the alchemist and the priest.

Jeiros bowed to her. 'Queen Shezira, you have issued the challenge. Which king or queen do you call to your side?'

'I call King Valgar.'

Valgar didn't bother to say anything. He simply got up and

walked to stand with Shezira. Jeiros bowed across the table to
Queen Zafir. 'Which king or queen do you call to your side?'

Zafir stayed silent; it was Hyram who answered. 'King Sirion.
My cousin.'

Sirion was standing right next to Hyram, which meant that
Hyram couldn't see what Shezira could. He couldn't see the
tautness in Sirion's face, the whiteness of his knuckles. When he
didn't speak, Hyram turned slowly to look at him.

'I'm sorry, cousin. I've always felt this crown wasn't really mine,
that I was taking care of it for you, waiting for this day. But a pact
is a pact. I must declare for Queen Shezira.'

The warmth of victory blossomed in the pit of Queen Shezira's
stomach. Two out of two. Hyram looked aghast, his face frozen
in horror. Even Jeiros looked stunned; in fact, the only one around
the table who didn't seem surprised at all was Queen Zafir. *Thank
you, Jaslyn. At last you've done something useful.*

'King Tyan,' she said. As hard as she tried to avoid it, her voice
held a tremor of victory.

Jeiros bowed to Prince Jehal. 'As King Tyan's regent, you have
the right to speak with his voice.'

'Yes, I do.' Jehal grinned. He stood up, leaned over the table
and looked straight at Hyram. 'Old man, you've slandered
me, you've even tortured me. I'd like nothing more than to see
everything you value turn to ash before your eyes.' He glanced at
Shezira. 'Your Holiness, will you name someone to follow you in
turn? Here and now? A pact, such as the one Hyram here seeks
to break? For what they're worth.'

Shezira nodded. 'You, Prince Jehal. I name you as my chosen
successor.' It left a sour taste in her mouth. *But if Nastria is right,
I can relieve myself of that obligation. When I go, Valgar can have it;
Almiri will take his throne and Jaslyn and Lystra could yet be queens.
Antros, if you're watching, I hope you're smiling.*

Jehal's smile, when he looked at Hyram, was so broad it almost
split his face in two. 'Does that please you? Without your treachery I would never have had this. You've betrayed your allies. Your
own cousins have turned against you. What possible reason could

I have to ally myself with you? Think about that for a moment. Because that is what I choose. I choose Queen Zafir.'

Shezira didn't move a muscle. She couldn't; Jehal's words had frozen her solid. She heard King Silvallan declare for Zafir as well, and then King Narghon, but it all seemed so far away that she barely heard their words. She couldn't think. For a moment the world seemed to fade completely; when it finally returned, Jeiros was halfway through another speech. He'd opened the second of his two scrolls, and Zafir was the next Speaker of the Realms.

55

Undone

When he was done, Jeiros took the ring from the centre of the table. He bowed before Zafir and put it on her finger. One by one, the monarchs knelt before her and kissed the ring.

Nastria watched as her queen knelt and kissed like the rest of them. With calm and dignity, as a queen should. It was the most inspiring thing she'd ever seen. *To be so noble even in defeat.*

More noble than she could ever be.

There would be a reckoning for this, she decided. No matter what Queen Shezira ordered her to do, there would be a reckoning. If she'd been a man, with a man's strength, she might have tried to kill Prince Jehal with her bare hands there and then. As it was, it would have to be something more subtle.

She wondered briefly whether any of what she'd seen between Jehal and Hyram had been real, whether it had all been an elaborate charade designed for that one moment of treachery. Hard to believe, but whenever Hyram was around, everything always came back to King Antros and his unfortunate demise. Was that what was behind this? Was that why he'd betrayed the pact between their clans?

In the endless hours that followed, Queen Shezira let nothing show. Nastria wanted to take the queen and whisper in her ear: *It can be undone. Zafir is named, but she's not crowned! Until High Priest Aruch hands her the Adamantine Spear in the Glass Cathedral in front of the full assembly of dragon-knights, it can be undone.* But there was never a chance; they were never alone. So she watched Prince Jehal and she watched Queen Zafir. There were games and entertainments, a display of courage and skill from the Adamantine Guard, tournaments of horsemanship for the lesser knights and of flying skills for the dragon-riders. Queen Zafir watched them with the same blank mask she'd worn in the Hall of Speakers. Jehal, on the other hand, was animated, excited, intoxicated with his victory. The two of them never looked at each other. Not once.

Jaslyn. Princess Jaslyn had the key. When she came back from the alchemists with the flask of liquid silver. With damning words, signed and sealed by the master alchemists of the redoubt, naming it as poison. One of Jehal's knights had gone with Tiachas. She would find him and bring him back for Master Kithyr, and then they'd uncover the true depths of Jehal's villainy. The queen would have to believe her, and then so would all the rest of them.

And then she saw Jehal pass close to Queen Zafir and whisper something in her ear. For a moment Zafir's mask cracked, and something electric flashed in her eyes. It lasted an instant, and whatever Jehal said could only have been a word. But Nastria wasn't watching his mouth, she was watching his hands; and for that instant, in the press of knights and lords, Jehal's hand had alighted on Queen Zafir's thigh and stayed there for a blink of an eye longer than it should. And in that touch Nastria saw it all, and understood that Hyram was the biggest victim of all.

She grinned. She had four more days before the ceremony in the Glass Cathedral. Quite long enough. Still smiling, she set herself to following Prince Jehal.

56

The Caves

Dawn at the bottom of the ravine came late, and when it came, rained fire. Jaslyn stood in stupefied disbelief as the redoubt erupted around her. She glimpsed two dragons, a near-black and a perfect white, *her* perfect white, and then Rider Semian threw her to the ground and lay on top of her as the very air burst into flames. All she could think of was the white dragon, and how long she'd been looking for it, then a blinding heat seared her face. Her dragonscale armour kept her alive, and when she opened her eyes again, she could still see. She could see the two dragons burning down the alchemists' eyrie. Swallowing the three other dragons there in clouds of fire.

Silence!

She wanted to run, to hurl herself between them and her precious Silence, for what good it would have done. Rider Semian, though, was already dragging her back.

'The caves,' she heard herself shout. 'We have to get to the caves!' She glanced back as she ran. Silence was still there, shielding his head with his wings, but otherwise immobile. While the attackers stayed in the air, that was all a trained dragon would do, and so she willed them down, willed them to bring it to teeth and claws and lashing tails. *Then* Silence would show them.

The white had a rider. No, two riders. Jaslyn squinted, trying to make them out. She frowned. The dark one didn't seem to have any at all. Which wasn't possible. She must have made a mistake.

They were coming back. This time Jaslyn didn't need any prompting to throw herself down, and this time she remembered to cover her face. For a second time fire washed over them. As soon as the dragons had passed, they were up and running again. They reached the nearest cave.

'Deeper,' she gasped. 'There will be markings on the wall when we're far enough to be safe. And lamps. Alchemist lamps.' They stumbled on into the darkness, groping for the walls. The floor of the cave was uneven and treacherous, but at last they reached a point where the cave narrowed. A little further on Jaslyn felt the marks on the wall that meant they were safe. Groping around on the floor she found a crate filled with lamps, and when she picked one up and gave it a hard shake, it slowly started to glow with a cold white light. She gave it to Semian, then took another for Jostan and another for herself.

'That was our white,' she said once they'd got their bearings. 'The white for Lystra's wedding. What's it doing here?' She looked expectantly at her two knights, but they were clearly bemused. 'What about the other one? That wasn't one of ours. Whose was it?'

Still no answer.

'Who was riding them? Who was on the back of the black? I saw two riders on the white but none on the black. Who were they?'

Semian grunted. 'Last anyone saw the white, she was with her Scales.'

'A Scales would not attack his own order.' Jaslyn held up her lamp and peered into the darkness. As she did so, the tunnel back to the cave entrance lit up with an orange glow and a blast of hot wind slammed into them. 'We need to go back out. We need to get to Silence and Matanizkan and Levanter. There are three of us and only two of them. We'll kill the riders and force them down.'

'Your Highness, it would be death to go back out there.' Jostan's voice was flat.

'Coward!' Jaslyn took an angry step towards him.

'Rider Jostan has the right of it.' At least Semian had the grace to avert his eyes from her. 'The alchemists have their own defences. If we go out there alone, the dragons will kill us before we can reach our own mounts.'

'They were attacking Silence!'

'They were burning the saddles and harnesses so that we couldn't ride them, Your Highness. Silence will not have been harmed. She is too precious.'

For a long time Jaslyn stared back towards the cave entrance. She could hear noises from outside now, but they seemed very far away, as though the dragons were occupied elsewhere. Surely there was a chance? She tried to think about how far they'd have to run to get from the cave to the eyrie. Even in dragonscale it could be done, couldn't it?

But not if their saddles and harnesses were destroyed, and Semian was probably right about that. She would have done the same if it had been her riding the attack. She breathed a long sigh and turned around.

'Very well. We continue. The caves all come together. We'll find the alchemists and the soldiers they keep here.' *Prince Jehal has done this. He must know why I'm here. He knows I've found out about his poisons. Well, I'll let the whole world know what he's been doing, and then no one will stand with him. Mother will be made speaker. She'll destroy him, and then Lystra will come home again.*

Walking through the caves was slow and tedious. The lamps gave off barely enough light for them to see their own feet, and though the floor and the walls were smooth, the tunnels sloped steeply up in places. At times the cave became almost a chimney, rising vertically. Metal rungs had been hammered into the rock, but in dragonscale climbing them was almost impossible. Jostan dropped his lamp, which smashed to pieces on the floor. Then they reached a place so narrow that they had to abandon most of their armour. Jaslyn tried not to think how she must look, still in her gauntlets and helm and boots, the rest of her in plain doeskin, a bright red stripe across her face where the flamestrike had penetrated her visor.

It seemed like they spent half a day wandering through the cave, but at last, stopping to listen, they heard the rush of water somewhere ahead and she knew they were close. A few bends later they saw light, the sound of the water grew louder, and the next thing she knew she almost pitched over the edge of a chasm. Semian's hand on her shoulder caught her just in time.

The alchemists had built their tunnels along the underground river, she knew that much. She got down onto her hands and knees and felt over the lip of the chasm until her fingers found what she was looking for: a ladder secured into the stone. The water was more than a hundred feet below, and the cleft in the rock so narrow that her back sometimes touched the other side as she climbed down the ladder.

At the bottom a walkway of wooden boards hung over the swirling river. Little niches were cut into the walls, and after ten minutes of walking, the niches had lamps in them, filling the chasm with their ghostly white light. Rider Jostan stopped at the first lit niche and took the lamp.

'Someone must have come this way to light these,' he said. 'We must be close.' Then he wrinkled his nose. 'Does anyone else smell something?'

Jaslyn and Semian paused and sniffed the air. 'Smoke,' they both said. Jaslyn wasn't sure what to make of that. Smoke meant fire, and her first thought was dragons, but after all this walking they couldn't be so close to the entrances to the caves, could they?

The second thing she thought of was a kitchen firepit. She was hungry.

At a narrow point in the chasm, a little further on, they found the alchemists. The lamps stopped, the wooden walkway ended abruptly, and a voice from the darkness above challenged them.

'Who are you?'

'Rider Semian, Rider Jostan and Her Highness Princess Jaslyn, in the service of Queen Shezira,' shouted Semian. His voice echoed around the caves.

'Hold the lamps up so we can see your faces.'

Jaslyn hoisted her lamp. Her tongue twitched, prepared to lash out at these idiots who were getting in her way, but she stilled it. She was tired, hungry, covered in bruises and scrapes from countless stumbles and falls, and the burn across her face was hurting.

The smell of smoke was stronger.

After a second, lights appeared above them and she could see a cluster of armoured soldiers on a wooden platform. They threw down a rope ladder. When Jaslyn reached the top, she saw that they weren't just any soldiers; they were Adamantine Guardsmen.

'Your Highness.' Their captain bowed. 'I'll send a man ahead of you so there are no more mistakes.' So that everyone knew she was coming, he meant.

'How many of the Guard are here?' she asked.

The captain bowed again. 'Before the attack there were close on a hundred of us, Your Highness. Now I'm not so sure.'

'A *hundred*? Then why are you here and not outside seeing off these dragons? There were only two of them!'

'Your Highness, we did fight, but the rider of the white dragon was too clever, and the black dragon ...' He took a deep breath. 'Your Highness, there was no rider on the war-dragon. We formed shield walls against their fire, but they didn't stay in the air. The black one came down and smashed our walls. It was killing with tooth and claw and that murderous tail. We lost between a third and a half our number.'

'I had three dragons out there.'

The captain shook his head. He didn't say anything, but his eyes said that the dragons were lost to her now.

'What is it, Captain?'

The soldier sighed. 'Your Highness, your dragons are with the others now. They're trying to smoke us out.'

57

Turning the Knife

Sometimes Jehal felt he would burst. Sometimes his own clever-ness seemed overwhelming. Hyram, Shezira, he'd played them both, and they still didn't even know how.

He dressed himself carefully. Two layers. On the outside he looked like an Adamantine Guardsman, with his heavy quilted coat and his colours and his helmet. If he took all that off, he might pass, in the dark, as a pot-boy. Pot-boys often ran errands at night. He knew; he'd sent Kazah off on enough of them, after all.

The moon was setting. He didn't know how late it was, except that he'd waited for more than half the night, and if he waited much longer he wouldn't have time to do what he wanted to do and be back before dawn.

He wrapped the white silk across his eyes for one last time and looked at Zafir, sleeping, through the tiny ruby eyes of his Taiytakei dragon. She was alone. Good enough.

No. He stared at her and then slowly undressed again. *Too dangerous. Not until after tomorrow. Not until all the other kings and queens have gone.* He didn't take the silk off, even once he was naked. Instead, he made the little metal dragon flutter across Zafir's room and settle beside her head. It pecked gently at her face until she stirred. When she saw the dragon, she smiled.

'It's the middle of the night.'

The dragon nodded. As Zafir reached under her pillow for her own strip of silk, Jehal looked over his shoulder. Two ruby eyes glowed at him in the dark.

'You're naked,' she whispered.

'I wish you were.'

'I wish I could touch you.'

Jehal sighed. 'Soon, lover. When Hyram's out of the way.'

The smile faded from her face. 'The potions are already losing their effect.'

'That's not right. There should have been enough to keep him going for another month.'

'Yes. You gave him too much, so I've been stealing them and watering them down.'

'*What?*'

Zafir rolled her eyes. 'I want it done and over, Jehal.'

Jehal growled. He started to pace the room. 'Why did you do that? He wasn't supposed to get sick again until this was all long done.'

'You ask me why?' Zafir sounded scornful. 'Do you have any idea how dirty all of this make me feel? Sometimes, after he's finished with me and goes back to his own bed, I make myself sick to force the nausea away.'

'But now you're speaker – unless you fuck it up in the next couple of days. Isn't that what you wanted?'

'No, Jehal, it's what *you* wanted. What I wanted was you. Hyram disgusts me. I have to writhe and groan and call him the king of my bed when all I want to do is break his neck. And he knows something now. I don't know how, but he knows something.' She frowned. 'Something he didn't know this morning. He was asking questions.'

'Questions?'

'About you. Someone's put it into his head that we might be lovers, Jehal. Of course he doesn't believe it, but he won't quite let go of it either. He's put men on my door. He was enough of a bore before; now he's intolerable. Get rid of him, my prince. I've had enough. You've got what you wanted, so now give me what *I* want.'

Jehal leered at the little ruby eyes that watched him from the corner of his bed. 'I would like nothing more, lover. Nothing more at all. Even thinking about it ...' He glanced down. 'Well, you can see for yourself.'

'Don't you want to be here? Next to me, feeling my skin?'

'I'd like to feel more than your skin.'

'Sliding under silken sheets together?'

'You know I would.'

'Then *come!* Now!' She pushed back the covers of her bed, slowly revealing herself to him. When they were at her feet, she lay back and ran one hand slowly from her neck down to the soft hair between her legs. 'Do I have to show you what to do?' she breathed, and then laughed as Jehal's Taiytakei dragon fluttered up into the air and flew erratically around in circles for a better view.

'We have to wait, lover. Wait until it's safe'

'No.' Zafir suddenly sat up and snatched Jehal's mechanical dragon out of the air. She blew Jehal a kiss and then everything went dark and muffled.

'What are you doing?'

'If I can't have you, you can't have me. I'm done with this. I'm tying your little toy up and putting him under my pillow. Then I'm going to take this silk off my eyes and go back to sleep, and if you want to see any of this again, you get rid of Hyram and your stupid starling-wife. And you do it soon, lover, or I'll do it myself.'

Jehal waited for a while, but all he heard was Zafir's breathing. After another minute he pulled the silk away from his eyes and took a deep breath. His heart was racing and his head spinning, and he wasn't sure whether it came more from lust or fury.

Get rid of Hyram. *She's too impatient.*

Could it be done? *If she does it herself, she'll botch it and every-thing will be for nothing.*

Could it be done?

He climbed back into bed and tried to sleep, but his head wouldn't stop. Thoughts blossomed and died faster than he could keep count of them. *Could* it be done?

And then it came to him, and he realised that yes, it could; and moments later he was asleep.

58

Patience

Kemir sat slowly whittling a stick into an arrow shaft. Somewhere nearby Nadira was pacing impatiently. Even from here he could feel the dragons' determination. Their focus on what they were doing was frightening.

When the alchemists had scuttled away into their caves, the dragons had been furious for a while, raging up and down outside, smashing the few buildings that remained intact, flying around the cliff face, searching for other ways in. Then they'd calmed down. Now they'd built enormous pyres at the mouth of each cave, set them alight, and were methodically blowing the smoke down into the tunnels. The frightening bit was that they'd been at it for two days, all five of them, without a pause for breath. Two of the new dragons moved from fire to fire, blowing the smoke. The other three went to and from the woods, tearing down trees to burn. Every few hours Snow soared up out of the valley. Sometimes Kemir and Nadira went with her. They flew above and beyond the ravine, looking for wisps of smoke leaking up through cracks in the ground. Whenever she found one, Snow sealed it shut, and then she'd circle for hours, looking for more. Kemir understood exactly what she was doing. He'd done it himself, except his victims had been rats and rabbits.

Ash lumbered past, dragging a fifty-foot tree towards the caves with his tail. The dragon looked at him greedily. *Kemir, I am hungry. Which one of you has more meat on you?*

'Me.' Kemir didn't bother to look up.

There's nothing left in the village, Kemir, and we need to eat.

'Then go and hunt.' When the dragons weren't tending to the fires, they were eating. In the first two days they'd eaten all the animals from the eyrie and the bodies of the men they'd killed. Today they'd gone back to the village at the mouth of the ravine. It seemed to surprise them that they'd found it deserted. The villagers couldn't have got far, but they had clearly had the sense to run and hide, and had even taken most of their animals with them.

'Hey, Ash,' shouted Kemir. 'You know, I'm hungry too. What does dragon taste like?'

The dragon paused in his labours and turned to look at Kemir. It was impossible to read anything from a dragon's face, but Kemir got the impression he was laughing.

Suddenly, the dragon froze. He dropped the tree and rose onto his back legs, staring intently towards the caves.

Kemir stood up as well, but he couldn't see anything through the rubble and the smoke. 'What?'

Ash began to run. *The smoke has worked. They're coming out!*

59

The Assassin

Side by side, two dragons shot across the Mirror Lakes. They barged and snapped at each other, looking for an advantage. Three more came after them, strung out in a line. Jehal squinted as they hurtled towards him, trying to work out which was which. Now and then he glanced sideways. Hyram was watching the dragons; so was Queen Zafir. In fact almost everyone was watching. The race was going all the way to the finish.

One person, though, wasn't watching the dragons. Among a group of messenger boys standing at the back among the guards, one wasn't jumping up and down and cheering. He was more interested in Zafir, and in him. Jehal smiled to himself. He wasn't sure who the boy was spying for, Hyram or Shezira. Both of them perhaps. In the end it didn't really matter. What mattered was who the boy really was.

The dragons were getting closer. An hour ago they'd launched themselves from the top of the Diamond Cascade. Ten immense wooden frames, each one a hundred feet high and a hundred feet wide, lay strung across the Hungry Mountain plains and around the lakes. Ten frames, one for each of the Kings and Queens of the Realms, and the last one for the speaker and her guests. Jehal was supposed to be out in the plains, at King Tyan's frame, but he'd quietly slipped away to be here instead. He'd made some effort not to be seen, but the boy had followed him here anyway.

Around him everyone was shouting. He peered over the water, trying to see whether there were any more dragons on their way, but there weren't. The point of the race was to fly through all ten frames. From the ground they seemed enormous; on the back of a speeding dragon they became suddenly small. Accidents happened. Sometimes a dragon would be lost, but more often a rider. Losing four, though … Jehal felt briefly wistful. He'd ridden in these races and knew exactly how the riders fought for position. It must have been a particularly good battle over the plains, and for a moment he wished he'd been there to see it.

He shook himself. The two dragons fighting for the lead were still neck and neck heading for the last frame. They'd reach the finish in less than a minute. Time for him to go. He slipped away while everyone was watching the finish, and almost no one noticed him leave.

Almost. As he scurried away into the woods Jehal heard the roar of the crowd reach a peak and then a crash as one or both of the dragons hit the frame. He felt a flash of irritation. They'd be talking about this race for years, and he'd missed it.

He peered around among the trees. As he did, two figures began to rise from the undergrowth; hastily Jehal motioned to them to stay hidden. 'Another minute,' he whispered as he walked past them. 'Dressed as a messenger boy.' He stopped for a moment and held the white silk up to his eyes. Zafir was already on her way, walking quickly with a pair of her riders at her heels. Doing her best to seem furtive. He put the silk away and crouched down amid the ferns and brambles.

'Have you got it?' he asked. One of the men handed him a large sack. He thought about reminding them all how dangerous their quarry was, but he could already hear Zafir coming along the forest path. She passed barely a yard from where Jehal was hiding. He held his breath and waited.

And waited.

He was on the point of reaching for the silk again when the messenger boy finally appeared, creeping silently down the path. Jehal tensed, ready to spring.

The boy must have had a sixth sense. As Jehal and his men launched themselves, he was already spinning around, jumping away with a knife in his hand. He lashed out and one of Jehal's men grunted and staggered. Then Jehal had the sack over the boy's head.

'It's a woman!'

'I know *that*. Pin her *down!*' Jehal hissed. She was deadly quick but no match for three strong men. 'Get her hands. And get that bloody knife off her!' For a few seconds the four of them wrestled in grim silence, and then Jehal punched at where he guessed the woman's face would be and the struggling stopped. Together they wrapped another sack around her waist, pinning her arms.

'Shit.' The wounded man was looking at himself, at his hands. His shirt was soaked in blood. He stood for another second and then slumped to the earth, lost among the bracken.

'Stay here,' growled Jehal. 'Deal with him.'

'He's dead, Your Highness.'

'Yes. Unfortunate. And he's a rider of Furymouth. We can hardly leave his body here, can we? Deal with him and then come back to me.' He searched the woman carefully for more knives, made sure her arms were properly pinned and tied a rope around her neck. Then he dragged her away through the trees. Whenever she seemed to be coming to her senses, he pulled on the rope and made her fall. *I don't need you looking pretty, not that you ever were. Just alive and able to run, that's all.*

He'd come to the woods the day before, looking to see how far he'd have to go. There was a long-abandoned forge not far from where the dragon race ended. With a cellar. At the time it had seemed perfect. It had also seemed a lot closer to the place he'd chosen for the ambush.

Finally, after it seemed he'd been dragging the woman for an hour or more, he reached it. He pulled her inside and threw her down the stairs to the cellar, then closed the door behind them. Finally he pulled the sack off her head and threw a bucket of water over her. He smiled and gave a little ironic bow.

'Lady Nastria. Queen Shezira's knight-marshal. What a pleasure to have your company at last. Shame about the circumstances.'

She looked at him. Her lips were broken, her face bloody and bruised. One of her eyes was already so swollen she could barely open it. She spat out a tooth and opened her mouth.

'Scream if you want, but no one will hear you. That's what all women do in the end, isn't it? Scream for help?'

Nastria closed her mouth. 'Traitor,' she slurred.

'Traitor? Me? Because I gave your queen my word and then didn't keep it? Just like Hyram, eh?' He laughed. 'Traitor? You don't know me, Knight-Marshal. Not at all. No, no treachery here. All I'm doing is righting a very old wrong.' He shook his head and sighed. 'I've been watching you. Would you like to see how?' Without waiting for an answer he took out the white silk and pressed it to her eyes. 'Look. Look hard. A little bit of sorcery that someone gave me. And don't pretend to be shocked. Does Queen Shezira know about your blood-mage?' He took the silk away. 'You understand, don't you, that I wouldn't have shown you that unless I was going to kill you?'

She looked at him, defiant and sullen at once. 'What do you want, Jehal?'

'Here.' He held out a cup of water. 'Water. I thought you might be a bit of a mess by the time I got you back. You know you killed one of my riders back there.'

Nastria looked at the cup and turned her face away.

'Lady, you and I both know that good poison is expensive and nowhere near as easy to come by as others may think. When I kill you, it'll be with steel.' He picked up a sword from the corner of the cellar and drew it from its scabbard. 'This was my father's, back when he could hold it.'

'Then get on and use it, Jehal. Your fate is already sealed and you can't change it.'

'I'd sooner destroy the palace itself than murder an artist such as yourself. But as I cannot have you following me... A lady knight-marshal. I've often wondered what it must be like for you, surrounded by riders who are all so much stronger. In full armour I imagine you can barely stand up. But you're quick, I'll give you that. And you can do something that almost no other rider could ever do: dress like a serving boy and slip through the palace, and no one gives you a second glance. Sometimes you're Lady Nastria, knight-marshal. Sometimes you're a pot-boy, a scullion, a maid.

I admire you, I really do. You and I are alike.' He smiled. 'If you want to be sure that something is done properly, there's nothing like doing it yourself.'

'How long?'

'How long what?'

'You and Zafir.'

Jehal laughed. 'A long time, Knight-Marshal. Long enough that we glance at one another in a way that only lovers do, no matter how much we try not to. It pleases me that you're the one to see through it. I suppose you've already told Hyram.'

Nastria shrugged.

'Well I'm going to feel very silly if you haven't.' He held out the cup again. 'Please.'

She spat and looked at him with scorn.

'No, you *have* told Hyram, and I know you have. "Your wife and the Viper, Lord Hyram. Watch them closely." That's what you said. He didn't take it very well. It's all falling apart for him, isn't it? He's ill again. The potions aren't working any more. Zafir is young and he's old. And then there was the vote. I wish, I really do, that I could have read his mind just that once. Just to know what went through it right then.'

'I know things, Prince Jehal. Things about the Taiytakei. Things you don't. They're not the friends you think they are.'

Jehal laughed. 'Poor Knight-Marshal.' He held out the cup one more time. 'Are you going to drink this or not?'

'Not.'

He nodded. 'It would have been a disappointment if you had. I don't suppose there's anything I could offer you that would make you betray your queen and bow your knee to me. To have someone of your abilities I would give a great deal. I'd have to know you meant it of course.'

Nastria simply stared at him. He knew that look. It was hatred.

He sighed. It would have to be the hard way then, and yet, in a way, that made him feel better. As he forced open her mouth and tipped the cup down her throat, he knew that he'd have felt dissatisfied somehow, if she'd crumbled.

She fought and spat, but she couldn't stop herself swallowing at least a little of the water, and slowly her struggles subsided. Her head lolled onto her chest. Jehal waited until she started to snore, and then tipped the rest of the cup on the floor and put his father's sword away.

'I told you it wasn't poison, Knight-Marshal. Although you're going to wish it was.'

60

The Embers

Tears streamed down Jaslyn's face. However much she wiped her eyes, it never helped because the smoke was always there. Semian had shown her how to breathe through a damp cloth like the others, and yet she was still constantly coughing. Even in the vast space of the central cavern, the air was becoming unbearable. Unpleasantly warm too, despite the river of ice-cold water running though the caves. Sooner or later the dragons were going to work out how to foul that as well.

'Turn back, Your Highness,' rasped Rider Jostan. 'There really is no need for this. Go back to the higher caves. Stay there with the alchemists. This is soldiers' work.'

She knew he was right. She didn't even have most of her armour any more. Yet, watching the figures moving through the smoke around her, she knew she had to go. 'Do you want to die slowly in this smoke, Rider Jostan? I, if I *must* die, will do so quickly and with clean air in my lungs.'

'The Embers will defeat the dragons, Your Highness,' said Semian quietly. 'One way or another.' That's what they called themselves, these soldiers of the Adamantine Guard. Jaslyn had never heard of them before, but she recognised their weapons. No swords or axes or daggers, only huge shields as tall as a man and giant crossbows that fired bolts as long as her leg and needed three soldiers at a time to move them through the caves. Scorpions.

'How many soldiers *are* there, Rider Semian?'

'I don't know, Your Highness.'

'Then guess. Sixty? Seventy?' As they stumbled along, the smoke grew thicker and the air hotter. Jaslyn had no idea where she was going. They were simply following the soldiers, and if they got lost they'd probably never find their way out. It wasn't a cheering thought.

'Around that number, yes.'

'Against five dragons. So twelve soldiers for each one. Do you think twelve men could ever defeat a dragon, Rider Semian? Never mind that there were a hundred of them and only two dragons in the first place, and they achieved very little then.' After their first meeting in the caves Jaslyn hadn't been allowed near the Guardsmen. They were a special legion, the alchemists said. The best of the best, trained from birth solely to defend the redoubt. They couldn't have a woman, even a princess, in their midst, she was told. And however much she insisted, the alchemists always found a way to stop her from talking to them. They never flatly refused, of course, but they might as well have done.

However special they are, they aren't going to win. Jaslyn's only hope was that she might be able to slip away in the confusion. Or get close enough for Silence to hear her voice.

'I suppose it *is* unlikely, Your Highness,' said Rider Semian reluctantly.

'They're not going to fight the dragons, Your Highness,' said Rider Jostan. 'They will kill the riders.'

Jaslyn shook her head. Rider Jostan hadn't quite understood what everyone else now knew, what the alchemists had explained with careful patience so there could be no confusion. That the dragons were acting on their own. That there were no rogue riders commanding Silence and Matanizkan and Levanter, but rogue dragons instead. Despite everything he'd been told, Jostan still firmly believed there were men outside, and all he had to do was kill those men and everything would be sorted out.

'One rider will do,' growled Semian. He understood perfectly; Jaslyn had seen his face when the message came to him. Someone *was* out there, and Semian clearly knew the man. Just a sell-sword, he said. One of the knight-marshal's more foolish ideas. He'd waved it away as unimportant, but his eyes were fierce.

They reached the river. The soldiers, apparently, were following it to get to the outside. As they left the vast space of the cavern and entered the river tunnel, the smoke grew even thicker and the air became scorching. Jaslyn could feel the hot wind on her face, steadily blowing in from the outside. Before long they were wading up to their waists in the freezing water and splashing it over their arms and faces simply to keep from burning. They didn't need their lamps any more; the caves and the smoke here were lit up by a flickering orange glow.

'They've lit a fire at the cave mouth, haven't they?' The thought hadn't occurred to her before. 'How are we going to get out?'

'The river, Your Highness,' said Rider Semian.

'They're going to swim? In full dragonscale?' Despite herself she started to laugh, but her guffaws turned into a coughing fit as the smoke choked her.

'Highness, they're not wearing dragonscale.'

'What?' She sat down at the edge of the river and splashed water in her face and down her throat until the coughing stopped. When she looked up, they'd lost sight of the soldiers in the gloom. Not that they needed any help to find their way out now they had the river to guide them.

'They are not wearing their armour, Your Highness.'

'Then they'll be killed before they even climb out of the river! This is futile! Madness.' Jaslyn punched the water. They'd come all this way, gone through all this pain, and now they'd have to make their way back through the smoke. They'd probably get lost in the main cavern, and even if they didn't, the smoke would get them in the end. Without armour the soldiers wouldn't last long enough for *anyone* to slip away.

'Perhaps not as futile as you think.' Rider Semian started to strip off his armour. 'Your Highness, it seems we will have to swim.'

'Swim *where*, Semian?'

'Past the fire at the cave mouth, Your Highness.'

'And then? Perhaps you think we could float down the river without the dragons noticing us?'

'That's exactly what I think,' said Semian. He picked up his shield and poked two fingers through a hole that had been cut through it. Then he showed Jaslyn the two straps around it. 'When the time comes, lie on your back in the water, Your Highness. Hold the straps and press your mouth to the hole. The shield will float, and you will be able to breathe. Don't swim, just drift. Let the water carry you away.'

'When the time comes?'

Semian finished taking off his armour and waded deeper into the water. 'If the Embers somehow fail, I will try to distract the dragons. If I can get close enough that Matanizkan hears my voice, maybe she'll still obey me. You'll know if I've succeeded. That's when you should go.'

'They'll catch you.' Jaslyn peered at Semian. She could only make out the shape of him in the haze now, head and shoulders still clear of the water. He was doing this for her, she realised. This wasn't some plan the alchemists had devised, this was *his* plan. He was doing it to save her. The revelation left her feeling strange inside. She half rose to order him not to go and then stopped. Either way they were most likely all going to die.

'Better to die on my terms than someone else's,' he said. Those had been her own words when she'd insisted on coming down with the soldiers and somehow trying to escape. He was almost naked, armed only with a sword around his waist, a bottle of something on a string around his neck and a shield the size of a door. Jaslyn watched speechless as he lay back in the water and pulled the shield over him.

Madness. She bit her lip and watched him go dutifully to his death.

61

Disintegration

Climbing the stairs to the top of the Tower of Air was harder than it had been a week ago. Halfway up, Hyram paused to catch his breath. He looked at his hands. They were trembling. He could feel it in his legs too, and it was starting to affect his speech again.

Is it harder because of the sickness, or because of what I know?

No, that wasn't right. He didn't *know* anything. He only suspected.

No, that wasn't right either. He *knew* that Prince Jehal had given him his support. He *knew* that Jehal had betrayed his pact with Shezira and made Zafir speaker. And he *knew* what Jehal had said, there in the Hall of Speakers, as he did it.

He knew too what had been whispered in his ear, that Jehal and Zafir were lovers. At first he had simply refused to believe it. Then he'd sought the source of this whisper. He couldn't be sure who'd started it, but it seemed to originate from the Tower of Dusk, which meant it came from Shezira. Sour grapes then, besmirching Zafir in a last desperate attempt to overturn the decision of the kings and queens? It wouldn't work. Silvallan wouldn't care and Narghon would probably be pleased to hear it.

It's too late, Shezira. I couldn't change it now even if I wanted to.

He started on the stairs again and eventually reached the top. Usually the tower was loud and busy with servants running up and down between the levels, but today it was quiet and almost empty. The doors to the two topmost floors were guarded. The soldiers hurried to let him pass but they weren't usually here. *I have to keep an eye on her. I have to know where she goes. I have to know what she does, who she sees.*

'My lord.'

He stopped. He'd been so lost in his thoughts that he hadn't seen Zafir. She was sitting in the little anteroom that separated her private rooms from the stairs.

'W-What are you doing out here?'

Zafir stood up. She lowered her eyes demurely and showed him what she had in her hands. 'Embroidery, my lord.'

'Embroidery?' Hyram shook his head. 'And I-I don't have to be your l-lord.' She'd taken to calling him that as soon as the wedding was over. He'd liked it at first, but now it seemed to make her into a servant. It was almost as though she was using it to build a wall between them.

'Isn't that what you want? Aren't I supposed to sit quietly in my nice airy tower, doing nothing very much while you rule the realms?'

'One of those r-realms is yours, Zafir. You don't have to relinquish it.'

'The other kings and queens will expect it from me. It is what the speaker is supposed to do, after all.'

'Y-You could be d-different—' He stopped himself. This was nonsense. This wasn't why he'd climbed the tower. 'Y-You sent word to me, my queen. A-About the potions?'

'Yes.' Zafir smiled and beckoned him into her rooms. Past the anteroom was another staircase that led to the very top of the tower, to the queen's dressing room. Beyond that, most of the rest of the level was one large open audience room. Or bedroom, as it had lately become. Zafir snapped her fingers. A man came running with a pair of goblets. He seemed rather large and ungainly for a servant, Hyram thought, and the face was unfamiliar.

'Your manservant is n-new.'

'He's hardly a manservant, my lord. He arrived very recently and brought a gift for you.' She took the goblets and offered one to Hyram, then sat down and picked up her needlework again.

'A g-gift? I know of no riders r-reaching my eyrie in the night.'

'*Your* eyrie, my lord? And I did not say he came on the back of a dragon.'

Hyram sniffed the goblet that Zafir had given him. His eyes widened. 'S-So you *do* have more.'

'Yes, my lord. Drink. There's plenty more now. I have reached an arrangement with Prince Jehal.' She glanced up at Hyram from time to time as she spoke, but mostly her eyes were fixed on what her fingers were doing, on the stab and thrust of the needle through the cloth.

'The Viper.' Even hearing his name was like being stabbed. 'W-What arrangement have y-you reached, my lady?'

'One that suits me, my lord.'

'There have been w-w-whispers, Zafir.'

'Whispers, my lord?' She stopped and looked up at him, as innocent as a child. For a moment Hyram wondered what he was doing. He had everything, didn't he? Everything he wanted. Why sully it with baseless suspicion?

But it was the Viper, and so he had to know, even if it ruined everything. 'Yes, my lady. Whispers. About you and J-Jehal.'

'The Jehal who murdered my mother?' Her eyes held him fast.

'I-I had not forgotten, my lady.'

'Drink your potion, my lord. Recover your strength a little.' She smiled, stood up and came towards him. 'It is true I have an arrangement with Jehal. If you want to know, I will tell you everything about it.' She briefly touched his hand, then went to stand behind him and put her hands on his shoulders. Hyram sighed and drank deeply as her fingers kneaded his muscles. 'You must be exhausted.'

'Yes.' Hyram put the cup to his lips and drained it. He could feel the potion coursing through him almost at once, hot and fierce.

'So here is the arrangement I have with Jehal. There will be no more potions for you. Not ever.' Her hands stayed at their work. 'Your sickness will take its course, just like King Tyan's has. I will be speaker; Jehal will be my lover. In time he will follow me. And you, my lord, will be kept perfectly alive, trapped in the prison of your own body, to watch it all unfold.'

A numbness filled Hyram's head. He had to run the words through his mind two or three times before he understood that there hadn't been a mistake, and that she'd meant every word. He lurched out of his chair and staggered forward. Something was desperately wrong. The room was spinning. He could hardly feel his arms and legs. As though ... He reached for her and she sprang away from him, snarling and spitting like an angry cat.

'Don't touch me! Never touch me!'

'T-The s-sickness ...'

'Is getting worse, is it? Yes, my lord, this potion is a little different. It'll happen much more quickly now. I pray that the Ancestors leave you as useless as King Tyan, and quickly.'

He had a dagger on his belt. Somewhere. He had to reach for it three times before his hands closed on the hilt. 'Y-You ... y-you ...' he gasped, 'vile ... w-wicked ...' There was a chair between them, but he had the dagger in his hand now. A huge pressure was building in his head.

'Me? And what about you, my lord?' she hissed and darted away behind a table. 'You betrayed Queen Shezira, the most powerful friend you had. You've broken your clan's pact. And for what? Who do you think I am? You take me in my own bed and then you moan my mother's name in your sleep. I was never anything more to you than some *thing* to keep your memories burning. Oh, and the potions, let's not forget the potions.'

Hyram stumbled around the table and lunged. Zafir jumped nimbly out of the way. 'I-I ... l-loved—'

She sneered at him, dripping scorn: 'You loved yourself, my lord.'

'I l-loved A-A-Aliphera.' He felt obscenely drunk and his head was about to explode. Zafir's face swam in and out of focus. He wanted to reach out and grab it and destroy it, to smash her into bloody pulp, but his arms and legs felt as though they were made of lead. Sometimes it didn't seem to be Zafir's face at all that he saw, but Jehal's, laughing at him. He took another few steps and slashed the air with the dagger; Zafir was too quick for him.

'Well she never loved you, my lord. She despised you. You made her sick.' She darted forward and spat in his face at the same moment as he launched himself at her. He felt the dagger snag on her clothes and she gave a little yelp. He staggered a few steps forward as Zafir twisted away. She cursed and he heard the crash of something falling over. The pressure inside his head was crushing. The world was slowly losing its colour. He turned around. Zafir was scrabbling on the floor, trying to get up, clutching her side.

'You cut me,' she hissed.

'I'll do ... more th-than c-cut you, y-you w-whore.' He was made of stone, but inside was pure fire. His vision seemed to compress as he stepped over her, until all he could see was her face and everything else had dissolved away. He was splitting, falling away into elemental pieces. He raised the dagger to plunge into her flesh and brought it down, and then something crashed into him and everything went dark. He couldn't move and he couldn't see, but for some reason he could hear voices. He could hear Zafir shouting for her guards. And he could hear the Viper.

62

River Treasure

Kemir watched from a distance. Men were emerging from the river, clutching their enormous shields and struggling to pull their ridiculous crossbows from the water. They weren't wearing any armour. In fact, when he squinted he could see they weren't wearing anything at all. They were painted, however, covered in swirling patterns that had somehow resisted the water.

He frowned and idly strung his bow. They were mad. He wondered, for a second or two, whether the patterns painted onto them were some kind of blood-magic so that dragon fire wouldn't hurt them. Only for a second or two, though, before Snow felled a dozen of them with a single blast.

Then Ash was among them, and Snow backed away and left him to it. The other three dragons, the ones they'd found at the eyrie, stopped what they were doing and watched. Even as Ash was finishing off the soldiers one of them scuttled forward and snatched one of the bodies, gulping it down. Ash turned and roared. For a moment the last few Guardsmen were forgotten as the dragons squared up. Then the other dragon lowered its head and backed away.

In the space of a minute the soldiers all died. They didn't manage to erect a single one of their crossbows; Kemir wasn't even sure they'd tried. It was almost as though they knew they were doomed, and preferred to die quickly in battle than slowly choke to death. He stretched and ambled towards the aftermath in case any of them had had anything worth looting. Not likely, since they were all naked, but there might be a ring or a talisman on a chain. Pointless really, robbing the dead out here. Even if he did find anything, then what? He stared at the river, as bodies and shields floated past. *So futile* ...

One of the shields moved. At first Kemir thought his eyes had played a trick on him, but when he stopped and watched carefully, he could see feet sticking out from underneath. They were kicking.

Slowly he pulled an arrow from his quiver and drew back his bowstring. He fired the arrow into the middle of the shield. Even at such a short range, it didn't go in very far, but it went in far enough. The water thrashed and splashed, and suddenly there was a man scrambling to his feet on the far bank. Kemir drew out another arrow and then stared in amazement.

'You! Murderer!'

Rider Semian stared back at him. He was naked apart from a long thick shirt that reached his knees and a sword belt. He still held his shield and had a bottle hanging around his neck on a piece of string. Kemir held an arrow in one hand and his bow in the other. Semian was only a few yards away but the river was too wide to jump. Kemir grinned.

'You're a dead man.' Without looking away, he put the arrow to his bowstring. 'You can't reach me, and you need to be a lot further away before I'm going to miss. So what's the matter with you? Too much of a coward to die like the rest? Or is that what they were for? Were they all supposed to die, all the *little* soldiers, so that you, a *rider*, could live?' He drew back the bowstring.

Semian didn't move except to shift behind his shield so that Kemir could only see his head. 'Who are you working for, sellsword. Who bought you?'

'No one.' Kemir laughed. 'For the first time in far too many years. Just settling an old score.' He might have gone on – tried to explain to the rider why he was helping Snow, how dragon-riders had destroyed his family, his friends and everyone he knew. There was a courtesy to killing a man, and part of that was making sure that he understood why he was marked to die.

Then again Semian hardly deserved any courtesy, so Kemir just released the arrow.

Semian yanked up his shield, which quivered as the arrow hit it exactly in front of his face.

Kemir's arm shot back for another arrow. At the same time Semian took a huge leap into the middle of the river. In mid-air he flipped his absurd shield sideways and hurled it at Kemir. As Kemir nocked his second arrow, he ducked and twisted sideways, but the shield was so big it caught the top of his bow, almost tearing it out of his hands. He dropped the arrow and nearly fell over.

By the time he'd regained his balance, Semian was scrambling up the near bank of the river.

'You'll have to do better than that, sell-sword.'

Kemir hesitated. *Knives or arrow?* Arrows were more certain, but Semian was maybe too close.

He went for another arrow anyway. *No shield to hide behind this time.* Semian drew his sword. He sprang the last few yards between them and swung. As Kemir let the arrow go, the tip of the sword clipped his bow. The arrow went went wide, and then the rider was on him. Kemir launched himself at Semian and the two of them tumbled to the ground, arms locked around each other, rolling back towards the river. Kemir had one hand around Semian's wrist, pinning his sword. His other hand went to the rider's throat. Semian let the sword go and punched Kemir in the face, hard enough to make his vision swim. They rolled apart. Kemir sprang to his feet and drew out his knives. Semian was up too. Unarmed. His sword lay between them.

'Last time you were the one surrounded by allies and dragons. Now it's me.' Kemir tipped back his head and roared, 'Hey, Snow!' then bared his teeth at Semian. 'Show me which dragon is yours, so I can feed you to him after I've killed you.'

'I don't see you surrounded by allies,' said Semian. He took a step back. He still had the bottle on a string around his neck; now he lifted that over his head. 'I see only you.'

'This time, *I* have the dragons.'

Semian kept his eyes on Kemir as he flicked the stopper out of the bottle. Kemir lunged forward. Semian skittered backwards.

Kemir shook his head.

'Ah ah! No special potions from your friends the alchemists. You should have drunk those before you came out.' Semian was even further from his sword now.

'This is poison, sell-sword.' He slowly put the bottle to his lips and tipped it back.

'Is it slow and painful?'

'I believe so, yes.'

'So I could still carve you up and watch you bleed slowly?'

'Oh, you misunderstand.' Semian glanced back towards the caves. 'It doesn't kill *humans*.' He dropped into a fighting stance. 'I'm unarmed. Are you going to try your luck with those knives of yours, sell-sword? Or do you have something else you should be doing?'

63

Fangs of the Viper

Cold air brushed Hyram's face. He opened his eyes. He was flat on his back and Jehal was crouching over him. They were outside in the open air somewhere. It was night, and he was alive, barely. When he tried to throw out an arm to grab the Viper by his throat, he could barely move. His limbs tingled. They weren't really awake yet.

'You're shivering, old man.' Jehal spoke softly and quietly, as through someone was sleeping nearby. 'Are you cold? Or are you sick? Which is it, do you think?'

'I-I have n-nothing to s-say to you, V-Viper.'

Jehal smiled. 'That *is* a relief. If you'd got it in your head to make a long speech about what a terrible person I am, I might just have thrown myself off the balcony here. Anything to make it end.'

'Y-Y-You'll …' He couldn't make his mouth work properly. His face was turning numb.

'Never get away with it? Is that what you were going to say? You must be losing your mind, old man. I already have. Do you know where we are? We're in your palace, old man. You're surrounded by your own guards.' Jehal frowned and shook his head. '"There goes our lord, so drunk he can't stand straight again." That's how easy it is.' He laughed. 'Of course we're friends ever since I backed your speaker, aren't we? I wonder if any of the soldiers I've just walked past were the same ones you had with you down under the Glass Cathedral when you tortured me.' Jehal reached down and picked up something from the shadows beside him. 'You've been wanting to know this for a long time.' He held up a small round bottle made of thick smoky glass. Then he pulled a sack out of the shadows as well. When he tipped the bottle over the sack, a glittering silver liquid dripped out. 'Yes, I *have* been poisoning you. You've got two very fine poisons in you already, in fact. A little Nightwatchman in your drink to start. Then a little prick from a needle dipped in Frogsback.' Jehal held a needle in front of Hyram's face. 'Gave you that just a couple of minutes ago, when you started to stir. It should be working by now. If you stop breathing, that means I've got the dose wrong, and I'm going to feel quite foolish. If you don't, well then you should recover from it in a few hours. I do like Frogsback. This though ...' Jehal stroked the bottle of silver liquid. 'This is special. It's the vapours. Even in tiny doses they slowly destroy your mind. Very, very slowly. Of course in bigger doses they act rather more quickly.'

With that, the Viper straddled Hyram and forced the sack over his head. Hyram tried to struggle, but he was so weak that he might as well not have bothered. He also tried not to breathe in, which was equally futile.

'You can't smell them,' said the Viper. Hyram felt the rest of the bottle being tipped over his head. 'A little pot of this in your bedroom for a year, that's all it took. That and someone to stir it up from time to time. A sort of scum forms on the top after a while which keeps the vapours from forming. Otherwise it's perfect, don't you think?

'Didn't you start to have a problem with your pot-boys about a year ago?' Hyram could tell that Jehal was grinning, simply from the sound of his voice. 'Kept disappearing, didn't they? I don't suppose you thought anything of it. A different one every few months. Did you even notice? No? Shame on you, old man. You should always pay attention to your pot-boys. They're almost invisible yet they know all your secrets. They know who you take to your bed; they know who you talk to in the middle of the night. They sleep in the same rooms as us. They know every nook and cranny and corner of our sleeping lives. They breathe the same air.' The Viper chuckled. 'So you had to keep having new ones, before the vapours could affect them. Don't worry, they've all been well looked after. Oh, but then you probably don't care, do you, because you didn't even notice them. No, you're probably too worried about your own predicament just now. I suppose I can understand that.'

The Viper's voice receded, as though he was standing up.

'Don't bother trying to move or shout out, old man. I hope you've learned by now that a Viper's bite is poison.' He laughed. 'But you had one little victory. I assume it was you who stole Queen Shezira's white dragon. Since it wasn't me, and it wasn't Zafir, and I sincerely doubt that King Valgar would dare do such a thing. But you ... What was it? You couldn't bear the thought that I should own such a prize? And now Shezira's never going to know. Pity.' He patted Hyram on the shoulder. 'Goodnight, old man, and goodbye. I'm going to leave you now, surrounded by your Adamantine Guard. In a little while Zafir will come and take your hood off, and then she'll call in some of your loyal men, the ones you set to guard her door. They'll carry you back to your bed to sleep off the stink of wine that's on you. Sleep in peace. By tomorrow morning, when you see me again, you won't even know who I am.'

The Viper walked away. Hyram heard his footsteps fade to nothing. Inside the sack he tried to turn his head, twisting it as far as he could from the fumes that he couldn't even smell. When he tried to pull off the sack, it was like slapping himself with slabs of dead meat. His arms flailed with a will of their own. They wouldn't do what he wanted them to. He couldn't move his fingers at all. He tried shouting but all he could do was rasp. Out here on the balcony, no one would hear him.

Frogsback. He's paralysed me.

He kicked with his feet. He could do that at least. Hopelessly uncoordinated, but he could move them. After a few minutes he'd managed to push himself a few inches. Exhausted, he gave up. If anything, the numbness was getting worse, and the more he struggled, the more fumes he breathed.

Shezira. Time and space became a blur. He wasn't sure where he was any more. At some point he thought he felt strong arms take hold of him. They must have taken the sack off too, because he could see stars again. And faces.

Shezira. She was the only one left he could trust. The only one who could make it all go away. Even after everything they'd done to each other, after everything he'd done to her, she'd do the right thing. She'd have the strength that he lacked.

He tried to struggle, but the thoughts never got further than his mind, while the rest of his body slumbered in peaceful stupor.

'Shezira ...'

64

Smoke and Poison

Kemir turned and ran, sprinting towards the caves and the dragons. 'Don't!' he screamed. 'Stop! Don't eat the bodies!'

He was too late. Of course he was too late. Rider Rod wouldn't have told him if there was any danger he might stop it. All of the dragons had bloody muzzles. There were still a few corpses littered around the river, but there had clearly been a lot more. He clenched his fists in furious frustration. *No armour, no sword, I should have carved him up.*

And that was the point. That was *why* Rider Rod had told him. *Because I had him. Because for a moment there, with no sword in his hand, he was mine for the taking. Because this time I could have carved him up. And now I'm too late* and *I let him go. Shit!* The realisation made him clench his fists again and scream.

'They're poisoned,' he shouted when Snow and Ash both stopped and peered down at him. The other three dragons didn't understand. They still did what they were told, whether it was by a rider on their back or another dragon in their head.

Snow spat out half a knight. *How are they poisoned?*

'I don't know.' Kemir pointed back down the river. 'There was a rider. He got past you in the river. He told me.'

Ash lifted his head and snorted fire at the heavens. *Perhaps he lied.*

'Perhaps he did!' Kemir shrugged. 'Wait and find out if you like. Or go and find him and ask him. Last time I saw him he was a few hundred yards that way, behind those rocks and heading for the forest. He can't have got far.' *He murdered Sollos.*

The dragons didn't say anything else. Ash stamped a clawed foot, shaking the earth, then the whole valley trembled as he and

Snow pounded away towards the trees. The other three dragons went back to the cave-mouth fires. Kemir cast a nervous glance at the cliffs towering over them, wondering if they were about to come crashing down. As soon as he convinced himself that they weren't, he ran after Snow. *That's what they should have done. Not fire but stone. Shake the whole mountainside down and bury the place. Could they have done that?*

He reached the place where he'd found Semian and picked up his bow. He left it strung, just in case. Ash and Snow were at the edge of the trees and launching themselves into the air.

He is in there. Not far. I can feel his thoughts. He is cold, very cold, that is all I can sense.

Where?

Distant. Exactly where I cannot be sure.

Then burn it. Burn it all.

Burn it all.

'The river,' shouted Kemir. Semian's shield was gone. 'He'll be in the river.' Except the river was so shrouded by trees that the dragons probably couldn't even see it from above. Kemir stood at the edge of the wood and watched. A part of him wanted to give chase himself. *Let Sollos rest in peace at last.*

'You want him alive, remember!' he shouted as the first lance of fire stabbed down into the trees. Semian would have his sword again and Kemir might not even see the knight until they stumbled into each other. And did he really want to hunt down a desperate rider while two dragons were raining fire down from above? No, probably not.

He took a deep breath. If Rider Rod had been telling the truth about the poison, and *if* all the dragons had eaten it, and *if* they all died, then what? Stuck in a valley full of angry soldiers and alchemists hadn't seemed too bad with two murderous dragons on his side. Stuck there without them he'd be the hunted one.

'Bugger.' He growled. 'Another day, Rider Rod. One day, if the dragons don't get you, I'll still be waiting for you in those shadows.' He sat down to watch as Snow and Ash burned the forest. They'd give up soon enough. That was the trouble with the pair of them. No patience. Were all dragons like that?

Ash suddenly lurched in the air. He turned sharply, flew almost straight towards Kemir and landed heavily next to the river. Before he'd even come to a halt, he had rolled over into the water. *Hot! Too hot! I am burning inside!* Ash pressed his head into the ice-cold water, took a long swallow and then splashed more water over his back. A second later he was gently steaming.

Kemir backed away.

'It's the poison, you stupid greedy dragon. That's how dragons die. They burn from the inside.' He wrung his hands in frustration and looked around for Nadira. It was hardly a surprise that Ash was the first, since he'd probably eaten more than the rest of the dragons put together. But he hadn't thought it would happen so quickly. How long had it been? Ten minutes? The alchemists in the caves, though, they'd know exactly how long the poison would take. Exactly when to come rushing out to finish off anyone stupid enough to remain.

He jumped up onto a rock and glanced around the valley. 'Nadira!' he shouted. He couldn't see her. 'Snow!'

Ash. Here, I will cool you. Snow landed to squat beside Ash, pouring river water over him. Over by the cave mouths the other three dragons didn't seem troubled. Yet.

'Snow! Did you eat the bodies of the dead?'

Yes.

'How many?'

I did not count mouthfuls, Kemir. Does it matter? Their poison is in me.

'Not as many as Ash, though.'

Far, far fewer.

'Then perhaps not enough to do to you whatever it's done to him.' Kemir looked around the valley for Nadira again. This time he saw her, not far away, sitting with her back to a tree, brushing her hair. He wondered, for an instant, where she'd found the brush. 'Nadira!'

Ash! You must stay awake! Kemir could feel frustration in

Snow's thoughts, and a deep sadness with it. Strangely little anger, though. *Kemir, I begin to feel it too. I must destroy the alchemists quickly now, while I still have the strength.*

'No! You should fly away, while you still can.' He waved Nadira towards him. By the caves, one of the dragons had gone to lie down in the water as well.

I cannot leave Ash. He is sinking into torpor. It is our way of stopping the heat inside when it grows too strong. If they find him alone like this, they will feed him their potions again and he will be lost.

'Or they might get both of you. Or you might die from the poison. You don't know what it does. You don't know anything. We have to go.'

I understand your fear, Little One, but I will not leave. There is too much undone.

'Then stay here and die! Or be enslaved again. For myself, I wish for neither.' Kemir got up. He trotted to Nadira and took her hand. 'Come on! We need to go. And quickly.'

The poison is in me, Kemir, and it will do what it will do. If I am to die, I will die in battle against my enemies. I am a dragon, and that is my nature.

'In battle?' Kemir threw up his head to the heavens. 'They're not going to come out and fight you, you stupid creature. They're going to wait and watch as you fail. They'll hide in their caves and come out when you're too weak to lift yourself off the ground. Is that battle?' He was shouting now, filled with a bitter sense of loss that he didn't understand. 'Fly up into the mountains! Find a lake by a glacier and immerse yourself in it! If that doesn't keep you cold, nothing will. If you want to fight, fight the poison.'

No, Kemir. I will stay with Ash.

Kemir stamped his foot. 'If the poison doesn't kill you, you can come back and try again! You can free Ash, free them all. If you die, you're dead, and everything you want dies with you.'

Snow stared at him. For a second he thought she was going to eat him. He could feel the thoughts in her head, the rivers of anger and desire, the knotting indecision. Then, slowly, she nodded.

It is not our nature to flee, Little One Kemir, and I do not under-

stand why you would betray your own kind. But yes, then. Let us leave. She lowered her head and shoulders to the ground. Kemir scrambled onto her back and hauled Nadira after him.

65

The Night of the Knives

Almiri tiptoed across the floor. She was shaking, still sweating from running up the stairs. And from what had gone on before. She held a single candle, and the flame flickered restlessly, casting dancing shadows across the walls. Her hands were trembling. She approached her mother's bed and felt like a young girl again, a child looking for a comfort she rarely received.

Shezira tossed and turned. Almiri knew those dreams. She'd had her own dreams, of being at home in the far-off north. Of someone tapping on her window, of the tapping growing louder, and then the rooms shaking and swaying. Of pictures falling off the walls, candles tipping over, ceilings cracking, beams breaking. *Of castles falling and of the earth splitting open.*

She knelt by the bed and gave her mother a gentle nudge. 'Your Holiness ...'

Shezira twisted violently away. *Someone in her bedchamber. In the middle of the night. Ill deeds ...*

Almiri tried again. 'Mother!' This time Shezira heard her. She sat up, wild-eyed.

'Almiri?'

'Yes. Mother, you have to wake up.'

Shouts outside. Swords clashing. Men screaming. Hiding ...

Shezira rubbed her eyes and squinted at her daughter, shielding her eyes from the candlelight. 'Almiri,' she said again. 'What are you doing here?'

'Mother, someone has tried to kill the speaker.'

'Hyram's dead?'

'No, mother.' Almiri tried to keep her voice steady, but she couldn't hide the tension. 'Queen Zafir. Someone has tried to kill Queen Zafir.'

Lying on the floor in the dark, trying not to breathe. Armoured feet in front of her eyes. Vicious words and bared, bloody swords ...

'I don't suppose they succeeded?'

'No, mother. She was wounded but not killed.'

Shezira chuckled. 'Pity.'

'Mother! This is not a joke.' Almiri's voice sounded shrill to herself. She wanted to scream.

'Who did it?'

'They say it was a rider disguised as a messenger boy. They say it was your knight-marshal.' She could see the coldness blossom inside her mother and sweep across her face. *How long has it been since you were afraid, mother?*

Her own husband, a king, dragged from his bed and thrown to the floor with a sword to his neck.

'Nastria?'

'Yes, mother.'

'No!' Shezira threw off her blankets and got up. 'No, Nastria would never do such a thing. Not without my order.'

'Yes, mother. They say that too.'

'Servants!' Shezira peered at her. 'I ordered no such thing. You look frightened, daughter. Why?'

'Because ...'

The sword is lifted up ...

Because I am. Because I'm terrified. Petrified. Paralysed. But she could never say that. Not to her mother. Shezira couldn't begin to understand. She wouldn't even try.

'Because the Adamantine Guard have seized our tower, mother. Valgar's riders are either dead or taken. They dragged my husband out of his bed.' *... but never comes down. The feet march away and take him with them and she is alone in the dark, still silent and unbreathing.* 'When he fought, they beat him like a common criminal. I hid under the bed. I heard them talking. They didn't see me in the dark.'

Servants were coming in now, sluggishly, rubbing the sleep

from their eyes. Shezira scowled at them. 'Dress me,' she snapped. 'Awake my riders. Awake everyone. Daughter, you're not making much sense. Why would Hyram's guards do such a thing?'

Almiri sat on the bed and held her head in her hands. No matter how hard she tried, she couldn't keep it all clenched up inside her for much longer. 'They're Zafir's Guard now, mother. Your knight-marshal tried to kill her. They *saw* her. She fled, and they saw her come to our tower. But she's not there, mother. When they don't find her, they'll come here.'

'I'm quite sure you're right, especially if they saw *you* come here too.'

'What was I supposed to do, mother? It was dark. I wasn't asleep. I saw them take Valgar and so I ran. They killed our riders!'

Shezira held out her arms to be dressed. 'Yes, so you said.'

'Where *is* Lady Nastria, mother?'

'Missing.'

What's that, mother? A touch of fear? It is, isn't it? So you do *remember what it feels like from all those years ago.*

'Missing,' Shezira said again. She frowned.

'Would she—'

'No, daughter, she would not. She would never be so mindlessly stupid.'

Someone ran into the room and grovelled at Shezira's feet. 'Your Holiness—'

'What?'

'The speaker's soldiers are hammering on the door, Your Holiness. They demand—'

Shezira waved him away. 'Tell them that I am dressing and that when I am ready they may enter. Tell them that the person they're looking for is not here, but I shall be happy to allow them to see that for themselves. Tell them that my riders shall not be the first to bare their swords. And remind them that I have a good few more than King Valgar did.'

Another servant approached. 'Your armour, Holiness?'

'Are we at war? Don't be foolish.' She waved that one away too.

'Mother—'

'*Enough*, Almiri. The Guard may take their orders from Queen Zafir today, but for the last ten years they've answered to Hyram, and old habits are not so easily forgotten. Does he think I plan to go to war with them? That would be absurd. I will speak to Hyram in person, and if he intends to imprison everyone who disagrees with his foolishness then he can do it himself. No, daughter, something else is afoot here. Hyram will release King Valgar and Zafir will pay compensation to the families of his dead riders. I will see to it.' Finally she was dressed. She shooed all her servants away and marched out and down into the body of the Tower of Dusk. She swept down the stairs into the great hall with Almiri on her heels. A dozen riders were already there, some of them armoured, some of them still in their nightclothes, but all armed. Most of them were pressed against the doors to the outside. A heavy bar was braced across both doors, and the riders were shouting at the soldiers outside, such a cacophony of cursing that Almiri couldn't make out a single word. When the queen reached the bottom of the stairs, she snatched a spear and banged it on the floor. 'Open the doors,' she shouted. 'Let them in.'

'Mother, don't go outside.' Almiri almost snatched at Shezira's sleeve, but that would have earned her nothing but contempt.

The riders fell silent. Shezira glared at them. 'What are you waiting for?' She pointed at the nearest two knights, who'd managed to scramble into their armour. 'You come with me. The rest of you—'

'*Mother!*' Almiri almost screamed. It was a mistake to shout at a queen, but she couldn't help herself any more.

Shezira rounded on her. 'Queen Almiri is our guest,' she said very clearly. 'See to it that the Adamantine Guardsmen understand that. And we are not King Valgar, but the Queen of the North, the Queen of Sand and Stone, with twelve score dragons at our beck and call. See they understand that too.' She swept her cloak around her and marched towards the door. 'Why is this door still closed? Must I open it myself?'

She would have lifted the bar with her own hands if some of her riders hadn't hastily removed it. The doors swung open. Outside, dozens of Adamantine men stood waiting, fully armoured and with bared steel in their hands. They paused and then parted as Shezira strode towards them, and after all the shouting an eerie silence fell. Almiri watched her go into the gloom of the night. Tears stung her eyes.

You're wrong. Mother, this time you're wrong.

She kept her thoughts to herself, though, and as Shezira vanished into the darkness, she quietly slipped away.

66

Jostan

For a time that felt like forever, the smoke was unbearable. In the caverns Jaslyn sat by the river, a wet cloth wrapped across her mouth, and tried not to cough herself to death. Not coughing was almost impossible, and whenever she succumbed, she inevitably took in lungfuls of hot smoke and that made it a hundred times worse. Jostan sat beside her. The first time she fell to coughing, he had wrapped his arms around her ribs and then pressed his lips to hers. She tried to fight, pushing him away, thinking he'd lost his mind, but he wasn't trying to kiss her. He blew air out of his lungs and into hers and then drew away. His air still reeked with smoke, but at least it was cool and moist, not bitter and dry. When she'd regained her composure, he had knelt at her feet.

'Forgive me,' he whispered.

'I should have your head,' she rasped. But the coughing fit had gone, and anyway the only person who could have defended her honour was Semian, and he was gone too.

The second time she began to cough, he did it again, and she realised that a part of her liked the closeness of it. Instead of fighting him off, she found herself wanting to pull him to her, to have someone to hold on to at last, if only for the last hours of her life. Eventually she pushed him away, firmly but gently this time. After that she made sure that she didn't cough any more. In the end she lay beside the river, eyes closed, listlessly splashing her face whenever they started to sting again. The water tasted delicious. She tried to pretend that Jostan wasn't there and think only about that.

'Princess! There is a breeze,' he said at last. 'Do you feel it?'

She lifted her head. He was right. A gentle wind whispered along the river from the depths of the caves.

'What does it mean?' she asked.

'It means that the fires are drawing air out of the caves. It means the dragons are no longer tending them, Your Highness.' He could barely contain himself. 'The Embers have won!'

Jaslyn wanted to cry. Coming down here had been stupidity. *Her* stupidity. 'I'm sorry, Jostan. I know we should have stayed with the alchemists.' The Embers were dead. She hadn't seen it with her own eyes, but the shouts and the screams and the roars of the dragons had echoed far into the tunnels.

'No, Princess. This means the dragons are gone. The Embers have won.'

'The Embers are dead, Jostan.' Speaking was a trial. Her throat was raw and burning, and every word was a battle against the smoke.

'Yes.' He was smiling, she realised. 'And the dragons ate them.'

She was missing something. She struggled upright. 'Why is that a cause for happiness, Rider Jostan?'

He frowned and peered at her. Twice he opened his mouth to speak and then closed it again. At the third attempt words finally came out. 'I'm sorry, Your Highness. I thought you knew.'

'Knew what, Rider?'

'That the Embers ...' He wouldn't look at her. 'Highness, the Embers took poison. The bottle that Rider Semian had around his neck, that was poison too. Dragon poison.'

'What are you talking about?' *Dragon poison? No such thing. I would have known.*

'The Embers, Your Highness, they went out there to die. They knew what awaited them.'

'Poison?' *Would she have known?*

He bowed his head.

And then it hit her – far, far later than it should have. 'Silence!'

Jostan stared at the ground. 'And Matanizkan and Levanter. I am sorry, Your Highness.'

'Sorry?' For a moment even the smoke didn't matter. *Sorry? What use is sorry? My Silence! You've poisoned my Silence. Graceful, elegant, beautiful, perfect—*

And trying to kill us, she reminded herself. *Or was.* No, best not to think about it. Would she ever have sacrificed Silence to save her own life? No. To save Jostan? Semian? No. To save anyone at all? She didn't know.

'I have to see!' She was already getting to her feet.

'No, Your Highness. Wait. It's not safe.'

She screamed at him. 'You've poisoned my Silence! I want to see him.'

'We have to wait.'

'Wait for what?'

'Wait for Rider Semian, Your Highness. He went out to watch. When they're all dead, he will come back and tell us.'

'*When they're dead?!*' She was rigid with fury. If she'd had claws, she would have torn Jostan to pieces. 'So they're still alive?' She pressed her face up close to his. 'There must be something to take this poison out of them. Poison the white if that's the only way, but not Silence. Not my Silence!' But there wasn't something. The alchemists wouldn't have an antidote. Why would they? And even if they did, it would take hours to walk back to where they were hiding, and hours more to get back to the mouth of the caves.

She turned and ran towards the entrance, heedless of the smoke, but Jostan pulled her down. 'Your Highness!'

'Silence!' She screamed and fought and tore at him. 'My Silence! Don't eat them! Don't!' But Jostan was strong, much too strong, and he wouldn't let her go. She ordered him, cursed him, berated him as best she could before the next coughing fit seized her, but his arms stayed wrapped around her and all her struggles were useless. 'Silence,' she whispered. Tears streamed down her face. Jostan still held her, but his arms were gentle now, and suddenly welcome. She rested her head on his chest and wept. Here in the murderous choking dark she didn't want to be a princess any more.

They crept down the river until they could see the massive pyre at the cave mouth, and there they waited for an hour, maybe longer, before she decided she couldn't bear any more. She was careful this time, waiting until Jostan was distracted before she ran, sprinting along the river bank and then diving into the water when the heat from the fire was too much. She heard Jostan shouting after her, but she didn't look back. By the time he finally caught her, they were already outside, thrashing in the river alongside the fires.

'Keep your head down!' shouted Jostan, and then they were past, and the air was suddenly cold and crisp and deliriously fresh. It felt so gloriously clean that she wanted to gulp it down as fast as she could. For a second she almost forgot about Silence.

And then she saw him. A hundred yards from the river, flat on his belly, eyes closed. Still.

'Your Highness! Wait!' But she didn't, and this time Jostan didn't try to stop her. She hauled herself out of the freezing river and ran as fast as she could, collapsing to the ground by the dragon's head. Silence was gone. She could already feel the heat burning him from the inside.

Jostan came towards her, then saw the look on her face and stopped dead in his tracks.

'Is he ...'

Jaslyn shook her head. She couldn't speak.

'I ... I should look for the others, Your Highness. Please be careful. The others ... They might not ...'

He should have taken her back into the cave, and they both knew it. She should have stayed there until all the other dragons had been found. He should never have let her escape in the first place, and her mother would probably have his head for being so careless. But for a moment Jaslyn loved him more than anyone in the world simply for leaving her alone.

67

The Balcony

Jehal watched through the eyes of one of the Taiytakei dragons. He saw the doors of the Tower of Dusk open and watched Shezira storm towards Hyram's keep. He grimaced. *Like an arrow from the bow of a master archer*, he mused. *Straight and deadly and utterly predictable. And when Hyram cannot be roused, what then, mighty Queen?* He took off one strip of silk and put on the other, to see through the eyes of the little dragon that he'd left watching over Hyram's bed. The Adamantine Guardsmen had taken Hyram from Zafir's rooms back to his own and put him to bed, just as their new mistress had ordered them. He should be snoring nicely by now. Everyone would assume he was drunk.

The bed was empty.

It took Jehal a couple of seconds and a close inspection to believe what he was seeing, but Hyram was gone. Despite all the poisons, somehow Hyram had woken up and got out of bed. The dragon found him a few minutes later, out on his balcony, leaning over the parapet. His face was slack and vacant and he was shaking; it was all Jehal could do not to laugh. Hyram could have ended up anywhere. As it was, it was a miracle that he hadn't simply tipped over the parapet and dashed himself to pieces on the ground below.

Now there's a thought.

He tore off the silk and fumbled for his boots. 'Kazah! Help me get dressed.' If Shezira got to Hyram and Hyram could actually string a sentence together, there was just a chance that everything might unravel. He ought to feel afraid, he supposed. Or at least annoyed, alarmed, worried – something like that. Exhilarated though? *Not good.*

Which only made the feeling stronger. He grinned at Kazah. However this ended, he was definitely going to miss it once it was all over.

Shezira reached Hyram's keep expecting to have to take the place by storm and quite prepared to do so, single-handed if she had to. Instead, the doors were flung open for her, which made her pause. But Hyram was not a murderer. Whatever else he might do, despite all his betrayals, he wasn't a killer.

Nonetheless. She whispered to the two riders she'd brought with her, 'Stay close to me.'

Inside, an old man was waiting for her, so withered and bent he made even Isentine look young. She took a moment to recognise him.

'Wordmaster Herlian?'

He bowed, as best he could. 'Your Holiness.'

'I am here to see Hyram.' She could demand that now. Of course, the Guard might not see it that way.

'He's ... Your Holiness, he's not himself.'

Shezira snorted. 'He's not the speaker and he's not a king. I can march straight into his bedchamber whenever it pleases me, Wordmaster. Whoever he is.'

Herlian bowed again. 'Your Holiness, I wouldn't dream of trying to stop you. He's been asking for you. Or at least he's said your name. But he's not well, Holiness. His mind has wandered. He talks of you and of Antros and of Aliphera and of dragons, and makes little sense.'

'He'd better make sense when I ask why his soldiers are hammering on my doors.'

Herlian shrugged. 'I will take you to him, Your Holiness.'

Hyram was flying. He was on the back of a dragon high in the sky with the wind streaming past his face. He didn't know the name of his dragon. It belonged to someone else; he wasn't sure who. His brother, perhaps. Antros. The giant of his life, always casting him into shadow.

Maybe it was the wind that was making him weep, or maybe not, for hadn't Aliphera ripped out his heart and torn it to pieces in front of his very eyes, flaunting herself with that dashing prince from the south, Tyan. She'd wanted Antros, but Antros wasn't for having. She should have wanted him instead, but no, no, she didn't, and now she'd left him with nothing, just an empty shell, devoid of feeling.

No, that wasn't right either. There hadn't been any feeling for a long time, but now it was back, all of it, decades and decades of pain, all at once.

'Hyram.'

The dragon was talking to him. That must be it. There couldn't be anyone else with him, up here in the sky. Except suddenly there *was* another dragon, flying alongside him, with that frightened young slip of a girl from the north that Antros was off to marry. Not much to look at, but they had dragons, lots of dragons.

'Are you drunk?'

That made him laugh. If only he *was* drunk. Now there was a way to take all that pain, round it up and throw it back into the box from where it had escaped. *Back where you belong. No business being out here after all this time.*

'You are, aren't you? Drunk again.'

'No!' he screamed at the stupid girl on her dragon, wishing she'd leave him alone. 'Go away!'

'I'll go away when you explain to me why your Adamantine Guard have taken Valgar, have killed his riders, and why they were hammering on my door.'

'Guards?' He didn't know anything about that. 'Ask the speaker. He must know. They're his men.' He grinned. 'My brother's going to be the speaker one day.' Then he looked away. That was a stupid thing to say. The girl was about to marry Antros. Of course she knew about the pact.

The dragon underneath him suddenly banked and sank through the air. Hyram swayed and clutched at the harness. For some reason he hadn't strapped himself in. He had no idea why he'd forget a thing like that. That was the sort of thing Antros would do, except Antros didn't forget; he did stupid things on purpose and then mocked Hyram for being a coward. And he always got away with it too.

The girl grabbed hold of him. He couldn't even remember her name, but she must have jumped off her own dragon and landed on the back of his, and now she was pulling at him.

Hyram lurched violently and stumbled towards the parapet of the balcony. Shezira caught him, stopped him from falling to the ground, and then let go as he fought her away.

'If it's not you, then who's doing this?' But she could see in his eyes that he was somewhere else, somewhere far, far away.

'Get off my dragon,' he shouted at her. 'Get off it! Stay on your own!' She backed away from him. 'Yes, that's right. Back where you belong. Stay away!'

The hairs on the back of her neck rose. She'd seen Hyram drunk often enough. This was something else. 'Hyram? If you didn't send the Guard, then who did? Zafir?'

'Zafir?' he looked at her blankly, as though he'd never heard the name. 'Prince Tyan, that's who did this to me. And that little bitch Aliphera, with her flashing eyes and her stone-cold heart. She did this. And Antros, always blocking out the sun, wherever I stand. You're welcome to him. Take him away and leave me be, all of you.' He lurched again.

'Aliphera's dead, Hyram. Tyan's mad. Antros has been gone for fifteen years. What are you talking about?'

'Death.' For a moment his eyes focused on her. 'Death, Shezira. Life is like a wheel rolling through time, and sometimes little pieces stick to it. They stick to it all the way round and come back again when you least expect them. I'm sorry I betrayed you to them. Aliphera and Tyan.' He reached out to her, and then his eyes went wide and she could see him fall away back to whatever place held him. A door closed behind his face. He wasn't coming back.

Shezira shook her head and pursed her lips. 'You mean Jehal and Zafir, don't you? I'm sorry too, Hyram. Sorry for you, but I don't have time for this. Whatever they're—' Hyram's face had gone rigid with terror. He was looking past her.

'Get away! Get away!'

Something fluttered past her and flew at Hyram. In the darkness she couldn't see what it was. Some sort of bird perhaps, but it glittered like gold and made a strange sound as it flew, more a clattering of metal than the fluttering of feathers. It buzzed at Hyram's head.

'Get away!' He flailed at it, stumbling towards the parapet.

Shezira took a step towards him. Somewhere inside the keep a commotion had started. It was rapidly getting closer.

'Get away! Get off my dragon!'

He was going to fall.

'Hyram!' She lunged at him, trying to grab his arm. He shrieked and hurled himself away from her, straight into the parapet. His head and arms kept going, tipping over into the emptiness beyond. His legs flew up. It all seemed to happen very slowly, so slowly that Shezira couldn't understand why she couldn't do anything about it. And then he was gone. He didn't scream at all, but she heard the thud, a few seconds later, as he hit the ground.

There were people running into Hyram's bedchamber behind her.

'Murder!' shouted a woman's voice. It was Queen Zafir. 'She's murdered my husband!'

For the first time in many years Shezira didn't know what to do. She stood staring over the edge. Behind her she could hear her riders trying to defend her. There were only two of them, though, and Zafir had come in force. It didn't last long.

Jehal unwrapped the silk from his eyes. Then he lay back on his bed while Kazah pulled his boots off again. He stared at the ceiling filled with immeasurable satisfaction.

I win.

68

The Glacier

She was getting hotter. Kemir felt it. They hadn't gone very far before Snow's back grew first uncomfortable, then painful and finally almost unbearable. He'd made a mistake, he thought. She *was* dying, and there wasn't much to be done about it.

At least we'll be far from the alchemists when they finally come out of their caves. We can just die slowly from cold and hunger instead.

He could live with that, he decided. Better to die out here, fighting to survive in these harsh lands, than rot in some dungeon. Nadira probably wouldn't see it that way, but there wasn't much she could do about it now. They'd tried, him and Snow. They'd tried and they'd failed, and that felt so much better than not having tried at all. He could die happy with that.

Snow flew higher and higher, arrowing deep into the World-spine. The mountains and valleys grew more wild and broken, the peaks higher, until they arced into a narrow valley filled with an azure lake. Snow dropped through the air until she was skimming the water. Her flying had become erratic. She was aiming for the end of the lake, where a glacier stretched down from the mountainside and immense chunks of grey ice drifted lazily in the brilliant blue water. As she reached it, she crash-landed close to the shore. Even as Kemir and Nadira were struggling out of the freezing water, Snow was backing away into the deeper parts of the lake, towards the ice cliff of the glacier. There was madness in her thoughts now, mixed in with the fury. She wasn't afraid, though. She was sure she was dying, but she wasn't afraid.

Goodbye, Little One Kemir.

Kemir spat and shook as much water as he could from his clothes. The air up here was so cold the wet furs were already starting to freeze. 'Live, dragon,' he hissed. 'If you live, you can free as many dragons as you want. But if you're gone, who else will do it?' *Never mind that there's little chance of us surviving on our own up here.*

She was sinking beneath the freezing water. When she finally lifted her head and looked up, she was instantly wreathed in steam. She must have read his thoughts, though, for with one last gasp, she spat a stream of fire at the trees nearby, setting them ablaze. Giving him warmth and fire and a chance, at least, to survive. Then she gave Kemir a look and cocked her head. Her thoughts felt distant and vague, and also a little confused, as if the answer to his question was obvious. *You, Kemir. You will do it.*

Kemir laughed. 'I don't think so, dragon.'

He pulled Nadira after him into the forest and didn't look back. Behind him, the dragon sank with barely a ripple and was gone.

Epilogue – The Perfect White

'Where is she?' Almiri had barely landed. She wore full armour and had nearly fifty dragons with her: Shezira's from the encampment in the Purple Spur, and a detachment of Valgar's riders. She started to take the armour off. The weight of it left her almost unable to walk.

Rider Jostan glanced towards the caves and bowed. 'She's still with the body, Your Holiness.'

Almiri wrinkled her nose. The valley still stank of smoke. The alchemists were out of the caves now. Some of them had left; most had stayed to rebuild the ruins of their homes.

'Did you find all the others?'

'No.' Jostan sounded solemn. 'We found four dragons. The fifth is missing. The white.'

'The four you found, were all of them dead?'

'Yes, Your Holiness.' Then he smiled a little. 'We even found Rider Semian. Or he found us. Naked and half-dead from the cold, but he recovered quickly enough. It was hardly a problem to get him warm.'

'So one more to find. And the riders? The ones that brought the dragons here in the first place?'

Jostan shrugged. 'Left on the back of the white. Semian saw them go, heading into the deepest parts of the Worldspine. He says there were two of them. A man and a woman. The man used to work for—' He didn't finish, but Almiri knew what he had been going to say: Queen Shezira's knight-marshal. For the assassin who'd tried to murder Speaker Zafir, who'd died rather than be taken when she failed, and who might just have started a war.

Jostan bit his lip. 'I'm afraid Semian took the Ember poison, Your Holiness. His mind is—"

'I need to speak to her.'

Jostan looked uncomfortable. 'Yes, Your Holiness.'

He left her presence and headed for the caves.

Almiri took her time with her armour. They couldn't stay long; the alchemists' eyrie was tiny, and all the cattle they'd kept to feed visiting dragons were gone. She wasn't entirely sure what to say to her sister. She'd waited for a couple of days, hoping that Jaslyn would come to her, but she hadn't.

Eventually she couldn't put it off any longer. She walked towards the cave mouths and the dead dragons that lay there. The ground around them was already blackened from the heat. She could still recognise Matanizkan, Levanter and Silence, all three hatched and raised in Outwatch. Jaslyn was sitting, legs crossed, beside the river, as close to Silence as she could without being scorched. She was soaking wet. Sweat, Almiri thought, until she saw Jaslyn scoop handfuls of water from the river and splash it over herself.

She sat beside her sister. The air was burning hot and hard to breathe. There wasn't any wind.

'This is as close as I can get,' said Jaslyn quietly.

Almiri felt herself begin to cook under her flying clothes. 'You have to leave him,' she said uncomfortably. 'He's gone. We can make sure you get his scales.'

'I want to take them myself, when he's cooled enough.'

'I ...' Almiri stood up. The heat was intolerable. 'Can we go back to the eyrie?'

'Have some water from the river.' Jaslyn splashed some over her own face. She made no move to stand. Almiri sighed and sat down again.

'We fought our way out of the Adamantine Palace, Jaslyn. After they took mother and Valgar. Out of a hundred riders, twenty of us reached the eyrie and our dragons. We took as many as we could. I have Mistral. They say our mother murdered Hyram, and that our knight-marshal tried to kill the speaker. They mean to put mother and Valgar on trial. They'll be executed. They won't even be given the Dragon's Fall.'

Jaslyn didn't move.

'Our mother is imprisoned, Jaslyn. King Valgar too. Valgar had less than a hundred dragons, but you—'

'You're the eldest. Mother's realm is yours.'

'No.' Almiri shook her head. It was hard, sometimes, not to be bitter. 'No, mother has made you her heir, and she has given you away. To Prince Dyalt, King Sirion's youngest. You have to use him. You and Sirion have five hundred dragons between you. You can fight them. Make them give mother back to us. The realms need you, Jaslyn. Mother needs you.'

'Mother never needed anyone.'

Almiri bit her lip. 'Then I need you, sister.'

For a long time Jaslyn didn't say anything. Then she took a deep breath. 'The dragons weren't dead when we found them. Did anyone tell you that?'

Almiri shook her head.

'They were still alive. In torpor. And you know what? Just before he died my Silence woke up. Somehow, he woke out of his torpor. He was nearly gone, and he woke up, and he spoke to me. He spoke to me, Almiri. I heard his thoughts in my head.'

'Dragons don't speak, Jaslyn.'

'Yes, they do. When we don't poison them. He spoke as though he'd plucked the words out of my head. He told me a lot of things that I didn't know. About our dragons. He was beautiful before all this, but when he spoke ... I would have saved him if I could. I would have done almost anything. *Even if there was something to take this poison away, I would not go back to what I was.* That's what he said.'

'You've seen what one rogue dragon can do. Look around you. We have to do what we do, Jaslyn.'

'You know, don't you? You know all about it. What we do to them. Why didn't anyone tell me?'

Almiri shuffled her feet. 'You're not a queen, Jaslyn. Only a princess. And there are secrets even queens do not hear.'

'He asked me why I was so sad. "Because you're dying," I said to him. And he lifted his head with what little strength he had and looked at me. *And you will follow me*, he said. *One day. The difference between us is that I will die today and be reborn tomorrow. You will not.* That was all. An hour later he was gone. Do you suppose that's true? Are dragons reborn when they die? Or is that another secret too dire for a princess?'

'If it is, then it's too dire for this queen as well.' Almiri chewed her lip. 'I don't know, sister, but if they do come back, then one day there will be another Silence.'

'That's what I thought at first, when he died. Perhaps, at that moment, another dragon was born in some eyrie.' Jaslyn slowly got to her feet. 'But will he remember me, Almiri? I don't think so.' They walked away side by side, as sisters should.

'I don't want a war, Jaslyn. None of us wants that. But they can't do this.'

Jaslyn wasn't listening. 'If it's true, then the white will remember me. She will remember us all.'

Very slowly, they were dying. Nadira couldn't see it yet and Kemir didn't have the heart to tell her, but it was true. He'd kept them alive for five days now, since Snow had vanished beneath the frozen waters of the lake, but it couldn't last. The weather had been kind to them, but wind and rain were always fickle in the Worldspine. One day he'd run out of arrows, or his bowstring would break. Or one of them would get hurt or fall ill. He wasn't catching enough food, and they didn't have the clothes or the shelter to stay properly warm. A hundred things could go wrong, and sooner or later one of them would.

They had to move. He tried to break it to Nadira, to make her understand that Snow wasn't coming back, that their only chance was to leave and head for lower ground. A boat, he thought. Or at least a raft. Water always found the quickest way down the mountains.

She screamed in his face. Shrieked at him that Snow *was* coming back. He backed away. One more day, he promised himself. One more day and then he'd leave, with or without her. He could force her to come, he knew, but he'd let her choose. She could stay and die if she wanted. That's what Sollos would have done.

As that last day began to fade he made his weary way back to the lake, carrying with him what little food he'd been able to hunt or gather. The forests here were harsh and hostile, and yielded little. He was hungry. They were both hungry. They'd eat and they'd still be hungry.

He reached what passed for their camp at the edge of the lake, and the hairs on the back of his neck bristled. He couldn't see Nadira. The forest was silent except for the wind and the ever-present creaking and groaning of the glacier. He stared out across the lake. And suddenly he felt the fire and iron of her presence, a moment before the water began to churn.

Little One Kemir, I am hungry.